# HONOR AMONG

# THIEVES

A novel by

J.M. Aucoin

*Hope & Steel: Book One*

HONOR AMONG THIEVES

*Hope & Steel Book One*



Headshot photo by Vander Photography

Edited by Julie Tremblay & Joyce Shafer



ISBN-13: 978-1512172379

ISBN-10: 1512172375

Published by Sword & Cape Press

Published in the United States of America

www.JMAucoin.com

For Big Poppa Pizz & Mrs. Libby,
Thanks for the love, the laughs, the hospitality,
And putting up with all the childish shenanigans.

You'll be eternally missed.

Fencing makes those who want it
Spry and well-rounded, light and thin,
Flexible, ready for all things.
Stout and undaunted against enemies,
Brave and jaunty, who dare manfully.
Bold and noble in War,
To win praise, honor, and victory.
Make fresh several hundred beside him,
You wonder at the Fencing Art without distress.

— Christoff Rösener, 1589

# France 1609

# I.
# Fat Men and Fat Purses

*All we had was hope. Hope and steel.*

What these words meant to Darion Delerue de Tarbes occupied his mind as he leaned back in the country tavern chair. His scuffed brown leather boots rested at an angle atop the rough wood-hewn table before him. A broad-brimmed hat tilted low masked most of his face from patrons coming and going but did not block his ability to watch them. Within easy reach on the table were a well-oiled wheellock pistol, a powder flask, and his sheathed rapier.

Heavy curtains partly drawn across the windows kept winter's chill out. Pale moonlight poured through the uncovered glass. The room was lit, albeit barely, by a crackling fire in the hearth and tallow candles flickering on tabletops. Darion kept his cold blue eyes focused on the courtyard beyond the window his table was next to. His feigned expression was one of indifference. He was motionless, except for the long dagger, a main gauche, nicked and scarred from previous bouts, which he twirled slowly in his hands.

*All we had was hope. Hope and steel.*

He must've heard his father utter that phrase a hundred times or more growing up, back when the Catholic League and its army waged war against the French Calvinists. Darion's father was part of Henry of Navarre's cavalry during those religious, civil wars. The battles ravaged the French countryside, but the wars also took its toll on the Delerue household to the point where Darion's father said they owned only two things of worth in this world—hope and steel. Years later now, Darion still uttered that same phrase, more out of tradition than reverence. The wars of religion were over; Henry of Navarre was now King Henry of France, and the Huguenots got the tolerance they fought, bled, and died for a decade earlier.

But hope was for fools. Only steel mattered in this world. Steel and the jingling of coin in one's purse.

"All we have is hope and steel," he uttered.

"What was that?"

Darion's gaze shifted from the courtyard to the man who'd spoken.

Jaspart de Tremear, captain of the infamous Falcon Highwaymen, sat solemnly across from Darion. He set his mug of warm wine next to his short-brimmed hat and waited for an answer. Candlelight cast shadows onto his weathered face and ebony eyes. The perpetual half-grin he seemed to wear was an illusion. A dangerous illusion created by the scar near the left side of his mouth and poorly hidden by a bushy mustache.

"Nothing, Captain. Just mumbling."

"Mumble quieter." Tremear turned his attention back to the others in the tavern. Some men drank their chill away. Others jested with companions or flirted with barmaids. A few gambled away what little coin they had on them.

Darion sipped his wine and studied his captain. Tremear had been a soldier for the Catholics during the civil wars. During those days he'd been known as a man of determined character. Like many soldiers in days of peace that followed war, the captain had fallen on hard times. This led to an insatiable thirst for action to rid him of far too many moments of boredom. He now led thieves and highwaymen and fought for gold instead of glory.

Darion's history hadn't the grandeur, prestige, or misfortune of Tremear's. But it did have a promising military career shattered by a few honeyed words from a woman.

Darion's watchful eyes moved back to the unoccupied courtyard. The Gray Mule Tavern was ideally located. People traveled to and from Paris, the Low Lands, Calais, and England, and all of them had to pass the tavern. Many stopped in to meet their needs. Fat men with fat purses to be lightened, among them. Rumor was that the Chevalier d'Auch, his business concluded in the Low Lands, would pass by there in the next day or two. A good reason for the highwaymen to set up shop in the country haunt.

The two men passed the next hour in silence, speaking only once to order more wine.

Clopping hooves came to a stop in the courtyard. The driver of the black coach pulled by a team of four gray horses hopped down and opened the carriage door. A young man dressed in plain clothing stepped down. A well-polished rapier protruded from the black cloak he wore. A second man, older, followed him. Despite his age, this man moved with the grace of one in his prime. A gust of wind ruffled his white pointed beard and the sparse white curls beneath his short-brimmed hat. He hiked the high collar of his dark wool cloak around his neck, shielding his face from the bitter air. Silver trim and buttons on the cloak glinted in the moonlight when he turned briefly to pull the caught hem free.

The highwayman captain pulled back the rest of the curtain, and watched. The older man spoke to the driver. He gestured toward the stables around back of the tavern then gave the man a friendly pat on the back. The younger passenger followed the older as they made their way toward the tavern. Tremear let the curtain go when the driver began to unhitch the horses.

"Promising start."

The younger of the two men stepped in, followed by a flood of moonlight and a gust of brittle air. Nearly everyone in the tavern turned and scowled. He gestured to his riding companion to enter then closed the door behind him.

The barkeep ran forward and wiped his hands on a grubby towel. He glanced at each of the two men and asked, "What can I do for you this evening, messieurs?" He swiped his towel ineffectually across the table where the older man seated himself, facing away from where Darion watched.

"We need four fresh horses for Paris. Immediately," the younger man said.

"Of course, monsieur!"

"Our driver is already around back."

"Excellent! I'll send my boy to him. Anything for you while you wait? Supper? Wine?"

"We'll take whatever meat you have already cooked, and some wine. But be quick about it. We leave as soon as the horses are ready." He took out a velvet purse from the folds of his cloak and tossed it at the barkeep.

The barman's eyes glowed with greed and joy at the weight of the purse. He scurried across the room and into the kitchen.

"I think we have ourselves a victor," the captain said.

"You sure it's him?"

"I'm certain." He threw back the last of his drink and picked up his belongings. "I'll round up the others. Be sure to get Andre before you leave, eh?"

Tremear strapped his sword belt around his waist and headed for the front door. He tipped his hat to the two men as he passed them.

Struck by the stranger's unusual grin and odd attention, the two men watched with curiosity as Tremear disappeared into the frigid night.

Andre Bauvet sat alone at a table on the other side of the room. This allowed him to keep an eye on the rear door and windows of the tavern and the stables behind it. He took a sip from the flagon of wine he'd nursed to keep his senses sharp. His other hand stroked the raised scar, lighter than his dark skin, that ran from cheek to chin and interrupted his thick black beard. He glanced at Darion, who gave a subtle, quick nod of his head. In response, Andre scratched at nothing in his short, messy black hair atop his square-shaped head then once again focused on the stables.

Darion let a few minutes pass then collected his weapons, cloak, and mug. He wanted to catch a glimpse of the old man—his mark—but the thickening pockets of men and women in the tavern prevented this. He maneuvered his way between tables, where he could pass, which led him behind the old man. Something about the man's posture and air was familiar to him.

Darion lowered himself onto the bench across from Andre, who took his attention off the stables.

"What news, Gascon?" he asked, pouring Darion a small mug. Gascon was the moniker Darion's friends used for him, a reference to his home in Gascony. The soldiers in his old regiment started it, and the highwaymen continued it.

"Over my shoulder. The older gentleman in the black and purple striped doublet and his man next to him carrying the long blade."

Andre peered past Darion. "The chevalier?"

"Tremear seems to think so. Either way they have coin. He tossed a hefty purse at the barkeep when he entered. He's also in a hurry to leave."

"Urgent business then?"

Darion sipped his wine. "So it would seem."

"As long as he's willing enough to turn over more of his purse, that's all I care about." Andre held up his mug in toast. "*Salut,* Gascon."

Darion smirked and clanged his mug into Andre's.

"*Salut.*"

Darion cast a quick glance at the two men. Something about the older man made him uneasy. He gulped wine then reminded himself not to dull his wits before the take. He told himself it was just nerves. But why now? He had been a highwayman for nearly five years; though, he grew tired of the life each day. He had no other place to go. His brother wouldn't be pleased to see his face again. He had no trade skills beyond soldiering, but he'd be arrested for deserting the army if he tried to sign back up. He could register under a different name, but someone would recognize him eventually. Darion's only hope for a new life was across the sea. He had just enough coin for passage across the Atlantic and a little extra to start his life over. More coin in his pockets would be even better.

"You look like you have a devil in you, Gascon. What's on your mind?"

Darion considered his friend a moment, weighing how much to share. "I'm leaving, Andre."

Andre's laugh grew from a chuckle then loud enough to draw the attention of several men nearby. His amusement vanished quickly: Darion was not laughing or smiling. "Fuck me. You're serious?

"As serious as a papist."

"Jesus. Where the hell would you go?"

"New France somewhere. Maybe the new colony, Quebec."

Andre flashed a roguish smile. "Now I know you've lost your wits. What the hell would you do there, eh?"

Darion shook his head. "Not sure yet. I'll figure it out."

Andre raised his mug to his lips. His scowl remained fixed.

The tavern door opened. Clothing and hair billowed in the numbing wind let in. The coach driver waved from the threshold at his two passengers. One of the drunker patrons cursed and told him to close the fucking door lest he wanted a bloodied face. The older and younger men joined the driver, who slammed the door behind him, after making a rude gesture at the complainer.

"Looks like our benefactor is on the move," Andre said. "We should provide an escort."

Darion took a final swig of wine. "Get the horses. Meet me out front."

Andre flipped a coin onto the table. Cloak and hat donned quickly, he left through the back door.

Darion shifted his way between patrons and barmaids. Before he reached the courtyard door, someone tugged on his cloak. It was the barkeep.

"Thank you, monsieur! Come again."

"Pardon. The older man who just left. By chance, do you know who he is?

"No, monsieur, just that he's a generous soul. I wish more men were like him."

Darion nodded once and ran his hand through his long brown hair. He exited the tavern and shut the tavern door behind him quickly. Frigid wind whipped at his face. He pulled his cloak tighter around his shoulders and stamped his feet to keep warm. A useless action. Where was Andre? The coach was leaving.

A few minutes later, Andre appeared with their two mounts and a complaint about the time it took to get them saddled.

"Ready, Gascon?"

Darion secured his pistol into the saddle holster and hoisted himself up onto the horse. "They're heading south to Paris."

"Well, let's not leave them waiting now, eh?"

Andre whipped the reins. His horse reared then sped down the frozen dirt road.

Darion's wine provided little warmth against the bite in the air. At least it wasn't snowing. He raised his woolen scarf over his bearded face and nose, put his boot to his mare, and followed in fast pursuit.

# II.

## Cornered Prey

The full moon gleamed silver on the road, its light shattered by the occasional dark shadows of thin pockets of trees that lined the verge. This made for easy travel on the well-worn route: Darion and Andre rode at full gallop. The coach appeared as a black smudge against the dim glow of the small town ahead of them. The carriage would never reach the town, however. Captain Tremear and several other highwaymen waited for them well before that could happen.

With the help of the night—out of sight and out of ear range—Darion and Andre quickly gained ground on the coach. Soon, however, a sharp crack of a whip rang out and the carriage bolted forward.

"It seems we've been spotted, Gascon," Andre yelled.

"Was only a matter of time."

The riders kicked at their horses' flanks, sending the excited beasts speeding down the road. Even with four horses, the coach could not overcome the weight of carriage, men, and luggage. If the occupants of the coach believed they'd find sanctuary ahead, they were sorely mistaken.

Andre drew his wheellock pistol from his saddle holster and fired as one might over a ship's bow. The warning was clear: Business was meant and blood would be spilled if the coach didn't comply. But the carriage raced on with the two highwaymen closing in. Hooves thundered. The coach frame rattled. All sounds familiar to the chase.

Darion reached the right side of the carriage as they all rushed down the slope.

"Pull off, man!" The driver looked over his shoulder, his eyes alarmed but lips frozen in a harsh scowl. He whipped the reins, but his team had no more speed to give. "Pull off, you mad bastard!"

The driver ignored him. He leaned forward. Determined.

Darion roared a curse, grabbed his pistol, and aimed it at the coach. The driver briefly glanced his way. Fear flashed in his eyes, but to his credit, he kept on. Darion adjusted his aim and fired.

The driver flinched as the lead ball whizzed by his head. He looked at Darion, his face pale.

"That near miss was deliberate. The next one won't be."

Turmoil raged in the driver's eyes. He swallowed hard and pulled up on the reins until the coach came to a complete stop.

Andre halted on the other side of the team and held onto the bit of the first horse. Darion leapt from the saddle. His temper flared. He drew his rapier and stormed to the coach. There was a certain dance to these scenarios and he didn't appreciate the young driver improvising to the tune of his own madness.

The driver shifted in his seat. Darion glared at him.

"Don't be a fool, man."

The driver nodded and sat back on the bench.

Darion stayed behind his horse. It was possible that both men inside had pistols at the ready, if they had any brains about them.

Andre trotted his horse to where Dorian stood then dismounted. "How d'you want to play this one, Gascon?"

Darion scowled. "I don't. You in the coach, come out. Now."

"Like hell we will." It was the younger man who spoke.

"Come along, messieurs. Let us take care of business so we can all quickly get on our way and out of this damn cold."

"Bah! To hell with you."

Darion signaled Andre to grab the driver. Andre acted quickly and soon had the edge of his rapier against the man's neck. He pressed the blade closer to make the man cease his whimpering.

"I make this offer, messieurs," Darion said. "Leave the carriage—with caution and your hands raised—and we'll let your driver see morning."

The silence was broken by the thundering sound of Tremear and his men approaching.

"You hear that, messieurs?" Darion asked. "You'd be wise to act with haste. Our captain isn't as forgiving as I am."

Still no sounds or movement came from within the carriage. Darion sighed. The chevalier and his retainer had nowhere to go, nor could they hope to win, outnumbered as they were. It was in their best interest to submit. What reason caused them to refuse? Were they stalling? Perhaps waiting for someone to arrive?

"Messieurs, I will count to five. After that, the grass will be watered with your blood. One... two... three–"

"As you say, you damnable scoundrel. But you are to let the driver be."

"Wise of you, old man. First, your pistols. Out the window, please."

Two pistols clattered to the ground. Darion inched closer, rapier in hand. He knew better than to trust them. He threw the door open and the younger man leapt out, sword drawn, cloak billowing behind him. The man moved like quicksilver. Darion barely had time to deflect the attack.

"Fucking shit." Darion retreated a few steps. "You are an ass," Darion said. "The role of hero is played by fools and corpses."

"And you, sir, are a coward! You hide your face." His blade flicked forward and back, like a serpent's strikes.

Darion fought to parry the feints and blows, but the other man's swordsmanship was superior. This was unexpected from a courier, a lackey. The highwayman managed just enough hilt-to-blade to keep his hellish opponent from hitting his mark.

"I shall skewer you like a pig for roasting, you black-hearted bastard," the man said.

Darion drew back a few steps then sliced his blade left to right. His rapier tip just missed the man's abdomen. This caused his attacker to hesitate from bearing down on him.

Not twenty feet away Andre crossed blades with the chevalier. The old man had used his retainer's distraction as an opportunity to sneak out the coach and flank Andre from behind the team of horses. The highwayman had no choice but to let the driver go, so he could properly defend himself. So while Andre and the chevalier exchange pleasantries with steel, the driver flattened himself against the side of the coach in fear. The chevalier showed obvious signs of a skilled swordsman. The way he took his stance, held his guards, thrust and parried all looked like plates straight out of a fencing master's treatise. But his age betrayed him in his motions. His feints weren't inviting enough and his ripostes too slow. At one moment Andre beat the chevalier's blade away, took a step back, and held his sword straight forward, waiting to see if the old man would run into his point. The chevalier stopped, struck out at Andre's sword with his own, but caught nothing but the cold air. A smile appeared on Andre's dark visage as he disengaged the old man's attempted beat. Only his love for a little sport held his hand in check and kept the chevalier breathing.

Darion did his best to keep his adversary in check. He didn't need to best the retainer; he just needed to delay him long enough for Captain Tremear and the rest of the Falcon Highwaymen to arrive. And in the distance he could already hear the low rumbling of hooves on frozen ground.

The other man feinted to Darion's sword arm and circled his blade below with a thrust toward Darion's chest. Darion avoided the thrust and responded with a quick, short lunge, which the man parried, as was Darion's desire—it left the young man open for the brief moment needed. The highwayman's left fist connected and blood streamed from the surprised attacker's nose.

"Damn cad!" The man swiped at the blood on his lips then launched into a flurry of attacks, his sword action sharpened by fury. "I will gut you."

Darion whirled his rapier. His opponent's blade rested against his sword's hilt. The highwayman warmed to the familiar sensation of knowing he'd won before he finished his move. The attacker tried to muscle Darion's rapier out of the way. This relieved Darion of any effort as his sword glided forward.

The blade sliced into the man's upper arm. He dropped his sword and pressed the already bloodied hand to the wound. Darion smashed his hilt into the man's face. The mad bastard collapsed and lay in a heap, shivering, on the frost-covered grass.

The highwayman stood over the man, his hidden smile one of scorn. The man writhed in pain and made no effort to rise. Darion glanced at Andre, who threw the chevalier to the ground. The old man's hat tumbled off. Moonlight reflected on his head, which was bald except for the sparse white fringe. He looked up. Darion's breath caught. Though he could not see them, even with the full moon, he knew the man's eyes were green and piercing. That the man's brow was weathered from years as a soldier—and as a surrogate father to a rowdy youth.

"Uncle?"

The desperate chevalier lashed his rapier at Andre. Andre blocked the move with his boot, forcing the sword onto the ground. He stomped on the blade, breaking it in two

"Enough!" Andre said. His arm drew back, ready to deal a wicked, if not fatal blow. The old man raised his arm in defense.

Darion rushed forward and held Andre's hand in check. "No!"

"What the hell, Gascon? Are you mad?"

"Let him be."

"Darion?" The old man lowered his arm. "It is you. Scoundrel." His shocked expression shifted to joy. He smiled at the highwayman gazing down at him.

"You know this man?" Andre asked.

"There is no point in further pretense." He pulled his scarf down. "This is my uncle."

"Your uncle's the damned Chevalier d'Auch?" Jaspart asked.

Darion's skin crawled at the sound of the captain's voice. He didn't notice the captain or the rest of the Falcon Highwaymen arrive. But there they were. Still mounted on their horses, masked in their scarfs, and with bewildered looks in their eyes.

"So it would appear." It had been at least five years since Darion had seen his uncle, Jean-Girard Lecroix. He'd last seen him before he abandoned the army for a highwayman's life. And before his uncle was dubbed a chevalier—a knight. He did not share his uncle's joy at this dubious reunion. The gravity of the situation was too severe.

The captain looked no more amused by the revelation.

"Your valuables, Chevalier. Now. Delay any further and your companions will be escorting a corpse back to Paris."

Lecroix considered the captain with a penetrating gaze. He got off the ground and reached into the coach.

"Easy now, old man," Tremear said. "Easy."

Lecroix scowled before pulling out a canvas satchel and dropping it on the ground. He then pulled out a velvet pouch from his doublet and threw it at the captain. Tremear flinched but caught the purse.

"What else?" Tremear said.

"That is all. I'm not a rich man. I'm a man of peace, not gold."

"I know. So where is it?"

"Where's what?" Darion interjected. What more could they want beyond coins and jewels?

"Captain!" one of the highwaymen said.

Tremear whirled. "What is it?"

"Riders. And plenty of them. Fifteen or so. We need to go, Captain. Now."

Tremear growled. The highwaymen were outnumbered two to one, far from the odds a band of thieves wanted to get involved in. The captain pulled his pistol from his saddle's holster. "Where is it? You're running out of time, old man."

The chevalier's eyes glimmered with defiance. "From the sounds of it, it is you who is running out of time."

Tremear snarled. He aimed his pistol at the driver still flushed against the side of the coach and fired. A bright flash lit the area. Smoke wafted from the pistol's barrel, and the driver screamed, grabbing his hip. He pulled his hand away from the wound slick with blood and slowly slid down the side of the carriage. A grotesque look of shock fixed on his face.

"Murderer!" Lecroix cried. He lunged at Tremear with arms extended, ready to pull the captain from his horse and strangle him, but Darion rushed between them. He grabbed his uncle by the cuff of the doublet and held him in place.

"At ease, Uncle," he said in a low voice. He turned back to Tremear. "Captain—"

"You have a lot to answer for, Gascon," Tremear said. "Back to base camp, men. Quickly now!"

Darion looked crossly at his captain from beneath his wide hat. The sound of the horsemen grew closer. They'd arrive in a couple minutes at most.

"Move out!" Tremear yelled. The highwaymen spurred on their horses toward Clermont.

Darion lifted himself into his saddle. He frowned at his uncle hunched over the young driver, pressing his wool cloak over the lad's wound.

"Uncle."

Lecroix shot daggers with his eyes. Darion hadn't seen such a look in his uncle's face since he was a child. So much disappointment. Regret. Anger.

Darion replaced the scarf over his face. Fifteen horsemen pulled into the field, all donning dark doublets with silver trim. Three silver fleur-de-lis were embroidered over the left chest, and crimson cloaks over their shoulders. Darion recognized the company instantly. *The Forty-Five Guardsmen.* The king's personal bodyguard. A few held fiery torches, but he knew all were armed with pistols and steel.

The company seemed confused at first, their eyes jumping around at the scene before them.

"Highwaymen!" Lecroix said. "They headed north!"

"There!" one of the Guardsmen said, pointing at Darion and Andre. "There's two of them!"

"Shit," Darion said. "Move!"

He and Andre put their boots to their mounts. The horses dashed off. They wouldn't be able to lose the Guardsmen through the wide-open fields, but a thick patch of woods rested not far off from the road. If they had any chance of escaping, it was in there.

Several shots fired. Darion heard the lead balls zip past his head. Andre was still with him, leaning low over his horse's neck. Not far behind them were the Guardsmen, barreling down with their crimson cloaks billowing in the moonlight.

On they charged. Darion could see the break in the trees ahead. Just a few more yards and they'd have enough cover to make their escape.

The Guardsmen fired another volley just as Darion hit the tree line. He closed his eyes, expecting one of the shots to bury itself in his back. All missed. He sighed in relief. He rode deeper into the forest before looking over his shoulder. He had hoped to exchange a friendly quip with Andre, but he was accompanied by nothing more than the trees around him. Darion pulled on the reins. There was no sign of Andre. No shadows lurking about the woods, nor the sound of a horse's whinny in the darkness. A harsh breeze picked up as a dreadful thought came to mind. He kicked his horse's flank and headed back.

He stopped several yards from the edge of the forest and

dismounted. He crept to the threshold and hid behind a large tree. Andre's horse was lifeless on the ground, and Andre was slowly pulling himself up from his knees to his feet. Several Guardsmen surrounded him, their pistols and harquebuses leveled at Andre. Two men dismounted and approached with fetters in hand.

"You're under arrest, in the name of the king."

Darion swore softly. He wanted to run to Andre's aid–two friends fighting side-by-side like in the old tales Darion's mother used to read him when he was a child–but they would've been cut down on the spot. He'd be no good to Andre if they were both choking on their own lifeblood.

Andre started drawing his blade, but a Guardsman walloped him across the face with the end of the harquebus. He collapsed, blood trickling from his forehead. He groaned and looked toward the woods while his hands were shackled together.

"Where are your friends now, eh?" he was asked.

Andre smiled through the pain–that insolent, roguish grin he was so wont to share. Another Guardsman grabbed him by the hair. "Answer him, asshole."

Andre hocked bloody spit at the man's feet, earning him another dose of the harquebus stock. This time to his gut.

"Search the woods for the other bastard. Bring this one back to Paris."

Darion had lingered for too long already, he knew. Looking back is what got men killed. He mounted his mare, put boot to flank, and took off into the night.

# III.
# A Thief's Loyalty

Darion arrived at their usual meeting spot, an old and abandoned farm northwest of Paris, a few leagues from the Seine River and Rouen. It was one of the areas decimated by the religious wars. Catholics would destroy farmsteads and commerce loyal to the Huguenots, and the Huguenots sure as hell did it right back to Catholic landowners. So much blood and ash, and all over whether God prefers his loyal subjects to speak to him in Latin or French. In the end, no one won. The Catholic League lost. The Huguenots lost. But the real losers were the poor, hard working men and women who saw their lives turn to dust in an instant. For a moment, Darion felt lucky that all he lost in the war was his father.

He crossed the moonlit yard to the large farmhouse overlooking the ruined pastures around it and dismounted, throwing the reins around the fence. The farmhouse interior was shrouded in shadow. Only a few faint strands of silver light filtered its way through holes in the curtains, catching the edges of a table, a couple of chairs, and the railing by the stairs. As he stepped in he heard the clicking of a pistol near his head.

"Hold it right there."

"Easy, Simon. It's just me. Darion."

"Blessed be, Gascon. I almost shot your brains out."

Darion patted his friend on the shoulder. "I'm glad you didn't."

"Who's there?" Even through the darkness, Darion could make out Tremear's silhouette against the weak light. Behind him came a few other highwaymen, one holding a lantern to light the way. All were still armed to the teeth.

"Just the Gascon, Captain," Simon said.

"Were you followed?" Darion shook his head. "Where's Andre?"

Darion felt the gazes from his brethren fall on him. "He fell behind."

"What do you mean he fell behind?" Simon asked. "He was with you."

"We weren't able to get out of there before the Forty-Five showed up."

"The Forty-Five Guardsmen? Damn my soul."

"We made for the forest nearby, hoping to lose them in the trees, but Andre's horse was shot down before we got there."

"You should've gone and got him, Gascon," Tremear said.

Darion nearly laughed at the irony. It was Tremear's decision to linger longer that got Andre caught. Had they left at the first sign of trouble, they'd all be safe and sound in their little thieves' den.

"Against those odds? All it would've done was give the gravedigger extra work."

"Is Andre dead?" Simon asked.

"No, but the Guardsmen detained him. They're taking him back to Paris."

"We need to leave here. King's men will be on us."

"We're not leaving," Tremear said. "They don't know where to find us."

"What if Andre talks?"

"If you're so worried about that, Simon, then you can scurry away. No one's stopping you. Hell, I'll even give you some coin to measure yourself for a new petticoat. How about that?"

"What are we going to do about Andre?" Darion asked. "We can't just let him rot in prison."

"The stupid bastard got himself caught. Let him get himself uncaught," Tremear said. He looked at the men around him. "We've run into king's men before and haven't had any issue. They'll be looking in the wrong area for us anyways. Tomorrow morning we head back to base. Anyone who wants to leave is more than welcome to leave."

⚜⚜⚜

Darion rose early the next morning and packed what few belongings he owned. An extra cloak, an old doublet, breeches, and a thick leather jerkin he used as light armor. He also had a few additional daggers and swords he collected over the years. Some from his days as a soldier; others taken from his victims as a highwayman. He placed his extra steel in heavy wool blankets.

He opened a drawer and pulled forth a couple of books he owned, the only items tied back to his childhood in Gascony. He started putting them into his satchel when he noticed a bit of paper jutting out of the top of one of the books. He flipped it open and pulled out a small portrait of a young woman with raven hair, fair skin, sapphire eyes, and a delicate and welcoming smile on coral lips. Darion smirked. It was a face that brought him joy, but it was also the face that brought him the most sorrow.

"Who's that?"

Darion slammed the tome shut and turned to see Simon standing in the doorway. He had a crooked grin beneath his full, reddish beard.

"No one of importance. Not anymore, anyways." He placed the book in his satchel and buckled it closed.

"Where you off to?"

Darion stared at the leather purse on the table beside him, nearly full from a long, arduous task of saving every coin he could. It was his savings to start a new life, but, as much as he wanted to leave to start anew, he couldn't leave France. Not yet.

"Paris, I think. I have some unfinished business there."

"Does this business have anything to do with the comely girl in that there portrait?"

Another wry smile appeared on Simon's face.

"Believe it or not–no."

"Of course."

Despite Simon's mocking conclusion, Darion wasn't lying. He wanted nothing to do with that old life, a life that held so much promise but led him down the dark road to becoming a thief and highwayman. His business rested in his current life. It rested with his uncle, and with Andre. Darion couldn't leave his friend to rot in prison or be tortured beyond recognition.

Darion threw his satchel over his shoulder and placed his wide-brim hat on his head.

"Will you need some help finishing this business?"

Darion considered his friend with a long glance. A little sword play would probably be needed, but he didn't want to put any more of his brethren in harm's way. He shook his head in a convenient lie.

"I'll manage. Thanks."

He patted Simon about the shoulder before heading downstairs. The farmhouse slept while sunlight poured through the breaks and tears in the drapes, and the brisk wind rattled the windows. Darion grabbed a piece of bread from the kitchen and stepped out to the stables. He had a long ride ahead of him, and he wanted to get to Paris before sundown.

To his surprise, he found Tremear saddling a horse.

"Jaspart," Darion said. "I'm surprised to see you about this early in the morning." The captain quickly glanced at Darion but continued going about his preparations.

The sun was warm, but Darion didn't feel its heat above Tremear's frigidness. "Where do you think you're going?"

"I'm leaving."

The captain scoffed. "Shit. Turning tail and running is it? And to who, I wonder. Your uncle–the fucking Chevalier d'Auch?"

Darion scowled. "I didn't know. Last time I saw my uncle, he was merely a retired lieutenant from the king's guards. Don't put Andre's arrest on me. He would be here if you ordered the retreat at the first sign of trouble. We got the chevalier's coins and valuables. What more could he have had?"

"Doesn't concern you. You're running, remember?"

"Eat shit, Jaspart."

Tremear stepped around his horse and threw back the fold of his cloak. Morning light caught the guard of his rapier. Darion had no doubt that the captain meant for that. Darion dismissed the gesture with a chuckle. He placed his satchel on the ground and threw back his own cloak.

"Everything alright?" Simon stepped into the stable. Darion and Tremear didn't break their stare. "What's going on?"

The ends of Tremear's mustache upturned and his stance softened.

"Just saying adieu to the Gascon." He led his horse out of the stable and mounted the saddle. "I'll be gone for a few days. I need to talk to some contacts to see how badly Andre and the Gascon fucked us."

Without another word, he rode out. Darion grabbed his saddle and headed for his horse's stall. His skin singed, infuriated by everything that happened. Still, a small part of him was glad he didn't have to draw blades against Tremear. Men who crossed steel with the captain often found themselves measured for a pine box.

"Darion," Simon said. "What was that about?"

Darion's blue eyes flared in vexation.

"Like the captain said. We were just saying adieu."

# IV.

## The Chevalier & the Lieutenant

Jean-Girard Lecroix, the Chevalier d'Auch, paced back and forth in an antechamber of the Louvre. He had arrived early in the morning, nearly beating the sun back to Paris, but decided to wait a few hours before returning to the palace. It gave him time to freshen up from his long trip from the Low Lands and to plan what he wanted to say to King Henry and the Duc de Sully. He couldn't keep the attack on his coach a secret. Not when one man's head was still in a foggy haze and the driver barely held onto his life, and definitely not with almost a score of the Forty-Five Guardsmen as witness to the incident.

There would be questions in the coming days. Lots of them. Lecroix had plenty of his own, in fact.

Mostly why his nephew and surrogate son, Darion, was with the highwaymen. The lad had such a promising career in the new standing army, but disappeared, suddenly, one night. None of Darion's companions knew where he was, and Lecroix thought him lost to the afterlife, no doubt at the end of a sword or a pistol's barrel. It seemed peculiar that he would leave his life with the military to become a thief and an outlaw. It didn't seem in Darion's nature. He was always a young man of honor, loyalty, and duty—much like his father. Yet there was Darion last night, shadowed in a cloak and mask, and baring steel against his uncle. Death was, perhaps, a far more acceptable fate than what Darion had become—to Lecroix anyways.

The old chevalier sighed. If the king and duke had no other missions for him, maybe he would travel back to the countryside and look for Darion, get some answers, and smack some sense into the boy if need be.

Morning light shown through large windows, cutting through the shadows of the Louvre in long, golden streaks. Lecroix stood in one of these strands, letting the sun warm him as he waited. When he first arrived, he had passed the queen, Marie de Medici, her household, and most of the royal family. She looked agitated, and shuffled at a pace that made it difficult for her ladies and children to keep up. When Lecroix arrived at the antechamber, he was told to wait. Several minutes went by before he noticed a pale man garbed in all black leaning against a pillar in the shadows. The fellow stood there like a statue, his eyes fixated on Lecroix as if studying him. He made the chevalier feel so uneasy that he didn't even notice his own hand moving toward his rapier.

The drawing room doors opened. Don Pedro Alvarez of Toledo, the Marquis de Villafranca and the king of Spain's emissary to France stormed out. His face was bleak and cross, and he looked aghast at the chevalier as he passed. The marquis muttered in his native tongue and kept on, passing the pale man in the corner who finally showed signs of life and followed Don Pedro like a shadow.

Several more minutes went by, and still Lecroix wasn't given access to King Henry.

Footsteps echoed behind him. Antoine Castel, lieutenant of the Forty-Five Guardsmen, rounded the corner. He was dressed in the typical Guardsman's uniform. Long dark hair dangled about his shoulders, while a scowl held firm beneath his heavily bearded face.

"Chevalier," Castel said.

"Lieutenant. It's good to see you again."

The lieutenant nodded. Castel and Darion were friends once. Good friends. But the morning that Darion vanished, Castel was found bleeding on a field. He told officials that the two incidents weren't related, that he didn't know where Darion was, but Lecroix always had his doubts. He wondered if Castel knew about Darion's more recent activities.

"Something the matter, Chevalier?"

"No, no. Just a bit tired from my travels."

Again the lieutenant nodded, seemingly uninterested in any sort of conversation.

The chamber door opened. The Duc de Sully—the king's right hand man and most trusted friend—stepped through. His face had kept its youthful appearance, despite the stress and worry of his ministerial position. But the duke's typically tenacious gaze seemed veiled in irritation; nonetheless, he managed a friendly smile beneath his bushy, brown beard.

"His Majesty will see you now, Chevalier," Sully said. "And you, Lieutenant."

The duke led the two men into the king's drawing room. His Majesty sat on a large velvet covered chair, dressed all in black with a stiff, white ruffle jutting from beneath his doublet's collar. He held a small glass of dark wine. Henry was a joyful fellow for a monarch, a rarity in those days. A smile was readily on the king's lips when he was with his children or his soldiers, and he often amused himself with friends during hunts, or flirting with his mistresses. Despite those frequent moments of rapture, his early life of battles had taken its toll. His raven hair and beard were now heavily streaked with grey, and rumors swirled around court that he wasn't as fit and able as he once was. Rumors that the king did all he could to quash.

"Chevalier. Welcome," the king said, his bright blue eyes smiling.

Lecroix bowed. "Your Majesty."

"I'm pleased to see you again, my friend."

"As am I, Your Majesty."

"We were expecting you yesterday afternoon. I was starting to get worried that something happened."

Lecroix cleared his throat uncomfortably. "We had a broken wheel by the border. It delayed us several hours, sire."

"Well, I assume you have some excellent news for me. Otherwise you would've been off waiting until *after* I spent some time with my wife and children."

"Of course, Your Majesty. I wouldn't have interrupted unless it was vitally important, and I do have good news." He pulled a leather tube from under his arm. "We've reached a tentative agreement with the Low Lands."

Sully took the scroll case and stepped to a large table off to the side. "What are the terms?"

"It's a defensive contract. Ten thousand men should Spain continue their aggressions on the Providences. And five thousand men in the form of infantry or able ships, should Phillip turn his eye toward Your Majesty."

The king chuckled. "That'll get that haughty Spaniard, Don Pedro, in quite a fit."

"We're also to continue facilitating peace between the Low Lands and Spain."

"That'll be a bit more difficult."

"Sire?"

"Don Pedro has been pushing for a Franco-Spanish alliance," Sully said, his eyes scanning over the document. "No doubt he will bristle and bluster at this news."

"He proposed a double marriage. The dauphin and my eldest daughter to Phillip's children," Henry added.

"And, are you considering his offer, sire?"

The king's face soured. "As if I would let my own children mix with Hapsburg filth."

"We didn't have enough leverage before, Chevalier," Sully added. "France is still recovering from our wars and the populace has no interest in going to battle with anyone. Not to mention the money we send to the Low Lands is draining the royal coffers. It's better spent on roads and commerce. But the promise of men or ships may put Phillip in check. If nothing else, it'll make the Spanish think long and hard about poking the embers in the Low Lands." Sully finished reading and rolled the document back up. "Well, this all looks well and in order, Chevalier. You and President Jeannin did excellent work."

"Thank you, Your Grace."

"You may go unless there's anything else."

Lecroix hesitated. "There was... an incident on the road. Not far from Clermont. We were attacked by highwaymen."

"What?" the king said, nearly leaping from his seat.

"Why haven't my men informed me of this?" Castel asked, finally finding a reason to break his soldierly silence.

"I told them to delay their report. I wanted you to hear it from my mouth first. My apologies, lieutenant, if I've forced your men to breach protocol."

"Was anyone injured?" Sully asked.

"Our driver, Phillip, was shot. He's alive, albeit barely. We had to leave him at an inn in Pontoise."

The king turned to Sully. "Send my surgeon to Pontoise, Maximilien. Immediately."

"And Gaston?" Castel asked, a hint of concern in his voice.

Lecroix studied the lieutenant a moment. Castel's eyes had narrowed. His jaw slid back and forth in a nervous grind. Gaston was an initiate for the Forty-Five, hand recruited by Castel himself. The lieutenant wasn't wont to have many friends, but he had a fondness for Gaston. This escort mission was part of his training.

"Injured. A sword thrust to the arm and a broken nose. His head is still a throbbing mess, however. We thought it best to leave him at Pontoise, as well, until he recovers."

"And the men at fault?"

"About a half-dozen riders or so. All masked. All well-armed. And not just nicely polished swords and a few pistols. These men rode as well-armed as any of His Majesty's Guardsmen. We were only able to apprehend one of the scoundrels. He's been given lodgings in the Prison de l'Abbaye."

"Who is he?"

"He wouldn't talk but we did take this off his person."

Lecroix reached into his doublet and pulled out a singular long falcon feather, clipped at an acute angle near the end of the plume. Castel snatched it from the chevalier's hand and gave it a long look. Lecroix was hoping to get a read off the lieutenant, on if he knew anything about this band of men his nephew rode out with, but the lieutenant remained as inert as a sitting stone.

"Question him, Lieutenant," Sully said.

"Yes, please do," the king said. "I want to know what sort of men dare attack one of my emissaries."

"With pleasure, Your Majesty."

Castel bowed and left the room with purpose in his stride. Lecroix didn't envy the prisoner one bit.

"Any other surprises for us, Chevalier?" the king asked.

"None, Your Majesty, but I have one request. A favor."

"That so? Name it, my friend."

"If you have no other use for me, I was hoping for a holiday. I've been away from France for so long, and I'd very much like to catch up with some old comrades."

Henry looked at his favorite minister. "What do you think, Maximilien? Shall we give this chevalier his due?"

"I believe we can do without his presence for a short while longer," the Duc de Sully said.

"We shall wish you to present the signed treaty to the Low Lands in our name, of course," Henry said.

Lecroix bowed. "I thank you for the honor, Your Majesty. I shall try to keep it a concise holiday."

# V.
# The Auld Horse Inn

The Dog's Inn was a popular haunt for soldiers in Paris. It was owned by Captain Charles de Fonte, a middle-aged Gascon, who, after the final cannon blast was fired between the Huguenots and Catholics, turned in his commission from the cavalry and opened up the tavern on the Rue de Saint Andre. Many men who fought alongside Fonte were as faithful as patrons as they were comrades in arms. Even those who once traded carbine shots and sword thrusts with the old soldier found themselves enjoying the comforts and entertainment Fonte's establishment provided.

When Darion joined the infantry to fight against the Duc de Savoy, mockingly known amongst his enemies as *Testa d'feu,* the Head of Fire, he was quickly introduced to the tavern by his companions. He spent nearly every night there toasting with friends and flirting with mademoiselles. Darion looked forward to staying there once more.

Darion rode into Paris through the gate at the Port de St. Martin. The sun started to settle back down for the night, painting the sky in scarlet and casting long shadows across the city landscape.

Darion hadn't seen the city in several years, but not much had changed. Paris was still fairly dirty from the years of neglect at the hands of the Valois, albeit it began to shine a bit brighter under Good King Henry. Four hundred thousand citizens crammed the narrow and crooked streets. Ill-paved and poorly drained, some roads felt more like marshland than city streets. Lofty houses of lath and plaster jutted into the sky, nearly blocking out the sun and trapping the rank air. In the summer it would get even worse. Carpenters, cart-wrights, and smiths would practice their trade along the streets, while artisans, tanners, and cleaners pushed their wares on anyone who was foolish enough to stop and listen. Packs of dogs would fight over scraps of fetid meat in the same alleyways young boys and girls chased after each other and laughed. It made traversing the city aggravating and riding a horse nearly impossible.

Fortunately, winter still had its cold clutch on Paris, so pushy vendors who enjoyed having all their toes kept to the warmth of their workshops instead of the lanes, and the putrid stench from the craftsmen workshops and work sheds remained at a minimum. Still, the streets were crowded with men, women, and children going about their business. Within a few hours, however, most would be locked inside their houses. For as dirty and foul as the city was during the day, at night it became even more dangerous. Rogues, swordsmen, cut-purses, and assassins plied their trade by moonlight, and the incompetence and corruption of the local authorities made bringing the ne'er do wells to justice nearly impossible.

Darion looked forward to seeing old Fonte's face and perhaps other familiar—if not outright friendly—faces, like that of Rolland Hazart d'Orthez, another fellow Gascon. Unlike most second born sons of Gascony, however, Hazart didn't join the army; rather he became a sailor where he found himself exchanging knife thrusts with the Spanish and Turks who used the Mediterranean as their personal gold mine. When Hazart made his way to Paris to "look for his golden egg", he met Darion where the two bonded over long nights of heavy drinking and a few tavern brawls. Darion heard Hazart had found himself a respectable woman to marry, though he didn't hear where they were living.

Then there was the infamous Peppin Petite, a name both fitting and ironic, for he was small in stature but not in breadth. He was from Caen in Normandy and was part of Darion's infantry regiment when King Henry took up arms against Savoy. Alas, Peppin had the ill luck one afternoon of having his harquebus blow up in his face while practicing his marksmanship. The small explosion burned the right side of his face, including his aiming eye. After that he began wearing a black cloth tied around his head to cover the useless, maimed eye. Fortunately for Peppin, the explosion did more in injuring his features than it did his marksmanship. His ability to line up and hit a target was just as impressive when he used his left eye. The stout and bawdy soldier was also proficient with a sword, cutting and thrusting his enemies like he was possessed by Archangel Michael—or perhaps Lucifer himself, for when the guns are firing, the horses trampling, and steel clashing it is hard to tell the difference between one and the other. A score of other men and women flashed in Darion's mind.

He turned on the Rue de Saint Andre. The buildings all looked the same as Darion remembered, just as run down as ever, and the streets just as filthy. But where a sign once hung inviting travelers to enter for a quick drink at the Dog's Inn was replaced by another sign—The Auld Horse. Darion stood there for a minute, staring and wondering what happened to his old haunt. He probably would've continued staring if it wasn't for a young woman breaking him from his trance.

"Would you like to come in, monsieur?" she asked. She looked no older than seventeen. A few wisps of dirty blonde hair peered from the ends of her crimson hood while her eyes, like ice crystals, sparkled in the fading sunlight.

"My apologies, mademoiselle," he said, "but it's been many years since I was last in Paris. But I remember this tavern being called the Dog's Inn."

"You are correct, monsieur."

The front door opened. An older man walked out with a long candle in hand to light a few lanterns outside. His face was slightly reddish and was framed with white hair and beard.

"Oh, good. You're back, Catherine," he said. "You're later than I would've liked."

"Sorry father but I was helping Madam de Cambon cut vegetables."

"Aye, and you should've been doing that here. We have patrons of our own, you know." His attention turned to Darion. "Who is this young gentleman?"

"I came looking for the Dog's Inn," Darion said. "Captain de Fonte's is an old friend of mine."

The old man's face dimmed. "Ah, yes. Of course. Come on in and out of the cold. I'll see to your horse and then will explain all."

Darion handed the reins to the old man before following Catherine into the inn. He was instantly struck by the strong aroma of roasting chicken and wood smoke, a far cry from when the tavern was overrun by soldiers and reeked of oiled leather, steel, and wine. The front counter was still just a few feet inside the door. A few ledgers rested on top of it next to a burning candle. To the right was the kitchen. To the left through a narrow doorway was the tavern area. Darion saw only a few people sitting at a table along the wall, sharing in an intimate conversation near the cracking fire of the hearth.

Darion pulled off his gloves revealing a few, light scars. Catherine's eyes seemed drawn to them.

"You're a soldier?" she asked.

"For a time."

"Cavalry or infantry?"

"Infantry."

"Who did you fight under?"

An amused half-smile appeared on Darion's lips.

"Go see if anyone needs something, Catherine," the old man said. The young woman's eyes pleaded with her father, but he didn't relent. She curtsied and disappeared into the tavern hall.

"Forgive my daughter, but she's young and reads far too many tales of adventure."

"Quite alright, Monsieur..."

"Claude de Lasset at your service. I'm afraid I didn't catch your name."

Darion balked. As a highwayman he cherished anonymity, but he wanted to put those days behind him. Small steps. "The name's Darion Delerue."

"From the south no doubt?" Darion searched for meaning behind the old man's words. The innkeeper grinned warmly. "I spent some time in Gascony when I was younger. Your accent is as thick as pastry batter."

"Last time I was here, Monsieur Lasset, it was still called the Dog's Inn and was run by Captain de Fontes. Does he no longer own this place?"

"No. I'm afraid to bear such ill tiding, but the good captain passed away last spring."

Darion's heart sank. "How unfortunate. And his wife and daughter?"

"They sold me the tavern and moved to Brittany where the madam has relations. I've been running this place ever since."

"I see. I hope the men have been treating you as well as the captain."

"More or less. Business hasn't been quite the same since the captain died, but it's good enough."

Darion took out a few coins from his satchel. "I'd like to rent a room, if you have any available."

"Certainly. How long will you need it for?"

"Only a night or two I suspect. Three at most."

"Of course, monsieur. Let's get your room situated and then we can go about dinner, eh?"

Darion nodded and followed the old man across the tavern floor. Darion had never seen it so empty. Only a handful of patrons were dining. Most looked to be other tradesmen. One man sat in the shadows in the corner of the tavern, drinking alone. All were silent or conversing in low whispers to each other—a far cry from the rowdy and bawdy soldiers who once overran the tavern, drinking and carousing their way to an early grave. The ghosts of those days echoed in Darion's mind.

"Down this hall we have a very nice room," Lasset said at the top of the stairs.

"How about this one?" Darion asked. He stopped in front of a smaller room just at the top of the steps.

Lasset looked at Darion dubiously. "It's available, but the room down the hall is much nicer, and I'd give it to you at the same rent."

"That's quite alright." Darion stepped into the room. It was sparsely furnished with just a bed, a wardrobe, and a small writing desk in the corner.

"It's yours if you wish, monsieur. Make yourself at home. I'll have Catherine fetch you some fresh linens."

The room was, as the keeper said, smaller than the other rooms in the inn, but it was the same room Darion rented out when the building was still the Dog's Inn. It was also close enough to the tavern floor, so he could keep an ear out for trouble. And the large window on the far wall overlooked a narrow alleyway in case he needed to make a quick exit. But inside the room there was another perk. Darion dropped his saddlebags and dragged the bed from the against the wall, the feet scratching at the wood beneath it. He dropped to a knee and groped the floor, pressing against the boards and scraping at the seams. After a little searching, one of the boards dipped. He scratched at the edges and, with a little work, pried it free.

Darion smiled. A knock came at the door.

"Monsieur Delerue?" Catherine said from the other side. "I brought you some linens for your bed."

"Just a moment."

Darion placed a greater portion of his purse in the cavity before replacing the floor board and dragging the bed back to its spot by the wall. He opened the door. Catherine walked in, large white sheets in her arms. She looked around.

"Redecorating already?"

"Excuse me?"

"The bed. You've moved it. It's a little further to the window than before."

Darion gaped at her. "You're a perceptive one."

"I try to be. Father says my mother was very much the same way." She dropped the sheets and started making the bed. "You must've rented this room before."

Darion crossed his arms. "And what gave that away? My boots, perhaps?"

She shrugged. "Why else would you want one of the smaller rooms when the biggest is available?"

"Why else, indeed."

She placed a pillow by the headboard. "There. Finished. You'll sleep well on that, I'd wager. Your food is also ready, as you please, monsieur."

# VI.
# The King's Wager

Jacquelyna Brocquart followed the king and queen, and a score of their closest friends into a large, open hall. "My little gambling den," the king called it as they entered. Stacks of dice and playing cards were already placed on tables in anticipation of the evening's festivities. A roaring fire blazed in the hearth, warming the party and illuminating the fine tapestries of red, blue, and purple velvet trimmed with gold tassels.

Jacquelyna had been at court a little over a year and knew the faces around her quite well. The Princess de Conti, Madame de Guise, Maréchale de la Châtre, Duc d'Épernon, Monsieur de Joinville, Concino Concini, and Monsieur de Bassompierre all filed in, chattering and laughing to one another. Not a single ambassador or emissary, groom or lady-in-waiting remained in the room, not even the queen's favorite, Leonra "Galigai" Dori. A minimal number of servants were allowed to enter the den, to serve drinks and refreshments, but only at the king's wishes and by the ringing of a small bell. His Majesty enjoyed his time with just his close friends and wanted as few outside distractions as possible.

Jacquelyna, however, was the exception to this royal policy via a special dispensation from King Henry to be part of this little soirée. The privilege irritated the queen who berated Henry for not doing the same for her beloved Galigai. Henry merely smiled, as he was wont to do during his wife's tantrums in her native tongue. He didn't know Italian but took great joy in irritating his wife when it suited him.

Jacquelyna sat on a low velvet stool near the fireplace, just on the outskirts of the group. She struggled with her longing to gain influence at court and her desire to not make enemies at court. Besides, she had her own interest in mind, namely conversing with Martin Lorfeuve, the Comte de Mauriac, who instantly sought her out when he arrived.

"May I sit with you?" he asked smiling.

"Of course. Please." She couldn't help but return the smile. His radiant amber eyes flickered with an adventurous longing, and his crooked grin hinted at dashing rogue hidden beneath the finery of his doublet. He was well built from the hours spent hunting, riding, and practicing swordplay. He was, at his core, a man of action, and Jacquelyna had a soft spot for such men. She always had ever since she was a little girl listening to her mother's stories of heroes and monsters. Lorfeuve was a dream come true and, like the young woman she was, she fell quickly for the count, smitten by his charm and coarse elegance.

"I'm glad to see you," he said, taking a seat beside her.

"I'm surprised to be here. Ladies-in-waiting aren't usually allowed at these soirées. But the king invited me."

"I know." The count's smile changed, grew a bit wider. More whimsical.

"Did you ask him?"

He took her hands into his own. "I may have earned a debt with His Majesty that I called in. I hope you don't mind."

Of course she didn't. Why would she? Her father spent nearly his entire small fortune to secure her a spot at court. He called it an investment and hoped she would marry into a wealthier family. Jacquelyna was a dutiful daughter and shared in her father's interest, but if she could find love at the same time—so much the better.

Lively conversation ruled the first hour of the gathering, starting off with a new dress the queen had ordered made special for her pregnancy, then onto the latest portrait of the king painted by Francois Porbus, and then news and gossip from around France and beyond.

All the while Jacquelyna and Martin remained in their own little world until the king, invigorated by a few drinks, began to dominate the night's conversation with talk of a recent hunting trip.

"This stag was a beast of a creature," he said. "It had to weigh upwards of five hundred pounds. It took half the men to drag it back to the palace. And it had antlers longer than Bassompierre's sword, I tell you, or perhaps something else!" The king winked, and the men laughed while some of the women blushed. "It took us nearly three hours to track the wretched thing. I swear if it wasn't for Monsieur

Lorfeuve I might never have caught him. The fellow has a nose like a scent hound. Isn't that right my dear count?"

The count was so lost in his own conversation with Jacquelyna that he didn't hear the king call him.

"Eh! Martin!"

Jacquelyna smiled and gestured toward His Majesty with a slight tipping of her head. Lorfeuve turned a deep shade of red when he saw all eyes had fallen on him. He leapt up from his seat and bowed.

"Your Most Christian Majesty called for me?"

"I did, Lorfeuve. I was comparing your tracking skills to that of a scent hound, but it's obvious your hearing is a bit... lacking."

Lorfeuve chuckled at the jest. "Your Majesty does me too much justice. I may have helped track the stag but, as they say, it's not the hound that puts the ball in the beast."

The small crowd applauded. Martin bowed before returning to his seat next to Jacquelyna.

"I'm bored!" the queen said. "Perhaps we should play a game."

"A splendid idea, Your Majesty!" Bassompierre seconded. Monsieur François Bassompierre had the rare gift of being a favorite of both the king and queen. He was a spectacular commander on the battlefield, and his skill with a blade was well spoke of at court. He had shown some interest in Jacquelyna until His Majesty found another target for his affections—a certain Charlotte de Montmorency.

"Of course," the king said. "What Madame the Queen wishes, Madame the Queen shall receive. Cards anyone?"

"Oh, I think I could partake in a little fun," Bassompierre said, twirling the ends of his mustache.

"As shall I," Concini said in a thick Italian accent.

Henry rolled his eyes. "And you, Madame la Maréchale?"

"Of course, Your Majesty."

"And how about you, Mademoiselle Brocquart?"

Jacquelyna stood and curtsied. "My apologies, sire, but I'm afraid I'm not very skilled at cards."

"Nonsense. Come. Sit at my table and play. 'Tis my royal decree. Perhaps our dear blood hound will assist you."

"It would be an honor, sire," Martin said. He led Jacquelyna to the table. In a soft whisper added: "Do as I say and you'll do just fine."

The table tops were cleaned of drink and glass, and cards were dealt. Lady Luck favored the king and Bassompierre that night and frowned upon the queen—who typically dominated her husband in cards—and Concini who, according to Martin, made some foolish mistakes, most likely to keep the queen's purse full. It was no grand secret that Concini was courting the queen's precious Galigai, and his fortune was entirely linked to Galigai's future and the queen's mood.

There were a few inquiries as to the nature of Don Pedro's visit, but Henry merely shrugged and said the Spanish ambassador wished to catch up on the news and to know how negotiations with the Low Lands were going.

"So peace is at hand then?" Concini said.

"One can only hope," Henry replied.

"That is good to hear."

A thin, smug smile nestled itself on Concini's lips that made Jacquelyna's stomach turn. His devilish eyes, aquiline features, and thin mustache set her on edge. He reminded her of a snake resting in the garden, waiting for the right moment to lunge and bare its fangs.

"I believe it's your turn, monsieur," the king said.

Concini peered at the messy pile of cards in the middle of the table and fiddled through his hand. He snapped a card upon the table. "There. Eight of spades. I win."

"Bah!" the king said, throwing the rest of his hand down. Concini shoveled the coins toward his corner. Henry looked away in disgust and stroked his beard. Mischief glowed in his bright blue eyes as his gaze fell upon his wife. "Madame la Reine, there's an issue of the utmost importance with your household that I wish to discuss, and that is the role of Mistress of the Robes."

The queen beamed. "I'm glad that you bring this up, my dear. I was thinking Galigai would take on that responsibility."

The king burst into laughter. "Galigai? Surely you're joking."

"I rarely jest when it comes to such decisions, husband. Galigai is one of my dearest friends. I can think of no one better for it."

"And I can think of about a hundred souls better suited to be your mistress." He picked up his cards and shuffled them into the deck. "I'd say I rather see François here be your Mistress of the Robes than that Italian witch."

"And what has the poor child ever done to you?"

"Her presence at the palace is offense enough."

"Your Majesty, I must protest," Concini interjected.

Henry's nostrils flared in anger. "And you! You, Signore Concini. I have seen and heard enough of you and Galigai than my stomach can abide. I bid you go and marry the girl and be gone back to Florence, lest she marries a Frenchman first and continues to poison this court."

"Husband!"

Concini sunk in his chair and attempted to fend off the rouge that leapt to his cheeks.

"I will not have her in such a capacity at my court." His eyes fell on Jacquelyna. "Mademoiselle Brocquart. How would you care being named Mistress of the Robes for the queen?"

Jacquelyna stomach fluttered. "I, Your Majesty?"

"Yes, you! And why not, I ask? You are of the finest noble birth and Martin here speaks very highly of your character. Your beauty illuminates these otherwise dreary hallways and your life is as pure and scandal free as we'd ever find. You are more than suitable."

Jacquelyna glowed at the thought. "I would be honored, Your Majesty."

"There! It's settled then." The king leaned back and put his hands behind his head in victory. The queen tightened her lips until they turned a sickly white. She flipped through the hand she'd been dealt. Jacquelyna knew Marie de Medici favored Galigai over her—the queen and maid had been long-time friends after all. "My dear—"

"There's nothing left to be said," the queen interrupted.

"Very well. How about we put it to a bet, eh? If I win this hand, Mademoiselle Brocquart becomes your Mistress of the Robes. If you win, you can name Galigai."

The queen slammed her cards down on the table. "I grow tiresome of this game and it's nearly eleven. I think I'll retire to my apartments. Come, Jacquelyna."

Everyone but the king stood to bow or curtsy. Jacquelyna made to follow her queen, but the king snapped his fingers. "Stay put, mademoiselle. You are my guest tonight. I'm sure my wife the queen can survive one night without you. You will be with her every day and night soon enough."

The queen stamped her feet. The folds of her skirt swished

together as she bustled across the marbled floor. Concini bowed toward Henry, but the king ignored him—or didn't notice, at least. Concini followed the queen, nearly running into the guards standing outside the door.

Silence gripped the room. The king's eyes darted around, lively now and full of humor. "Well, I don't remember commanding the merriment to end. Drink! Sing! Gossip! D'Epernon, I believe the deal is yours."

The duke, who wore his starched collar high around his neck, inclined his head. He wasn't always a friend to Henry IV. They had long been bitter enemies during the religious wars, and d'Epernon fought tooth and nail to keep Henry off the throne after Henry III's murder. But, like all men, he had a price worth making peace over.

The king leaned toward Jacquelyna. "I fully intend on making you the queen's Mistress of the Robes. I wasn't merely using you to prove a point with my wife. That was just gravy on the main course."

He chuckled and leaned back into his seat, jumping into a conversation with Bassompierre. Lorfeuve picked up his glass. "I suppose congratulations are in order."

Jacquelyna picked up her glass for their private toast and sipped her wine.

The gaming and drinking slowed about two hours later. Nearly all of the party had fallen asleep in chairs or couches by the fire. Bassompierre fought slumber in a futile effort, slumped in an armchair, eyes fading. The only ones who remained alert and active were the king and the Duc d'Epernon, who sat silently with mugs in hand, and Jacquelyna and the Comte de Mauriac, who fell back into a lover's conversation near the warm, crackling fire.

A retainer arrived and stood silently at the door.

"I think you're being summoned, my dear duke" the king said.

D'Epernon turned around and nodded to the retainer. "It appears so. I hope Your Majesty will pardon my absence from court the next several weeks. I need to attend to my estates before the spring."

"You will return in time for my sons' birthday celebrations next month, will you not?"

"Of course." The duke bowed and left with the silent servant.

The king stretched out his arms.

"I'm retiring," he bellowed. Bassompierre nearly jumped out of his seat. The rest of the room shook from their dreams. Even Jacquelyna and Lorfeuve broke from their conversation to look upon the king. "I advise you all to do the same, eh?"

Tired groans emanated from the party members. They filed out to an atrium and kicked their sleeping servants awake. As Jacquelyna followed the king grabbed her attention.

"Best to see to the queen before you retire for the night," he said. "You know how awful her temper can be."

"Yes, Your Majesty."

"And I'll speak with her in the morning to make sure you see no ill-repercussions by all this."

Jacquelyna curtsied and headed for the queen's rooms, but the Comte de Mauriac leapt in the way.

"Leaving without as much as a good-night?" he asked.

She blushed. "I'm sorry. I forgot. I was heading for the queen... the king..."

"I know. I heard." He grabbed her hands and lifted them to his lips for a delicate kiss. "I'll see you tomorrow?"

She nodded. He backed away, never taking his eyes off her. She left through two large doors and up the stairs, crossing several long halls, cold and dark but for several lanterns burning along the walls.

When she reached the queen's chambers, she heard two low voices speaking in Italian. She made out an *Il mio amore* here and a *Troveremo qualcosa* there, but her Italian wasn't fluent enough to understand their conversation. Still, it was obvious who the two lovers whispering in the dark were.

Jacquelyna hid behind a pillar. She didn't want to interrupt what was obviously a personal and serious conversation, but her movements were detected. Concini wrapped a cloth around his face and backed away into the shadows of the room, while Galigai stormed forward, her fists clenched.

"Spying on me now?" she asked.

"No, I–"

"Is that why the king named you Mistress of the Robes? Because you're spying for him?"

"No. Not at all. The party just ended and His Majesty ordered me to attend to the queen before retiring and—"

"So, you decided to stalk in the shadows like a thief and spy?"

"No, I heard voices and I didn't want to intrude."

"You failed. Besides, the queen has been asleep some time now. You're not needed here."

The true meaning of Galigai's words wasn't lost to Jacquelyna. She twiddled her fingers.

"My apologies. I... I will retire to my room."

She made to leave, but Galigai motioned her to stay. Like a spell Jacquelyna's feet felt as if they turned to stone.

"Just because the king named you Mistress of the Robes doesn't mean you'll gain the queen's favor or her ear. That role belongs to me and only me. I'm her favorite, and no amount of doting and favoritism from the king will change that. She'll only grow to despise you for it. Ponder on that before you accept the king's offer."

# VII.
## Masked Men

Don Pedro paced back and forth outside a closed warehouse by the Seine River. Harsh light from a nearby torch flickered across his face, accentuating the petulant expression on his brow and lips. He had been waiting by the docks in the cold for nearly an hour, and he was not a man accustomed to waiting. But he had little choice in the matter, and that only added to his vexation.

Standing solemnly a few feet away and holding the burning torch was the ambassador's retainer, a fellow dressed in all black except for the blood red sash around his waist. He was nicknamed the Spanish Viper, though born Gonzalo Yanez de la Cruz de Madrid. He watched with a bleak air as his master swore and paced. Neither the ambassador's foul mood nor the wicked chill seemed to bother the Spanish swordsman.

"Are you sure you signaled them correctly?" Don Pedro growled.

"Yes, Excelencia."

"How many lanterns did you light?"

"Three, Excelencia. As usual."

"And were any of the curtains drawn?"

"No, Excelencia."

"Cursed sons of whores. They'd let me freeze if they could."

Gonzalo remained silent. He had been in the ambassador's services for some months now, sent to Don Pedro by Dominican monks who described Gonzalo as better suited for a tavern brawl than a quiet priory.

Despite knowing Gonzalo as a devout Catholic, Don Pedro rarely felt comfortable around the swordsman. Gonzalo's face was unnaturally pale; his cheeks—bedecked with more craters than a full moon—were partially framed by a black mustache and goatee trimmed into a perfect spade; his eyes, one blue and one a pale green, probed his surroundings with scrutiny. The only sound that routinely came from his person was the clinking of the long cup-hilt rapier at his side.

"If they don't show up soon, we're leaving," the ambassador said. "The Duque de Lerma will not be pleased."

A cold breeze came off the riverbed. Don Pedro shivered and hiked the collar of his cloak around his face. Flame from the torch danced wildly.

"You beckoned an audience?"

Don Pedro spun on his heel. Standing at the shadow's threshold were two men in long black cloaks, masks over their mouths and noses, and tall crown hats on their heads.

"I did," Don Pedro said. "I've been waiting out here in the cold for more than an hour."

"You forget yourself, señor," the second, taller man asked. "We do not serve you nor do we have to answer your every beck and call."

"But the note I gave you—"

"Yes, the note you received from the Spanish Inquisition says that we would help you should you need it. We have and will continue to do so at our own discretion. Remember that you are in France, not Spain. We are far capable of accomplishing our own goals without seeing to yours."

Don Pedro balled his fists beneath the folds of his cloak.

"Very well," he said. It was the closest to an apology the old Spaniard could muster.

"What is it that you want?" the first man asked.

"The Chevalier d'Auch has returned."

"We know."

"With a treaty with the Low Lands."

"We know that as well."

Don Pedro gawked at the two masked men. "You don't seem overly concerned."

"We're not."

"This brings France and the Low Land rebels closer together. If the treaty is signed, it'll be a blow to Spain."

"We care little for Spain's interests."

"A misfortune to Spain's interests is a misfortune to God's interest."

"Yes, yes, yes. We heard that's what you told Henry de Bourbon." The taller of the two masked men crossed his arms. His brilliant eyes smoldered like fresh coals. "Spain's interest and God's interest aren't always one in the same, señor."

"Now you sound like that damned Béarnaise king of yours."

"What is it that you wish, Don Pedro? We grow tiresome of your bold tone. It's late and, as you've noticed, it is cold out here."

"I hired the highwaymen to attack the chevalier's coach."

"Yes. The Chevalier d'Auch's guard was injured in the ambush and his driver waits to enter Saint Peter's Gate. We know all, Don Pedro. It's why we remember suggesting to you to not put that plan into action."

"Do you know that the Forty-Five Guardsmen arrested one of the fools?"

"We had heard such rumors."

"What if he talks?"

"Does he know anything?"

Don Pedro shrugged. "One can never be too sure."

The two masked men exchanged glances. "We fail to see how this is any of our concern."

"What if I talk?"

The masked men fell silent, but Don Pedro could read the rage in their eyes. One of them gestured with a gloved hand. From out of the shadows all around them came other men in all black with masks over their faces and hats low over their eyes. They were all armed, of course, with rapiers and halberds glimmering in the moonlight and finely crafted harquebuses in hand. Don Pedro glanced back at Gonzalo who hadn't as much blinked since the two masked men arrived. He knew Gonzalo was a devil in a fight, but not even Gonzalo could take on a dozen men on his own.

"Threats do not go well with us," the first masked man said. "We will help you, but for our own reasons."

"What reasons are those?"

The taller fellow raised his hand and flicked his wrist. One of his guards stepped forward into the light and doffed the wool cloth around his mouth and nose. His face was grimy, swathed in stubble and a large, bushy mustache. Don Pedro thought the rogue was smirking at him until he spotted a jagged scar at the corner of his mouth.

"Captain Tremear," Don Pedro said.

"Excellency," the highwayman captain replied.

"Working for these men now are you? Life as a highwayman not pay well?"

Tremear shrugged. "Thieving keeps my coffers full and my belly full of wine. This? This I do for personal reasons."

"Fighting the old wars still, I see. Does your man imprisoned know anything?"

"I tell my men only what they need to know. As far as they're all concerned, we got a tip about a rich chevalier who needed his purses lightened."

"You should've killed them all."

"Those weren't my orders."

"Those were the orders I gave you."

"But not the ones we gave him," the tall masked man interjected. "We will help you free the captured highwayman because he is a member of our associates and not because Don Pedro Alvarez of Toledo, the Marquis de Villafranca, demanded it of us."

"What about the treaty?" Don Pedro asked.

"What about it?"

"An alliance between France and the Low Lands will only strengthen the king's resolve. He's Catholic in name only and would still be an open heretic if it meant he could wear that crown on his head without fear for his life. I hear rumors that he may even turn back to his Huguenot past anyways."

"We will consider it."

The man raised his hand over his head and twirled it in a circular motion. The dozen armed men backed away into the shadows whence they came, followed by the two masked men. Tremear lingered a moment, eyeing Gonzalo before replacing the wool mask over his face and melding in with the night.

# VIII.
## Phantoms

Darion stared out his bedroom window, watching the sun rise over the tall buildings surrounding the inn, the light shimmering off the frost covered windows. He had been up for a few hours. In fact, the entire night proved to be a long and sleepless one for Darion. He had spent most of the night awake, contemplating a way of getting Bauvet out of whatever rat nest the king's men threw him into. But first, he needed to know where Bauvet was being held.

He wrapped his long, wool cloak around him and stepped out into the narrow street. The air felt colder than it had in previous days, the sun's rays weak and barely warming to the skin. In the distance a group of clouds rolled in as if stalking the sun like a pack of wolves to a stag.

He made his way down to the quays lining the Seine River, the breeze coming off the water brisk and strong. He crossed the Ponte de l'Hotel Dieu just as bells rang at Cathédrale Notre Dame. A few birds fluttered away from their perches in the tower. The cathedral doors swung open and out poured a stream of men, women and children. First the poor and downtrodden filed out in their patched breeches, ratty hemmed doublets, and thinning cloaks. Their faces were particularly glum—either from the promise of eternal damnation or stepping into the frigid air. Several guards and armed retainers dispersed the city rabble ahead of the flow of gentlemen and ladies parading out of Notre Dame in a wave of silk, velvet, fur, and embroidered wool. A few dawdled in conversation, while most hopped into their carriages.

Darion grumbled and sifted his way through the herd. A woman caught Darion's eye—a head of wavy black hair beneath blue, fur-lined hood. He caught just a glimpse of her face—fair skin with peached cheeks—before she turned to speak with an older woman beside her.

*It couldn't be.*

He followed the two women. After seeing a ghost from the past, how could he not? He trailed them at a distance, but his inquisitiveness sped his legs. He shoved people unknowingly out the way, trying to get closer.

An unmarked coach pulled up. The side door opened. A young man, finely dressed with fair hair and a matching, pointed beard, stepped out, brandishing a wide and impish smile. He offered his coach with a sweeping gesture of his arms. The women curtsied in thanks. The older woman, who Darion didn't give a fig about, stepped in first, and then the raven haired lady who caught Darion's thieving eye. As she stepped on the foot stool, she turned, as did the man next to her, and several others around the coach. Something caught their attention. They gaped in Darion's direction.

"Jacquelyna," Darion said to himself softly.

As if the wind carried his soft words to her ears, her blue eyes locked on him for a moment. A wrinkle appeared on her forehead. Darion couldn't help but smirk.

Rough hands grabbed Darion by his shoulders.

"You hear me, you asshole?" an angry fellow slurred. "Watch where you're going. Fucking idiots."

It took Darion a moment to realize his situation—this drunkard lout prostrating before him in front of the mass of Parisians fresh out of God's grace. But his mind was still with the carriage. A whip cracked, and Darion turned to find the coach rumble away. The drunkard shoved Darion, sending the Gascon swordsman stumbling a few steps.

"You hear me? I piss and shit on the whore that bore you."

Now the bastard had Darion's full attention.

"What was that? I can't understand you beneath your slurring."

"Like a fucking Gascon should talk about speaking proper French."

Darion measured the man challenging him to see if he was a battle tested veteran or little more than some foppish young braggart who thought having a beautiful sword was more important than knowing how to wield it. In a match of inches—and sword play is very much that—every bit of knowledge is as sharp as the blade that does the piercing.

This particular brand of drunk was a stout man, decked in a dark maroon doublet and a disheveled wine-stained shirt untucked beneath an old and fading cloak. What Darion cared about, however, was the military broadsword hanging at the rogue's hip, its guard scratched and scuffed from well use. Darion then surveyed the man's face; his mouth, chapped from the winter, twisted in an aggravated grimace beneath cheeks of grimy stubble. A wool hat rested scrappily across his head, and a black cloth covered one eye.

Darion laughed.

"What are you fucking laughing at, eh?" The man's hand reached for his sword, but Darion didn't care. "Is your death that amusing?"

"'Sblood, Peppin. You haven't changed a bit."

"Eh? I know you?" He squinted, attempting to focus the one good eye he had left. A wide grin crept to his dirty countenance. "By all that's holy and their little shits, it's you, Darion!"

The two men embraced in laughter, no doubt to the dismay of the crowd around them who anticipated a little sport.

"It's been how many years?" Peppin asked.

"Far too many, I'm afraid."

"How you been, eh? You have a few more scars since the last I saw you. Obviously your temper hasn't changed."

"You're not looking much prettier either, Pep. Your hair is starting to thin out."

Peppin scratched the back of his head. "Bah! What do you know about such things? Awful haircut is all. You would think the barber was the one with only one eye."

"What were you doing at church? You haven't turned into a holy man, have you?"

"The damn place would burn down if I took a step in it. I fell asleep beneath one of the arches. The bells woke me. Lord knows how I got myself here." He readjusted the wool cap covering his head. "Have you eaten yet?"

"No. Not yet."

"Ah good. You can join me for breakfast, then. I could use a drink after my night. Your treat."

⚜⚜⚜

Jacquelyna rode in silence, staring out the small sliver of space between the black curtain and the coach's window. Her companion, Véronique Ricard du Jardin, the Comtesse de Civray, and Martin Lorfeuve, the Comte de Mauriac, spoke in earnest conversation, but it was all noise to Jacquelyna.

She could've sworn she saw Darion in the thick of the post-service mob, staring at her with his sharp blue eyes and flashing that roguish grin of his beneath a beard that was foreign to her. She also could've sworn she saw Darion and Peppin almost draw blades on one another. Darion and Lieutenant Castel perhaps, but Darion and Peppin? That's how she knew what she saw couldn't be real. But for a brief moment she felt her chest flutter. She missed Darion's company and Peppin's laughter, even if his laughter came at the end of an untasteful joke. Even Castel was more agreeable back then, before he became lieutenant of the king's bodyguards.

She felt a tap on her shoulder, and she almost leapt out of her skin.

"By Heavens, you are jumpy," Véronique said with an amused grin. "Father Noiret's sermon must've struck a chord with you."

"Oh my. Yes," Jacquelyna stammered. "It was quite moving."

Véronique and Lorfeuve stared at her, waiting for something. The countess chuckled. "You didn't hear a word I said, did you?"

"No, I'm afraid not. Sorry."

"The good count here was just praising the king's decision to name you Mistress of the Robes. You must be excited, child."

"It's an honorable and desired position amongst all the queen's ladies in waiting," Martin interjected.

"I am most humbled by the accolade," Jacquelyna said, still a bit flustered.

"Oh come now, my dear, no need to be modest among friends. His Majesty could've done a lot worse in naming someone. We all know that. He could've named that witch of a woman, Galigai."

Jacquelyna sunk her head between her shoulders. She recalled Galigai's words to her. The coach came to a stop, and the doors popped open.

"Will you join me for breakfast, my dear?" Véronique asked.

"I would love to, but I can't. I need to attend to the queen first."

"Practicing for your new role? I jest, of course." She put a gloved hand on Jacquelyna's arm. "Call for me later today if you can."

"I will."

"And you, Comte?"

Lorfeuve eyed both women and placed a solemn hand over his heart. "I'm afraid I, too, have other engagements."

"Mmhm." Véronique tried to play the fool while her eyes gleamed in knowing delight. "I'm sure you do."

She stepped out of the carriage and shuffled up the stairs and into the palace. The count stepped out next and offered his hand to Jacquelyna.

"Thank you," she said.

"I'll escort you, if you wish."

Warmth from a fire greeted them as they entered the palace. Jacquelyna pulled back her hood and took off her gloves.

"Her Majesty should still be in her chambers," she said.

"Then by all means, lead the way."

They moved through the grand halls of the palace, their steps echoing off the decorated walls and stone steps. They passed a few courtiers conversing while servants threw back the heavy curtains to let in the morning sun. The light highlighted the beautiful murals and portraits hanging off the walls.

"What troubles you, darling?" Lorfeuve asked.

"Hmm?"

"You didn't say a word the entire ride. I didn't want to say anything in front of Madame du Jardin, but it's obvious that something troubles you, and I don't think it's Father Noiret's sermon either."

He always was good at reading her. "It's nothing." He gave her a long, disbelieving look. She sighed. "I just thought I saw someone. Someone I used to know."

"Don't think any more on that."

Jacquelyna's brows creased. "Why?"

"Obviously this person has done you much harm. Otherwise you wouldn't look so pained." He stopped and turned her softly by the shoulders, so they faced each other. "You're better off looking forward, Jacquelyna. You have a grand future now at court. Besides, if I stumble across this brigand, I might be tempted to teach him some manners."

Jacquelyna chuckled at the count's gallant humor. She did have a grand future at court. But he was wrong about one thing. It wasn't Darion that harmed her. She harmed him.

# IX.
# Prison de l'Abbaye

Darion and Peppin stopped at a nearby tavern—the Black Lamb—not far from the Seine River. They ordered some warm stew and a little wine for breakfast. Not that Peppin needed any more wine in his stomach, but Darion obliged him anyways. They hadn't seen each other for five years. They sat in silence at first, old comrades with so much to say but not knowing where to begin. But not even long, friendly calms in conversation could stand up to the verbose, one-eyed marksman for long.

"So, where have you been, eh?" Peppin asked.

"After I left, I joined up with a band of highwayman in the countryside." He shrugged indifferently; the details filled themselves in, he figured.

"Horseshit. You? The brave and honorable Darion became a common thief?"

Darion's temper smoldered a moment at being called a thief—even if it was accurate. He swilled his wine.

"What about you, Pep?"

"Still soldiering. It's all I know, but there hasn't been an overabundance of wars to fight. Not for France anyways. I spent some time in the Low Lands, helping the Dutch fight those blasted Spaniards. Would still be there but heard a rumor that Good King Henry is planning on taking up arms against Spain himself. Figure I'd come back and join the old regiment if I could."

"Still a soldier of fortune then, eh?"

"Fortune my ass. Barely have a *sous* to my name. I'd be on the street if it weren't for my ol' woman lodging me. You think your merry band of cut purses could use another good eye?"

"I'm hoping those days are behind me, Pep."

Peppin gulped his drink and poured himself another round. "So what brings your hairy ass back to Paris then, eh? The women? The wine?"

"A friend."

Peppin leaned back with a giant, dumb grin on his face. "Ah, well, you're too kind, Darion."

Darion chuckled. Clearly time hadn't decayed Pep's humor—nor his ego. "Not you, though I am glad to see you again."

"Who then? Not Antoine I hope."

Darion grimaced at Castel's name. He should go visit Castel, but not alone. Lord knows how Castel would react to seeing him after all these years, especially after he deserted Castel and Pep without a word or reason. Pep wasn't one to hold grudges with friends, but Castel would take a sneeze as a personal affront if in the proper mood.

"One of the men I've been working with the past few years. He got caught the other night."

"Any idea where he's rotting now?"

"Not a clue. I need to try to get him out, though."

"Darion—"

"It's the least I can do, Pep."

Peppin considered his friend with a long and understanding gaze. He threw his head back and downed another draught.

"I may know of someone who can help. He's a gaoler and he owes me a favor. He might be able to tell us where to find your friend. Still, this favor won't come cheap. We'll need to grease a few palms."

Darion thought of the purse he stored away below the floorboards of his room. "Doable."

"And this meal is on you."

Darion grinned. "That may be a bit more difficult."

"Asshole." Peppin's eyes shone with laughter. Despite his rough demeanor, Pep was a good man with an honest soul, and the most loyal friend Darion had ever known.

"You'd really do this for a man you never met?"

"Fuck that. I'm doing this for an old friend in need."

Darion held out his mug. "To old friends."

"And new adventures."

Lecroix stepped into the eastern entrance of the Prison de l'Abbaye just after noon and shook off the cold the best he could. The stone walls seemed to reverberate the frigid temperature with the exception of a few patches of warmth from torches lining the walls. It had been ages since he stepped foot in a prison. He had called Bastille home for a time, or to more accurately put it, he was a political prisoner during the religious wars. For nearly a year he remained idle in his cell, his mind, body and soul decaying beneath the heavy stone walls until his services were deemed necessary once more. He had no wish of returning to barred windows and doors, but at least he was returning under slightly better circumstances. Still, he shuddered.

"This way, Chevalier," a guard cloaked in wool and leather said.

The dank, musky smell emanating from the walls engulfed his nostrils. He could almost hear the rats that had rustled around his cell at night and taste the thin and putrid stew handed out for meals. He fought back vomit that rose in his throat. Foul memories. Foul days.

"Is Lieutenant Castel here?" Lecroix had been packing for his holiday to find Darion when a Guardsmen appeared with a hastily written note from the lieutenant. In it, Castel demanded the chevalier to attend him at the Prison de l'Abbaye. And like the dutiful soldier he once was, Lecroix halted his packing and headed for priory-prison.

"He is, sir. He's with the prisoner–Andre Bauvet."

The gaoler fumbled through the keys of his belt. The large iron gate groaned on its hinges as it opened. Lecroix heard voices coming from a room not far off. One was loud and harsh, the other calm and defiant.

Two Guardsmen with their scarlet cloaks draped over their left shoulders stood on either side of an old, wooden door. Both held harquebuses in their arms while a trail of thin smoke led to slow burning matches around their wrists. It seemed a bit much for a simple prisoner, but, then again, an attack on a king's ambassador was a serious affair.

"Chevalier d'Auch is here," the gaoler said. One of the

Guardsmen nodded and opened the door before stepping through first. Lecroix followed into the cell lit by a couple of torches against the walls. Surprisingly, Bassompierre was there. He stood leaning against a wall near the door, twisting the ends of his long, thin mustache in an attempt to hide the look of aggravation about his face. Just outside a halo of light stood the lieutenant, his back toward Lecroix. A pile of old hay was in the corner.

"The Chevalier d'Auch," the Guardsmen announced.

"You summoned me, messieurs?"

Bassompierre motioned for the Guardsman to leave.

"You, too, Monsieur LaPointe," Bassompierre added. "We are in need of nothing else presently." The gaoler grumbled as if he didn't care if they needed his help on anything. The door closed with a familiar thud that forced the chevalier's teeth to clench. "Recognize this man, Chevalier?"

Lecroix's attention turned to the cad seated in the middle of the room, his arms and legs manacled. Despite being in the Prison de l'Abbaye and having stared down Castel's wrath, the highwayman didn't look worse for wear. Just a fat lip and a black eye. The lad was lucky his bones were still in one piece.

"This is one of the scoundrels who attacked me the other night."

"Yes, but do you know his name?"

Lecroix raised his brows. "Of course not. I never saw this man before he and his compatriots thrust pistols in my face and shot my driver."

"Well, he knows your name. He requested to see you, specifically."

"What?"

"You're Jean-Girard Lecroix d'Auch," the highwayman said in a pained voice. "A chevalier, appointed by King Henry himself."

"You know an awful lot about me for a common highwayman."

The highwayman smiled. "I also know that Darion Delerue is your nephew and that you let him go free. Yet here I am. Am I to be your nephew's whipping boy?"

The lieutenant whipped around. "Darion was there?" Castel said, his lip quivering in ire. "And you let him go free?"

"Is this true, Chevalier?" Bassompierre inquired with a more composed and dignified grace.

"Yes, Darion was there," Lecroix said, "but he escaped with the rest of their band. I didn't let him do anything."

"You failed to mention that yesterday morning," Castel added.

"And for good reason."

"We can discuss the reasons later, gentlemen," Bassompierre said, pushing himself from the wall and locking eyes with their highwayman prisoner. "What I want to know is what a bunch of knaves think they were doing attacking a king's emissary."

"Trying to survive," Bauvet said. "Not all of us can live off silk and fancy titles."

"Does it have anything to do with France's relation with the Low Lands? Or Spain?"

"I don't know what you're talking about. I know little of the Low Lands and wouldn't help a Spaniard if it meant saving my soul. They're not exactly fond to my kind."

"Many aren't too fond of you here, either, monsieur. You'll be transported to the Bastille where you'll undergo further questioning under the supervision of Monsieur Bassompierre here. He's the governor of the Bastille and will see to it that your stay is long and uncomfortable."

"I didn't kill anyone!"

"That's of little consequence in these matters. Someone needs to hang and you're all we have. Think on that while you say you don't know anything."

Castel knocked on the cell door. It opened. He and Bassompierre stepped through. Lecroix lingered a moment, his eyes probing the highwayman staring blankly at the wall. It was a look he recognized in himself for a time. Back when he prayed for a reprieve he was sure he'd never obtain.

As he left the cell Lieutenant Castel grabbed him roughly by the arm.

"You let him go."

"I gave my nephew a chance to turn back."

"But he got away."

"It appears so." He crossed his arms as he considered the lieutenant. "You two used to be close. Monsieur Petite, as well. Then

Darion disappeared and you were found bleeding on the ground the next morning. What happened, I pray?"

Castel bit the end of his mustache. "You do something like that again, Chevalier, and I'll have you arrested. I don't give a fig or not if you're in the king's good grace."

# X.
# Hospitality of Prisons

Darion and Peppin huddled beneath the shadows of a stone gate not far from the Prison de l'Abbaye. Peppin's contact, Henri LaPointe, agreed to aid in their attempt on a limited basis. He wouldn't show them in and out of the prison—too much risk for a lowly gaoler—but he'd stack the deck in their favor. For a hefty price, of course. LaPointe told Peppin he'd meet them by the gate after sunset to give them details and receive payment.

It had been snowing for several hours. The lack of visible tracks indicated it had been a quiet evening for the Prison de l'Abbaye. Alas, the snow would give anyone looking for them later an unwelcoming advantage. Not that they could change the weather or the timing. Peppin made it sound like it was a now or never deal for LaPointe.

Darion and Peppin stood flush against the archway as an unmarked coach rumbled past and toward the prison. Darion shot Peppin a wary look.

"Probably another prisoner being sent off to their hell," Peppin said.

"Let's hope we won't be among them. You sure you don't want out of this, Pep? This doesn't concern you."

Peppin inspected his harquebus. "And let you run in there all by yourself like a fool? Like hell."

"Better two fools than one then, eh?"

Peppin grinned. A half hour went by, but LaPointe never showed. Darion grew impatient.

"Don't worry your hairy Gascon ass. He'll be here. He's probably occupied by whatever business that coach brought. You bring the money?"

Darion pulled out a small purse full of coin that hung from his belt.

"Good. We'll need it."

"Your friend has a sweet tooth for coin, Pep."

"What do you expect? *Your* friend is a political prisoner and *this* is Paris. It's not like buying a pastry."

Darion tightened the cloak around his shoulders. He hated the cold and hated the snow.

In the distance Darion saw the black coach exit the Prison de l'Abbaye gate. A whip crack split the air. The two horses leading the carriage lurched forward. Again Darion and Peppin flattened themselves against the wall in the shadows. The coach zipped through the arches and back into the city depths, creating a long and continuous track in the snow.

"Someone's in a hurry to get home," Pep muttered.

Darion looked back to the Prison de l'Abbaye. If the coach was LaPointe's delay, he should appear from the prison soon.

Fifteen minutes went by, and the Prison de l'Abbaye still hung in silence. A breeze picked up, slashing Darion's face with snow and ice.

"Where the hell is he?" Even the ever jovial and optimistic Peppin began to look worried. "You sure this is the right gate, Pep?"

"Of course I'm sure. I know what fucking gate to go to. Maybe we should go look for him."

"Or maybe he's not coming. We can't just stroll up to the Prison de l'Abbaye. What would we say to get in?"

Peppin thought a moment. Then his eyes lit up, and a crooked smile crossed his face. "You leave that to me, eh?"

Darion took a deep breath and sighed. He didn't like being left out of the loop but knew better than trying to question Peppin when Pep felt like he had a grand idea. Whatever it was, it was easier to just go with it.

They made their way to the Prison de l'Abbaye.

"Just let me handle all the talking, Gascon," Peppin said. Darion ignored him, or didn't hear. His eyes were locked on the large oak doors of the prison's southern entrance left ajar.

"Hmm."

"What is it?"

Darion gestured to the door with a nod. "The door's open."

"Fucking animals and their lack of manners."

Darion shot a sidelong glance at his one-eyed friend. The courtyard was empty, but several torches lit a nearby wall in a warm, orange glow.

"Where the fuck is everyone?" Pep asked.

"A changing of guards."

"Any idea where your friend is lodged?"

Darion pointed to several tracks in the snow, leading to another open door across the cloister's courtyard.

"Let's try there, eh?"

The two men moved silently and swiftly. Darion checked his sword, pulling it partly out of its sheath. It glided smoothly with no hitches or snags. Peppin blew on a match cord that smoldered around his wrist.

Inside they found the hall as deserted as the courtyard. Some of the wall candles had blown out, painting the hallway in patches of black and orange. At the far end Darion spied an iron gate thrown open and, beyond that, a wooden cell door left ajar.

"This way," Darion said.

Their feet echoed off the stone walls. To Darion's surprise, they hadn't seen or heard a single soul since they arrived. Whatever plan Monsieur LaPointe put into motion was a damn good one, but the tomblike silence only set his nerves on edge.

They stopped at the doorway. Darion peered into the cell shrouded in shadow but for one wall washed in a candle's glow. Darion flashed a hand signal. Peppin attached his cord to the serpentine of his harquebus while Darion unsheathed his rapier. The prison was so quiet that even the muted dragging of steel on hardened leather sounded like a cannon's blast to Darion.

Like a phantasm, Darion slid into the cell, his rapier raised for a quick thrust should it come to it. Peppin fell in alongside him, his firearm poised. The cell looked deserted.

Darion picked an upturned candle from the stone floor. The flame sputtered, glowing a little brighter for a moment, revealing a faint impression of another man resting in the corner. Darion stepped closer and crouched, letting the weak light illuminate the figure. The man's right hand clutched his chest while his left gripped an unpolished sword. Darion lowered the candle to the floor. A coagulating pool of crimson shimmered. A few feet from that body was a second corpse.

"Shit. Pep, we have a problem."

"What?" He stepped near Darion, the steel dangling from his belt clinging together in a light jingle. "Goddammit. Is he?"

Darion nodded. "It's not Andre, though." He looked around for any other evidence of what happened. "We should go find LaPointe."

Peppin moved closer to the body. A hard grimace etched itself on his face. "I'm afraid we already have."

Bells rang from the prison courtyard. Loud cries of panic and ferment followed. Footsteps slapped against the stone floors, and long shadows of men armed with swords, harquebuses, and pole-arms flickered against the wall at the end of the hallway.

"We need to go, Pep."

Darion jerked Peppin by his doublet sleeve to wake him from his mourning. They sprinted down the hall and into the court. Three men stood in the courtyard, barring Darion and Peppin from their escape. They gawked at Darion and Pep, wide-eyed and amazed.

"Halt there!"

"All we have is hope and steel," Darion said before charging forth with sword and dagger gleaming in the moonlight.

"Finally. A little action!" Pep leveled his harquebus and fired, dropping one of the three guards to the snowy mantle. The man reeled in pain as he groped at his shattered knee. Peppin flung his harquebus around his shoulder, drew the broadsword from its scabbard, and joined Darion in the fray.

Darion had hoped to catch the guards by surprise. He did, compliments of Peppin's quick trigger and immaculate accuracy. He was upon the other two guards before they knew what was happening. One man had three feet of steel through his shoulder before he could draw his sword. The other managed to start the process of unsheathing his weapon, but Darion backhanded him with the pummel of his rapier, cracking the man's jaw and knocking him unconscious.

"You could've saved me one," Pep quipped.

A clatter came from behind them. Darion pointed over Peppin's stout shoulders.

"Be careful what you wish for."

Another six men surged out a side door, some holding flaring torches and others their swords or halberds.

"Mother of Jesus," Pep swore. "This is more like it!"

Pep grabbed his harquebus and powder flask and began loading it.

"We don't have time for that, Pep."

"Keep 'em busy, Gascon."

"Peppin..."

"Just fucking hold them off."

"Dammit." He readied himself while six men charged forth with flame and steel. He didn't stand a heathen's chance in Spain at fending off all six guards.

"Pep–"

"Few more moments, Gascon."

The men were close enough for Darion to see murder in their eyes.

"Peppin..."

"Don't rush me, dammit!"

"Fuck this."

Darion drew his pistol from his belt and fired. The courtyard lit up in a bright flash. When his eyes readjusted to the darkness, only five guards stood. The sixth lay in shock on the ground, but still alive.

The guards were scattered now; some had continued to rush forward despite the pistol blast while others flinched at its thunder. Darion threw his pistol aside and primed for more swordplay. He met the first three guards head on with a large, sweeping cut of his rapier. Two men retreated back to avoid the strike, but the third parried with his sword. A guard armed with a halberd thrust forward. The large metal head burned red in the light from the torch. Darion barely voided the blow. He flicked his wrist out, drawing a small, circular cut underneath the guard's wrist. The man carped. The head of the halberd fell to the ground. Darion parried two thrusts from the other guards and thrust back, nearly striking the sentinel in the eye. His momentum took him past the guards just as the remaining two guards arrived to the fight.

"Peppin!"

The harquebus fired, staggering one of the guards back. Darion beat his partner's blade away and drove his rapier into the man's leg. Blood pooled around the blade as he withdrew. He whipped around as a sword tip came dangerously close to his face. He leaned to the side, parried, and slid forward. His blade scraped off the guard's doublet, opening up the man's arm.

Peppin rushed forward and swung his harquebus like a giant club. His adversary raised his rapier, glancing the blows away in a desperate fashion as he fleeted back. The guard held his sword straight forward, a failed attempt to repress the one-eyed man's assault. Pep hammered down with his heavy stock, knocking the rapier out of the guard's hand. He then slammed the butt of the harquebus into the guard's side. The guard doubled over, gasping for breath. Peppin struck another blow against the man's face.

And like that, Darion and Peppin found themselves surrounded by nine wounded guards sprawled across the snowy soil stained red.

Another eight men spilled into the courtyard just as Darion caught his breath. Two raised their harquebuses and fired. Lead balls fizzled by, smashing into the stone walls nearby.

"I think we've outstayed our welcome, Pep."

"Never cared for the hospitality of prisons anyways."

They sprinted out of the Prison de l'Abbaye, slamming the gate behind them and knocking over a few wooden casks resting on the other side. They rushed by the stone archway, nearly slipping on the snow in the process. Darion peeked over his shoulder. Orange flashes appeared at the front gate until the darkness of the foyer was overcome with torchlight.

"What the fuck happened?" Peppin said between labored breathing.

"No idea, Pep."

"Think it had to do with the coach?"

Darion shrugged. He hated jumping to conclusions, but it certainly seemed that way. He looked over his shoulder once more. A man stood outside the Prison de l'Abbaye, his arms alternating between waving wildly and pointing toward Darion and Peppin.

Darion and Peppin ducked into a dark lane between a couple of tall buildings. Two watchmen rushed by, heading for the prison.

Darion and Peppin slinked through the darkness, peeking around corners and keeping a sharp eye out for any guards or watchmen lurking about. Darion used to have safe havens for situations just like this, but it had been years since he had any interaction with his contacts, and he wasn't even sure if they still lived in Paris—or were even alive at all.

"Is Divines still open for business?"

Peppin's eyes grew lustful. He let out a single loud laugh before covering his mouth.

"Jesus Christ, Gascon. You want to go to Divine's now? You are a dirty son of a whore."

"Shut up, Pep. Is it open?"

"Of course. But—"

"Does Maretta still work there?"

"She does. Why?"

Darion took a deep breath and cringed. He didn't like the idea, but they had little choice.

## XI.
## Divine's Absolution

Divines, as the name may imply, was one of the local brothels in the *Cour des Miracles*—the Court of Miracles—an area of town known for its crime and debauchery. Darion, Peppin, and even the uptight Castel spent their fair share of time at Divines, back when they were all posted in Paris and under the service of the king. Darion's preferred companion those days was fiery and strong-willed Maretta la Mandesta, also from Gascony—a woman who had provided refuge to Darion on several occasions when life got a little too heated, and cold steel made things worse.

Darion and Peppin crept through the streets like vaporous specters, avoiding the city guards at all costs. News of the incident at the Prison de l'Abbaye spread like fire and within a quarter of an hour, the streets swarmed with guards and watchmen. Even a few of the king's Forty-Five were on the prowl.

Darion and Peppin finally reached Rue de St. Jean. They hid in the shadows of two tall, deteriorating buildings across from Divines. Two men with swords on their hips and lanterns in their hands stood just outside the brothel's small, shoddy courtyard. Darion took the time to glance over the old parlor. The building itself was large, its façade comprised of crumbling stucco and lath, broken up by rows of wide windows. Candles illuminated through several thin curtains, exposing the inviting figures of the mademoiselles on the other side. It signaled to passersby that there were warm beds—and warm women—available for the night. Rooms that were occupied had windows covered with thick red curtains, giving the impious couple some privacy—relatively speaking. From the looks of things, business was busy at Divines.

Eventually the two watchmen moved on, seemingly deciding that going about their business was more important than a late night romp with a local cocotte.

"Let's go," Darion said

They crossed the street and courtyard to the brothel's front door. Darion went to knock on the door, but Peppin stopped him.

"Better let me handle this."

He stepped in front and gave three confident knocks. The door opened. Heat from several fireplaces walloped Darion in the face. Also greeting them was a tall and robust man, bald with a curled mustache, and dressed in run-down finery. A long dagger and a small pistol hung from his belt. In hand he held a lacquered walking stick.

"Welcome to Divines," he said, his voice sounding like it came from the depths of a cavern. His eyes quickly fell to the numerous weapons at Darion and Peppin's sides. "I'm going to have to ask you to leave your effects with me. You can retrieve them before you leave."

Darion didn't like the idea of being unarmed, but it was either hand over his sword and dagger or take his chances with a few score of king's men scouring the city streets for him.

He undid his sword belt, as did Peppin.

Inside the brothel was warm and fragrant. The walls were much nicer than the bordello's façade. Vines and other potted flowers hung from the walls and ceiling, and the rooms were divided by long, sheer drapes, hinting at the charms and indulgences that lay ahead. A few of the courtesans passed through the vestibule, dressed in loose bodices and skirts hiked high by their chasers. Others were covered from neck to ankle in long, silk robes. It had been years since Darion last visited Divines, but also a while since he had been with a woman. If it weren't for the unseemly situation waiting for him outside, he may have very well been tempted. Peppin, on the other hand, salivated like a wolf.

"Wait here, messieurs, while I fetch the madam," the warden said.

Peppin slapped Darion hard on the back.

"You are one wayward bastard, Gascon. Hiding out in a whorehouse? 'Sblood. I didn't think you had it in you."

"It was the closest asylum I could think of, Pep. I didn't come here for pleasure."

Peppin shrugged his massive shoulder. "No use wasting a

perfectly good opportunity, I always say."

The warden returned with Madame Yolente la Rossa de Tors, the procurer of the parlor. She was older than any of the other girls in Divines, but not old herself. In fact, despite her life she remained youthful and pleasant to the eyes. Her wavy, fiery red hair dangled over her bare shoulders and just above her breasts.

"Ah, Monsieur Peppin," she said as she descended the spiral staircase. "I haven't heard your bawdy voice in here in some time. And who's your new friend?"

Her eyes, an icy blue that had a habit of piercing through everything she gazed upon, grew wide.

"By Heaven," she uttered. "Darion Delerue. It's you, isn't it?" Darion doffed his hat and bowed slightly as he always did when he visited. "I haven't seen you in years."

"None of us have," Peppin added with a quick elbow to Darion's ribcage.

Yolente put her hands on her hips and drank Darion in, no doubt taking note of his ratty clothing, his beard, and the extra scars on his face.

"You haven't changed a bit," she said with a friendly smile. "What brings you back?"

The two men shifted uncomfortably. They were hardened men who could lie through their teeth to the authorities, but they couldn't—or perhaps refused to—even tell a half-fib to Divine's madam. She cocked her head to the side and crossed her arms.

"Jesus Christ. You're jesting, right?"

Peppin looked at his feet. Darion shook his head.

"We need to hide out here for a little bit," Darion said. "Is she here?"

"Maretta? Yea, she still works here. Same room as always." Darion headed for the stairs, but Yolente held out her arm. "She's with a benefactor at the moment. You'll have to wait your turn."

Darion looked back at Peppin, but the one-eyed soldier's attention was drawn elsewhere. Two women—a curvaceous brunette with skin the shade of milk and a youthful black with tight braids wrapped around her head—walked by. One licked her lips while the other traced the curve of her breast. Peppin bared a crooked smile and shrugged.

"I'll see your Gascon ass in the morning," he said. He stepped between the two mademoiselles, placing his arms around their waists. They led him to a side room; cooing and giggles soon reverberated from the opposite side of the closed door. Darion looked back at Yolente who merely raised her brows in allure.

"Do yourself a favor, Darion, and stay out of trouble while you're here. We have plenty of other girls that will meet your fancy."

The madam vanished between violet sheer curtains, leaving Darion alone in the foyer with the large warden who sat on a couch beside the hearth, one leg crossed over the other and staring at Darion.

Darion groaned. He needed a drink.

In the middle of Divine's second floor was a wide, open chamber with velvet covered couches, down-filled pillows, and old, Turkish rugs. Several men reclined about the room flirting with or being fawned over by a handful of girls and women looking to earn their coin. At the far end of the room stood a long oak table full of cheese, fruit, and several decanters of wine. Darion strode to it, putting the blinders on to the woman who ogled him. As he reached for a decanter, a soft and slender hand covered his own. He looked over his shoulder. A young girl with dirty blonde hair and light eyes bit her lip between smiles.

"Drinking alone?" she said in a gentle voice. She looked so much like Catherine de Lasset, the bar-maiden at the Auld Horse, Darion thought. Kindly, he removed her hand from his.

"Tonight I am."

"You sure, monsieur?" She caressed his arms and let her hand wander to between his legs. Darion moved her hand a second time.

"I'm certain."

The mademoiselle frowned and her warm, inviting look turned to a cold gaze.

"Your loss then." She strolled over to another set of women and whispered to them. They eyed Darion with sour looks. Darion poured himself a full glass of wine and quickly shot it back before refilling it. A few more ladies smiled and waved flirtatiously at him. He felt the heat beneath his collar get to him; he needed some air.

He left the room with a full glass of wine. He did his best to ignore the moans and whimpers of pleasure creeping between closed doors and thin draperies. In the back of Divines, overlooking a small courtyard, was a balcony where he hoped to find some refuge and quiet.

He sidestepped a couple of men who had each just left their respective rooms and were still tidying up their dress. He didn't recognize them, but they gave him a polite nod just the same. As he neared the balcony access, a door flew open. Out backed a man holding his hat, doublet, and cloak in hand. He bumped into Darion, spilling wine out of Darion's glass and onto his jerkin and boots.

"Goddammit."

"My apologies, monsieur," the young lad said. Darion looked up, prepared to send the fear of hell into the boy, but his eyes flew by the young boor and to the blonde behind him. His eyes locked with hers, deep like honey. Her mouth fell open.

"You!" she said. "You son of a whore!"

Maretta la Mandesta slapped the wine out of Darion's hand. Glass shattered into a hundred pieces across the floor. Heads poked out of their rooms to see the commotion.

"You know this churl?" the young man said. How fast a lad so green took on the role of gallant knight. Darion's brows creased, and his hand reached for the sword he didn't have.

"Shut it, Josse," Maretta said. The young man's face lost its pallor. He hurried down the hall with his tail betwixt his legs.

Maretta's face was full of repulsion and resentment. Without uttering a word Darion felt thoroughly chastised. She shook her head and stormed back into her room, slamming the door shut. Darion stood there a moment, like a callow boy. He was unsure if he should follow or leave her be and seek solace on the frigid balcony. Either way he expected a frosty reception. He swore to himself before entering.

Maretta's room hadn't changed in the years gone by. It still had emerald walls with gold-colored borders, an old sofa with azure cushions, a few silver candelabras on nightstands, and a large, well-used bed with lavender sheer drapes around the four corners. Maretta herself was leaning over a black table with a large mirror. Her long blonde hair dangled forward, almost covering her face. She looked up into the mirror, scrutinizing Darion without ever turning around.

"Maretta–"

"You think that after all these years you think you can just walk back in here and have me? Is that it?"

Darion scratched his chin. It was a peculiar line from a courtesan. "I didn't exactly come back for you."

"Well, that's just charming of you. I shouldn't expect any less, should I now? Why are you here then? The other usual? Of course. Does Yolente know you're here?"

"She does."

"And she still let you in? *Fantastic*. And what of your wife? Does *she* know you're here?"

Darion raised a brow. "I'm not married, Maretta."

"Well, that's some bullshit if I ever smelt it. Then who was the strumpet that caught your gaze? I know you just didn't lose interest in me."

"You heard of that?"

Maretta turned around and leaned against her desk with crossed arms. "Of course I did. I have my sources as good as any other whore. People talk, Darion. And just because you stopped coming here didn't mean your friends stopped."

Darion was a regular of Maretta's for quite a while. Then he met Jacquelyna, and things changed. For a long time he thought things were changing for the better. Because of that, he felt guilty visiting Maretta so frequently. So he just faded away. He didn't expect Maretta to take it so personally. She had others...

"I started courting a young woman, but it... it didn't end well, shall we say."

"No. I can see that it did not," Maretta said, her voice softening a little.

"Maretta, I'm not looking for anything, but a place to rest—someplace quiet and away from those purse vultures out there."

"They're good girls, Darion... mostly. They're just looking for a way to survive the only way they can. Just like me." Her eyes pored over Darion some more before she sighed in resignation. "Fine. You can stay here for the night."

Darion put his hat against his chest in thanks before placing it, and his cloak, on a peg against the wall. Maretta poured two glasses of wine and handed one to Darion.

"So what did you do this time that you need hiding?" Darion stared at his wine—Anjou from the smell of it—before looking back up in silence. "I just agreed to let you stay here and you won't answer the simplest of inquiries?"

Darion shook his head. He preferred keeping his private affairs private. She knew that.

"Very well. Keep your damned secrets. It's no skin off my back. You can at least tell me where you've been all these years. If you didn't run away with your love, where did you go? I deserve to know that much."

"Making a living... the only way I know how."

# XII.
## Unwelcomed Guests

Despite the thick curtains, morning sunlight found its way into Maretta's bedroom, waking Darion. He rolled over and leaned his elbows on his knees, rubbing the sides of his temple. He threw on his clothes, and staggered to the nightstand where his empty glass and a quarter-filled decanter of wine sat. He poured himself a drink and sniffed it, its aroma perking him up a bit. He sipped it and pulled back the edge of the curtain and glanced below. Four horses were tied to posts outside the brothel, and a few men armed with swords stood waiting below.

"The hell do you think you're doing?" Madame Yolente said from the floor below, her voice loud but muffled.

Someone replied, a deep and calm voice, but the words weren't distinguishable. A carriage with windows barred by iron rods rolled next to the swordsmen.

"You can't come in here armed like this!"

"We're not here for your girls," a man said.

Darion felt his blood chill for a moment. He picked up Maretta's stiletto from the desk drawer and hid it beneath the cloak he draped over his shoulder.

"What's going on?" Maretta asked, lifting herself from her pillow.

"Unsure." It was only half a lie. Darion grabbed his hat and placed it on his head. "Stay here, eh?"

He slipped out of Maretta's bedroom and down the hall. The commotion had grabbed the attention of several other girls and patrons. Heads poked themselves out between doors to eavesdrop while a few others remained passed out in the center room. Darion tiptoed down the top few steps. Two armed men stood just inside the brothel. Madame Yolente pointed incredulously into their faces. Behind her stood the brute of a warden. He held a large wooden club in hand that seemed eager to meet someone's skull.

"This is an important matter of state, madam," the watchman said, "and the quicker we can start the quicker we can finish. We're looking for two men who were seen leaving the Prison de l'Abbaye last night after murdering several men and releasing a dangerous prisoner. We have reason to believe they may have come here after."

"You think they slit a few throats and then go for a quick fuck, is that it? We haven't any men of the sort come by here."

"We need to verify that for ourselves, madam."

"You'll have to get through me first then, coward."

Their debate was cut off by the jingling of spurs from outside. The watchman turned and parted way as a tall man in a dark doublet and a crimson cloak stepped forward. Darion couldn't see the man's face from beneath the fellow's hat, just the thick beard that covered his cheeks and jaw. Yolente's demeanor changed from fiery to anxious. That told Darion all he needed to know of the man.

"Madam," he said.

"Lieutenant. Haven't seen you in ages."

"No, you haven't. My apologies for the intrusion, but I need to search your establishment." The Guardsman spoke to Yolente, but his head moved back and forth, scanning the room.

"Is this really necessary? You know how sensitive the patrons can be."

Maretta crouched beside Darion on the steps. "What's going on?"

"Trouble."

"Your sort of trouble?"

Darion gave her a look that said, "No. Worse."

Back at the brothel's threshold, the lieutenant shrugged. "I also know you harbor men in trouble."

"You would know. You and your friends used to look for sanctuary here far too often."

"You can either tell me what room he's in, or we can overturn every table, bed, and cushion in this entire hold. I'm fine either way, but the choice is up to you, madam."

Yolente looked around her. It seemed obvious that she didn't want to give Darion and Peppin up, but she had to look out for herself, and her girls. A tree that didn't sway with the breeze was bound to break in a storm, and Yolente was staring down a tempest that was the Forty-Five.

Before she could answer a side door creaked open. A loud, drawn out groan mixed with a few girlish giggles came from the other side. Peppin popped out of the room, naked as the day he was born, and with each hand firmly gripping his two companions' buttocks.

"Holy mother of god, what does a man got to do to get some sleep around here," he grumbled. "And close the fucking door, it's cold as a Spaniard's heart outside."

Peppin stopped in his tracks when his foggy eye recognized the man standing in the doorway. Pep chuckled.

"Fuck me. Antoine?"

Darion's mouth fell ajar. He couldn't believe it. Antoine? A Guardsmen?

"I should have known he'd drag you into this," Castel said.

"Who drag me into what? Not a soul alive that needs to drag me to a whorehouse. You know that."

Castel forced his way passed Yolente and headed for the stairs. No doubt he'd know which of Yolente's girls to question first. Peppin stormed forward to cut him off, but the lieutenant pulled out a pistol from the folds of his cloak and pointed it at Pep's head.

"I loved you as a brother once, Peppin, and a part of me still is fond of you, but I will paint the walls with your brain if you get in my way."

Pep ground his teeth in a defiant act of silence.

"Arrest him and get him some clothes," Castel ordered two of his men. "You other two with me. I know where to find him."

"No!" Yolente screamed. She grabbed at Castel's arm. He shrugged her off violently, sending her falling into the warden's arms.

"Leave her be!" Maretta yelled from atop the steps. She covered her mouth, realizing what she had just done. She turned to Darion. "I'm so sorry."

A malicious grin appeared on Castel's face. He pointed a gloved finger right at Darion. "Arrest that man!"

Three guards rushed toward the steps. Darion leapt to his feet and sprinted down the hall. There was no backstairs or hidden passageway for him to escape through, just the balcony and the jump that followed. He shoved aside a few of the women in the hallway and bulled through a patron trying to pay his respects to his mistress. Cries of anger rained from each. Darion threw the doors open and stepped onto the balcony. He looked down. It wasn't a far drop, but it wasn't exactly a safe endeavor either. He hesitated and peered over his shoulder. The three guards were barreling down at him with swords and daggers drawn. He didn't stand a chance armed with just Maretta's thin stiletto.

*To hell with it.*

He leapt over the balcony, his hat flying off his head. He rattled off a curse as his ankle twisted in the snow as he landed. He stumbled to his feet and picked up the stiletto from the ground. He took a step and nearly fell over. He groaned and hobbled to the tall stone wall at the end of the courtyard.

"Halt!" Castel said.

Darion tried reaching for the top of the wall. He jumped, missed, and did all he could to not scream like a small child when he landed on his injured ankle. A pistol fired. Darion recoiled. Antoine's pistol was pointed safely at the ground a few yards from where he stood. He handed it off to one of his men and grabbed a second pistol. This one he aimed at Darion.

"I said halt. Then again you were never good at taking orders."

"Bullshit, Antoine. I was great at taking orders."

The rest of the guards poured into the courtyard with either swords drawn or firearms leveled at Darion. Half a dozen men now surrounded him.

"Why don't you toss your little knife down, so we can finish this like gentlemen. Trust me when I say it's more than your blackheart deserves."

Darion stared at his old friend for a moment. He had no clue what Antoine meant, but he wasn't getting out of this by running away. *This is what loyalty gets you.* He threw his dagger down and leaned against the wall to take pressure off his ankle.

Castel handed the pistol off to one of his men.

"Sword," he said.

"Excuse me, sir?" the guard replied.

"Your sword. Give it to me."

The guard did as ordered. Antoine took the rapier and studied it as he marched toward Darion. Satisfied with what he saw he threw the rapier at Darion's feet.

"Take it," he said. Darion gaped at Antoine. Was Antoine really giving him a chance to fight his way out? "Take it!"

Darion winced as he bent over and grabbed the sword. Antoine untied his cloak and let it fall on the snow-covered mantle. He unsheathed the long swept-hilt rapier at his side and took an *en garde* stance. Darion considered his old friend a moment. He didn't know what any of this was about. He knew Antoine would be angry in their first encounter—for leaving without warning—but he didn't expect this level of resentment. With much effort Darion took a guard. He did his best to keep weight off his front foot, but it was a futile plan. He was as good as dead if he couldn't move.

The resolve in Antoine's eyes subsided, but the embers of ire still remained. He dropped the tip of his sword and stood straight.

"You're injured, aren't you?"

"If you're going to fight me, Antoine, then fight me."

The lieutenant sheathed his rapier and strolled forward. Darion shot him a baffled look.

"No. Not like this." Antoine snatched the sword from Darion's hand "Arrest him. No mistakes this time. We bring them both to the Bastille."

# XIII.
## Ghosts and Old Friends

"That's terrible," Véronique Ricard du Jardin said, lowering her wooden embroidery hoop to her lap. Jacquelyna had just finished recapitulating an incident with the queen from earlier in the morning and her subsequent confrontation with Galigai. Every dress Jacquelyna chose for the queen was rejected and tossed into a huge mountain of silk and brocade. Eventually the queen dismissed Jacquelyna. She recalled the wicked smirk on Galigai's face as she closed the door. Jacquelyna did her best to hide her emotion, but Véronique was sage in the ways of court—or perhaps Jacquelyna was an open book.

"That's truly terrible, but I can't say that I'm surprised. Rivalries aren't saved for the gentlemen of court, my dear. Ladies can be just as vicious and cutthroat. They may not end in silly wars or duels, but they're just as passionate—and sometimes lethal. I know it from experience."

Véronique finished off with a quick wink that made Jacquelyna chuckle. Véronique always knew how to make Jacquelyna smile when things got rough. The aging countess was there for Jacquelyna when she had first arrived at court, and she often turned to Véronique for her courtly knowledge and guidance. Véronique used to be a lady-in-waiting for the former queen, Catherine de Medici, but left the queen's service after wedding the Comte de Civray some years back. The count had tried taming Véronique into being an obedient caretaker of his country estates, but he soon learned that taming the wind of a tempest was a far easier task than trying to domesticate his wife. So he allowed her—in the most liberal use of the definition—to attend to him in Paris. It proved a shrewd move as Véronique had helped parley several political and business compromises for her husband.

"I know," Jacquelyna said in almost a sigh. "I suppose I'm more irritated that I lost my tongue in front of Galigai. I knew she and the queen never cared much for me, but when Galigai started berating me like that my mind went blank."

She turned to look out the window of the countess's Paris home. The sun was out once again. The rays pouring through the glass warmed her face.

"Haven't we all." Véronique sipped of coffee and inhaled in the heavy aroma of its brew. Jacquelyna never enjoyed the smell of coffee but indulged in a cup or two every so often when her spirits needed a lift. Today was one of those days. She joined Véronique in sipping a bit from her warm drink. "You just need to learn to stand up for yourself a bit more, Jacquelyna. You have a strength in you. I can see it. You've let it out a few times and it's as bold and robust as a lion. You just keep it caged for some reason. It's that polite country upbringing of yours."

Jacquelyna shrugged. She wasn't convinced she had strength, but she knew she needed to stand up for herself more. Galigai walked all over her, and the queen walked all over her. There wasn't much Jacquelyna could do about the latter; as for Galigai, she was a witch inside and out, and it did Jacquelyna no good to let Galigai get under her skin so easily.

Véronique eyes flashed in excitement. "Shall I give her a talking to? I've never liked her anyways and this would give me an excuse to exercise some vehemence."

"No. I appreciate the offer, but, as you say, I need to learn to stand up for myself. I can't be the queen's mistress of the robes and let Galigai dictate my mood."

"As you wish. If it makes you feel any better I heard that His Majesty gave her an earful recently."

It did make Jacquelyna feel better. At least a little. Galigai may have had the eye and ear of the queen, but Jacquelyna had the attention of the king. "What for?"

"Apparently she got a little too close to the king and queen arguing over His Majesty's mistress."

"Again?"

"It's the foundation of their royal relationship. His Majesty, for as good as he is for France, has the vice of all men—women. Alas, Marie doesn't turn a blind eye to her husband's infidelity, and he's not very discreet. Part of me thinks they enjoy their little spats. What's a relationship that doesn't have a little fire to it, eh? Besides, I don't think the queen has much to worry about. Henriette d'Entragues has tired of His Majesty's affections."

Jacquelyna blushed. "You're such a gossiper."

Véronique raised her brows, feigning affront. "Gossiper? I merely stay informed, my dear. When a man gathers court news is he called a gossiper? No. At worst they're labeled spies, and more likely they're called shrewd politicians. It pays to be well informed, Jacquelyna. Trust me." The countess put her cup on a table. "Do you want to talk about what was vexing you yesterday?" Jacquelyna gaped at her friend a moment. Véronique was in an extra inquisitive mood. "I don't need *gossip* to read you, my dear. You wear your emotions as plain as day."

"It was nothing. Really." Jacquelyna picked up her embroidery hoop and continued where she left off, but she could feel Véronique's warm, tawny eyes raking her over. She looked up. Véronique lifted her dark brows in friendly scrutiny. Jacquelyna sighed in resignation. "I thought I saw someone yesterday morning. After Mass and in the crowd outside."

"This person must've been important to you in some way. You looked as white as a sheet in the coach. Was this someone supposed to be dead?"

For all the parts of court life Jacquelyna still needed to adjust, she at least wasn't fazed by Véronique's candor. "No, but I haven't seen him in some time now. Five years or so."

Véronique flourished a teasing grin. "Him, is it?" She picked up her own hoop and started embroidering while she spoke. "That explains a lot now. A lover, no doubt?"

Jacquelyna unconsciously reached for the brooch that typically fastened her cloak together. A cloak that she wasn't currently wearing.

"Something like that."

Véronique wasn't wrong by any means, but Jacquelyna's relationship with the then young Gascon soldier was more than just a lustful love affair. Perhaps even more than she knew. Jacquelyna added a few more stitches through her linen, sewing as fast as her nimble fingers could manage. It was almost as if she was stitching the wounds of her past through her embroidery.

"Very well, we don't have to speak of it if you wish. You were just obviously troubled yesterday and I wouldn't be a good friend if I didn't ask, now would I?"

Jacquelyna smiled. "I appreciate it. I do. It's just..." She wasn't even sure who she saw. What good was it to get distressed over a mere ghost? Besides, what does it matter? She has Martin Lorfeuve, the Comte de Mauriac, courting her. "Anyways, I should go. The queen will be needing me shortly. At least, she's supposed to be needing me."

"I'll send for my coach. I should go in search for my husband at the palace before he decides to spend his afternoon and evening swimming in wine."

Jacquelyna found the rest of the queen's ladies-in-waiting outside a parlor that overlooked the Jardin des Tuileries—the Tuileries Garden. The Tuileries Palace itself had been in almost constant reconstruction since Henry IV took the throne, but the king adored his gardens and liked to gaze upon it whenever he could—even when covered in snow. The gardens had fallen into decay during the final stages of Henry III's reign, thanks, in part, to the long and expensive civil wars that plagued France. But the good King Henry IV saw to bring the garden back, planting mulberry trees in an attempt to develop silkworms for clothing, and a large fountain to add a little tranquility to an otherwise hectic palace. It was one of the king's safe havens when he couldn't go hunting but needed to get away from things and relax.

So Jacquelyna found it surprising when the parlor doors flew open, and Don Pedro marched out in a punitive stride. Anger burned in the Spaniard's eyes.

"Cousin," the queen said, rustling her way out the door to follow the ambassador. Galigai followed in tow, looking crossly at Jacquelyna as she passed, but Jacquelyna stood firm beneath the Italian's cold gaze.

Don Pedro spun on his heel. "My apologies if I lost my temper with your husband, my lady. I just wish he listened to reason and logic."

The queen placed her arm under the ambassador's. "My husband has a tendency to be dense in these matters. I think an alliance would be beneficial to both our nations."

"I'm glad to hear you say so."

"Alas, he has a soft spot for his Huguenot lackeys. Getting him to turn on them is a mountainous task."

"So I've noticed."

Jacquelyna and the rest of the queen's ladies fell in line behind Marie de Medici and Don Pedro. Jacquelyna nearly started as a dark figure materialized from the corner of the room. She hadn't noticed him when she first entered. He didn't look back at the queen's ladies-in-waiting, but there was a coldness exuding from him that almost made Jacquelyna shiver.

"Did you see them?" one of the ladies behind Jacquelyna asked.

"No, but I heard about it. Did you?" another responded.

"I did! They were out all night. It was so exciting!"

Jacquelyna wanted to ignore their idle gossip, but she remembered what Véronique said. *It pays to be well informed.*

"What happened?" Jacquelyna asked.

"A prisoner escaped from the Prison de l'Abbaye last night. I heard a hundred men forced their way in and slain the entire guard. The king doesn't know of it, but they caught two of the wretched villains."

"A hundred men? A hundred men broke into the Prison de l'Abbaye and the king knows nothing of it? Louise, that's impossible."

Louise blushed. "Well, maybe the story is a little exaggerated, but it's mostly true."

"Louise–"

"No, she's right," Pieronne, another of the queen's ladies, interposed. "My brother is part of the guard and was there when they arrested two men. Lieutenant Castel of the Forty-Five challenged one to a duel even!"

Jacquelyna stopped dead in her tracks. "He did what?"

Pierrone looked strangely at her. "He challenged the churl to a duel."

"My God..."

"I know! How fearless and gallant."

Jacquelyna grabbed Pierrone by the shoulders, not caring that the queen's party still moved forward. If the young lady was confused before, she must've thought Jacquelyna was downright mad now. "Did your brother say what this fellow's name was?"

"I... uhh... no, he didn't. I don't think he ever knew."

"What about the second man? Did your brother describe him at all?"

Pierrone looked at the other ladies gathered around them. "Yes. In fact, I think he said the other man was missing an eye."

Jacquelyna felt her flesh prickle.

⚜⚜⚜

Don Pedro and his retainer stepped out of the shady corridors of Louvre Palace and into the frigid afternoon air. As they walked the ambassador let the anger that he dammed so well in the presence of the king flow. He muttered oaths and curses. His nose wrinkled into a wicked snarl. His sun-drenched face flushed a deep livid.

Behind him moved Gonzalo, his cloak flapping and weapons singing their metallic song.

"That damned Béarnaise king is bullheaded, unrelenting, and all too foolish," Don Pedro said.

"Negotiations not going well, Excelencia?" Gonzalo replied, his voice sounding like it'd been worn out by gravel.

"He refused my proposal of a France-Spanish alliance—again. He still holds hope for a formal alliance with the Low Lands. I pressed him for an answer of a marriage alliance and he delays. He is maddening. He hasn't admitted it yet, but I suspect he's close to a deal with the Dutch heretics. He insults me with one hand while he holds a damp cloth to soothe the wounds in another. He wishes to humble Spain and therefore me. His predecessor should have never had named that Huguenot asshole his heir. It should have gone to a true defender of the faith, a true Catholic. Not this heretic *converso*."

"What will you do now, Excelencia?"

Don Pedro threw his arms up in the air. "I don't know. I need some time to think."

They stepped into the Spanish embassy. Several members of the household and royal envoy wandered the halls.

"I could always deal with Henry myself, Excelencia."

Don Pedro looked long and hard at the swordsman.

"When the Dominican monks referred you to me they counseled me of your dedication to the Lord and His work. They also told me you were a prime soldier, the very definition of the *Domini cane*. But listen to me, señor, and listen to me well. You keep your fangs to yourself. We will triumph over this false Catholic, but we won't do it with his blood on our hands. We want an alliance, Gonzalo. Not a war."

He held his gaze with the swordsman waiting for a response, but the latter remained statue like. After a spell Don Pedro began to feel unnerved as he stared into the man's heterochromatic eyes.

"Your Excelencia seems to be in a foul temper this afternoon. Perhaps I should wait to give you this dispatch then." Gonzalo pulled out a small parchment sealed in red wax.

Don Pedro snatched the letter from the swordsman's hands. Color drained from his face as he noticed the Duque de Lerma's seal imprinted in the wax. He stepped toward an open window for light, broke the seal and read its contents:

*Don Pedro Alvarez de Toledo, Marquis de Villafranca,*

*I write this with a heavy heart for you have been at King Henry's court for the greater part of seven months now. His Catholic Majesty, King Phillip III, grows eager to have an alliance with France. He also grows more impatient with each day you fail to secure said alliance. He wishes to know of any advancements you've made with King Henry and when he can expect to take the king's hand in friendship.*

*Please advise us as to your current state. We expect nothing less than another achievement we've grown accustomed from you. Should you feel you are not up to the charge assigned to you, we will find a more suitable replacement.*

*Good day to your Worship,*

*~~ Don Francisco Gomez de Sandoval, Duque de Lerma*

Don Pedro crumpled the note and rubbed his brow to ease the pain that suddenly appeared.

"Unpleasant news, Excelencia?"

"Duque de Lerma writes. King Phillip wants to know of our advancements. He grows impatient."

"How will your Excelencia reply?"

The ambassador's eyes bulged from his head as he searched for an answer. "I need more time to reap some fruit from our hard work. We need to find some way to press King Henry toward Spain. Arrange another meeting with our local friends."

# XIV.
# The Warmth of Old Flames

A few stray strands of sunlight leaked through the small barred window carved high into the stone wall. One of these faint beams found its way across Darion's face waking him from his agitated sleep. He stirred from the pile of old straw he was laying on and sat up. Unfortunately for him, his nightmare of being locked in the Bastille was a reality.

"How'd you sleep, Gascon?"

Darion looked into the cell next to his own. Peppin sat slumped against the wall and was tossing a small stone in the air and catching it.

"Not well. You?"

"The accommodations are comely, of course, but I much prefer the warm bed of Divine's with a naked woman on either side."

Peppin smiled. Not even the dreariness and gloom of the Bastille could dampen his spirit. The buoyant mood was quickly overshadowed, however, by the murk of their cells, the coldness of the floors, and the gravity of their situation.

"Pep–"

"Fuck you, Gascon. Don't even think of apologizing. Lord knows you've gotten me out of more trouble than I care to remember. It was usually me getting us into troubles. Only seems fair to turn the tables, eh?"

"Nothing like this, though, Pep."

Peppin grunted. "Yea, well." He tossed the stone in the air again and caught it without even tracking it. "First time for everything, eh?"

Footsteps patterns and keys jingling cut short their conversation. One of the gaolers stepped in front of Darion's cell. Falling in beside him was Castel—his red wool cloak thrown over one shoulder—and Darion's uncle. For a moment Darion wasn't sure who he was less thrilled to see.

"Open the door," Castel ordered. The gaoler shoved the key into the lock and turned. The cell door screamed as it was pushed open. The lieutenant and the chevalier stepped in.

"How's your ankle?" Castel asked Darion.

Darion didn't answer. He was in no mood for idle chat with the man who threw him into the Bastille.

"Get some fresh straw and wood for a fire," Lecroix ordered. The gaoler looked past the chevalier and to Castel. The lieutenant thought a moment before assenting.

"And our cloaks, too," Peppin said from the cell over. Darion and Peppin were stripped of their cloaks when they had first arrived. "Cold as a witch's teat in here, you know."

The lieutenant looked at both men with a calculated smile. Darion recognized that look, and it hardly meant pleasantries.

"That depends on how accommodating you both are," he said.

"We don't know anything, Antoine," Darion said.

"That's lieutenant to you. Besides, you don't even know what I was going to ask you."

"Doesn't matter, *lieutenant*. We don't know anything."

Castel crossed his arms. "Normally I'd agree, but not this time. I want to know where he is."

"Who?"

"You know who. Andre Bauvet. Your friend that you helped escape."

Darion paused for a moment, pretending to be in great thought. "Apologies, but I don't know of such a man."

"Don't bullshit me, Darion. He knew your name and he had no qualms informing on your uncle. Despite that you still lifted him from his cell. You both must be quite the chums. Funny that you were willing to risk your own life to save his. Last time I saw you, you were more prone to sacrifice your friends to save your own skin."

"That's not fair, Antoine," Peppin interjected.

"No one's talking to you, Pep."

"Well I'm talking to you, you oaf, and I said quit it."

"You son of a–"

Castel made for the door, but Lecroix jumped in front of the lieutenant and pushed him back. "Lieutenant, this outburst is beneath your rank," he said.

Castel backed off and readjusted the positioning of his cloak. He grimaced at Pep who didn't even budge from his seat in the adjacent cell. Castel turned his attention back to his prime target, and Darion found the ire and resentment in the lieutenant's stark gaze to be genuine.

"I don't know what you're talking about, Antoine."

Castel opened his mouth to fire another volley of insults, but Lecroix once again stepped in and whispered something into the lieutenant's ear. Castel looked at the chevalier like he was mad but nodded. He then gave Peppin and Darion long, scrutinizing glances.

"You both look fairly well put together men," Castel said.

"Thank you, Antoine," Peppin said, pulling at the hem of his ragged sleeves and doublet. "Ain't let no one say you can't be a charmer."

Darion, however, wasn't as amused. He could read between the lieutenant's words. Slowly, he stood up and brushed the straw clinging to his breeches and doublet.

"What's that supposed to mean, Antoine?"

A wide and wicked smile spread across Castel's face. "It means that there were nine prison guards injured last night and two dead. And the guards here think you two are responsible."

"So?" Peppin asked.

"So, it means the only thing keeping you both from being mashed into a bloody pulp is my hand. But my arm tires easy you see."

"Maybe you should exercise more." Peppin laughed at his own jest, but no one else joined in. Darion shook his head; Pep's laughter faded.

"Try my patience and we'll see how long that smirk lasts." The gaoler returned with two other armed men, holding a few small logs and a hay bale. "Think on that while you rot in here."

Antoine started to leave the cell. The gaoler and guards tossed the supplies on the ground. There was barely enough material for one man for half a day, let alone two.

"Where's mine, eh?" Peppin said.

"Pep–" Darion rebuked.

Castel stopped at the cell threshold and looked over his shoulder toward the one-eyed marksman. Peppin and Antoine had their fair share of arguments over the years–nothing worse than friendly spats–but neither one could ever let the other have the final word.

"Share it. You're lucky you get even that."

Castel disappeared down the hall, not waiting to see if Peppin would try to continue the discussion. The two guards and the gaoler followed the lieutenant, but not before flashing murderous looks at the two prisoners. The cell gate clanged closed leaving Darion, Peppin, and Lecroix alone in the dim light.

"Come to chastise me, Uncle?" Darion asked.

Lecroix crossed his arms as he leaned against the iron bars. "No. I'm actually here to help you."

"Help me?" Darion laughed heartily. "I know you're a religious man, Uncle, but not even God can work miracles such as escaping the Bastille."

"You're not helping yourself, Darion, arguing with the lieutenant."

"Antoine's an asshole," Peppin grumbled.

"That may be so, but he also holds your lives in his hands."

"There's nothing we can say that'll convince him that we know nothing," Darion said.

"So you truly have no knowledge of the incident?"

"Even if I did, it wouldn't matter. I'd be hanged as a deserter anyways."

"You may, but he wouldn't."

Lecroix gestured with his chin to Peppin who was still huddled on the mound of old straw in the corner of his cell. The one-eyed soldier didn't show any sign whether or not he cared if he was executed alongside Darion. There were worse ways to go than beside an old and trusted friend, but Pep was fairly innocent in the matter. A man shouldn't be convicted of a friend's crimes. Darion sighed in resignation.

"We were at the Prison de l'Abbaye, and our plan was to break in and free Andre. We had arrangements set up that would give us an easier time getting to Andre's cell. But when we got in we saw two corpses in a cell. We encountered several of the guards where things turned, shall we say, heated. A few blows were exchanged and we ran to Divine's to weather the storm we knew was coming. We didn't even check to see if Andre was still there or not."

"Well, he's not. He was sprung from his cell or your friend got out of his cell on his own and fought his way out."

Andre had the prowess to fight his way past two lightly armed guards, but slipping out of a cell in the Prison de l'Abbaye wasn't as easy as picking one's way through an old woman's strongbox. Darion was about to write it off as a mystery when he remembered the black, unmarked coach.

"There was a carriage..." Darion began.

"That's right. Damn thing nearly crushed our toes as it barreled its way out," Peppin added. "It had the devil driving that team."

"It was unmarked, but it showed up around the time we were waiting for Monsieur LaPointe to give us a sign to move. The carriage came and went, but LaPointe never did. We investigated and that's when we found his corpse splayed out on the ground."

Lecroix took all this in with a soldiery blank expression, but his light eyes seemed topped with alarm and thought. He stroked the ends of his wide, white mustache.

"Who other than you would want Monsieur Bauvet free?"

"We have friends, but none that planned on coming to Paris. Other than that..." Darion shrugged. Who knows. Why would anyone want to break out a lowly highwayman from the Prison de l'Abbaye?

⚜⚜⚜

Fire danced at the end of a torch against the wall, the flames spitting and crackling the stock it clung to. Long shadows flickered against a stone wall—two men and two women. A cold breeze picked up and ran its way through Jacquelyna's fur-lined cloak. She couldn't help but shiver.

"We don't have to go if you don't want to, my dear," Véronique said. Jacquelyna shook her head. She needed to go. She needed to be sure.

A carriage led by two gray horses pulled up and splashed into a small puddle of slush on the road. One of two men, bundled up in wool and leather, stepped forward and opened the carriage door. As she stepped in, Jacquelyna caught a glimpse of the steel at his side. Véronique sat across from her and soon the coach pitched forward and rumbled away from the palace.

"Will the queen miss you?" Véronique asked.

Jacquelyna once again shook her head. If anything the queen would be pleased to be rid of her for a few more hours.

The two women sat in silence. Jacquelyna had hardly said a word since she learned that Darion may be in the Bastille. She rushed from the queen's company as soon as she was able and tracked Véronique down, just before she and the Comte de Civray were about to depart for their Parisian estate. In a rush, Jacquelyna tried to explain everything to Véronique, but she was sure it came out sounding more like spewed gibberish. Nonetheless, Véronique agreed to help. After that, Jacquelyna did her best to remain in solitude, even avoiding the Comte de Lorfeuve's calls in the evening.

She could hear the water rushing beneath them as they passed by the northern quays of the Seine. She pulled back the curtain of the coach and gazed out. The sky was clear, letting the near full moon rain down its silvery gleam onto the street. Men in long, dark cloaks and various hats stood on the side of the road, while lurid women showing more skin than the weather permitted eyed the coach as it drove by. It was a blunt reminder that life outside the palace walls and gardens wasn't so plush and pleasant. Life was cold, dark, and she was relieved that Véronique brought two of her armed retainers along with her.

For the next few minutes, all she could see were the tall, densely populated houses that shrouded the narrow streets in a blanket of black. She knew most of the guards and catchpoles didn't bother perusing this part of the city. Full of thieves, murderers, and prostitutes, the watch was more worried about finding a dagger sheathed into their back than helping the innocent citizens who couldn't afford to live anywhere else. Soon, however, the thick mass of buildings gave way to the open sky, and in the distance, not far off, stood the Bastille, looming high against the horizon.

The coach passed underneath an old stone arch and up the trail to the prison fortress. Several windows glowed orange from candles and torches, and Jacquelyna felt herself gasp as the carriage came to a stop. A retainer opened the door, but Jacquelyna couldn't move.

"We can still turn back," Véronique said.

Jacquelyna shook her head. With that final forbearance, she stepped out. She walked beside Véronique, trailing behind the two armed men to the Bastille's front gate. One knocked and a slot for a window opened.

"State your business," a man with a petulant tone uttered.

"Our lady has come to see one of your prisoners," the retainer answered.

"At this hour?"

Jacquelyna heard an iron bolt being pulled back, and the large wooden door pushed open. A fire burned in a hearth in a nearby room, providing the vestibule with a little warmth. But the greeting her party received inside the prison was anything but. Three guards stood on watch in the foyer, each armed with a pole arm, a sword, and a pistol. Even the gaoler was extraordinarily armed with a rapier and dagger.

"Expecting a war?" one of the retainers asked.

"After the other night we can't be too careful," the gaoler answered. "Now who do you want to see."

The retainer looked back at Véronique who nodded. "Monsieur Darion Delerue and Monsieur Peppin Petite."

The gaoler suppressed a laugh. "No one's to see those two, by royal orders."

Jacquelyna's stomach fluttered a moment—first in excitement that it was indeed Darion she saw outside the cathedral, but at the same time it sank, knowing he was locked away in the Bastille.

"Perhaps we can come to an accommodation." The retainer pulled out a large, velvet purse from beneath the folds of his cloak. He loosened the strings to show the contents inside. Light from torches along the wall glimmered off the polished gold surface of the coins. There must've been well over a thousand *sous* in there, Jacquelyna thought. She whipped her head around to face Véronique, but the countess's expression ordered to her to remain quiet.

The gaoler rubbed his chin staring at the purse. There well may have been more gold in that one pouch than he would've made in an entire year's wage.

"No, it's not worth losing my job over. Or my life."

Véronique's retainer released a curt exhale. "What more could you want, monsieur? This is—"

The retainer stopped at the touch from Véronique's hand. She pulled back the hood from over her head and smiled. The gaoler looked at her with a distrusting gaze and gripped the end of his pistol a bit tighter. She placed her hands on the man's arms and leaned in. He looked anxious but not quite bothered by her proximity to him. She whispered in his ear. He grimaced at first, but as the retainers shifted in their own stance, new shadows cast over the gaoler's face. When light illumed him once more his eyes had widened and his jaw had fallen slack in unadulterated fear. The gaoler struggled to swallow the lump forming in his throat.

"Of course," he said, accepting the private offer the countess gave him. "But your men have to say here. Only the guards are allowed further into the prison armed."

Véronique inclined her head in acceptance of his small compromise and gestured for her men to remain put. The guard opened a small wooden door that led to the main corridor of the Bastille. Much like the vestibule, the corridor was poorly lit, and the flames from torches danced at the command of a draft breeze.

"What did you say to him?" Jacquelyna asked in a whisper.

Véronique smiled. "I merely gave him a little more incentive to cooperate."

"He looked like he saw Death itself. If you had him so feared, why did you agree to leave your retainers behind?"

"My dear Jacquelyna, sometimes it's best to let the men *think* they're in charge. Besides, we have no need of them in here anyways."

They passed several old wooden doors with small holes to see inside. A few grimy faces pressed their faces to the slits, their noses poking between the rusty iron bars. The deeper into the Bastille they went, the colder it got. Jacquelyna could see her breath plume before her face in an opaque cloud. Eventually they came up to a row of larger, open cells. The gaoler stopped in front of one.

"I'll be around the corner if you need anything," the countess said, stepping into the shadows of the hall.

"Thank you, Véronique," Jacquelyna said softly.

The gaoler banged his dagger between the bars.

"You awake, you bastards?" he said. "You have visitors."

"Is it my dear friend the lieutenant again?" a man's voice said.

"No," Jacquelyna answered, stepping around the corner. "But a friend nearly as old and dear, I hope."

A dark figure shifted in the shadows, two outstretched legs jerked forward before curling inward to stand. The man got to his feet slowly and limped his way into the strip of pale moonlight from above. His face and hair were caked in dirt and grime, but his eyes gleamed like elegant sapphires. *Darion.*

"Jacquelyna?"

She pulled back her hood and nodded emphatically. She thought she caught a glimpse of a smile on his face as he crossed the patches of light. Her eyes surveyed Darion, looking for answers that she knew he wouldn't give up on his own. The scars on his hands and one above his left brow were all foreign to her. When she saw him last, his cheeks were smooth and child-like, but now he donned a dark beard that poorly veiled another small scar on his chin. It answered many of her questions but also sprouted several more. She looked around his cell, noticing the pile of fresh hay on the floor and the small bundle of wood smoldering on the opposite end of the cell.

"You must be as cold as death in here."

"No worse than some of the nights during a campaign. I'll survive." He paused for a moment, his eyes darting around, studying her now. At first they seemed warm and tender, just like he used to look at her years ago. Then his eyes changed; they hardened and burned with a resentment she had never seen in him before. "What are you doing here, mademoiselle? Come to mock me?"

*Mademoiselle*? All those years in love and he reverted back to formalities?

"Mock you? Why would I do that?"

"You didn't answer my question."

"Well... I... I'm here to see you, of course." He considered her a moment before backing away from the iron bars. "Aren't you going to talk to me?"

"There's not much to talk about," he said from the outskirts of the shadow.

"You've been gone for five years. Five years, Darion, and you have nothing to say?" She took his silence as enough of an answer. "How about how you found yourself in the Bastille?"

"It's not all that interesting. Nothing worth speaking about.

Nothing compared to your fanciful life, I'm sure. Your father has done good by you, it seems. I'm glad."

"You won't even say why you left? I haven't seen you since the night before the duel. You left without a word to anyone." More silence. "Why?"

Darion chuckled in disbelief. "If you don't already know then—"

"You vanished like a phantom! Like a dream you were there one night but gone the following morning. You didn't even leave a letter—not to Antoine or myself. Not even to Peppin." She stopped and looked around. "Where is Peppin anyways?"

"Right here, love," the one-eyed soldier said, stepping into the soft glow of candlelight near his cell. He held his stocking cap in his hand and bowed in as much of a gentlemanly fashion a grubby soldier could. "Apologies for not speaking up earlier, but I didn't want to ruin the special moment."

"Apparently it was already ruined. Have they been treating you both well?"

"Well enough for two men charged with murder."

"Murder!"

Peppin held a hand to his chest. "It's a long story, love, but we didn't have anything to do with it—mostly. Let's say we got mixed up in a problematic situation. We didn't kill anyone, though."

"Then why..."

Peppin tried to gesture toward Darion subtly, but subtle had never been Pep's finest skill. Nonetheless, he got his message across. Ever since Darion deserted his post, Antoine held a burning hatred for the man he used to be inseparable from. Jacquelyna knew it all too well.

"I'll speak to Antoine," she began.

"No," Darion said. "We don't need you fighting our battles."

Jacquelyna's eyes scanned the room in a dramatic and mocking fashion. "Yes, I can see that. You seem to have everything well in order."

Darion turned away and crossed his arms.

"While Darion may be content with rotting away here, I for one yearn for freedom," Peppin said. "I'd be forever in your debt if you pry the bars for me in whatever way you can, love."

"I'll see what I can do."

"And if I'm not out in the next couple of days can you send word to my lady, Marguerite? She runs the Artillery Foundry tavern by the river."

"Of course."

With a crooked grin, Peppin held a hand out through the bars. Jacquelyna placed her hand in his, and he gave it a gentle kiss.

"Still the charmer, Peppin?"

He shot her a friendly wink before backing from the prison door. Jacquelyna gazed into Darion's cell one last time. He still leaned against the stone wall, his eyes fixated away from her and Peppin. *I've missed you,* she wanted to say, but instead she merely sighed and left.

# XV.
## The Bitter Taste of Freedom

The Chevalier d'Auch arrived at the Louvre shortly before noon. The winter weather that had grasped the city in an icy clutch finally showed signs of fragility. The air was milder than in days past. The sun felt warm to the old chevalier's skin, so much so that he draped his long wool cloak over one shoulder instead of wrapping it around his torso.

Lecroix spent nearly every waking moment pondering over what his nephew and Peppin had told him about the Prison de l'Abbaye incident. He had no reason to doubt their story, but he wasn't the one needing convincing.

He swung by the barracks of the Forty-Five Guardsmen which stood just west of the old Louvre fortress walls. Fifteen Guardsmen were always on duty to protect the king while the rest relaxed in their barrack lodgings or went about their personal errands. When he was a much younger and idealistic man, Lecroix was a member of the Forty-Five. He served Henry III well and faithfully—until one cold December night nearly twenty-years past.

Lecroix was on duty that evening when he received orders to go directly to the Chateau de Blois in the heart of the chateau's namesake. There, he and fourteen other Guardsmen were met by the Duc d'Épernon to be briefed of their mission. Once Henry III's true and faithful allies, the De Guise family—backed by the power of the Catholic League—had taken control of most of France in the spring of 1588. But Henry III refused to be a marionette for the League, and he set about to put an end to his strife. The king had requested the Duc de Guise and Cardinal de Guise to meet him at the chateau for a private audience to discuss the future of France. As for the Forty-Five, their enterprise was simple—when the duke and cardinal arrived they were to ensnare the treasonous dogs and dispatch them, sending them to Heaven or Hell.

And so the Guardsmen carried out their task with all the effectiveness and tenacity the corps had been known for. As Duc de Guise stepped into the council chamber, the door was locked behind him, and the Guardsmen, once shrouded behind floor-length drapes, marched on the duke with naked steel to end the threat against their sovereign. The next day they painted their blades red with the blood of the Cardinal de Guise.

Lecroix partook in the assassinations with the utmost horror and disdain. It wasn't justice; it was murder. To kill a man in battle or a duel when they had an equal opportunity to kill him, Lecroix had no issue with, but to hoodwink a respected noble of France and a man of the cloth, and to kill them in cold blood was blackhearted. Shortly after the assassinations he resigned his commission and tried entering the priesthood, but that venture fared no better.

Lecroix passed through the barracks' gates. A handful of the Guardsmen were taking advantage of the mild weather and practicing their swordsmanship in the garrisons' courtyard. Their eyes all focused on the chevalier as he entered. He tipped his hat to them and marched up a set of outer wooden steps to the second floor of the garrison. It overlooked the royal palaces and the gardens, and in the near distance the old fortress loomed against a bright blue sky.

He knocked on the door before entering. The office smelled of old paper and leather oil. A few murals of ancient French battles hung on the wall while bookshelves full of old notes, anecdotes, and theories on warfare strategy stood in the middle of the room. At the far end was the lieutenant's desk, and behind it, the standard for the Forty-Five Guardsmen.

"Can I help you, Chevalier?" a man said.

Lecroix turned to find a younger gentleman standing at the threshold. The man wore the uniform of the Forty-Five but was bare of their signature red cloak.

"I'm looking for Lieutenant Castel."

"I'm afraid he isn't here at the moment."

"Where can I find him?"

"He's at his daily meeting with Duc de Sully, but should return within the hour. I'm Sergeant Loys. Maybe I can help?"

"Where do they meet?"

The sergeant shrugged. "It fluctuates, but when the weather is nice they take a stroll through the gardens."

Lecroix doffed his hat in thanks and left the barracks. Lieutenant Castel was the one who held Darion and Peppin's life in his hands, but if Lecroix couldn't sway the lieutenant, an extra push from the duke may suffice.

The key would be to somehow convince either of them to release his nephew.

He crossed through a couple of courtyards and cut through one of the palace halls, barely acknowledging his friends and acquaintances that greeted him as he passed. Back outside, he stepped around two carriages that waited along a row of bushes. On the other side was the Tuileries Gardens and down below he saw a man in a flowing scarlet cape standing next to an older gentleman in dark clothing. Both men were listening attentively to a woman in an emerald gown, her arms animated as she spoke. Whatever she was saying didn't seem to please the lieutenant one bit.

The chevalier quickened his stride, nearly skipping down the stone steps. As he drew closer he noticed it was Jacquelyna Brocquart speaking fervently with the two men. Castel caught a glimpse of Lecroix approaching and rolled his eyes. Duc de Sully, however, greeted Lecroix with a sunnier disposition.

"Ah, Chevalier. Good to see you this morning."

Lecroix removed his short brimmed hat and bowed. "Your Grace. Lieutenant," he said. He turned to Jacquelyna. "Pardon the intrusion, mademoiselle, but I must speak with these fine gentlemen privately."

"If you're here to plead for your nephew's life you can save your breath for something more useful," Castel grumbled. "The mademoiselle has already tried. And failed, I might add."

"But I spoke with Darion and Peppin myself," Jacquelyna said. "They both had no part in whatever murder you charge them with."

Castel crossed his arms. "I have nine witnesses with deep cuts, broken jaws, and cracked ribs that say otherwise. However you bring up a larger issue which is how you were granted access to the prisoners in the first place."

"He wouldn't lie to me, Antoine."

"No, I suppose he would just disappear instead." Jacquelyna

stiffen at that verbal barb. "And does your new love, the count, know you're having secret trysts with murderers and deserters in the middle of the night? Does your father know?"

She slapped the lieutenant hard across the face and glowered at him. When she didn't elicit a reaction from Castel, she wound up for a second blow, but Lecroix hooked her by the arm and held her in check.

"I think you made your point clear, mademoiselle," he said.

Jacquelyna forced herself free from the chevalier's grip. Castel rubbed his face flushed red from her handprint, but he never showed signs of anger or pain. His eyes were soft, yet calculating in his gaze, as if *he* provoked the response he desired. The duke fingered the edge of the livery collar he wore around his neck. Per usual, he took in his surroundings in a sage silence, but now he seemed to have seen enough.

"Clearly there is some personal history here that I know little of, nor do I care to know it," Sully said. "I only care what's good for the state of France. What have you learned about Monsieur Delerue and Monsieur Petite's involvement in the attack on the chevalier here and the murder of the prison guards?"

"Not much beyond what you already know, Your Grace," Castel said.

"I spoke with the boys after the lieutenant left, Your Grace," Lecroix said. "They had forth a plan to rescue the prisoner, but never put it into action. Apparently, a black coach was in a bit of a hurry to arrive and depart the prison."

"I wasn't aware of this," the lieutenant said.

"Because you were too busy provoking your prisoners instead of trying to gather information."

Castel sneered and rested his gloved hand on his sword.

"Did they get a look at who was in the carriage?" Sully asked.

"Alas, no. They said the curtains were drawn and the coach unmarked."

"Another of Darion's lies, no doubt," the lieutenant said.

"I also spoke with some of the other guards and they remember seeing carriage tracks leading from the prison, but there was no schedule arrivals or transfers, and no new prisoners on record."

"Your Grace—" Castel began.

"It seems to me, Lieutenant," Sully said, "that there has been an unfortunate misunderstanding."

"Your Grace, with all due respect, of course the chevalier believes what his nephew has said, but–"

"But nothing, Lieutenant. You have no evidence linking these two men to the killings. Just conjectures and prejudice. However, one should be prudent in these matters. Let this Monsieur Petite free, but make sure you have two ununiformed men following him at all times. If he is in connection with the highwaymen fugitive, he will lead us to him. Now if you will excuse me."

Duc de Sully gathered the edges of his robe and started for the palace, but Jacquelyna rushed by the duke and cut off his exit.

"What about Darion?" she asked.

"Unlike Monsieur Petite, Monsieur Delerue is directly connected to the attack on a royal ambassador returning from mission for the crown, as well as a deserter to the army. He must answer for those crimes. Be glad I don't send them both to the gallows." A moment passed before the fire in the duke's eyes subsided. He looked almost pained by the decision he had to make. "That's the best I can do. Perhaps if Monsieur Delerue is a bit more forthcoming with information we seek, we can come to some accommodation. But for now he's where he belongs. My apologies to you both. And don't think of warning Monsieur Petite of his escort, Mademoiselle. It would be most unfortunate for you if you did."

Jacquelyna took a hard step forward to continue her crusade, but Lecroix grabbed her by the wrist and bowed at the duke. Jacquelyna looked at him in bitter disbelief but followed suit, curtsying with all the grace and class she could muster in her anger. When the duke was out of earshot, she yanked her arm free from his grasp. Her eyes were so full of betrayal in that moment.

"You? Of all people..." she said. She stormed away with heavy steps slamming against the cold ground. Castel, too, had daggers in his eyes as he looked at the chevalier. And without even as much as a polite bow, the lieutenant put on his hat and walked away.

"There's little to do when one is locked away in the Bastille, but sleep, eat, shit, and feel sorry for oneself. And I refuse to do the latter of the group."

Peppin was still tossing the small stone, sometimes banking it off the stone walls and catching it as it bounced back. The *clink, clink, clink* of the stone ricocheting was enough to keep Darion from napping through the afternoon, but Peppin continued his little game and talking for the sake of filling time.

"I bet Marguerite is worried sick about me," he continued. "Poor lass can't go more than a few hours without seeing my face and now it's been a good two or three days since I last visited. She'll probably send the watch looking for me."

"That's nice, Pep," Darion mumbled from beneath the hat covering his face.

"She's a good woman, my Marguerite. Unfortunately for you, she'll wring your neck when she finds out you're responsible. I'd say getting sent to the scaffolds may be a more doing you a kindness compared to what she'd do to you after all this." Peppin fell silent a moment, no doubt waiting for Darion to react to his little gallows humor. It never came. Peppin mumbled. "Mighty fine of your woman to come visit us like that last night, eh?"

Darion took a deep, riled breath before removing the hat from his face. In truth, his restless night was more due to Jacquelyna than the frigid cell. Her visit disturbed him more than he would've cared to admit. Once he was deeply in love with her. Just the sound of his name passing through her lips would melt his soldierly stoicism. Even the previous night he wanted nothing more than to press his lips to hers and feel her arms around the back of his neck in a warm embrace. But she had broken his heart, and he refused to let it happen again. Besides, he was locked in the Bastille, and the only way out of the Bastille was with hemp around one's neck.

"What do you want, Pep?"

"What do I want? A little high spirits and conversation would be nice."

Darion looked at his friend in disbelief. Peppin may have had only one good eye, but he couldn't have been blind, too. "High spirits and conversation? We're in the damn Bastille, Pep."

"I know that."

"So?"

"So, we've been in worse shape before."

Darion couldn't help but let out a single chortle. "When have we been in worse shape?"

"There was that tavern brawl with some self-righteous fops who got a little more steel in their diet than they probably planned. Or the time we were pinned down by Savoy's men with two shots each left and wet gunpowder. Or how about the night I got caught with that English dignitary's daughter in the stables? Then there was that night with the nuns—"

"All right, all right. You've made your point, Pep, but if you recall, we were at least armed in each of those times, and we never got locked away in the goddamn Bastille."

Peppin shrugged as if that was of little consequence. "Between the chevalier and Jacquelyna, I'm sure we'll be dancing in the streets of Paris in no time. I shall return to my beloved Marguerite and you to the arms of your treasured Jacquelyna."

"Little luck in that even if we do get out."

"I do recall you being a giant ass last night, yes."

"You don't know anything of it, Pep."

Keys jingled and two gaolers appeared at their cell gate with old wooden bowls, two tankards, and a pot of stew. Escorting them were a couple of guards armed with halberds and swords. The gaolers plopped two spoonful of stew into the bowls and poured water from a skin bladder.

"*Bon appetite*, messieurs," one of the gaolers said. He aimed his spit at Darion's bowl, but missed.

"Nice shot," Peppin jested. The gaoler glowered at him before kicking over his mug and stew. Water and steaming, viscous meat and broth splashed against the stone. Peppin smiled. "Thank you. The rat shit on the floor gives it extra flavor."

The warden's nose wrinkled. He and the three other men marched away. Darion crawled over to the gate and picked up his food and drink. He gave the water a sniff and recoiled from its wretched stench. He flung the water from the mug, then dumped half his *pot-au-feu* into it. He held it out to Peppin between the bars of their cell. Peppin inclined his head in thanks and took the mug. Both men picked at the meat and soggy vegetables before the silence got too much for Peppin.

"What I do know is that you disappeared for five years without a note or word."

"Jesus Christ, Pep."

Peppin held out a hand. "Let me finish, Gascon. This is important. We all feared you dead at first, but Jacquelyna swore she knew that you were alive—just gone. She said she didn't know where, and wouldn't say why, but she was damn sure you were still alive. She waited for you for several months before disappearing to her father's country estate for a spell. She wrote to me during that time, wondering where the hell you were."

"You can't read, Pep."

"I know people who do. Anyways, she never stopped caring about your Gascon ass. Was only recently that she started being courted by the Comte de Mauriac."

Darion cringed at the thought of her being courted by anyone, let alone a count. This Comte de Mauriac must've been the gentle-fellow Darion saw get into the carriage by Notre Dame, Darion thought. He knew he didn't like the look of the fellow, and now he had a reason why. He looked up at the small barred window above his head.

"Even if she wasn't, I'm done with her."

"Bullshit, Gascon. I can tell seeing her pains you. She was the reason you left in the first place, isn't she?"

"I don't want to talk about it, Pep."

"Too fucking bad. You know Antoine almost died because you took off?"

Darion whipped his head around. "What?"

"The stubborn bastard stood in for you at your duel. He took his duties as your second seriously and took a thrust through the right side of his chest. He was at Death's door for two weeks. He nearly got discharged from service because of it, but the captain took it easy on him, speaking that he was standing in for your sorry ass."

That explains the bad blood coming from Castel, Darion mused. A chamber door opened and slammed closed. It was followed by the drumming of leather boots and shoes against the stone floor, and the familiar ring of sword and dagger. The gaoler returned with the two guards.

"Come back with seconds?" Peppin asked. "I'd love to have more of that stew of yours."

The gaoler scowled, but was moved aside by Lieutenant Castel who stepped forward. His sharp gaze penetrated into the cells, examining its two occupants.

"Have anything to say yet?"

Both men remained silent. Castel shook his head. He gestured to the gaoler who waddled to Peppin's cell. He fumbled with his keys before finding the right one and opened the cell door.

"What?" Peppin asked.

"You're free to go, by order of the Duc de Sully, the king's minister," Castel said.

A wide, crooked grin appeared on Peppin's face. He wiped the grease off his hands and onto his wool doublet. He popped up to his feet and adjusted the cloth that covered his spoiled eye.

"See, Gascon? I told you we'd get out of this."

A rare hint of a smile flushed in the lieutenant's face. "Not him. Just you."

"What? Why not? We're both innocent."

"Innocent of breaking Monsieur Bauvet out of his cell, perhaps. But Monsieur Delerue is also implicated in the attack of a king's ambassador and need I remind you that he's also a deserter and a coward."

Castel laid the last phrase on thick with a heavy dose of menace in his voice. Darion peered at him from beneath his wide brim hat.

"This is bullshit, Antoine," Peppin said.

The lieutenant rested his hand on the pummel of his sword. "You can return to your little rat's nest in the cell if you prefer, monsieur. I don't give a fig at this point."

"*Monsieur*. When the hell did you turn into Monsieur Formal?"

Castel turned to the gaoler. "Officially discharge him and send him on his way. If he even sets foot near the Bastille you have my permission to shoot him on sight."

"Well that seems a bit harsh now, don't you think?"

Castel gestured at the gaoler who started down the hall. One of the guards gave Peppin a heavy shove, sending the robust soldier stumbling a step. He threatened to snap the guard's neck with a single look from his good eye, before he turned to Darion's cell.

"Don't worry, Gascon. I'll figure something out."

"No doubt that you will, Pep," Darion said, never taking his eyes off the lieutenant.

Castel lingered while the other four left down the hall. He leaned against the bars of the cell.

"I look forward to watching you hang, monsieur."

Darion grabbed hold of the iron bars to his cell's gate. "Antoine, I'm sorry for what happened to you. I didn't know."

The lieutenant stepped back, his face aghast. "No, you only think you are. But you will be before long. Trust me."

# XVI.
## Royal Ambuscade

"Please, you must do something!"

Jacquelyna found Véronique sitting in a parlor of the Louvre, enjoying a small game of cards with a few other ladies and gentlemen of the court. Her outburst shocked most of the women who looked at her as if she were going mad, while the men merely laughed at the incident. But Jacquelyna didn't notice, nor would she have cared if she did. Véronique smiled at her companions, excused herself from the game, and led Jacquelyna to a small bureau beside the wall.

"What's gotten into you, dear?" the countess asked.

"They're going to kill Darion."

"Yes, and his friend *Brontes*, too."

Jacquelyna shook her head emphatically. "No, Duc de Sully has rescinded Peppin's warrant, but not Darion's."

"How do you know all this?"

"Because I pleaded for their lives with the duke!"

Véronique looked over her shoulder to the group sitting at the table by the window. Sunlight through the windows nearly washed out their faces, but it was obvious they were interested in Jacquelyna's little drama.

"You did what?"

"Myself and the Chevalier d'Auch pleaded for their lives."

Véronique pulled Jacquelyna further away from the group. "My girl, I take back what I said yesterday. You're far too bold for your own good."

"You need to do something, Véronique."

The countess flashed a self-conscious smile. "Me? What in Heaven and Earth could I do?"

"I saw how you handled that gaoler. You struck the fear of God in him. Can't you do it again and get Darion out?"

"My dear, that is not a card to be played often. I did more than the situation warranted because I thought seeing him would put your heart at rest. I see that I had misjudged the situation. It's done nothing more than stoke the fire in you."

"So what if it has?"

"He is a branded criminal and if the king's favorite minister is unable to pull him from that fire then perhaps it is not meant to be."

Jacquelyna felt the tears in her eyes well. "But he is innocent of these crimes. Don't you understand? If anyone is guilty of them, it is me."

Véronique's visage went from shock to motherly concern. "My dear, you are not guilty of anything he has done. What he has done, he has done on his own accord, understand? You did not turn him into the mercenary that turned on his country. From what I've seen, you've shown more kindness than that churl deserves."

"But you could save him?"

Véronique's amber eyes betrayed the turmoil she felt inside. Even so, her next words were chosen carefully and void of any emotion within:

"Every action comes at a cost, my dear, and typically with interest. If I ask for a drink from someone, they will later ask for a meal in return. If I ask for a ride to stay out of the rain, they will later request sanctuary for a misdeed. And if I were to free a man deemed an enemy of the state, well... I need to weigh my investments."

"So you won't help him? Not even for me?"

Véronique frowned. "I'm sorry, my dear. Had I known this is the road your visit would've taken you, I wouldn't have suggested it at all."

The countess tried brushing a comforting hand on Jacquelyna's face, but Jacquelyna withdrew. She couldn't believe her best friend would desert her like this. It's not that Véronique couldn't do anything, but she *refused* to do anything. Jacquelyna's eyes raged in her ire. She spun around and rushed out the parlor door.

Jacquelyna had never known herself as one brought easily to tears, but she felt it difficult to hold them back now. She felt so helpless, so out of control of her own life. Between her father sending her away at court, to the queen not accepting her as her mistress-of-the-robes, to now Darion about to hang for a life she felt responsible for, it was becoming too much weight for her to bear alone. She needed to walk and let the cool March air soothe her aching head.

She stepped out back where the royal hunting dogs were let loose to run free and exercise. She never had a dog around when she was younger. Her father was never much for sport. He owned no livestock, so there was no need for one around the chateau. But she loved them just the same, and watching them romp amongst the bushes and trees provided a serene distraction from the trials of court life.

She sat on a small bench as the hounds took off in a mad dash across the lawn, turning hard to the left and heading back to their handler. One led while the pack trailed behind in a furry blur, barking and yipping as they sprinted by. Two stragglers hung back, engaged in a lively game of wrestling and play fighting. Jacquelyna smiled as the dogs enjoyed their carefree life. What she wouldn't give to be one of them.

Nearly a half an hour went by before her thoughts turned back to Darion rotting away in the Bastille. She tried not to blame herself, but she couldn't help it. If she hadn't begged Darion to call off the duel, perhaps he wouldn't have deserted his post. Perhaps he would've stuck around. They could've gotten married and lived happily ever after. But she was beginning to realize that the fairy tales her mother used to read her only existed in books and poems. There was no happily ever after and no gallant knights in armor...

"There you are."

Jacquelyna looked to her right and smiled. The Comte de Mauriac approached, dressed in a splendid blue and purple doublet and matching breeches with silver buttons running up the side. He doffed a black tall crown hat with purple plumes as he approached. Then again, she thought, maybe gallant knights do exist. She curtsied.

"Excellency," she said.

"Excellency? You must be troubled if you've fallen back to formalities. How many times have I asked you to call me Martin? Unless, of course, there is some deeper reason for reverting back that I'm unaware?"

Jacquelyna put a hand to cover her face blushing in

embarrassment. "No. No, of course not. I'm sorry, Martin. I've just been strained."

"So I've heard." He gestured to the bench and took a seat next to her. "I ran into the Comtesse de Jardin. She says you were visibly upset. I figure this is where you'd be."

Jacquelyna smiled. "You know me too well." She turned as another dog rushed by barking his furry head off.

"We missed you last night, you know. His Majesty was hoping to see how your card game has improved."

"I was visiting an old friend who I haven't seen in many years."

"At the Bastille, no doubt?"

Jacquelyna froze in place. No one was supposed to know of her little tryst.

"Are you spying on me, monsieur?"

The count flashed an impish grin. "Not at all, but word gets around court quickly. I thought you'd know that by now. You should take more care."

"Perhaps you are right."

An awkward silence passed over them.

"So, why is your old friend in the Bastille?"

She shrugged. She was ready to blame herself again, but she wasn't in the mood to listen to someone else try to take the blame off her shoulders.

"How do you know this rogue?"

"We were friends once."

"And that is all?"

Jacquelyna hesitated. "We were in love... for a time."

The count took a deep breath. "I see. From what I hear, he murdered a bunch of guards. Not exactly a man that you—"

Jacquelyna shushed him with a single finger over his lips. The count may have forced a neutral disposition of the matter, but his eyes betrayed his worry and discomfort.

"Have no fear, Martin," she said, pulling herself toward him. "My heart belongs to you now."

"I'm going to miss you, you know," the count said. "Alas, my business in the country has been held off for too long. I shall come visit as soon as I can. You can have faith in that."

Jacquelyna answered in a soft smile.

The following morning, Jacquelyna woke up early, but the palace was already bustling. With the king and queen readying to head to Fontainebleau the following day, the royal household and its servants, groomsmen, guards, and courtiers were also readying themselves for the trip south. Alas, for Jacquelyna, the trip to Fontainebleau would be delayed. She was due to leave the palace in the morning to escort the king's mistress–Catherine Henriette de Balzac d'Entragues, Marquise de Verneuil–and her son to their country estate in Normandy before returning to the royal household in Fontainebleau. While the entire trip would take a week or so at most, she didn't look forward to being away from the court for that long. It felt like a ploy by the queen and her lapdog Galigai to get rid of her more than anything else, but the king approved the measure, and so she had to go. And, though she wouldn't admit it publically, a holiday from the queen's temper and Galigai's harassment might be exactly what she needed.

She swung by the queen's chambers one final time to see if Her Majesty needed anything, but the two guards that stood watch said the queen was still asleep and not to be disturbed. And with that, Jacquelyna made a silent exit. At the front of the palace, she found Marquise de Verneuil's household gathering. It was a modest household, but that was expected from an unwed woman who was falling from the king's favor. His Majesty always had a penchant for younger women, and at nearly thirty, the sun was setting on the marquise's looks and influence at court.

An older, gray woman with a staid look about her approached. She dressed in a solemn black from head to foot, and her hair was immaculately stylized in a large, tight bulb at the back of her head. Her light eyes scrutinized Jacquelyna from head to foot.

"You must be Mademoiselle Brocquart," the woman said.

"I am, madam." Jacquelyna curtsied.

"I'm Madame de Mailly. Thank you for being punctual. In the past the court's lapdogs have been less than appropriately prompt."

Jacquelyna's mouth dropped at the backhanded compliment–or

perhaps it was just a straight affront. But before she could decide either way and comment, the marquise's proxy continued.

"You will be riding in the coach with my mistress's daughter, Princess Gabrielle Angélique. We are—"

"I'm sorry, but I thought I was to ride with the marquise's son, Gaston Henri."

Madame de Mailly clenched her jaws. "The prince has a high fever, so he and his mother will be staying in Paris for the time being. Understood?"

"Of course."

"Good. As I was saying, you are to ride with Princess Gabrielle Angélique. We are to head to Marquise de Verneuil's estate just outside Évreux where your task will be over and you'll be discharged to return back to court. The princess can be a rather fussy child, but discipline isn't yours to distribute. You're to entertain the princess and entertain alone. Is that understood?"

*Princess*? Gabrielle Angélique wasn't exactly high royalty. She was merely a child of the king's mistress, a bastard of the king. Henry legitimized Gaston Henri several years ago but hadn't saw fit to do the same with the marquise's daughter. Perhaps it had to do with the marquise's involvement with some Spanish plots against the crown or maybe it was to pacify Marie de Medici. Either way, Jacquelyna understood her role in the journey and didn't wish to involve herself in a spat between the king's wife and king's mistress. She nodded.

"Very good. We are to depart in ten minutes. You'll be riding in that coach."

Jacquelyna's eyes followed Madame de Mailly's long, slender fingers and out the door to a set of dark coaches with silver trim and the marquise's coat of arms sewn onto the side door. Jacquelyna imagined her coach was the slightly less ornamented coach, bare of any trim, but still flaunting the marquise's arms.

Tiny feet echoed down the hall, followed by the voice of an overwhelmed maid calling out to slow down. A young girl rounded the corner and into the lobby. Her golden blonde hair was pulled back, and she wore a full, peach-colored gown. Her eyes twinkled in youthful bliss, and she skipped while swinging her arms back and forth.

"Mademoiselle Brocquart, this is the Princess Gabrielle Angélique."

"A pleasure," Jacquelyna said with a curtsy.

"Princess, this is the queen's lady, Mademoiselle Jacquelyna Brocquart," Mailly continued.

"Hello," the young girl said, doing her best to not fall over as she genuflected.

"She is to escort you to your mother's home in Évreux."

"Okay!"

She skipped off toward the open door and the coaches, her nanny hurrying behind, barely able to keep pace with the young girl.

"She's a lovely child," Jacquelyna said.

"She has her moments."

A man dressed in red and gold wool and a dark maroon cloak approached through the open doors.

"Madame," he said, bowing his head. "We are ready to depart at your word."

Mailly blew out a long, drawn-out exhale. "Better to leave a little early, I suppose."

Jacquelyna took her seat across from Gabrielle Angélique and Madame de Mailly. The young girl's nanny, apparently, was permanently placed at the Louvre, and by the look on her face when she handed control back to Mailly, she was both thrilled and relieved to be dismissed from her charge.

The coach rumbled forward as they passed through the Louvre gates. Two coaches and four armed retainers made up the escort. They pushed through the throng of people with the aid of yells, curses, and threats from the drivers.

"Foul mouth dogs," Madame de Mailly uttered as she peeked through the curtain. "They'll roast in Hell if they're not careful."

"I like doggies," Gabrielle said. "Sometimes mother will let me visit father's dogs."

"Do you have one yourself?" Jacquelyna asked.

"No. Mother says I'm not responsible enough."

"Your mother knows best, Princess," Mailly reaffirmed.

Jacquelyna fought back a frown as she watched Mailly's scrutinizing gaze bear into the child. Gabrielle lowered her head in embarrassment.

"Well, if you are ever near Sarlat, visit my cousin. He has the most wonderful and playful dogs you'll ever see. Would you like that?"

"Yes!" Gabrielle said.

Jacquelyna's smile was met by Madame Mailly's irritated sneer. The caravan passed through the city's northern gates. Jacquelyna had spent so much time at court and in the city recently, she hadn't gotten a chance to enjoy the vast openness of the French countryside. It's where she was born and grew up, and although she enjoyed the opportunities offered in Paris, a large piece of her still yearned for the open sky and rolling hills.

Jacquelyna did her best to entertain the young girl with childish conversation about clothes and dolls. She asked Gabrielle how her embroidery lessons were going, if she was reading any enjoyable books, and what sort of games she played with her brother and friends. The young girl replied with "Well", "No", and "Hunt the slipper." Soon, however, the conversation dwindled and instead of chatter, Gabrielle filled the coach with off key humming. The type of humming born in a heart full of thrill and excitement but sounding as sour as spoiled wine.

"Sshhh!" Madame Mailly leered at the girl with threatening eyes. "You will stop with that incessant droning."

Gabrielle slumped her head between the shoulders of her dress. *The poor girl.* Gabrielle was merely amusing herself enjoying the childish ignorance that allows them to live on so carefree, even under the iron watch of the men and women like Madame Mailly. She shouldn't be punished for being happy. No one should.

"Madame Mailly," Jacquelyna began. The old woman shot her a side-glance. "I think that that's a bit too far, don't you?"

The old woman's skin turned livid. "*What*?"

"She was just trying to distract herself. It is a long journey after all."

A vein in Mailly's forehead pulsated beneath her wizened skin. There was a storm brewing in that old woman, and Jacquelyna didn't look forward to its wrath.

"Who are you to question my judgment? I'll have you know—!"

The coach jerked hard to the side, cutting Madame Mailly short and nearly knocking the coach's three occupants over. Jacquelyna righted herself and gaped at the old woman. They were still moving forward and from the feeling of things, they were moving faster than before.

"What's happening?" Gabrielle asked.

Mailly pulled back the curtain of the coach. A cold gust of air rushed in.

"Driver! What's the meaning of this?"

But even as she asked the question the answer was staring them right in the face. Half a dozen riders draped in dark clothing and cloaks flanked the left side of the coach. Jacquelyna pulled away the curtain on the other side of the coach. Another half dozen horsemen and their mounts thundered next to them. A few held pistols in their hands but all wore masks around their lips and cheeks.

"Highwaymen!" Madame Mailly cried out.

"What's happening?" Gabrielle whimpered.

"Hush, child," Jacquelyna said with a forced, but warm grin. "Everything will be fine." She turned her attention back to the old woman. "Are they trying to rob us?"

Two pistols fired, dropping one of the retainers to the ground and underneath the coach. Jacquelyna nearly lost her breakfast as she felt the wheels roll over the body.

"I don't think so," Madame Mailly said. "Thieves and robbers aren't usually the killing type. These men are assassins."

"Do you think they know who we are?"

Madame de Mailly considered Jacquelyna's question. For a moment, Jacquelyna thought she saw fear in the old woman's bitter eyes.

"We can only hope that if they do, it's enough to buy us our lives." The old woman then dropped to her knees between the seats and lifted the bench cushion. She pulled out a small wooden box, a metal flask, and a small velvet bag.

"What are you doing?" Jacquelyna asked.

Madame de Mailly pulled out an ornamental pistol from the box.

"Defending ourselves."

Gabrielle began to shake and cry at the sight of the pistol. The riders screamed and cursed outside. Jacquelyna took the young girl by the arm and pulled her into an embrace, softly stroking the girl's blonde hair and cooing gentle words of encouragement. But while her words were warm and sunny, her heart chilled. She stared at Madame de Mailly as the woman's old, slender fingers loaded the pistol with the speed and nimbleness of a veteran soldier. She could've given Peppin a run for his money, Jacquelyna reckoned. Madame de Mailly shoved the ramrod down the barrel before placing it back in its sheath. She threw back the curtain, leveled her pistol and fired without seemingly giving it a second thought.

"That's one," she smirked.

"There are still ten or so more!" Jacquelyna said.

Madame de Mailly didn't say anything but instead went about reloading her pistol. A few more shots were fired by the brigands. The coach came to a stop. Jacquelyna peered back outside. The horses pulling the lead coach had been shot and killed, blocking the road and forcing their coach to stop. A few of the horsemen dismounted and rushed the drivers on each coach while others remained on their mounts with pistols and swords in gloved hands.

"What do we do?" Jacquelyna asked.

Madame de Mailly finished her reloading. Any fear she once held was again replaced with her typical rancorous assertiveness. "Not act like chickens who've spotted a fox."

The door to the coach flew open. A large man reached in and grabbed Jacquelyna by the shoulders. She screamed in protest. He hauled her from the carriage and flung her to the cold ground. She moaned as her knee hit the edge of a small rock. The man did the same with Gabrielle who started to cry. Jacquelyna wrapped the young girl up beneath her cloak. The brute then leaned in to seize Madame de Mailly, but as his head disappeared into the shadows of the coach, a flash like lightning lit the inside, complemented by a chilling boom. The highwayman stumbled back from the coach, half his jaw missing, and dropped to the ground. Jacquelyna's eyes grew wide. She felt Gabrielle squeeze her in fear.

"Son of a whore. This one's got teeth!" another of the men yelled.

Two men stormed the other side of the coach. They grabbed Madame de Mailly, jerking her backwards and–between her shouts of reproach–flung her to the ground. Her face slammed against the frozen mantel. A few of the men turned their boots into her ribs and head. She groaned and was slow to get to her hands and knees.

Several more pistols were fired as the remaining retainers, drivers, and servants dropped to the ground in bloody heaps. Jacquelyna gave Gabrielle a squeeze, rocked back and forth and continued to coo softly in hopes of calming Gabrielle's panic. In truth, she needed to compose herself as much as she did Gabrielle, but serenity was difficult in front of ten men with murder in their eyes and blood seeping into the snow.

A man on horseback trotted over. He wore no mask, but the large scar across half his mustache was enough to send a chill through Jacquelyna.

"Where's the boy?" he asked.

"The prince isn't here," one of the swordsmen said. "Just these two women and the little girl. This one blew Jacques's face clean off."

The horseman's eyes darted to the limp body on the ground, the snow around it stained in red. He then regarded the old woman and dismounted, marching toward her with a fearsome stride.

"My name is Madame de Mailly," the old woman started, slowly pulling herself to her feet and brushing the snow from her gown and cloak, "and I'll have you know this coach belongs to the Marquise—"

The horseman cut off the old woman's sermon with a pistol shot that thundered through the cold air. Mailly's eyes flared. The corners of her lips trembled in pain. She groaned and whimpered and fell to her knees. She withdrew her hands from her stomach and gaped at her own blood as if it was the first time she'd ever seen it. The horseman then put a boot to her chest and knocked her on her back.

"Don't lecture me, crone. I know who you are and who this caravan belongs to."

Gabrielle shrieked. Jacquelyna did all she could to keep herself and the young girl from losing control. The horseman turned his attention to them. His dark eyes smoldered.

"Where's the prince?"

"He... he's not here," Jacquelyna stuttered.

"I can see that. Where is he?"

"Paris. He's very ill."

The horseman's jaw tensed beneath his unshaven cheeks. Another of the brigands walked up to him. His skin was dark and one of his eyes was partially closed by a gruesome bruise.

"What do we do now?" he asked.

The scarred man, clearly the leader of the murderous band, waved him off.

"Who are you and who's the child?"

Jacquelyna swallowed the lump in her throat. "I'm... I'm Jacquelyna Brocquart, the queen's mistress of the robes, and this is... this is Gabrielle Angélique de Verneuil... the king's daughter. He would be very put out if any harm... if any harm were to come to her."

The man smirked. "Yes. I would assume he would be put out, wouldn't he."

He held out his hand, and a swordsman handed him a pistol. He inspected the firearm before aiming at Jacquelyna. She turned her body to shield the king's daughter.

"You don't have to worry, mademoiselle. No harm will come to the little brat. As long as His Majesty cooperates to the demands offered to him, of course. You, however, well... step away from the girl."

Jacquelyna felt Gabrielle's fingers dig into her side. She had no intention of letting go. Jacquelyna shook her head, and the highwayman's massive shoulders rose and fell in a rage-filled staccato. He gestured at the swordsman next to him.

The swordsman's eyes raked Jacquelyna over as he approached. He grabbed her by the shoulder and did his best to pull her free from the princess's grip, but Jacquelyna struggled and screamed, and Gabrielle screeched like a banshee along with her. The swordsman snagged a handful of Jacquelyna's cloak and wrenched back. The brooch popped free and tumbled into the snow. It glinted in the sun. He picked it up. He studied the brooch—a silver wolf curled into an oval and with a bright sapphire eye—as if he had seen it before.

"What the blazes are you doing?" the leader said. "Who cares about some foolish trinket? Pocket it and separate the bitch and the bastard."

The swordsman turned to his commander. "We shouldn't kill her."

"Don't grow a heart now, Andre. You know the plan."

"I also know that we need someone to look after the little brat while the king considers his options. I sure as hell am not going to look after her. Are you? Or you? Or you?"

Each of man's brethren shook their heads.

The brigand leader mulled over the idea, his jaw grinding back and forth. He lifted the muzzle of his pistol and moved the doghead into a safe position.

"Put them back into the coach, replace the dead horse, and let's be on our way. The woman's in your charge, Andre. Don't hesitate to shoot her if you see fit."

Jacquelyna wanted to sigh in relief, but it felt like it was only delaying the inevitable. She raised her gaze and met those of Andre which pored over her as if he were searching for something but not knowing what. She couldn't decide if she wanted to thank him or curse him, and her inner turmoil must've flashed on the surface for a brief moment. The swordsman inclined his head, as if hearing her thoughts, and pocketed the brooch.

# XVII.
## Crows & Corpses

Lecroix was finishing his breakfast when a messenger arrived from the palace. The note was from the Duc de Sully and only said to arrive at the palace as soon as it was convenient. Yet it was delivered by a Forty-Five Guardsman, men not accustomed to playing the role of courier. It only punctuated the summons's urgency. The chevalier threw on the first court-tolerable attire he could find and rode his horse from his lodgings through the busy streets and under the palace gates. He dismounted, tossed the reins to the first servant that approached and made right for the Duc de Sully's office.

The doors to the duke's rooms were closed. Several Guardsmen stood outside armed to the teeth and kept an eye out of every window and entrance. One of the palace guards let Lecroix in only after checking the chevalier's summons and without even announcing his arrival.

Inside, he saw several men dressed in rich clothing with polished steel at their sides. There was Lieutenant Castel, his face graver than usual, the Duc d'Epernon, who first assembled the Forty-Five Guardsmen, François de Bassompierre, and the Marquis de Noyers, a fellow who Lecroix knew little about and had little interactions with previously. Standing in the middle of them was a smaller gentleman he didn't recognize dressed in a plain brown doublet, soiled stockings, and a weathered hat in hand. Together they made a semicircle around a large, wooden desk. Duc de Sully stood on the other side, leaning over its surface. Even at a distance, Lecroix could see the gravity in the duke's gaze.

"My apologies, messieurs," Lecroix said, doffing his tall crown hat, "but I came as fast as I could."

"This is an urgent matter, Chevalier," Sully said, "and I expect you to treat it with the greatest respect and secrecy."

"Of course, but what's happened?"

"Tell him," Sully ordered the older gentleman.

"I was on my way from Rouen to Paris, monsieur, when I came across a small caravan off the side of the road and people laying down on the ground. Seeing folks napping isn't odd, monsieur, when the weather is nice, but they were just lying there in the snow and mud. I got off of my cart and investigated." The man shot worrisome looks at the rest of the room. "And they were all dead, monsieur. Every single one of them. Dead."

"Who was dead?" Lecroix asked.

"I wasn't sure, monsieur, so I stopped off at Paris and found the watch and told him what I saw. He brought me here."

"Thank you, monsieur," Sully said. "That is all we need from you now. Wait outside in the antechamber will you?"

The old man nodded and was led away by one of the palace guards. Lecroix eyed the men around him. Their faces were darkened by the news, but something still made no sense.

"I don't understand, Duke. Who were they?"

"The watch didn't recognize the arms posted on a coach at the scene, but was well informed enough to come here. He drew it." Sully grabbed a piece of parchment on his desk and spun it around, so it faced Lecroix. On it was drawn a coat of arms that Lecroix recognized as the Marquise d'Entragues.

"Does the king know about this?" Lecroix asked.

"No, but he will shortly. Thankfully, the marquise was not in that caravan, nor the king's son. It was a caravan of mostly servants. Alas, it also had the king's daughter, Gabrielle Angélique, and the queen's mistress of the robes, Mademoiselle Brocquart."

Lecroix felt his veins chill. "Dear God. Are they among the dead?"

"We don't know, but we need to find out so we have answers. I can't keep His Majesty in the dark for too long. Not about this."

"When did they leave?"

"Yesterday morning."

"My men are already getting ready, Your Grace," Castel said.

"We leave within the hour."

"The Chevalier d'Auch will accompany you," d'Epernon said.

Castel shifted his stance. "With all due respect, that's unnecessary, Your Grace."

"Nevertheless, it's been decided."

"This is the second attack on coaches connected to the crown," Sully said. "I want to make sure we don't miss anything. The chevalier can be an asset."

Castel bowed and made for the door. Lecroix hung back, waiting to see if there was anything else they wanted to tell him, but Sully waved him off. Lecroix followed the lieutenant out of the palace and toward the Forty-Five's barracks. He had the stable boy bring his horse to him and mounted, putting his boot to the beast's flank and sending it into a trot. He eventually caught up with Castel striding faster than usual and paying no attention to the chevalier as he approached. Lecroix dismounted and followed at Castel's side.

"Same agreement as before, Chevalier," the lieutenant said. "This is my operation and if you get in the way I'll have you dismissed. Physically moved if need be."

Lecroix grabbed Castel by the arm. "I'm not my nephew, Lieutenant. Don't treat me as such. We're on the same side."

Castel considered Lecroix for a moment. "You're right. I offer my apologies. I shall try to conduct myself in a more appropriate manner in the future."

"Think nothing of it."

They continued their way to the barracks. Grey skies blanketed the horizon. A curt breeze cut at his face.

"I know you and Darion used to be close, but had a falling out. Mind if I ask what happened between you two?" Lecroix continued.

"I do mind, actually. Listen, Chevalier. I understand and respect the devotion you hold for your nephew, but I am not so sentimental. The rift between Darion and myself can only be solved by a matter of honor and with steel in our hands."

Lecroix, Lieutenant Castel, and fourteen Guardsmen rode out from

Paris late that morning, the sound of sixty-four hooves thundered against stone paved streets of Paris and then the frozen dirt in the countryside. There was just the one main road from Paris to Évreux, so they followed it northwest through the countryside. A couple of hours passed. The chevalier worried that whoever conducted the massacre went back to clean up their mess. Or, perhaps, the old man who reported the scene was just losing his faculties.

The band of king's men rode up a hill, most of the snow on the road having fallen down the slope or partially melted from the sun. At the top, all sixteen men and their mounts stopped and gazed down. In the wide, sloping valley, by two trees bare of leaves and buds, rested one coach, a dead horse, and several bodies strewn across the ground. Even from this distance they could see the snow stained in a dark cerise.

"Dear God," Lecroix muttered.

They rode to the saturnine scene. A murder of crows cawed and flew away from the bodies. Lecroix quickly counted the corpses, about a dozen in total.

"Find the king's daughter," Castel ordered. He dismounted and scanned the scene before them. There was a hint of sorrow or perhaps abhorrence in his eyes. Lecroix knew the look well. He had seen it in many men during his years as a soldier, and no doubt he sported that same, repulsed look himself in his younger days. But he hadn't seen a sight this stomach churning since St. Bartholomew's Day nearly four decades earlier.

The Guardsmen went about their orders, identifying the bodies, and looking for anything that may be lost or missing that could give them clues on the attackers. Most of the bodies were already in an early state of decay, their eyes plucked out by the crows and flesh nibbled on by woodland creatures hungry from their hibernation. The cold had fended off most of the maggots and other insects that would hollow a man from the inside out. A small silver lining. But each man and woman looked to have died brutally by pistol shots or sword thrusts. It was a massacre.

Lecroix noticed one body away from the rest, an old woman whose face was frozen in perpetual anguish. Her eyes were closed, at least, lest they'd also be pecked from their sockets.

"I don't see the child," Lecroix said, crossing himself.

"Over here!" one of the Guardsmen yelled.

Lecroix's heart sank. Two Guardsmen stood several feet off of the road near two bodies wrapped in black cloaks. They looked too big to be for a child, but Jacquelyna and Gabrielle Angélique were the only two people unaccounted for.

Castel pulled back the cloaks and stared for a moment. "Who are they?"

Lecroix sighed in relief. That moment of reprieve was quickly overcome by the fact that the king's daughter and the queen's mistress of the robes were still missing.

"No one I recognize, sir," the Guardsman said. "He's not dressed well either."

"The escort took at least one of the bastards to Hell with them," Castel said. "Where the hell is the king's daughter?"

"Two coaches left the palace, right?" Lecroix asked. "There's only one here. Whoever attacked the caravan took one. And hopefully with Jacquelyna and Gabrielle Angélique with it."

"*Hopefully.* This isn't good."

"It could be worse."

"We need to find out who did this. Look around and see if there's any sign of who these cowards were. And look for any tracks on which direction they would've traveled. With all these bodies, there must've been a dozen or so of attackers. I need some answers before we head back to Paris."

"We know who did this, Lieutenant," Lecroix said.

The chevalier heard the pain in his own voice as he said those words, and he knew who would feel the brunt of the king's wrath when it came to light, but honor compelled Lecroix to divulge all. He had a duty to his family, but also to his king.

He crouched down and pulled out a falcon feather tucked into the corpse's doublet.

## XVIII.
## Secrets in the Louvre

Lecroix heard the king's uproar from down the hall, cursing and swearing in a manner that would make even a hardened sailor blush in shame. No secrets could last long in the Louvre, and it seemed the king caught a whiff of this one.

Only Lecroix and Lieutenant Castel returned to Paris. Castel sent the remaining thirteen Guardsmen in opposite directions in search of the highwaymen—half north and half south—and each with a plan to alert the rest of the regiment should they catch scent of the murderers and kidnappers. A thorough plan, but Lecroix expected nothing less from the lieutenant.

As they approached the king's drawing room, another voice reached their ears—a woman's voice grated in wrath. Two of the palace guards crossed their halberds across the doorway.

"No one's to enter," one said.

"I'm Lieutenant of His Majesty's Forty-Five," Castel answered. "Move aside."

"I know who you are, lieutenant, and my apologies, but the king ordered no one to bother him."

"I must speak with the king. This is urgent."

"And I have my orders, monsieur."

"Let them pass," Sully said from beyond the doorway. "But trust me, messieurs, you don't want to enter there presently."

The guards looked at each other, wondering if the duke's word was as good as the king's in the current situation. They relented, pulled back their halberds and let the lieutenant and chevalier through.

"For the love of God, I hope you have good news," Sully said.

"That would depend on your definition of good news, I'm afraid," Lecroix said.

A glass shattered. The three men turned. A handsome woman in a red and white gown decorated in pearls rushed by them. The men bowed their heads in respect, but she paid them no attention. She shuffled by without as much as a glance, followed by two young women and an armed gentleman.

"The Marquise de Verneuil knows?" Lecroix asked.

"She was the one that told His Majesty," Sully replied.

Lecroix cringed. He could only imagine the anger and embarrassment the king felt finding out from his mistress that their daughter had been attacked and taken. No doubt Duc de Sully would be at the receiving end of King Henry's temper later. An occupational hazard, alas.

"His Majesty is in a foul mood, as you can expect, so act tactfully," Sully added.

They moved through the antechamber and into the drawing room, warmed by a crackling fire in a large hearth. His Majesty was in his riding boots still, his shirttails messily untucked from his breeches, and doublet hanging off the arm of a chair. He leaned over a wooden table, his head sunk between his lean and muscular shoulders. A few glass vases, a candelabra, and several loose sheets of paper decorated the floor.

"Your Majesty, Lieutenant Castel and the Chevalier d'Auch have returned."

The king turned around, the lids of his eyes rubbed red and raw, and a vulgar look of pain on his face.

"Please tell me you found my daughter unharmed."

Lecroix and Castel shot each other sidelong glances. Neither one wanted to be the bearer of ill news. Castel moved first.

"We found the marquise's household caravan heading north. We found no survivors, however, your daughter was not among the bodies. Nor was the queen's mistress of the robes, Mademoiselle Brocquart."

"Where could they be?"

"Unsure, but we are almost positive it was the same band of brigands who attacked the chevalier's coach recently."

"Highwaymen?" Sully interjected. "What the hell do highwaymen want with the king's daughter and the queen's lady?"

"Gold, most likely. Or land. We're not sure yet."

"This doesn't seem like a routine theft and certainly not by a regular band of highwaymen either," Lecroix said. "They're organized and well-armed. They seem more like soldiers than thieves. Thieves don't go after prey this big. Too many risks."

"So you think this is political?" the king asked. "My enemies are going after my family now?"

Lecroix shrugged. He wasn't prepared to say either way.

"Just what we need," Sully grumbled. "Another war on our hands."

"It's entirely possible that these brigands merely want to ransom your daughter, Your Majesty. They may not know who they're holding just yet."

"Gabrielle is not some piece of cattle to be bartered!" the king roared. "I will not tolerate this, understand? I will not. I want to know who did this and why, and I want them punished severely."

Silence clung to the air like a thickening fog. Each man was frozen in their stances, afraid to move into the path of the king's temper.

"We do have a prisoner tied to the men we think are responsible for this, Your Majesty," Castel said.

"Question him, dammit. Question him and torture him if you must."

"Your Majesty, please—" Lecroix spoke up.

The king's eyes flared. "I will not be questioned in this, Chevalier! Do what you must, Lieutenant, and do it quickly."

Lecroix expected a victorious smirk to appear on Castel's face, but instead he found the lieutenant's expression to be distant and void.

"As you wish, Your Majesty." Castel bowed and strode out the room, no doubt glad to be out of the king's reach. Lecroix, however, felt nothing but knots in his stomach at the thought of Darion being tortured, but he could do little to help his nephew now. Darion made his own bed.

"His Excellency, Don Pedro Alvarez de Toledo, Marquis de Villafranca," a herald announced.

The king's eyes darted to the Spanish ambassador as he passed and back to the Duc de Sully. They had a hardness to them that ordered the duke silently. Sully nodded, fully comprehending his charge, and he met the ambassador near the door.

"His Majesty is not in a proper mood to speak politics today, Ambassador," Sully said in a low voice.

"*Sí*, I know," Don Pedro said. "That is why I have come. I heard about the attack."

Sully shot a cautious glance back at the king. "I'm not sure he's in a mood to speak of that either."

"What do you want, señor?" Henry said, his temper rising to impatience.

Don Pedro stepped forward and bowed as low as his legs would allow.

"Your Majesty, I have just heard about a rumor that your mistress's carriage was attacked."

"Rumors spread fast, I see."

"Is it true?"

"And what business is it of yours, Ambassador?"

"I merely wanted to extend my condolences and offer any help in bringing these brigands to justice."

"And why would you do that?"

"As I have said many times, Your Majesty, it is my sovereign's greatest wish for Spain and France to put aside our differences and become friends. I know how much you love your family, of every branch from the Bourbon tree. If there's anything I or my master Phillip III can do, I beg you to call upon me as you would any other faithful servant."

The king crossed his arms and contemplated the ambassador's offer.

"Consider your offer marked, my friend."

⚜⚜⚜

Don Pedro quickly turned on his heel and headed down the hall. Servants rushed down the hallways, lighting the wall-mounted candelabras that lined the entire palace and lightening halls into a yellow glow. In many ways the ambassador saw his mission in Paris as being much like that of the candle boys'—bringing France out of the darkness of Protestantism and into the light of the True Faith.

The candles gave the Louvre an eerie glow. Most of the hallways were abandoned and silent. A stiff wind blew outdoors. Some of the windows shook. The breeze rushed through small cracks in the walls and glass, making the candlelight flicker like a fervid dancer. A few of the candles blew out, draping the passage in partial darkness. As if the shadows opened a portal to the netherworld, a dark figure appeared from between two pillars. The ambassador stopped in his tracks, noticing the tip of a sword peek through the long, wool cloak around the man's shoulders. His mind was put to rest, however, when he saw a silver cross glinting around the man's neck. The swordsman stepped into the light.

"Gonzalo," Don Pedro said.

"Excelencia," the other replied, placing a solemn hand over his heart and bowing his head.

"You have returned later than I anticipated."

"My apologies, Excelencia, but I ran into some unforeseen obstacles on my return back to Paris. Additional precautions were needed."

His somber tone only added to the already gloomy ambiance. Don Pedro moved to a corner of the hall and gestured his minion to follow.

"Obstacles?"

"King's men. More than a dozen of them. They're heading north to Évreux."

"Did they stop you?'

The swordsman shook his head. His pale blue and green eyes looked even more lifeless in the faint light.

"They never saw me, Excelencia."

"Good. And your mission?"

"A complete success, Excelencia."

"I heard there was more cargo than you expected."

"That is true. A young woman."

"What happened to her?"

"Taken."

"Did she recognize you?"

Gonzalo shook his head. "I kept my distance. They're keeping her to look after the bastard, but will want to ransom her, too. These French thieves have no honor, Excelencia."

"They won't fetch a pretty penny for her. Her father is practically in the poor house from what I gather. When you return make sure they keep the affairs separate. We don't need greed getting in the way."

"Of course, Excelencia."

"There is another item of the utmost importance to our mission."

"I am at your command, Excelencia."

"Apparently the highwayman we released had a friend in Paris planning on doing the same. The idiot got himself caught in the process and is now rotting in the Bastille. He knows the highwaymen, Gonzalo. He could pose a serious threat."

The Spanish swordsman smiled wickedly. "I understand, Excelencia."

# XIX.
## A Proposition

Darion groaned as he slowly regained consciousness. His vision was blurry at first, or so he thought, but then he realized he just had awoken to nightfall. Three tallow candles on short nightstands were his only source of light.

He tried lifting himself to his feet but felt weak and sore. Another groan escaped him. He peeled off some straw stuck to his face. His face burned as he pressed his hand to his skin, pulling back to find his fingertips sticky with dried blood. His lips twisted into a grimace; his afternoon started to come back to him. He had spent most of it in the company of his old friend, Antoine Castel, who was questioning him once again about the attack on Lecroix, but also something about an ambush on the king's mistress's coach. When polite discussion didn't give the lieutenant the results he wished, he moved on to more archaic techniques. Darion knew Castel was a man of resolve and that no god nor devil could keep him from achieving his goal, but Darion had never seen him turn to torture. And thanks to Peppin's little enlightenment about Castel's near-death wound, Darion wondered if the lieutenant was working on getting answers or just exorcising past demons.

The last thing Darion remembered was getting up close and personal with one of the Bastille's inquisitors and his wooden staff. The end result was waking back up in his cell, his face caked in dried blood, and with a few bruised ribs. It could've been worse, but he knew they were easing him into things. Future interrogations wouldn't go so smoothly.

He couldn't manage to pull himself to his feet, but at least he rocked himself backwards so his back rested against the stone wall. Toppled over at the foot of his cell was a dented tankard and a bowl with some brown sludge meant to pass off as stew. He stared at it for a few minutes, weighing whether it was worth the effort and pain to move for it or just stay put and get what little rest he could.

He chose sleep. Alas, his mind had trouble resting. He thought of how his idiotic plan almost got Pep measured for a noose. He thought of his uncle and how severely he disappointed his old caregiver. He even thought of Jacquelyna; he thought the flame that burned in his heart for her extinguished after he left. It had been five years, after all. But it seems that love never truly gets snuffed out; it merely dwindles into a smoldering coal, waiting to be stoked into a roaring fire once more.

But, above all else, what irked Darion the most was the path he had taken the past five years. He once was a proud and loyal soldier of the crown. A man of action and a man of honor. It was his honor and Jacquelyna's he fought for when she came to him and asked him to put aside honor for love:

Darion had found Sergeant Barrière speaking about Jacquelyna with far too loose of a tongue for his liking one evening. Words were exchanged between the two men, and plans to share steel was scheduled. Darion had looked forward to ramming three feet of steel through the sergeant's guts, but the night before the appointment Jacquelyna came to him and begged him to call off the duel. Darion couldn't understand why—he still didn't. Jacquelyna refused to give a reason. He was left with choosing between his love for Jacquelyna and his honor—and so he chose neither.

Love and honor. Two forces of life always at odds with each other.

Darion wasn't sure how long he wrestled with his past when he heard a faint creaking of a door down the hall. His eyes shot open. The candles burned low in their stands now. One had completely fizzled out. Darion strained his ears, waiting to hear steps move toward his cell or away, but he didn't hear a thing. Perhaps his ears were playing tricks on him.

The prospect of paranoia was comforting compared to the dark shadow that passed in front of his cell a moment later. The figure was short and dressed in black from head to toe. The faint candle light couldn't penetrate the heavy shadow from the hood the person wore. The figure stood there, motionless and silent, as if it were measuring Darion for some unknown reason. Then it took a step closer into the light, and Darion saw two amber eyes glow like smoldering coals in a fire. The figure pulled out an ornamented wheellock pistol from the folds of the cloak.

"Do I know you?" he asked.

"No." The figure spoke with a woman's voice. Darion's face betrayed his inquisitiveness and bewilderment. "However, we share a mutual friend."

Darion couldn't place her voice, and he couldn't see her face beneath the shadow of her hood. He hadn't met many since he returned to Paris, but still her identity eluded him.

"I'm afraid you have me at a disadvantage, mademoiselle. I don't recognize you."

"It's madam and my identity means little. What matters is our mutual friend."

A caustic grin appeared on Darion's face.

"And who is our mutual friend?"

"Mademoiselle Brocquart."

Darion smile vanished. He struggled to his feet.

"What of her?"

"She's been abducted. By some old friends of yours."

"I don't understand."

"No. I suppose you wouldn't, would you?" There was a mocking bite to her words. Darion lowered his brows. She reached into her cloak and pulled out another item. "Recognize this?"

"Should I?" He hoped to get more information from her before acknowledging anything. For all he knew, Castel sent her to trick him.

"I would say so. It's a falcon feather. That's what your band of thieves and cutthroats wear don't you?"

"Lots of folk wear falcon feathers in their caps, madam. Falconers for one. It's not all that peculiar."

"It is when it's been notched like so, isn't it?"

She outstretched her hand and held the feather in the halo of candlelight. Darion examined the rectangular notch on the top half of the feather. It belonged to one of the Falcon Highwaymen, or it was a well-constructed forgery.

"A fake," he said to test her. She giggled knowingly.

"Ah, Monsieur Delerue. I honestly do not know what Jacquelyna sees in you. Your blade must be sharper than your wit lest you'd be long dead and buried."

"Let's say I believe you, madam. Let's say this feather belongs to the Falcon Highwaymen and I, myself, part of their band. Let's say they did, for whatever unknown reason, decide to abduct Jacquelyna. What am I supposed to do about it?"

"Find her and bring her back home to Paris."

These words were so matter-of-factly stated that it took Darion by surprise. He stared into the blackness of her cloak, looking for a hint of a jesting smile, but the shadow gave no trace of one. All he saw were the smoldering amber eyes cutting into him like a winter's chill. He laughed at the absurdity of it all.

"And how am I supposed to do that from back here, eh?"

"You're not."

The woman cranked on a key she secretly put into the hole and pulled back. The gate groaned as it opened, but despite this gesture of goodwill, she kept her pistol leveled at him.

"This is a trap."

"A trap? Monsieur, you're in the Bastille. You already fell into the worst of traps."

"How do I know what you say is true."

The woman shrugged. "You don't."

"How do you know I'll do as you ask?"

"Because despite your pride and arrogance, monsieur, I see a glimmer of affection for Jacquelyna in your eyes. That is not a glimmer that many men share readily. It's a glimmer far beyond friendship and lust."

Darion considered the woman and her words. He didn't know what to make of it, or her, but he felt compelled to believe her. Better to trust this strange woman–offering him freedom at the end of a pistol, no less–than to stay put and try his luck with Castel and the Bastille's interrogators.

She gestured down the hall with the muzzle of the pistol. "You first."

"Don't trust me, madam?"

Darion thought he caught a faint outline of a smile on her face. He turned down the hall, painted orange from burning torches along the stone walls. The torches thawed him as he passed. What struck him as strange was that the Bastille halls were quiet. It felt like walking through a tomb more than a prison.

"Where are all the guards?" he asked.

"Paid off or scared silent. I'm a resourceful woman."

An understatement, Darion thought. To spring a man from jail was one thing. To break one out of the Bastille was another. But to do so without a drop of blood? That was beyond even the power of the saints. Darion could practically smell the fresh air of liberty as they turned the corner, but he stopped suddenly.

"What is it? Keep moving, monsieur. There's no time to dally."

"Did you bring a retainer?"

"What? No."

"Then we might have a predicament."

Darion stepped away to let the woman get a better view. Positioned at the far end of the hall was a man in black from hat to boot. Only a blood red sash around his waist gave his character any color. The silver cross around his neck and two long cup hilt rapiers in his hands glinted in the torchlight.

"Give me the prisoner, señora," the swordsman said in a thick Spanish accent. "I have no quarrel with you."

"I'm afraid he's mine for the evening," the woman said. "Perhaps you can borrow him another time."

The Spaniard stepped forward. The woman countered by aiming her pistol him.

"You have only one shot, señora. Men have shot me more than that, yet the Good Lord saw fit to resurrect me on the spot."

"Well, it's a good thing I'm no man."

She pulled the trigger. The pistol fired. The swordsman dropped to the floor in a pile of black wool and leather.

"Quick. There's another way out," the woman said.

Darion followed the woman whence they came. His knee felt fine now, but he could feel his flanks growl in pain with each step. They came to a row of small cells closed off by wooden doors and small bared windows. The woman started opening a few of the cells with her keys.

"What are you doing?" Darion asked.

"Buying us some time." She opened the last door and threw it open. "You're free, gentlemen! To liberty!"

The men all looked at her with defeated eyes, but slowly life came back to them as the thought of freedom replaced their shackles. The prisoners rushed for the door, some running, some walking, some dragging their bloody and blistered feet. Darion watched as the poor souls came across the Spaniard who, as he predicted, resurrected from the pistol shot. He marched forward with two bare blades in hand. Without a thought or look of remorse, the Spanish swordsman cut down the first two prisoners. He skewered the next man like a pig carcass on a spit. The final three fell into the fetal position or threw themselves flush against the wall, whimpering and weeping for their lives.

Darion didn't stick around to learn their fates. He followed the woman through another series of doors. At one inner door, she closed it tight behind them and locked it. Through the small opening between the wooden panels Darion spotted the Spaniard trudging forward. Streams of blood dripped down his blade like venom from a viper's fangs.

"This way, monsieur," the woman said. "We're almost free."

They rushed down one final hall and out into the night. The cool air felt like a relief to Darion's soul. He looked up, surveyed the massive prison lurking over him like a great watchman, and came to the easy conclusion that he never wanted to return to the Bastille.

"Who was that man?" Darion asked.

"No friend of yours, though I know the idea of friendship must be very different for men like you."

Darion scowled. "You presume much, madam."

Whoever this Spanish swordsman was, he meant death, and as soon as Castel caught wind that Darion escaped, he'd have every single soldier and watchman scouring the city for him. He had to get out of Paris fast, but the city gates were closed for the night. He needed help, and despite what this hooded woman thought, Darion had friends he could count on. Or at least one.

"Here," the woman said, reaching into the fold of her cloak. "You'll need this if you want to leave Paris without a fight. I suggest using it."

She pulled out a folded parchment sealed in red wax. Darion took it and inspected it, not sure what he was looking for or what he expected to find. When he looked back up to thank the woman she had disappeared like a phantom in the shadows.

# XX.
# The Artillery Foundry

"Oh no! You're not allowed back here."

Madame Yolente la Rossa de Tors, procurer for Divines, crossed her arms at the brothel's threshold. Her green eyes leered beneath her fiery red hair. Her lips tightened into a thin line.

"I'm not looking for refuge," Darion said, his eyes scanning the darkness behind him for the glow of a watchman's torch or the glint of a guard's polearm.

"Good, because Antoine gave me a lot of shit for harboring you and Peppin. I've had at least two visits from his men harassing me every day since."

"I just came to gather my sword and pistol."

"Not here, love. Peppin came by and took it. I told him the same thing I told you. Don't come back–least, not for a while."

She placed a hand on her hip and winked.

"Where's Pep now?"

"The Artillery Foundry, I'd wager. Northern shore on the east side of the river."

Darion put a hand over his heart as a gesture of thanks.

"You're not in more trouble now are you?"

"Best to forget I ever came by, madam."

Yolente smiled and shook her head.

The Artillery Foundry was a tavern by the docks of the Seinne River. Its placement by the piers made it an ideal spot for Paris's less than savory folk to mingle, plot, and carouse. The city watch rarely stepped foot near the Artillery Foundry—not worth the broken bones—making it an ideal spot to lay low for a bit. He could hardly believe Jacquelyna was abducted by the Falcon Highwaymen—kidnapping wasn't part of their repertoire—but he knew he needed to leave Paris, so checking out the story couldn't hurt.

Darion felt naked without his sword and dagger. The *Cour des Miracles* was a piss poor area to traverse without any sort of weapon at one's side, so he kept mostly to the gloom, hopping from one shadow to the next until he reached the Artillery Foundry by the quay. Through a thick window he saw the distorted scene of thieves, sell-swords, smugglers, beggars, fences, and others of the city's filth enjoying the tavern's hospitality. Darion wrapped his cloak around him, hoping no one would notice the lack of steel on his person.

He stepped into the tavern to the tune of cursing, singing, and roaring laughter from the patrons. Half-full jars and overturned tankards decked the tables, as well as a few empty wine bottles turned into candleholders.

"Get in and close the fucking door!" one man yelled.

Darion shot the fellow an annoyed sidelong glance before doing just that. He scanned the room, looking for Peppin, though he was sure he'd hear the one-eyed bastard before he ever saw him. A couple of men in wool and leather shuffled past Darion, but not before measuring him on the way out. Darion's hand instinctively went for the dagger missing from his side. He swore beneath his breath.

He reached the bar top along the side wall. A few men, rowdy and reeking of stale wine, leaned at its edge. Darion inclined his head to the men, and they went about their business at the bottom of their tankards. A large fellow, bald on his head but nearly ape like on his face, stepped toward him.

"What can I get you, messiuer?" he said.

"I'm looking for Peppin Petite," Darion said. "Do you know him?"

The man thundered in laughter. "Know him? Shit. The sonofabitch is practically a prince here." The barman's face then darkened a bit, and he looked at Darion with the utmost scrutiny. "Why? What do you want with him?"

"I'm a friend of his. I need to speak with him."

"Your business?"

"None of yours."

The barman half-grinned. "Bold words coming from an unarmed man."

The patrons next to Darion perked at this.

"I also have no coin, so I wouldn't bother, messieurs."

Some of the men grumbled—the prospect of easy prey dwindled away—and went back to their drinks. Two cloaked fellows held their steady gaze on Darion. The barkeep frowned.

"He's up stairs. Last door on your left." Darion tipped his hat in thanks and started heading up the wooden staircase. The barman yelled out to him: "He's a bit busy at the moment, though, so I'd watch yourself!"

Darion shuffled past a few men and women standing in the middle of the room and conversing among one another, while another table was silently at work in a game of cards. A few drunken louts bumped into Darion. He winced at the pain throbbing in his side. He made his way up the wooden stairs and down the hall that overlooked the tavern below. He finally came to the last door on the left. Through the door he heard wood creaking and scraping against the floor, and the faint ringing of a woman's giggle. He hesitated before knocking.

"Peppin! It's Darion. Open up."

Voices whispered on the other side in what sounded like a soft but furious debate. The door opened revealing a stark naked Peppin. His eyes were bloodshot and hazy, he reeked of wine, and he sported a large, goofy grin. Darion peered past his friend. A large woman lay in bed covered by only a thin white sheet. She smiled and waved her fingers at Darion.

"Fuck me," Peppin slurred. "How'd the blazes did you get out, Gascon?"

"We need to talk, Pep."

"Of course, of course. Just let me finish my business and then we can—"

"No. Now."

Peppin blinked. "Alright, Gascon. No need to get your petticoat all in a bunch."

"And put some breeches on, will you?"

Peppin looked down and grinned before shutting the door.

Darion took a seat on the first floor by the rear entrance, an area fairly shrouded in shadows, but for a few gleams of dancing light from the hearth along the wall. He took out the parchment the hooded woman gave him and studied it. There was no text on the front or rear of the paper, and it was sealed in a large red wax. He angled the paper around to get a better view of the seal itself—an eagle grasping a snake in its talons. He knew he'd seen that image before, but wasn't sure when or where.

Peppin staggered down the steps carrying two sets of sword belts, rapiers, daggers, and pistols. The tavern patrons parted for him as he made his way across the floor.

"Figure you'd be wanting this back," Pep said, sliding one set of gear across the table. He leaned the other set against a wooden column next to his seat.

"I went by Divine's to get it."

"Dear God, and Yolente let you leave in one piece? She had some choice words for me when I went to get our weapons."

"She had some for me when I showed up, as well."

"How in blazes did—"

Darion was about to answer when two massive hands placed a jug of wine and two tankards on the table. He looked up and saw the woman he caught Peppin bare ass naked with. She was tall and rotund, built like the sturdiest of sailors and with a rascally gaze.

"Here you go, you little shit," she said to Peppin with a smile. She gestured to Darion with a nod. "Who's your friend here?"

"Thank you, my dove," Peppin replied. "This is Darion Delerue, a gallant soldier and one of my oldest and best of friends. Gascon, this is the love of my life, my life's joy, my ray of sunshine, my little honeycomb, my—"

"Oh, you're full of shit, you little asshole." The woman held out her hand to Darion. "My name's Marguerite, but everyone calls me Mortar Marguerite, or Mortar for short."

Darion didn't bother asking why she was called Mortar. Her booming voice was enough evidence of that, though he was certain Peppin would attribute the nickname to the barmaid's well-endowed chest.

"Well, I'll leave you two boys be. Give a holler if you need anything. Especially you." Marguerite winked at Darion.

"Don't even think about it," Pep growled with a playful grin.

"Why? Are you?" Mortar Marguerite burst out laughing and left the table, forcing her way through the thick crowd with ease. Peppin watched until she was out of sight before turning back.

"What a woman." He poured two mugs full. "What shall we toast to? Our freedom?"

Darion clanked his mug against Peppin's and took a long swig. Freedom was fleeting.

"So, err, you going to tell me how the hell you got out of the Bastille?" Peppin asked again.

Darion took another long swig from his drink. He barely believed the story himself, but he recited to Pep what happened. How he woke up to a mysterious hooded woman, the story she told him about Jacquelyna's kidnapping, the Spanish swordsman hell bent on killing him for some unknown reason, and how they barely escaped the Bastille with their lives.

"That's quite the tale, Darion. Seems too fanciful for my liking."

"Me, too, Pep, but if there's any chance Jacquelyna is in danger..."

He trailed off and shook his head. Nothing made sense.

"I can make some inquiries."

"I can't stay in Paris that long. Antoine and his men will be looking for me by sunrise." He pulled out the parchment from his doublet again. "The woman also gave me this. She said it'd get me a way out of the city without harassment from officials."

"Us, you mean."

Darion cocked his head to the side. "You don't have to go, Pep."

"Fuck you, I don't. Jacquelyna's a friend of mine, too, remember."

"It might be dangerous."

Peppin shrugged his massive shoulders. "Life is danger, Gascon. If Jacquelyna's in trouble, I want to help. So, when do we depart?"

"As soon as you're done with your drink."

"As soon as you're done with your drink what?" Marguerite asked. She loomed over the table, an apron now tied around her waist. She placed a plate of bread and cheese on the table in front of them.

"Oh, nothing, my dove. The Gascon and I are merely going on a little holiday for the next few days, visiting some old friends in the countryside."

Marguerite crossed her arms. "That so?"

"Indeed! It's important to reconnect, don't you think, Gascon?"

Darion stared at him blankly. "Sure."

"Uh-huh," Marguerite said. "You two need anything else?"

"No, no. We're fine for now, my love."

Marguerite snorted before leaving.

"Lying now are we?" Darion asked. "That doesn't seem very like you."

Peppin put up a hand to silence Darion. He swung his head around to make sure Marguerite wasn't around to hear.

"Jesus Christ. You shut your fucking mouth. You're trying to get me killed?"

Darion leaned back in his seat and crossed his arms. A large smile spread across his face. "I never thought I'd see the day in which the great Peppin was scared of a woman."

"Oh, Gascon. You don't want to meddle with Mortar Marguerite. You wouldn't last five minutes with her."

"And you do?"

Darion laid the euphemism thick for Peppin. Not that Pep needed it. He found double entendres sometimes where there weren't any to be found.

"Sometimes that's all she needs." Peppin winked and threw back his drink.

"You were lying to her though."

"Don't have the heart to tell her the truth. She'd kill me before Antoine or your friends even got a shot. Where's the fun in that, eh? We should alert Antoine, though—about the kidnapping."

Darion gaped at his friend, waiting for a jest that never came.

"'Steeth, you're serious."

"He leads the king's bodyguards, second only to the king himself and the Duc d'Epernon. He has the manpower we need."

"He'd have me swinging from my neck sooner than he'd listen to me."

"Then I'll do it."

Darion shook his head. "We need to do this quietly, Pep."

Peppin scratched the stubble on his neck while his dark, single-eye gaze wandered across the room. Darion could read the concern on Peppin's face. For all Pep's traits and virtues, concealing his thoughts and feelings was not one of them.

"Very well, Gascon," he said in resignation. "Quietly."

## XXI.
## Snakes & Eagles

A tear nearly streamed down Peppin's face as they stood from the table and belted their swords. Darion and Pep were leaving a half-full jug of wine on the table–free wine at that–and there were few things that Pep hated more than wasted wine and turning down a handout.

Darion waited outside while Peppin paid his adieus. Through a foggy window, he spied Peppin speaking to Marguerite, her large hands in his own. He then raised them to his lips and said something that made the barmaid smile. Darion found it amusing that two coarse souls could act so tenderly to one another.

The tavern door opened. Peppin stepped out with a heavy heart.

"Everything well, Pep?"

Peppin rubbed his eyes. "Aye. Just really hate to see wine go to waste. Follow me. Mag gave us a couple of horses."

Around back was a large but old stable. Each stall was occupied by a horse of various colors and breeds–some belonging to patrons, others to Marguerite. The two Mortar Marguerite lent them were lean and muscular, built for speed more than for war. They'd have king's men on their heels soon enough, so speed was of the essence.

They finished saddling their horses when Darion felt an eerie presence prickling at the back of his neck. He peered over his shoulder to see two silhouettes standing at the stable's threshold. Behind them moonlight glistened off the Seine.

"Can we help you, messieurs?" Darion asked.

Peppin whipped his head around, almost startled by the two figures before them.

"You are Andre Bauvet," one said.

"Sorry to disappoint but I'm not."

"You are Peppin Petite," the figure said, pointing to Pep.

"At your service, messieurs," Pep said with a contemptuous bow.

"Then you must be the fugitive Andre Bauvet," the figure told Darion.

"Again, sorry to disappoint."

The two men threw open their cloaks. Pale light hinted at the cold steel at their sides. One drew out a long pistol from his belt. Darion made for his own pistol before remembering he had stuffed it into his saddle holster already.

"I say you are Andre Bauvet."

"Oh, Jesus Christ, his fucking name is Darion Delerue you dumb assholes," Pep yelled. The two men shot glances at each other.

"He's in the Bastille."

"Does he look like he's in the goddamn Bastille? Who the hell are you two louts anyways?"

"King's men," Darion said. "Regular ruffians wouldn't own pistols so ornamented. No doubt they were sent by Antoine."

"I don't care if you're Andre Bauvet, Darion Delerue or Duc d'Epernon, you're both coming with us. Hand over your swords, sirs."

Peppin leaned in over Darion's shoulder. "We can take these assholes."

"They got pistols, Pep," Darion whispered.

"Aye, but I refuse to go back to the Bastille."

"Your swords now, gentlemen," the Guardsman repeated.

Darion debated his chances of escape with that of having his bone shattered by a pistol shot from close range. He reached for the hooks on his sword frog when a third, massive figure approached.

"What's going on back here?" a thundering voice said. Mortar Marguerite stepped into the strip of silver light. A breeze blew off the river but even without a cloak Marguerite seemed unfazed by the cold.

The two men spun around, startled by the fact that someone so large was able to sneak up on them so silently.

"Turn back, madam," one of the men said. "This is no concern of yours."

"What did you say, you little shitstain?"

The Guardsman raised his pistol and aimed it at Marguerite. From the corner of his eye, Darion saw Peppin stiffen at the gesture and his face go livid.

"Easy, Pep," Darion whispered.

"Fuck you, Gascon."

"What was that?" the Guardsman said, turning to face the two men. As soon as he took his eye off Marguerite, she lunged forward and slammed a heavy fist into the man's skull. His jaw cracked under the force, and he discharged his pistol wildly into the night, lighting up the confined area in a bright, white light. It blinded Darion for a moment. When his eyes readjusted, he saw Peppin level his shoulder into the second man's gut. The Guardsman let out a hoarse moan before slamming the pummel of his rapier into Pep's back. Pep fell to a knee. The Guardsman raised his sword for a second blow. But Marguerite's hand shot out of the shadows and gripped the man's wrist as if he were a child. He grunted and whimpered as she squeezed the sword free from his clutch. When the rapier clattered on the ground, she torqued his arm backward, popping it free at the shoulder. The man's eyes flared. He screamed in unhallowed pain before a heavy fist from Marguerite shut him up.

And like that two of France's finest soldiers were sprawled on the ground, alive but unconscious.

Darion just stared at Mortar Marguerite. Now he fully understood the meaning of her moniker.

She helped Peppin to his feet. "So who the hell are these bastards?" she asked.

"King's men," Peppin said. "Guardsmen."

"They'll rain hell on you for this," Darion said. "You'd best to leave Paris for a few days."

Marguerite puffed. "The shit sort of advice is that? I can handle myself, have you no worries. Besides, can't trust anyone else to run this place. It'd burn to the ground without me. Can only imagine what sort of trouble you got into to have the king's bodyguards hunting you down."

"I'll explain all when I return," Pep said.

"Yea, you better return, you fool." Pep took her hands into his and gave them several gentle kisses. Marguerite blushed. "Oh, go on and get out of here."

Darion and Peppin took to their saddles and with a final blown kiss from Pep, left the Artillery Foundry. They rode through the city lit by a pale moon that shattered the shadows with silver gleams. A few watchmen and catchpoles walked by in groups of two and three, armed with pistols and swords, polearms, and torches. They spoke to one another and hardly paid any heed to Darion and Peppin. All the better, Darion thought. If they were so lax in their watch, then news of his escape hadn't left the Bastille yet.

They made their way to one of the gates on the southeastern quadrant of Paris. The Bastille loomed in the horizon, a cold beacon that made Darion shiver. Posted at the gate were three soldiers huddled around a small, open fire. Two picked up their halberds and stood in front of the closed access, while the third approached.

"Gate's closed, messieurs."

"We can see that. We have only one blind eye between us," Pep answered.

The sentinel looked annoyed by Peppin's boorish response.

"We have urgent business, monsieur, that requires us to leave at this ungodly hour," Darion said.

"Ungodly, indeed. My apologies, gentlemen, but the gate won't open until morning. You can leave then. By orders of His Maj—"

Darion reached into his doublet and pulled out the sealed paper. The guard took it and walked by the fire to get a better view of its contents. Upon seeing the seal his eyes grew to the size of plates, and he shot a nervous glance at his compatriots at the postern. He broke the seal and read the letter, his face growing paler with every word.

"Open the gate," he ordered in a mumbled.

The two other sentinels seemed confused by the order, but after their superior barked out the order a second time, they did as they were bid. The gates opened, and Darion and Peppin rode through without any more hassle. As the gate closed behind them, Darion gave the city one final glance. It was a brief visit and a cold reminder that sometimes you can't go back to the way things were.

The two men put their boots to their horses and trotted away from the city. A few minutes later, the bells in the Bastille rang.

# XXII.
## The Highwaymen's Hole

A few rays of morning sun shone through a wooden shutter, waking Jacquelyna. She found herself in the same godforsaken room the highwaymen threw her in the night before. It was old and musty, with just a simple bed, nightstand, a small writing desk, and wooden chair as furnishing. No decorations on the wall shedding paint chips. She found the room bleak, but what else did she expect from cutthroats?

She rose out of the chair and glanced at the peaceful and slumbering Gabrielle. Jacquelyna was surprised she managed to get any sleep herself, but that shock was also laced with guilt. She didn't want to leave her guard down around her captors. Not during the day. Not during the night. Not ever. They weren't men. They were savage animals without a shred of honor or a drop of compassion in their blood. Who attacks a coach full of women and children? Who murders the elderly?

She had remained vigilant the entire ride, consoling Gabrielle as best she could until the young girl cried herself to sleep. Jacquelyna had hoped they would stop along the way, somewhere she might be able to take off with the little girl, or at least get a message out for aid. But the caravan forged on like a dutiful army off to war until they reached a rundown chateau in the countryside. She was herded into a small room and locked in. While Gabrielle kipped, Jacquelyna huddled herself into the armchair in the corner, staring at the lonesome candle flame on the nightstand next to her until she drifted asleep. Her dreams were dark and restless, and like a ghost in the daylight, vanished from her memory when she awoke. All that was left was the sepulchral twinge in her gut.

She walked over to the window and opened it. A cold breeze

rushed in, turning her skin to gooseflesh. She crossed her arms and poked her head out. The sky was clear and bright, while a thin layer of snow covered the ground that went on some distance before hitting a wall of tall trees. It was a beautiful day if not for the fact that she was a prisoner among a band of villains and murderers.

Jacquelyna looked straight down and sighed. It was too far for her to jump safely. Not that she expected the highwaymen to be foolish enough to give her a room with easy access to escape. She closed the window and rubbed her arms to warm them.

The door opened. A highwayman stepped in with his doublet undone, revealing his undershirt stained with sweat and grease. Cold eyes surveyed the room from beneath heavy brows. When he was content with what he saw—or didn't see, perhaps—he gestured with his head.

"Follow me. Food is ready." Jacquelyna stood there, unmoving and unsure how to respond. Her stomach howled for food, but she didn't want to comply either. "Fine. Stay here and starve then. It's no skin off my balls."

He made to close the door.

"No! Wait," Jacquelyna said. "Give me a moment to wake the girl."

The highwayman ground his teeth together and waited with his arms crossed. Jacquelyna gently rocked Gabrielle out of her dreams.

"Wake up, princess," she said softly.

"Madam de Mailly?" Gabrielle cooed.

"No, my child. It's just me. Jacquelyna."

The young girl rubbed her eyes into focus. She blinked as she attempted to remember who Jacquelyna was and where she was. Then she saw the highwayman standing in the doorway. A flood of horror rushed to her face. She started to bawl and clung to Jacquelyna like an iron vise.

"Goddammit," the highwayman said. "Shut her up, will you?"

"She's scared."

"I don't fucking care. Shut her up or I'll shut her up for you. Understand?"

Jacquelyna stroked the girl's hair. "It's ok, darling. It's ok. You need to hush now, so we can go get some food. Does that sound good? Breakfast?"

Gabrielle's tears slowed, turning into periodic sniffles. She nodded.

"Good girl. Your father would be proud."

"I want my mother."

"I know, darling. I know. Let's eat breakfast first."

Holding Gabrielle's hand, Jacquelyna followed the highwayman through the hall and down a set of steps to the chateau's ground floor. Loud voices, laughter, and the banging of pots, pans, and mugs intensified as they approached the mess hall. The noise and sight of more than a dozen men–grubby from their ride–hit her like a wall. She stopped and surveyed the highwaymen enjoying their morning meal. Rough hands grabbed her by the arm.

"Sit," the large highwayman ordered. He pointed to an empty table along the short wall.

Jacquelyna led Gabrielle to the table while doing her best to ignore the stares from the highwaymen. For some reason she felt safer sitting behind the table. She let her eyes roam the room. The highwaymen reminded her a lot of Darion–in appearance, anyways. They had the same scars, the same greased hair, and stained hands from their pistols and swords. They smelled like him, too–a mix of oil, leather, horse, and steel. She always considered it a manly perfume that war gave soldiers as a badge of honor for their bravery and sacrifice. It clung to these men like it had clung to Darion. But there was something monstrous about these men. It was something in their eyes and the way they gazed at her, like salivating wolves. Where she saw a glimmer of love and tenderness in Darion's blue eyes, she saw the smoldering embers of lust and violence in the pupils of the bandits. She felt her skin crawl anytime they glanced in her direction. She noticed they stared at her breasts. She grew anxious, and began to breathe faster which only made her chest crest higher and more frequently, feeding into the cads' incessant ogling. She paled and adjusted her cloak to cover herself up.

Gabrielle whimpered.

"It'll be all right, love," Jacquelyna said.

"I want Nanny."

"I know. I know."

Jacquelyna couldn't help but think of Madame de Mailly and how the highwaymen dragged the old woman from the coach, lined her up and shot her like an old, useless dog. She could still see the pool of blood form under Mailly's body and hear the old woman's final groans as the highwaymen forced Jacquelyna and Gabrielle into the coach and rode off.

She lowered her eyes to the young girl, partly to see how the child was holding up and partly to help her ignore the licentious gazes of the highwaymen around her. A few strands of golden hair tumbled from beneath Gabrielle's bonnet; tears swelled around her eyes, blue as the sky on a summer day, but framed in red from incessant crying. Despite her sobs and whimpers, the king's daughter was holding herself together fairly well for one so young. And though Jacquelyna desired nothing better than to be home, a part of her was glad she was there for Gabrielle now. She couldn't imagine what it would be like to be alone at her age with these awful men.

Several highwaymen sat down at a table just across from Jacquelyna and Gabrielle. They dipped chunks of stale bread into their bowls of stew and mugs of wine. Their eyes fixated on her, however. She looked away. She didn't want them to see her fear.

"Richard. Henri. The mademoiselle and the girl don't need you both babysitting them. They're not going anywhere. The captain is calling for you."

"Both of us?" the larger of the two men asked.

"Both. Go."

The two men groaned and left. Jacquelyna kept her head turned to the corner of the room. She was counting the strands of cobweb to keep unwanted conversations at a safe distance. Nonetheless, a dark shadow loomed over her before shrinking as if the figure crouched to her level.

"Mademoiselle," the man said.

She did her best to ignore him. She didn't want to interact with these monsters disguised as men. She heard the highwayman place two bowls and mugs on the table. She glanced at him from the corner of her eye. It was the same man who spared her life after the attack, but he no longer wore the mask. His skin was like charcoal and his left eye remained partly swollen. His lip scabbed on the side and a few smaller wounds on his cheek were in the process of healing. Future scars to add to the man's impressive collection. *Andre*, she thought his name was.

"Some stew and spiced wine for breakfast," he continued. "My apologies for not having anything more suitable for you both."

"Here," Jacquelyna said to Gabrielle. "Eat. You must eat."

Gabrielle dug into the meal, not caring that it wasn't up to the usual standards of nobility. Jacquelyna, however, didn't as much as peek at the bowl placed before her.

"You should eat, as well," Andre said. "Did you sleep well, mademoiselle?" Jacquelyna kept shut. "Mademoiselle?" He looked at her as if he knew who she was, but for the life of her she couldn't pinpoint where they would've met. "Are you well?"

"I would be far better back in Paris," she finally grunted.

He sat across from her. "I'm afraid that won't happen for a while, mademoiselle. And sorry about the men. Half of them are unattached and the other half are married to women who look like the beasts they care for."

He smiled, but Jacquelyna didn't find it amusing. Nothing was amusing to her at that moment.

"Why did you abduct us?" she asked.

The man shrugged. "They were our orders."

"Are your orders usually to kill old women and steal children? Or do you do it for sport?"

The gentleness of the man's eyes quickly turned hard. She recoiled.

"You're surrounded by a lot of bad men, mademoiselle. A lot of bad men. Many here have murdered, thieved, raped. Possibly worse." He paused for a moment, setting his jaw askew. "I may be the only friend you have here."

Jacquelyna wanted to laugh at the irony of that statement. Instead she poked the stew with her spoon.

"You're soldiers then?"

"In former lives, yes."

"And who commands you?" The highwayman crossed his arms and leaned back in his seat. "What's to become of us then?"

Andre shrugged again as if he didn't really care what happened. "The bastard will return to her loving parents once the king gives in to certain demands."

"She's a child. Not a bastard."

The highwayman gulped his drink. "A child can be both."

"Will the king agree to your demands?"

"If he loves his children as much as folk say he does, yes."

Jacquelyna felt herself relax just a little.

"But you, mademoiselle, are a different matter," a darker voice interjected. Jacquelyna shivered and even Andre stiffened at the voice. Both laid their eyes on the man marching toward them. A large scar ran through part of his mustache.

"You weren't part of the equation and you're lucky you're not watering the trees with your blood."

"Captain," the highwayman said. "I was just—"

"Yes. I know."

The captain grabbed a chair and pulled it up to the table. He then grabbed an empty mug and the pitcher full of spiced wine and filled it. He considered the drink, breathing in its rich aroma, before taking a sip. Jacquelyna watched in silence.

"So, mademoiselle," the captain said, "tell me about yourself."

"What do you wish to know?"

"Your name. Your family. What your role is with the king's daughter. Everything."

Jacquelyna swallowed the growing lump in her throat. "My name is Jacquelyna Brocquart. I'm one of the queen's ladies-in-waiting."

"The queen, you say? And what do you do for her?"

"I'm her mistress of the robes."

The captain stroked his mustache. "And your father. Who is he?"

"His name is Marcel Brocquart, the Comte de Gien."

"A count. Ha!" The captain gave his highwayman brethren a slap on the shoulder. "That is good. Very good. Andre, get me ink and paper."

The highwayman left and returned a few moments later with a few loose sheets, a quill, and an inkwell. He placed them down in front of the captain who filled his mug with more spiced wine.

"I think we should write to the Comte de Gien," the captain continued. "What do you think, Andre?"

The highwayman nodded and sat down a bit more relaxed.

The captain scribbled a few lines on the paper. Impressive for a man who looked to be a lowly soldier at best. He stopped partway through and raised his gaze to the ceiling in thought.

"Andre, how much was the bill for the Comte de Broca?"

"A hundred and fifty *sous*, I believe."

"A bargain. I think the bill for a young and beautiful lady-in-waiting, the queen's mistress of the robes, and the daughter of a count would desire the best accommodations we have to offer. What say you, Andre?"

"Agreed, Captain."

"Two hundred and thirty *sous*," the captain said as he wrote each word. He leered at her. "Still a bargain, but we're not greedy men."

The two highwaymen who ogled Jacquelyna earlier returned dressed in riding boots and cloaks and armed with sword, dagger, and pistol. The captain rolled the parchment up and tied a ribbon around it.

"Bring this to our old acquaintance in Paris and have him deliver the message to the Comte de Gien." He held the parchment out over his shoulder and one of the men took it.

"What if the count desires proof, Captain?"

The captain thought a moment, smoothing out the end of his large mustache.

"You still have her brooch?" he asked Andre.

"I do."

"And your father would recognize this brooch?" he asked Jacquelyna. She nodded. "Give it to me, Andre."

The highwayman dawdled before reaching into the leather pouch on his belt. He pulled out the silver brooch and slid it across the table. The messenger grabbed it with a gloved hand.

"Go and be fast about it," the captain ordered. "The sooner this is over the better."

The two men left the room, their boots echoing down the hall. The captain's gaze turned to the king's daughter who ate in silence.

"An adorable little thing. A pity she had to be wrapped up in all this, but such is life. Though, I suppose, she should consider herself lucky. If her brother was in the coach instead of being ill, he would be here as our guest and she would be lying next to her bitch nanny. But such is life, eh? Very few of us are driving the coach and even fewer of us are inside the comfort of one. Most of us are the poor fucking beasts in the team, pulling and pulling and pulling."

"Who are you?" Jacquelyna finally asked.

The captain flashed a yellow smile. "I am Captain Jaspart de Tremear, formerly of the king's cavalry and now a man of fortune. These are my band of fellow fortune seekers better known amongst these parts as the Falcon Highwaymen."

"Why have you taken us?"

"It's complicated, far more complicated than a woman of the queen could possibly understand. Just know that there are some very powerful people who don't care for how the king runs things and wish to—how should I put this?—*pressure* His Majesty into certain political avenues."

"So you're using us as leverage?"

"We're using the bastard for leverage. You? You were unforeseen and are lucky that you don't have a lead ball in your brain right now. You can thank Andre for that. But don't test our hospitality, mademoiselle. I'm sure I don't have to explain what will happen if you do. Keep the girl quiet and in line, and when your father coughs up money for your bill you'll be on your way back to your fanciful life at court."

"What if he doesn't?"

The captain smoothed his large mustache as he gave that question a bit more thought. "Well. That would be quite unfortunate indeed, wouldn't it?"

# XXIII.
## Shadows

Rumors of an incident at the Bastille reached Lecroix's ears in the late morning. The stories ranged from a full-on assault by Spanish infantry to a ghostly assassin's sneaking past the guards, slitting their throats and releasing the poor, wretched prisoners from their cells. Few places could turn a simple affair into a marathon tale of action and intrigue better than Paris, but from what the city faced in past decades, it was easy to understand why. Still, Lecroix wrote it off as just old gossip resurfacing in a new form.

After a late breakfast, he decided to stretch his legs and walk through the city before making his way to the Louvre for new orders from His Majesty or the Duc de Sully. There was little point of spending a holiday searching for Darion when his nephew was tucked away in a cold, damp cell of the Bastille. He knew he'd have to head back to the Low Lands once the alliance was ratified, but when that would happen was anyone's guess. No doubt Sully was combing through every word and punctuation mark to make sure things were fair for France. The duke was nothing if not thorough.

A hint of spring clung itself to the ends of the sun's rays, its warmth battling a brisk breeze that blew from time to time as a reminder that winter hadn't quite yet retired for the season. That didn't stop the Parisians who opened their carts along the streets and chatted to one another at corners and in the squares. It was a long winter, and they took the mild weather as an excuse to poke their heads out from their lodgings to converse with the world once more.

The thick, sweet smell of wood burning in stoves and hearths filled Lecroix's nostrils while the hammering of steel and iron resonated from the bowels of blacksmiths' shops. Children giggled and dogs barked in alleyways. Snow and ice dripped from the rooftops, forming small pools of water that folks splashed as they walked by. The atmosphere was serene, yet Lecroix felt an ominous presence around him.

He continued down Grande Rue du Faubourg Saint-Honoré, which ran parallel to the Seine River. He tipped his hat to a few men and bowed to the ladies he came across. All familiar faces. All friendly. Yet he couldn't shake the feeling of being watched. He looked over his shoulder but found no one suspicious. Just more men and women going about their business in a sea of hoods, hats and bonnets.

"Well, if it isn't the Chevalier d'Auch!" a man called out.

Lecroix spun to see a fat and rosy face sticking outside a narrow window in a building across the street. The man was smiling beneath his white beard.

"Nicholas!" Lecroix replied.

"Jean-Girard. It's been a while. Come join me for a drink, eh?"

"I suppose I can spare a few moments."

Lecroix doffed his hat before stepping inside. The tavern wasn't well lit. The sunlight hadn't yet penetrated the depths of the room, and the fire in the grate was barely alight. He found Nicholas Joubert sitting alone at a table by the window, a mug in hand while a jug of wine rested before him. A plate with a few bread crumbs and chicken bones also lay on the table.

"Come. Sit," Lecroix's old friend beckoned.

Lecroix pulled up a chair while Nicholas signaled to the barman to bring another mug. In a few moments, both men were saluting to one another and enjoying the wine.

"Pinot Noir," Lecroix said, lapping his lips. "From Nuits-Saint-Georges?"

Nicholas laughed and slammed his hand against the table in exclamation. "'Sblood. You always knew your wine."

"More like know you. You're particular about your wine."

"Guilty as charged, my friend." He took another swig from his mug. "Guilty as charged. So where have you been, eh? I haven't seen you in a year."

"The Low Lands. Special assignment from the king."

"Oh, well haven't you gotten all fancy with your lavish

knighthood and your royal errands. Good to see you still fighting."

"Not so much on the fighting. I live the quiet life of a diplomat now."

Nicholas scoffed. "A pity if you ask me and a waste of your talents. The Forty-Five was never the same after you left."

Lecroix inclined his head while considering his friend's words. Nicholas was also a member of the Guardsmen during Lecroix's tenure, and like Lecroix he also partook in the assassination of the Duc and Cardinal de Guise. But unlike the chevalier, Nicholas had no guilt from it. He relished serving the king and would've thrown himself on sword and pike if His Majesty ordered him thus. Nicholas had argued with Lecroix over the matter of the assassination and did his best to keep Lecroix as a member of the Forty-Five, but in the end Lecroix's conscious won. It didn't keep the two men from communicating or staying friends decades later, however.

"It was for the best," Lecroix finally said.

"Perhaps, perhaps. So, what was this royal assignment?"

"Secure a defensive alliance with the Low Lands."

"Keep the Spanish in check?" Lecroix nodded. "And?"

"We succeeded, though the treaty hasn't been signed yet."

"Oh? And why's that?"

Lecroix shot Nicholas a glance that said the matter was sealed and secret.

Nicholas chuckled. "Of course. Can't give too much away, eh? I might be a spy! It'll be nice to know the Spanish won't be knocking on our door anytime soon, but, truth be told, part of me yearns for the battlefield."

"We're too old for that now."

"You're too old maybe. You're five years my senior remember."

Lecroix tipped his glass to his friend. He looked out the window as a few, young popinjays in all their finery rode by on their steeds, a hand on hip, and nose pointed to the heavens.

"So how long have you been followed for?" Nicholas asked.

Lecroix's eyes narrowed. "Excuse me?"

"Man in the corner. Dressed in brown and black. It looked like he was shadowing you down the road and he followed you in here. Has a mean looking sword, too. Made some enemies lately?"

Lecroix glanced over his shoulder. Indeed a man sat in the corner dressed in black and brown, and enough steel at his side to start his own forge. He took a long swig from his cup, but Lecroix was certain it was empty. *Had he been sent to finish the job the highwaymen couldn't finish?*

"I've made some new acquaintances lately, yes."

"Quiet life of a diplomat, eh? 'Steeth. Want me to handle him for you?"

"No. Not here. I'll lead him to an alley around the corner. You follow him from behind."

Nicholas smiled. "Just like old times."

"God, I hope not."

Lecroix tossed a coin on the table, bowed to his friend as if making his adieu, and left the tavern. He was tempted to see if his shadow followed, but that would tip his hand too early. So he strolled down at his usual pace, turning up a small alleyway between a butcher's shop and a bakery. There he waited until the man in black and brown turned the corner. The fellow's eyes lit up as Lecroix snagged him by the doublet and slammed him against the butcher's shop wall. The man grunted and fought back, pushing Lecroix's arms aside and unsheathing his dagger. He lunged at Lecroix, but the chevalier stepped to the side, dodging the blade. Lecroix whipped off his cloak and wrapped it around his arm in time to deflect a strong swipe from the assassin. The rogue pushed his advantage and forced Lecroix into a wall. The assassin then drove his dagger downward at Lecroix, hoping to stab the chevalier in the neck. Lecroix raised his cloaked arm, catching the man along the forearm and pushed back. The man was younger and stronger, however. Slowly the tip of the dagger inched closer to Lecroix's neck. The chevalier could feel sweat drip down his back.

"Drop it, monsieur, if you wish to live," Nicholas said, his sword tip digging into the assassin's back.

Pressure from the knife eased and the assassin raised his arms in defeat. He backed off from the chevalier and dropped the dagger to the snow and mud at his feet. With the threat of death gone, Lecroix was able to get a better look at the man who attacked him. The fellow was young, barely a man and had the look of someone who was in way over his head.

"You're late," Lecroix said to Nicholas.

Nicholas shrugged. "I thought you could've handled it. You used to be able to take on five men of his size at once."

Lecroix disregarded his friend's boast and unraveled the cloak around his arm. "Who are you and who hired you to kill me?"

The man looked confused. "What?"

"Come now, wretch," Nicholas said, digging the tip of his blade into the rogue's doublet. "Don't play the fool."

"You were following me through the streets for some time now," Lecroix added.

"I wasn't trying to kill you."

"The dagger at my throat said otherwise."

"I wasn't hired to kill you. I was hired to just trail you and then you jumped out at me. I was defending myself."

"Hmph. Likely tale," Nicholas said.

"It's the truth!"

"Who hired you then?" Lecroix asked. The young man hesitated. "Who hired you, or I bring you to the watch, and you can rot in a cell for the next year."

"Monsieur Castel!" the young man blurted. "Monsieur Antoine Castel, lieutenant of the king's Forty-Five Guardsmen."

"What? Why would he have you follow me?"

"Not sure, monsieur. Honest."

Lecroix regarded the young man for a moment.

"Go. Get out of here," he said with a shove. The young man jetted out of the alleyway without as much as a polite bow.

"'Steeth, Jean-Girard. Why'd you let the bastard go? He pinned you to the wall."

"I know all I need from him. He's young and stupid. Hopefully he won't be so eager to play the shade next time."

"Any reason why the lieutenant would want you followed?"

Lecroix placed the cloak back around his shoulders. "I have a sneaking suspicion."

The chevalier made straight for the Louvre after that. He stormed through the courtyard of the Forty-Five where several members practiced their swordplay. He stomped up the heavy wooden steps and into the Guardsmen's offices. A secretary tried restraining Lecroix from entering, pleading to the chevalier to let the lieutenant conduct his meeting in peace, but Lecroix soldiered through. He threw open Castel's office doors. The lieutenant was in the midst of a meeting with two other Guardsmen. The two men whipped their heads around, and Castel peered up beneath his heavy brows. Lecroix stood there in silence, his shoulders heaving beneath his cloak.

"Excuse me, messieurs," Castel said. "You have your orders. Prepare for them."

The two men looked at each other fleetingly before slipping by the chevalier. One wore his arm in a sling; the other a weird mask around his jaw.

"I'm assuming you're here because you met my page," the lieutenant said.

"Spy would be more accurate," Lecroix answered. "Would-be assassin is also in range. Want to enlighten me on why?"

"Not particularly, but since you're here I have some questions for you."

Lecroix chortled. "Questions for me? Ridiculous."

Castel grabbed a sheet of paper and a quill. "Where were you last night?"

"At home for dinner and then bed. I'm an old man. Why?"

Castel scratched notes on the paper. "When was the last time you saw your nephew Darion?"

"Couple of days back. You were with me."

Castel wrote some more.

"And you weren't near the Bastille at all yesterday?"

"What's this all about?"

Castel hesitated, seemingly debating whether he should answer the chevalier's inquiry or press on with his own.

"Last night there was a break-in at the Bastille. Or, should I say, a break-out."

"What? Another one?"

"Yes, it seems our prisons aren't as secure as we thought.

Something I mean to change in the near future. Seven prisoners were let go somehow. Three were killed in their attempt to flee, and three were found unharmed trying to escape through the eastern gate."

"That makes only six."

"The seventh was Darion."

Lecroix felt cold all of a sudden. "Where is he? Is he well?"

"So you haven't seen him?"

"God no, I—" Castel's questioning hit the chevalier like a wooden staff. "You think I had something to do with this?"

"You are on my list of suspects, yes."

Lecroix turned livid. "You question my honor, monsieur?"

"I know how much family means to you, Chevalier. I know that you would do anything to protect your loved ones, even social delinquents like Darion."

"You should've come straight to me first and not send a spy to follow me like a shadow."

"I needed to see if you would lead us to Darion."

"Now that I haven't, am I cleared of suspicion?"

Castel bared a cunning grin. "Of course! But your life may be in grave danger, Chevalier."

"No more than usual, I'm sure."

"Attacked twice in the past week. The king's daughter and a lady-of-honor disappeared. The Bastille soaked in blood. You are far too valuable of a diplomat for the king to leave your life to chance."

Lecroix's brow furrowed. "What are you doing, Lieutenant?"

Castel rang a bell on his desk. Two armed men walked in. "This is Emile and Remy. Two of my finest Guardsmen. And now, Chevalier, they are your protection."

"This is absurd."

"They are to stand on guard on a rotating basis. Follow you everywhere and seeing to your protection."

Lecroix scrutinized the two Guardsmen. They were young and coarse looking, but well groomed. Perfect for a job designed for protecting royalty. Lecroix would know. He used to be one of them, but he didn't appreciate Castel's underhanded tactics of keeping an eye on him. The role of the Forty-Five used to be one of honor to protect the king and France, but now it operated in the shadows like the rest of the vermin of Europe.

"The king will hear of this, Lieutenant."

"Consider that idea carefully before you act on it. The king's daughter has gone missing and I can connect it to your nephew and therefore you. You know how His Majesty is when it comes to family matters."

The chevalier placed his hat back on his head and stormed out of Castel's office. He trotted down the wooden steps and back into the heart of the city while his two new guardians followed closed behind. He didn't stop until he made it back to his lodgings where he slammed the door shut behind him. He refused to be followed and humiliated in public. Better he hermit himself in his apartments than be seen being watched like a criminal.

Lecroix started a fire while Emile stood on guard outside. He didn't envy the young Guardsman. Emile had the unfortunate and mundane task of standing in the wind and weather while Lecroix remained comfy by the fire.

Lecroix pulled the curtains over the windows to keep the Guardsman from prying inside. Then he sat by the fire and picked up a book. He read until his ire subsided, and he felt his thoughts drift to black.

⚜⚜⚜

Lecroix awoke some hours later. The fire was more a bundle of smoldering orange coals than actual flames, draping the room in darkness. He shifted in his seat and removed the book that had fallen in his lap when he heard a board creak behind him. He paused, letting his ears search for another trace of sound. None came. He tossed another log into the fireplace, then stoked the coals with a poker; a bright, orange flame shot up and licked at the wood.

He sat back down in his seat. He heard the faint rustling of fabric behind him, and he let out a heavy sigh.

"I know you're there, Véronique."

"You're being watched you know," she replied in a voice like honey.

"My new nanny, compliments of Lieutenant Castel and the king's Forty-Five Guardsmen."

Lecroix's eyes fixated on the flames before him, but he could feel Véronique's presence step out of the shadows behind him. She placed her fingers on the sides of his head and began kneading his temples. The chevalier moaned slightly.

"You always did like it when I massaged your head."

"There were a lot of things I liked that you did, but that was years ago. How did you get by the guard?"

"It wasn't easy, but I have my ways. But you knew that already."

Lecroix wanted to chuckle, but he was too busy enjoying the congenial bliss at Véronique's fingertips. After a few minutes she stopped and sat on a velvet stool beside the fire. She pulled back the green hood around her head. Lecroix studied her. It had been decades since they first met, loved, and then departed; yet to his eyes she still looked as beautiful as the day they met.

"What are you doing here?" he finally asked.

"I thought after what happened last night you'd want to talk."

The chevalier's brow furrowed as he tried penetrating the meaning of her words. A shadow crossed her face. He caught a glimpse of the cunning and illusive woman he once fell in love with.

"You let Darion go?"

She smiled. "Who else?"

"Did you also let Darion's friend escape?"

Véronique crossed her hands over her lap. "I'm afraid I can't take credit for that. My apologies, Jean-Girard."

"Why did you free my nephew? You don't even know him."

"I saw him once when I visited the prison with Jacquelyna Brocquart. Your nephew may have the pride and arrogance of a Gascon, but he also has your noble heart. He pretends not to love Jacquelyna anymore, but his eyes betray him. He's a singular man, cut from steel. He's also a good man, just one a bit tormented by his past."

"You could tell all that from one look of him?"

Véronique flashed a devilish smile. "It was what I was trained to do, remember?"

How could Lecroix forget? He met Véronique when they were

both much younger. He was still a member of the Forty-Five Guardsmen and she a maid-of-honor for Catherine de Medici, the queen-mother of King Henri III. Véronique was also a member of the Flying Squadron, an elite group of women under the service of Queen Catherine and used for political means. The Flying Squadron were alluring, guile, and as dangerous as any armed soldier, only their weapons were beauty and duplicity instead of steel and shot.

It was Véronique who seduced the Duc de Guise into meeting with Henri III at the Château de Blois. After the Guardsmen assassinated the duke, Lecroix spotted her in the shadows between two pillars. He confronted her, accusing her of having an affair with the duke and betraying his heart and his love. With cold, stoic eyes, she told him the truth of the matter, her position with the Flying Squadron as a spy for the queen mother, and her charge to get the duke to Blois for his reckoning. She proclaimed her relation with Lecroix wasn't political but true love, but he couldn't believe her. She betrayed his heart and his trust. He left the Forty-Five a fortnight later.

"But why did you free him?"

"Because whoever broke the highwayman prisoner out is also responsible for the attack on your coach as well as the kidnapping of Jacquelyna and the king's daughter."

"And you think Darion will betray his friends?"

"I'm gambling that he has enough of your heart to do what needs to be done. There's more going on here than we realize, Jean-Girard."

She reached and touched his hand. He pulled it back.

"And what is going on, madam?"

"I'm unsure."

Lecroix witnessed a change in her face. She seemed troubled, a rare emotion for the spy.

"Lieutenant Castel said there were six other prisoners released, some of which were cut down by sword thrusts. That doesn't sound like your mode."

"There was someone else at the Bastille. A man dressed all in black. He had a thick, Spanish accent and two long swords."

"Do you know who he was?"

"I recognized him. Fortunately, he didn't seem to recognize me or I probably wouldn't be here speaking to you right now."

"Do I have to ask you for his name?"

"Gonzalo Yanez de la Cruz."

Lecroix's mouth fell ajar. "God's blood. Don Pedro's retainer?"

"Assassin is a more accurate term, but yes."

Lecroix rubbed his brow. "None of this seems like the ambassador's style."

"I agree. That's why I think more is happening. More than any of us know."

Lecroix grabbed his cloak draped over the back of his seat. "We should tell His Majesty immediately."

"No! No, you cannot. You have no evidence. Just speculation and hearsay from a woman who was dining with friends when the getaway took place."

Véronique smiled. Lecroix knew she would not be obliging of the issue.

"So what do we do?"

She pulled the hood back over her head and dissolved into the shadows.

"We wait."

"For what? Véronique? Véronique?"

Silence. She had vanished as silently as she arrived.

# XXIV.
## The Return

Darion and Peppin's ride from Paris through the French countryside wasn't without its own adventures. Several leagues outside the city they came across a small unit of Forty-Five Guardsmen on their way back to Paris. They seemed in a hurry and paid no attention to the two men. A few leagues after that, the thundering of hooves alerted the two men of another band of king's men returning to the city. Darion and Peppin took to the safety of the shadows off the road until the silhouette of horse and horseman vanished against the dark blue sky.

Fortunately, the rest of the ride remained quiet. They headed north, across the Seine River, and through the open fields of Normandy. Eventually they came across a large, flat meadow. Fog hung low against the ground creating a soft, opaque veil. Standing on the horizon as a black smudge against the haze was the Falcon Highwaymen's chateau.

Darion took a deep breath. "We're here."

"Are you ready for this, Gascon?"

"Don't have much of a choice. If they have Jacquelyna we need to get her out."

"And if she's not in there?"

"Then we pay our respects and move on tomorrow."

"If she is here, how are we going to get her out? Ask?"

Darion shrugged. Telling Captain Tremear about it would probably set him and the rest of the men against him. They probably already saw Darion as being compromised thanks to his uncle. Lord knows what they would do if they found out he also had ties to one of their prisoners. He couldn't buy Jacquelyna out either. That would just make his highwaymen brethren suspicious.

The grass rustled and broke beneath the weight of their mounts as they rode to the chateau resting peacefully in the morning glow. Darion thought the place abandoned until he saw the puff of smoke emanating from a chimney.

They dismounted and led their horses around back. Darion's eyes bounced from the chateau to the stalls to the sparse trees nearby to anything that moved and caught his eye. He didn't want to tell Peppin, but he wasn't entirely sure he'd be welcomed back into the flock. Not after his last encounter with Tremear.

"Think they're looking for us? The Forty-Five that is," Peppin asked, leading his horse into a stall.

"I'd bet my life on it."

"Antoine must be fuming."

Darion gazed at Peppin, who sported his usual wide smile. Darion wanted to join Pep's amusement, but his stomach twisted and turned. He knew the men that lurked over Jacquelyna–if she was there. He knew their thoughts. Their tendencies. Their perversions. If they as much laid a finger on her...

He felt a hand on his arm.

"You well, Gascon? You look pale."

Darion forced a smile. "I'm fine, Pep. It's just been a long ride."

"I'd drink to that. Shall we go meet your friends?"

The chateau was quiet as a nunnery. A few wax candles burned low in their stocks while the morning sun illuminated the atrium in a soft, golden glow. The thick, smoky smell of bacon wafted down the halls. Saliva nearly dripped off Peppin's lips.

"This way."

They crossed a small antechamber into a larger parlor, bare of decorative paintings, statues, and artwork that usually adorned such rooms. Several old, beat-up chairs surrounded a round, old table full of upturned mugs and empty wine jars. Curtains were drawn over the windows, but were so tattered and frayed that small beams of light passed through.

"Jesus, Gascon. This place is a shithole," Peppin said.

It was, yet Darion called it home for years. The highwaymen weren't men who gave a fig about finer living. They worked hard and caroused harder, not wasting a single *sous* on trinkets or savings. They drank, ate, and whored away their keeps. All except Darion, who dreamt of a life beyond thieving.

In the dining area a few men had their heads down on the table, snoring, and still gripping their mugs. Another highwayman held playing cards in his hand, seemingly never finishing his round before falling to Morpheus's touch.

"Quite the soirée they had last night, eh?" Peppin asked.

Two men were awake, however, eating their breakfast quietly. They glanced over, their faces stuffed full of bread, eggs, and bacon.

"Holy shit," Simon said, his voice muffled from the food shoveled into his mouth. "Look who's back."

"Simon," Darion said, stepping forward and giving the highwayman a friendly embrace. "Good to see you."

"Didn't think I'd see your face after what happened. Thought you were going to cross the sea."

"Things didn't work out as they planned."

"Andre's back."

Darion raised a brow. "Is he now?"

"He's upstairs with our new guests." Guests was the word the highwaymen used when holding a valuable hostage. They had done so regularly in the past, typically provincial lords or their family members. It was a quick way of earning a large payout with little trouble.

Darion gestured behind him.

"Simon, this is an old friend of mine—Peppin Petite. I've brought him to be a new recruit."

"The captain is out for his morning ride at the moment. Up to him if your friend can join or not."

"I know the process."

"Process?" Peppin asked.

"Captain Tremear will want to see your skills to make sure you're not wasting our time. Simple enough," Simon added. "Until then you're more than welcome to eat and drink."

Peppin's face lit. They rode hard all night, not able to stop for food or drink.

"Go eat, Pep," Darion said. He leaned in and continued in a low voice. "Find out what you can from them. Be discrete."

"No need to tell me twice." Peppin picked up a nearby plate, dumped what remnants of food was on it and headed to the kitchen area.

"You going to join us, Gascon?" Simon asked.

"In a bit. I should see Andre first."

"He's on the second floor in the usual guest quarters. He just brought them some food."

Darion tipped his hat. A few of the passed-out highwaymen began to stir and gawked at him through hazy eyes as he passed. He trotted up the stairs and down the hall until he came to the guest quarters, the only real room with any true furnishings. The door was closed, but as he raised a fist to knock he pulled it back. Perhaps he should wait? *Fuck it.* He took a deep breath and adjusted his hat before finally knocking.

The door opened a crack and peering through was a dark brown eye encased around skin puffy in purple and yellow.

"'Sblood. Gascon?" Andre said. "Hold on." The door closed. A few moments later, Andre slipped through. "The hell are you doing here?"

"I could ask you the same thing." Darion scanned his friend's face, battered and bruised from his stay in the Prison de l'Abbaye. "You look like hell."

"Still feel like it. You look like you've gotten into a few scuffles recently, too."

Darion shook off the inquisition. "How'd you escape?"

Andre scratched the back of his neck. "A long story, my friend."

"Simon says we have some guests."

Bauvet looked back at the door. "We do. Bastard daughter of the king–"

"Jesus Christ, Andre."

"–and a woman named Jacquelyna Brocquart."

Darion doffed his hat and ran his hand through his long hair. He did his best to veil his exasperation, but he noticed a probing glint in Bauvet's eyes. He was looking for something.

"Do you know her?" Bauvet asked.

"Who? The daughter?"

"The woman." Darion shook his head. He had mention Jacquelyna to Bavuet on several occasions, but he wasn't sure if he could trust anyone—even Bavuet. "She's the queen's mistress of the robes. Her father is a count. Should fetch a pretty penny."

"I'd imagine so."

"She's also a fairly comely looking girl."

Darion ground his teeth. "This is senseless, Andre. This will do nothing but bring the wrath of His Majesty on us. The king's more likely to send soldiers than coin."

"As to that, we've already been paid."

Darion gaped a moment. "Then why do you still have his daughter?"

"The demands aren't financial."

"I don't understand."

"You don't have to," a booming voice said. Darion spotted Captain Tremear standing at the end of the hall. The sunlight pouring through the open window turned the highwayman captain into little more than a silhouette. "You just have to know that it fills our coffers plenty. Besides, I thought you were done being a highwayman."

"Plans changed. I also brought a new recruit with me."

"Oh? And you didn't clear it with me or the rest of the men first? We're in the midst of a delicate operation, Gascon."

"When I left for Paris I didn't realize we were in the business of kidnapping royalty and children."

Tremear crossed his arms. "Is that going be a problem?"

"Not if it fills my pockets."

"And your friend?"

"I've known Peppin for years. Won't find a more loyal man or a better shot than him."

"That so? Let's see what your friend has to offer. Bring him around back. I want to see how well this friend of yours shoots."

Peppin was on his second plate of breakfast when Darion returned to the dining area. He was gracing Simon with tales of his exploits in the Low Lands and some side work he did to keep coin in his pocket. Pep always had a way of seducing his way into a group. And among grubby men with skin full of scars and who reek of sweat and horse, Peppin blended in perfectly.

"Ah, Gascon. Hungry now?" he asked, pulling out a seat.

"Not yet. Captain wants to see you out back. And bring your harquebus."

⚜ ⚜ ⚜

Tremear was lighting a pipe he kept stuffed in his belt and watching as a few other highwaymen set up targets at different distances. He started laughing upon seeing Peppin.

"Holy mother of God," he said, nearly choking on the smoke from his pipe. "This Cyclops is the best shot you've ever seen, Gascon? He's a brute to be sure, but I'm surprised he can see anything let alone hit a target."

Peppin smiled as loaded his harquebus. He primed his pan, shook and blew the extra grains from it, and charged his piece with powder before ramming his shot down the barrel and cocking his match.

"We'll start you off easy," Tremear said. He puffed his pipe and pointed to the first target about twenty-five yards away. "Aim for that close one there."

Peppin gazed at Darion from over his shoulder with a crooked and impish smile on his face. He then raised his harquebus to his shoulder, took aim and fired.

A flock of birds scattered from a nearby bush, cawing and chirping in angst. As the smoke cleared, all eyes fell on the first target. Tremear leaned forward and then fell back in laughter.

"Best shot you've ever seen, Gascon?" the captain guffawed. "The sonofabitch couldn't even hit the first target."

The rest of the highwaymen joined the captain in his mirth. Peppin took off his wool cap and scratched his head.

"Oh, first target you said? Fuck me. I thought you said the last one way down there."

He pointed at the furthest target almost a hundred yards away. Everyone focused on the small target down the field, a small object on the horizon and not part of the original three marks the highwaymen set up.

"My eyesight is good. My hearing?" He cleaned out his ear with a pinky. "Not so much. I'll be finishing my breakfast if you messieurs need me."

He shot a knowing wink at Darion as he passed. One of the highwaymen jogged down the field and returned with the marker, a small hole just off its center. Tremear ogled at it before chuckling.

"Well, piss on my mother's grave," he muttered. "You just may be right, Gascon."

# XXV.
## Clash of Worlds

Jacquelyna and Gabrielle remained locked away in their chambers the entire day. It wasn't by force but by choice. After the lustful looks and lewd comments made by the highwaymen, she refused to be in their presence, even if Captain Tremear and Monsieur Bauvet swore that they wouldn't be touched. These men were thieves and murderers and kidnappers. What was their word worth? Their honor surely wasn't worth the breath they swore on.

Gabrielle spent most of the day in dreamland while Jacquelyna sat on an old armchair, looking out the window. The sun began to set, painting the sky in deep reds and purples.

Jacquelyna couldn't help but consider Captain Tremear's words to her. How she would be free and back at court when her father coughed up the money. *When.* A sound plan when dealing with nobility; a sound plan unless your father is little more than a pauper with an elegant title. After purchasing her a spot with the queen, Jacquelyna's father, the Comte de Gien, lived nearly broke and what little money he did have he saved for her dowry. He couldn't afford to buy her freedom. She was as good as dead.

But she needed to remain strong. Not for her own sake, but Gabrielle, a gentle lamb among a pack of wolves.

A light rattle came outside her room, followed by a key turning and the door opening. At the threshold was Andre. His dark eyes darted from Gabrielle to Jacquelyna.

"Dinner's ready," he said.

"I'm not hungry."

The highwayman's shoulders sulked. "Mademoiselle, you need to eat. So does the little one. She can't return to Paris a corpse."

"I'm amused to hear that, monsieur, considering you and your lot are so quick to make corpses."

The man's eyes hardened. "You will both eat even if it means I funnel the food down your miserable throats myself. Understand?"

Hair stood on end on the back of Jacquelyna's neck. Bauvet had shown the most compassion of all the highwaymen; she almost forgot he was also capable of being murderous and violent as the rest of his lot. She nodded and gently rocked the king's daughter awake.

"Momma?" she cooed.

"No. It's me–Jacquelyna. Are you hungry?"

In a sleepy haze, Gabrielle nodded and sat up in the bed. She looked in good spirits until she spied the highwayman at the door. Then she grabbed on to Jacquelyna's skirts with all the strength of a wild cat.

"It'll be fine, my dear. He won't hurt us. He just wants to bring us downstairs for some dinner."

"No!"

The highwayman scraped the top of his lip with his teeth and shook his head as if he had little choice in what he was about to do. He stepped into the room, his large build casting a heavy shadow over the bed. Gabrielle recoiled and hid her face in Jacquelyna's skirts and even Jacquelyna feared what might come next.

"You want to be strong and healthy when you see your mother and father, don't you?" Jacquelyna asked. Gabrielle nodded, though she still refused to show her face. "Well, you need to eat your supper then."

She peeked out from behind the folds of Jacquelyna's skirts. "When can I see mother?"

She glanced at the highwayman. "Soon, I hope. First you must eat."

Gabrielle loosened her grip, and Jacquelyna exhaled in relief. She took the child's hand and led her out the door. Bauvet followed, though he didn't look any more or less relieved at the outcome.

To Jacquelyna's pleasure, the mess hall was free of highwaymen, but she could hear their laughter and curses down the hall. Jacquelyna and Gabrielle took a seat in the corner where a few candles burned. They waited as Bauvet strode into the kitchen, returning with two plates of cold roasted chicken and soggy asparagus.

"Here," he grumbled, nearly dropping the plate on the table. "Eat. There's some wine in the flagon over there."

"Is there anything else?" Jacquelyna asked. "I'm not in the mood for wine."

"This isn't the Louvre."

Jacquelyna averted her eyes and picked at her food. Bauvet groaned.

"I'll check. Stay put."

The highwayman strode into the kitchen. She heard him open a hatch and descend into the cellar. Her heart leapt in restlessness.

"Come," she said, grabbing Gabrielle by the arm. "We need to move."

The young girl cried out as Jacquelyna's grip tightened, but she didn't resist. They rushed to a side door that led out near the stables. A cold gust cut right through Jacquelyna's satin dress and skin, but Jacquelyna didn't care. They needed to leave, and this might be their only chance. She spotted the stables across the yard, hidden in partial shadow from the chateau and fading sun. A hint of a smile flashed on her face as she could sense freedom just a few yards away. She sprinted, nearly dragging the king's daughter with her.

"Stay right here," she told Gabrielle. The girl nodded, though confusion painted her delicate, young face.

Jacquelyna looked around, hoping to find a horse already saddled, but they were all prepped for a night in. She scurried to the wall where several old leather saddles hung. She pulled one off the lower pegs and rushed to the nearest horse. She placed the saddle on top and groped for the billet strap when a dark figure shifted outside. Her heart froze. She whipped her head around, but the face she gazed into was one she didn't expect to find.

"Darion?" she said as if waking from a dream. "Wha- What are you doing here?" He just stood there, silent and examining. "Help me. Don't just stand there. Help me!"

Darion stepped forward and grabbed her arm.

"Not tonight," he said.

The chateau backdoor flew open and a handful of the highwaymen—half dressed and armed with swords and daggers—poured out.

"What are you doing? Help me get out of here!"

"I can't. Not now." He peered over his shoulder. "Over here, boys!"

Jacquelyna's eyes widened as things became clear. He was one of them. He was a highwayman. A Falcon Highwayman to be exact. But it made no sense that he was here in the first place. He was supposed to be locked away in the Bastille.

She pleaded with him, but he remained unmoved. His sword and dagger remained in their sheaths. Still, through his cold, blue eyes she saw a glint of pain. She wrenched her arm free.

"You bastard."

She slapped him hard across the cheek, jerking his head to the side. He raised a hand to feel the side of his face, and when he gazed back at her, his callous look sent a chill colder than the wind through her.

The highwaymen rushed to the stables, Bauvet at the head of the pack. He gave Darion a long, perplexed look before even acknowledging Jacquelyna's presence. It was almost as if he was as surprised to see Darion turn them in as she was.

"Where do you think you're going, mademoiselle? Out for an evening ride?" Bauvet asked. He turned to the men. "See her and the bastard both to their quarters."

The highwaymen pushed her back into the chateau and up the stairs, while dragging poor Gabrielle kicking and screaming behind. A few times Jacquelyna fell and slammed her forearms onto the stairs, but the pain she felt seemed dull compared to Darion's betrayal. Was this recompense for what she did to him all those years? Did his heart turn to stone after he disappeared?

Even so, she couldn't believe he would throw her to the wolves, salivating with greed and lust. Perhaps he was a more prideful man than she ever realized. Something had changed in him. That she knew now. She could see it in the way he carried himself, the scars left on his body, and his eyes that seemed a little duller of life. He wasn't the same man she once knew and loved.

She spent the next hour or so sobbing until the shadows of night hid her tears. Gabrielle spent the evening cuddling her legs on the chair, not making as much as a peep. The whole room was in darkness except for a strand of moonlight through the bedroom window and the orange glow of candles outside in the hallway. Soon, however, a dark figure blocked out some of the light from the hall.

The door unlatched before opening, and Jacquelyna felt her hairs stand on end as a short, stout man slipped his way in. He closed the door with his elbow before turning and letting the soft light from a candelabra light his squalid complexion.

"Peppin?" Jacquelyna said.

"Evening, darling," he replied.

"What are you doing here?" She then considered her question and crossed her arms. "Are you part of the highwaymen now, too?"

"No. Well, yes... sort of. Here, a little something to cheer you up."

He placed two plates full of meat, veggies and cheese, and two small tankards on the short desk along the wall. Jacquelyna stared at it a moment. She wanted nothing more than to refuse meat cooked and touched by the highwaymen, but her stomach cried to be filled, and it was brought by Peppin. With a bit of guilt, she grabbed a slab of meat and wolfed it down. Peppin waited by the door while Jacquelyna ate. After a few minutes of silence, her stomach began to calm.

"We were so close to escaping, Pep, and then Darion informed them where we were."

"I know. He told me."

"Does he hate me so much he'd rather see me locked here?"

"Far from it, I believe."

"But we were so close."

"Yes, and he also said you wouldn't have gotten half a league before you'd be run down."

"So, better to not try then?"

"Better to bide your time and stay alive. Sorry to say you're a loose end, darling. You might fetch them couple hundred *sous*, but the king's daughter is the real prize. As soon as they think you're a threat to their profit they'll slit your throat and leave you for the scavengers."

Jacquelyna had grown accustomed to Peppin's frankness, but to hear the reality of her situation didn't do much to settle her stomach. She pictured Madame de Mailly laying in the pool of her own blood. She frowned.

"My father doesn't have much money anymore, Pep. I'm afraid he won't be able to meet the ransom."

"If all goes well, he won't have to."

He reached into the doublet he wore loose around his torso and pulled out two small bundles of clothes.

"What's this?" Jacquelyna asked.

"Gifts. From Darion."

She recoiled back as if the bundles were laced in poison. "You can bring it back then."

"Jesus Christ, don't be such an idiot. You both have been acting like asses. Do you want to get out of here or not?"

"What is it exactly?"

"Clothes. For when you and the girl escape."

"Escape? But Darion turned us in. He—"

Peppin threw his arms in the air. "Holy Mother of God, you haven't been listening to a word I've said, have you? The damn Gascon came here for you. Shit. He could've gone anywhere when he got out of the Bastille, but he came here to get your ass away from this ilk."

Jacquelyna felt a lump lodge in her throat, keeping her from being able to voice the reproach in her heart. It also forced her to reflect on Peppin's words.

"How did he escape?" she finally mustered.

Peppin shrugged. "Some hooded woman got him out. They nearly got their throats slit in the process."

"A woman?"

Peppin nodded and handed her the bundle. She opened it to find wool breeches and doublets.

"Men's clothing?"

"It'll be a lot easier to flee in that than in your petticoats, I'd imagine."

Jacquelyna's eyes lit. "How are we going to escape? And when? Tonight?"

Peppin gestured for her to lower her voice. "Not tonight. Your little attempt has the men on their guard, but there's rumors that a caravan of merchants are crossing nearby. It has the men salivating at the thought of more gold in their pockets. It'll lessen the number of swords we need to deal with here."

She nodded. It all made more sense now that she had a cooler head and a full stomach.

"Where's Darion?"

"With the men. He thinks his pal Andre is suspicious and doesn't want to tip our hand. I slipped out, but I should get back before they get chary of me as well. Just be prepared to flee tomorrow night, after dinner, and when most of the men have rode off."

He turned to leave.

"Pep. Does he know?"

"What?"

"Does he *know*?"

Peppin frowned.

"No. I didn't tell him. Should come from you, though I don't know what telling him would do other than break his Gascon heart. Some things are just better left to the ashes of the past, love."

# XXVI.
## The Comte de Gien

It was a restless night for Lecroix. He debated what to do with the information Véronique had given him. Don Pedro's retainer, Gonzalo Yanez de la Cruz, was sent—for some reason—to kill Darion. It made no sense unless Spain was somehow involved with the highwaymen. It wouldn't be the first plot Spain had set against Henry IV, yet it also made little sense for Don Pedro to risk everything by kidnapping the king's daughter, even if she was just a bastard.

Alas, all the pacing and head scratching couldn't help bring serenity to his mind. He knew it was vital information, and he had his duty to king and country to disclose said information. Yet, part of him still trusted Véronique, despite her past lies. She would never admit it in a hundred years, but she was scared and bemused by the situation. He could sense it in her voice. She might've been an extraordinary spy, but he was still able to tell when something irked her. Whatever it was, it had her spooked enough to come to him for help.

By the time Lecroix came to a decision on what to do, the candles had burned to their bases and the sky smoldered in a mix of blue and orange. He buttoned his doublet, fastened his belt, and grabbed his hat and cloak off the chair. He figured he'd have one of his Guardsmen nannies waiting for him outside but to his great surprise he found no one. He waited a moment then walked around his building, but there wasn't a trace of his watchers. He found it odd, but decided to give it little more thought. He saddled his horse and took to the Parisian streets. He rode at a brisk trot until he arrived at the Louvre. He made straight for the barracks of the Forty-Five Guardsmen, but it was bare of the crimson capes and polished steel. Lecroix couldn't remember the last time the Guardsmen quarters stood so quiet and desolate while His Majesty remained in Paris.

He entered the palace, looking for anyone who would know the whereabouts of Lieutenant Castel and the rest of the Forty-Five. But the Louvre still slumbered except for a few servants preparing for another day of service. He eventually came across a few Guardsmen outside the king's rooms.

"Chevalier," one said.

"Where is Lieutenant Castel?" Lecroix asked.

"Indisposed, Chevalier."

"And the rest of your unit?"

The guard hesitated. "I'm not at liberty to say."

"Do you know when they will be returning?"

"Alas, no."

By saying nothing, the Guardsman told all Lecroix needed to know. Some new development occurred overnight. Castel wouldn't have pulled the two men commissioned with watching the chevalier and uproot two-thirds of the guards unless something major took place. Lecroix headed for the Duc de Sully's chambers, but it was guarded by a few members of the duke's household armed with halberds.

"I need to speak with the duke immediately," Lecroix said.

"My apologies, but His Grace has not returned to the palace."

Lecroix let out a noise that was as much sigh as it was a groan. "When do you expect him to arrive?"

The guard shrugged. "He left late last night and may wish to sleep longer than usual. You may leave a note with his secretary if you wish."

"I'll wait."

"As you wish, Chevalier."

Lecroix leaned against a pillar and stroked the ends of his white mustache. Something most certainly happened last night. Something crucial to the crown that involved the Forty-Five and Duc de Sully. Whatever it was, things were set in motion. The information he had would do little to change any of that. Still, the duke and king should know what Véronique divulged to him. He was duty and honor bound to do so.

An hour went by and still the duke remained absent. Lecroix sat against the wall, his hat low over his eyes and feeling the weight of his own sleepless night start to take hold. He almost yielded to his fatigue when he heard someone running down the hall.

"Your Grace! Your Grace!" the man yelled, startling the chevalier back to full consciousness. Lecroix raised his hat and peered beneath its brim. The man was of average height, long reddish hair that was streaked with grey, giving it a faded and mute tone. He wore a dull green doublet, unbuttoned along the sleeves, and an old, red velvet caplet over his shoulder. He wore no steel but for a dagger at his back. The two guards stepped toward the man with reproachful glares.

"Lower your voice, monsieur," one said, holding out his hand to keep the man from barreling past.

"I am the Comte de Gien and I demand to see the Duc de Sully... immediately."

"Unless you're the king, you demand nothing of His Grace."

"But I must speak with him. It is urgent."

"The duke has not yet arrived. If it is so urgent, you may wait quietly like the chevalier."

The Comte de Gien's gaze followed the guard's finger to Lecroix slouched against the wall. A frown appeared on the count's pale face.

"This cannot wait! I am the Comte de Gien!"

"I don't care who you are, monsieur. His Grace is not present."

A latch unlocked. Two wide doors swung open. Sully stood on the other side, partially dressed in his shirt and breeches, and a black velvet robe thrown over his shoulders. Heavy bags hung below his bright blue eyes that darted to each man in the hallway. Apparently he didn't go home after all, Lecroix mused.

"Apologies, Your Grace," the guard began, but Sully silenced him with a swift gesture of his hand.

"No matter," the duke said. "I expected the count to appear eventually. Now is as good a time as any. Please, come to my bureau, Gien. And you, too, Chevalier. Don't think I don't see you by the window."

Lecroix adjusted the hem of his doublet. He followed the two noblemen into Sully's office. Sully threw open the shades by the window letting sunlight pour in.

"I'm assuming you're here because of your daughter, Comte," Sully said. He broke a piece of bread and dunked it into his goblet.

"Is it true that she's been abducted?" the Comte de Gien asked in an almost demanding tone.

"As far as we know."

The Comte de Gien's eyes glazed over. For a moment, Lecroix thought the count was going to faint. But the man leaned against a chair and took a few deep breaths to right his mind.

"My daughter. My darling Jacquelyna," he mumbled. He reached into his doublet and pulled out a parchment. "I was ambushed last night by a man in a black mask and hood. I thought he wanted my purse, but instead he gave me this letter."

He handed it to the duke. Sully flipped it open and scanned the document. He nodded at certain parts and didn't seem the least bit surprised by its contents. He looked up and waited for the count to continue.

"Well?" Sully asked.

"Well?" Gien echoed, glancing over to the chevalier with a troubled face.

"How do you know this is from the real abductors and not some conniving purse swindler working off street rumors?"

The count reached into his purse and pulled out a small, silver brooch of a wolf's head with a sapphire eye. He thumbed it with a fatherly tenderness before displaying it in his open palm.

"This is her brooch, Your Grace. She's had it for years."

Sully rubbed the end of his nose. "Go on then."

"These churls want me to pay a ransom."

"Indeed. Two hundred and thirty *sous* it says. What do you wish me to do about it?"

"Well, I don't wish to pay it, Your Grace."

"Then don't."

"But they'll kill my daughter if I don't pay."

"Then pay."

The count fiddled with the brim of his hat in his hands.

"Your Grace, I am a proud but poor man. As you see, I'm wearing nearly rags. I gave all I had to the royal treasury to ensure Jacquelyna's place by the queen, and now I'm struggling to compile enough coin for a worthy dowry."

Sully made a circular motion with his hand. "And?"

"And, I'm afraid I cannot meet their demands."

"So you wish for a loan is it?" The count's eyes fell to his feet. "I understand your love for your daughter, Comte. I have one of my own. But the crown isn't a bank or your personal coffers. If you need money, I suggest you speak with a financier. Or try the Comte de Mauriac. He's a friend of your daughter."

"I have, Your Grace, but he isn't in Paris. I've sent word to his country estate, but it could be days before the message even arrives."

The duke held out the parchment as if to conclude the matter. The Comte de Gien moved slowly to take it back, as if the very gesture was pulling the trigger to kill his darling child. He bowed before staggering toward the closed door.

It pained Lecroix to see the count in such despair, but he didn't dare speak up and reproach the duke. Fortunately, the hopeless look of the count also moved Sully to add a memorandum to their conversation.

"We're doing everything in our power to bring her back safely, Comte," he said. "The king's daughter was also abducted."

The Comte de Gien's mouth fell open. "What?"

"It's knowledge not meant for public consumption and I trust your honor as a gentleman and a loving father to keep it that way."

"Yes, yes. Of course, Your Grace."

"I'm telling you because I want you to understand that the crown has an interest in this situation. We are doing our best to conclude this condition, but as a father I would consider all my options."

The count once again bowed and strode out of the room with a little more hope. When he was gone, Duc de Sully shook his head.

"Well, Chevalier, what brings you to the palace before the courtiers, or do you wish for a handout as well?"

"I came to inquire about Lieutenant Castel and the rest of his unit."

"He's indisposed, I'm afraid."

"So I've been told. This wouldn't have anything to do with the abduction does it?"

Sully's face broke into a disbelieving smile.

"You're not a fool, Chevalier. Why bother asking questions for which you already possess the answers?"

"My apologies, Your Grace, but yesterday morning the lieutenant had me followed and then in the afternoon and night he had two guards posted outside my lodgings. I leave this morning to find them both gone and two-thirds of the troop missing. Considering my life was almost sacrificed and Castel has implicated my nephew in all this, I'd like to know what is taking place."

"I cannot give you details, Chevalier."

"You didn't seem surprised by what was in the count's letter."

Sully crossed his arms. "You're perceptive. It's one of your finer qualities as an emissary."

"The king got a similar letter then."

"Yes, but the captors don't want money."

"They want a treaty with Spain?"

Sully hesitated. "No, they want the Edict of Nantes repealed. Why did you think an alliance with Spain was part of the demands? Chevalier, if you have any information that may aid us in this mess..."

Sully let his words trail as if he expected Lecroix to respond with some grand enlightenment into the matter. It was that exact reason he rushed to the Louvre in the first place, but after seeing the Comte de Gien despondent and helpless to save his daughter he began having second thoughts. Not that Lecroix wished to turn his back on His Majesty, but because of Véronique's plea to get more evidence.

"Chevalier?"

"Sorry, Your Grace. I was just trying to gather my thoughts. A source I trust believes that Gonzalo Yanez de la Cruz is responsible for the slayings in the Bastille."

The duke's brow furrowed. "Why do I recognize that name?"

"Because he is Don Pedro's retainer."

The duke's eyes grew wide. His skin livid. But just as quickly as his temper rose it vanished.

"Are you saying Spain is behind all this?"

"I'm saying Señor de la Cruz is involved to some degree."

Duc de Sully stroked his long beard. "Do you have evidence of this man's involvement?"

"No, Your Grace, just testimony from a trusted individual."

"Who is your source?"

"I cannot say."

"Chevalier, I must know who."

"My apologies, Your Grace, but I cannot tell you."

Sully looked shocked at Lecroix's refusal. "And if I threaten to throw you into the Bastille?"

Lecroix thought his heart stopped a moment. "Then I go with a heavy heart but my honor still intact."

"Dammit, Jean-Girard. You put me in a tough plight." The duke tapped his fingers against his desk while he thought. "Very well, but until you bring me hard evidence or reveal your source, I cannot go to the king with this. Nor can you. A false accusation could ruin the peace we've so long fought for and send us right back into war. Understand?"

"I do, Your Grace."

"Then go and don't return until you have something I can use. Go!"

Lecroix bowed and left the palace. Outside he found the Comte de Gien sitting against a low, stone wall. His head rested on his hands and his elbows on his knees. Apparently the duke's final words didn't bring as much solace as Lecroix first thought. He took a seat next to the count.

"I'm sorry about your daughter," he said.

The count looked up. "Why should you care, eh?"

"She is known to me. She and my nephew used to be friends."

"Who is your nephew?"

"Darion Delerue."

"Then I am sorry for you, sir." The count scowled before looking away, expecting Lecroix to leave at the slight, but instead the chevalier crossed his arms and stayed.

"Monsieur, I'm well aware that my nephew isn't the most honorable of men and that he and your daughter had a history that ended suddenly. I don't care about the details for they're not mine to know, but I do wish to help you get her back."

"Why do you wish to help me?"

"Because your daughter is an innocent and an unfortunate victim of a political plot."

"So you think my daughter wasn't who these cowards were after?"

"I'm afraid not. A band of highwaymen wouldn't risk attacking a royal caravan for just a lady-in-waiting."

"Does that mean—"

"She's perfectly safe, Comte. These highwaymen are more worried about the king's daughter at the moment, so Jacquelyna should be safe. It gives us some time, but it means we should move quickly while they're distracted."

"What do you suggest?"

"If there's a ransom, there must be a plan to deliver their demands."

"I'm supposed to leave two candles lit in my front window when I have the money. Then I'm to wait for further instructions. Alas, I have just two days to comply."

"Then you shall do just that."

# XXVII.
# Ransom

What Lecroix told the Comte de Gien was only partially accurate. It was true they needed to move quickly in rescuing Jacquelyna, but what he lied about was her safety. She was a loose end in the ordeal, a side prize that would be disposed of at the first sign of trouble. The king's daughter was far more valuable. The abductions were politically motivated and a lowly lady-in-waiting was of no value in that regard. But Lecroix needed to keep the count cooperative and his spirits high. He hated being deceptive, but sometimes a small fib was more a merciful blow than the cold truth.

He supped with Gien at the count's Parisian lodgings. It was a simple, nearly tasteless meal of boiled fowl and carrot—a dinner as modest as the count's household. Gien had just one servant, a middle-aged man named Jules Vernadeau who walked with a heavy limp, a souvenir from the religious wars. Jules had been with the count for nearly two decades, so when Gien felt the need to shrink his household, he knew he had to still keep the old soldier. Jules also ate at the table with them, a rare sighting among the nobility. It quickly became obvious to Lecroix that the Comte de Gien had few friends, but treasured the ones he did.

The count hardly touched his dinner. He mostly picked at the meat and fidgeted with the hem of the tablecloth. Every few minutes he glanced at the large spring-loaded table clock.

"Staring at the time won't make it go any faster, Comte," Lecroix said.

Gien's fingers wiggled as he looked for a place to wipe his hands, ultimately choosing the front of his wool doublet.

"I know, I know. I'm just anxious. This is my daughter we're talking about. If they as much as looked at her wrong—"

"All will be well."

After dinner, Gien put two lanterns in the window as the note demanded, and—under Lecroix's advice—pulled the drapes over the rest of the windows. All they could do now was wait for the messenger to see the signal and present them with the next move. The three men took to the small parlor for some sherry to help pass the time. The count downed three glasses well within the first half hour and prepared for a fourth glass.

"We need you lucid, Comte," Lecroix said.

Gien frowned and stared at the bottle as if he wished nothing more than to be the opposite of lucid. He handed the bottle and his glass to Jules who shambled his way into the kitchen. The Comte de Gien spent the next hour pacing back and forth and biting at his fingernails.

"When will he come?" Gien asked.

"He'll come when he comes," Lecroix replied.

"Do you think we should get more men?"

"The messenger is either not going to know anything or he is going to take a lot of precautions to make sure he isn't caught. The watch would just tip our hand. We must play this safely."

The count continued his pacing, his feet tipping and tapping against the wooden floor. Lecroix closed his eyes in silent praying, beseeching God to show mercy and light his way.

Two heavy bangs rattled the door. Lecroix's eyes flashed open and met those of the count, twinkling in concern.

"My God, he's here!" Gien said. "What should I do? Should I answer it?"

Lecroix put a finger to his lips. He stepped closer to the count, so he could speak in a hushed voice.

"I'm going to go to the second floor and see if I can get a look at him without being seen. Answer the door and try to get as much information from him as possible before he leaves."

Two more heavy thuds shook the door. The count headed for the entrance while Lecroix bound up the stairs with all the spryness his old, aging legs could muster. In the count's bedroom, he pulled back the drapes and peered below. A man stood there, dressed all in black with a mask across his nose and cheeks, and a large hood over his head. He also donned a polished rapier at the man's side.

The door creaked open. Lecroix shifted toward the top of the steps, so he could get a better position on the conversation.

"Comte de Gien," the messenger said.

"I'm he," the count replied. "Are you the messenger?"

"Do you have the money?"

"Not yet, but I'm working on gathering the notable funds. Where's my daughter?"

The masked man didn't answer, but rumbling wheels of a coach and horse hooves slapping the ground filled the void.

"Is my daughter in there?"

Again there was no answer. Lecroix rushed to the window in time to see the count throw open the door and thrust his head into the shadows of the coach. The hooded figure put a boot to the count's backside and pushed him in. The Comte de Gien let out a cry as he fell forward. The messenger leapt in behind the count and slammed the door close.

"Dammit," Lecroix groaned. He rushed down the stairs as the driver cracked the whip, and the carriage rolled away. "Jules, fetch the watch!"

The chevalier bolted after the coach, but his legs weren't as quick or strong as they used to be. He pushed hard, but the carriage still pulled away. He was certain he was to lose the coach when a pistol shot shattered the night air in a crackling boom.

Lecroix's heart sank. The highwaymen set the count up, abducted him, and then murdered him in the solitary bowl of the coach. The carriage came to a stop. Lecroix watched with horror as the door flew open. He expected Gien's bloody corpse to be thrown out, but instead the coach driver toppled from his post, landing lifelessly against the cold ground.

The chevalier rushed down the street and unsheathed his sword. Now the coach door opened. The count fell out, hunched forward and his arms in the air to protect a blow from behind. The masked man leapt out, his cloak billowing behind him, and drew his sword. He gaped at the driver's body bleeding in a strip of moonlight and whipped around, looking for something or someone. What the figure found was Chevalier Lecroix, sword in hand and a cold glint of determination in his light eyes.

"Where's Mademoiselle Brocquart?" Lecroix asked.

The figure answered with a thrust at the chevalier's chest. Lecroix retreated with a parry. He slipped in a slushy pile and nearly fell on his backside. It had been years since he regularly practiced swordsmanship—his new life of an emissary had warranted it obsolete—but now he wished he kept an edge to his former craft.

The masked figure continued his attack, flashing a flurry of half cuts and thrusts as the chevalier retreated. Lecroix defended himself with large, sweeping parries and a few ill-timed beats.

"Comte, flee!" Lecroix said, slashing his blade horizontally at his assailant's chest. The masked swordsman leaned back, letting the blade pass by him without harm. The Comte de Gien rose to his feet and hurried toward his home. Lecroix covered the count's escape with a few more broad strokes of his blade, moves more to keep the masked swordsman at bay than an attempt to maim or injure.

The first goal in any fight was to survive, and in this case Lecroix knew he was outmatched. His adversary was quicker at the wrist and stronger on the blade. Every move the chevalier attempted was countered before he could even complete it. It was as if this swordsman knew what the chevalier was thinking even before he did. Not a model situation to be in. Lecroix's best course of action was to run and fight another day, but duty bound him to combat. He needed to apprehend the messenger, to question him on who pulled the strings in this political plot, and to unravel its mystery. He needed to take the rogue alive, but he couldn't do it alone.

He only hoped Jules and his meager leg could reach the city watch in time.

The masked figure grabbed the edge of his cloak and whipped it at Lecroix's face. The chevalier retreated a step and raised his sword arm to protect his face. A folly he recognized as soon as he reacted thus. The cloak tangled around the chevalier's sword and his arm. He jerked his arm back in an attempt to free his blade, but it was caught, swallowed whole by the heavy wool.

The swordsman pulled Lecroix forward. The chevalier felt the heavy guard of the churl's rapier bash into his face. Everything went black a moment, and when he regained focus, he was on the ground, struggling to get to his hands and knees. A mud-splattered boot came into view and pushed against his chest. Despite the pleas and commands of his mind, Lecroix' body yielded to the gentle shove. He groaned as his head banged against the ground. His eyes fell in and out of focus.

The sky was clear as glass that night, letting the silver moon and the stars watch from high above in the heavens. Lecroix often wondered what the moon was like, what heaven was like, and if he would ever get to experience both when he died. It was an end he didn't expect for a good, long while, but he supposed the death he longed for as a soldier would be the death he earned in the winter of his life.

Lecroix felt the shadow of death fall upon him as the hood from the swordsman eclipsed the moon. The chevalier stared into the swordsman's eyes, bold and commanding. For a brief spell he couldn't help but think he recognized something about them. He waited for the swordsman to strike the killing blow, but all the man did was stare down on Lecroix with a gaze clouded by pity.

*Bang!*

The masked figure jerked back in a cry of pain. His sword clattered against the ground. He grabbed his shoulder, a trickle of crimson oozed from between his gloved fingers. He swore under his breath and dashed down the street and into the shelter of the shadows.

Lecroix lay there another minute, his head spinning and thoughts a blur. He tried to make sense of what just happened. Of why the swordsman didn't send him to God and if the gunshot actually happened. With a long, drawn out groan, he struggled to his hands and knees. Two hands reached out and helped him to his feet.

"Are you well, Chevalier?" Gien asked.

"I'll be fine," Lecroix placed a hand to steady his head. "What happened? Did Jules get the watch?"

"Not exactly, Chevalier."

The Comte de Gien stepped aside revealing Jules hobbling behind him, a spare match cord wrapped around his wrist and a well-serviced harquebus in hand. Two shots saved two lives; Lecroix stared at the man who fired both.

"What do we do now, Chevalier?" Gien asked. "What do we do now about my daughter?"

Lecroix spied back down the dark street and alleyway, unsure how to answer. More was at stake than just Jacquelyna's life. Her fate's sealed with the success or failure of the Forty-Five. What they lost, however—and there was no way he could reason such with a father's love—was their best prospect of finding out *who* plotted this all to begin with.

# XXVIII.
## Steel & Silence

Jacquelyna spent most of the night turning over Peppin's words. She had blamed Darion for her kidnapping and her failed attempt to escape, and she did it because he left her without warning, then returned as cold as winter. She also blamed herself for pushing him away to the highwaymen, and for being so naïve.

But none of that truly mattered until she could get back to Paris. *If* she could get back to Paris.

A scrawny highwayman with a gaunt face and light hair escorted her and Gabrielle to the mess hall late the next morning. The highwaymen were buzzing, a stark contrast from when they spent their days nursing their aching heads and their nights drowning their consciousness in wine and Armagnac. But this morning they were suiting up in their boots and cloaks, buckling their sword belts around their waists and lowering their hats over their eyes. About a half dozen in all were dressed for travel.

"What's going on?" Jacquelyna asked.

"None of your business," the highwayman said. "Now sit and eat."

She kept a sharp eye out of the comings and goings of the men. Peppin was one of them, armed lightly compared to what she was used to seeing. He had a saddlebag over his hefty shoulders and carried his harquebus in hand. Her eyes pleaded for information, but he did no more than shoot her a sideward glance while filing out with the rest of the men ready to ride. Shortly thereafter a whip cracked, the highwaymen urged on their mounts, and the horses galloped across the field.

The chateau fell into an eerie silence. No cursing. No oathing.

No mugs clinking or swords jangling. Just silence.

The light haired highwayman sat on a chair a table over from Jacquelyna and Gabrielle. He unsheathed his long main gauche and picked out a whetstone from a leather pouch. He kicked up his feet on the table and dragged the stone the length of the blade.

The grinding metal sent a chill up Jacquelyna's spine. He shot her a kinked grin. For a moment she missed the cursing and drinking of the rest of her captors.

"So, you're a lady-in-waiting, eh?" he asked.

"I am," Jacquelyna answered, more out of fear of remaining silent than wishing conversation.

"Must be nice, being at court with all the rest of the fancy folk."

He slid the whetstone up the length of the dagger, letting the steel hiss.

Jacquelyna nibbled at her chunk of stale bread. "It has its moments."

"Probably think you're better than the rest of us, eh? What's your father? A duke or something?"

"A... a count."

"A count! Well, that's mighty fancy if you ask me. That make you a countess?"

"No. My mother is the countess."

"That so? Where she at?"

Jacquelyna swallowed hard. "Dead."

The highwayman shrugged. "Must be rich though, eh?"

A chunk of bread nearly lodged in her throat. Once the highwaymen found out her father couldn't afford the ransom, she'd be discarded like refuse. Thieves have no use for excess baggage. Cutthroats even less so. And these men—these beasts—were both.

The highwayman ground a few burs out of the dagger's edge. Jacquelyna's skin crawled. A plate dropped onto the table, clattering loudly and breaking up the spine tingling music of the dagger and whetstone singing to one another. The fair-haired highwayman looked up and bared a friendlier smile.

"Gascon. Welcome."

Darion leaned his sword and dagger against the side of the table and sat. He didn't acknowledge Jacquelyna's presence. Not even as much as a cold, sideward glance. Was he truly ignoring her or just playing the part for the men, she wondered.

"You look like shit, Simon," Darion answered.

"Been up since before the sun watching these two." He gestured at Jacquelyna and Gabrielle with the tip of his dagger. Darion still looked straight ahead.

"When are you due off?"

"Not until Andre and company return from town."

"And you're going tonight?"

Simon chuckled. "Aren't we all?"

Darion dunked his bread into his mug. He then guzzled his drink and wiped his mouth on the back of his sleeve.

"Go get some sleep, Simon. You'll need it. I'll watch the brat and nanny."

Jacquelyna's skin flushed. Her lips tightened into a small slit. The fair-haired highwayman looked at her and burst out laughing.

"Looks like she doesn't appreciate that pet name there, Gascon, but I'll take you up on your offer. I owe you one."

"Think nothing of it."

The highwayman left without another word, and for a minute the only sounds in the hall were the birds chirping outside and Darion eating his meal.

"Am I dead?" Jacquelyna asked.

"What?" Darion replied.

"I said, 'Am I dead?'"

"Not yet, you're not."

"Oh good. Because you seem so uninterested in acknowledging I'm here that I was wondering if your friends killed me in my sleep and now I'm just a ghost, doomed to live among these cretins you call friends."

In the corner of Darion's eyes, Jacquelyna saw a flicker of annoyance, but it quickly evaporated as he swigged his drink. Still he fixated his gaze on the air before him.

"Where did everyone go?" Jacquelyna asked.

"To get supplies."

"I'm amazed you don't just steal everything you want."

Darion stuffed a chunk of bread into his mouth. "We just steal from the noble class."

"And murder and kidnap women and children."

Darion bit his lip. "I know nothing of that. That's not exactly our way. Not my way."

"Doesn't make it more pleasing."

"No, I suppose it doesn't."

"Peppin came to me last night."

"I know."

"So tonight–"

"Be ready to leave soon after sunset."

"That's all?"

Darion nodded, or perhaps he was just looking down at his plate. She leaned forward, trying to force her face into his view, but he turned away.

"Darion, look at me. Look at me. Look at me!" Like a child he continued to avert his gaze. "Why won't you look at me? Do you despise me that much? Have I grown hideous to you? Do you only think of me with hatred in your heart?" Darion clenched his jaw and dropped the chunk of bread in his bowl. "Look at me, Darion. You used to look at me so fondly."

At last Darion faced her.

"There are you happy?" he said. "Do I look like the same man you once knew?"

Jacquelyna frowned. He wasn't the same man. The man she once knew had bright, warm eyes that showered her with love and passion, but the sapphire orbs staring back at her now were as dim and distant as the winter sun. The man she once loved was honorable and caring, but the poor soul she observed now seemed void and yearning. It was just a mask for the pain she saw resting beneath his temperament. She had no doubt that the scars she caused his heart were far worse than those that peppered his body. She felt pity. Pity for a life not meant for him.

"I'm sorry for however I had wronged you," she said. Darion scoffed and ran his hand through his long hair. "Truly I am."

"Save your sympathy, mademoiselle. I don't want them."

"Then what do you want?"

Darion shook his head. "I think that's enough talk for one morning."

He grabbed her by the arm and led her to the stairs. Gabrielle followed, nearly squealing in fear.

"What are you doing?"

"Bringing you back to your room."

"Why?

"Because I tire of your games."

She dug her feet into the floor and jerked her arm free. "What games? I've never played games with you, Darion."

"You played one long ago, or do you forget? You made me think you loved me when it was Sergeant Barrière that you loved. Now come, follow me, please."

She stood firm. Her hands balled into fists, and her brow wrinkled with resentment.

"Are you absurd? I never loved Sergeant Barrière!"

"If that's true then why did you ask me to call off the duel, eh? Tell me that."

Jacquelyna felt her words swell in the pit of her stomach, turning and bubbling from years of pent-up suppression, but as her feelings rose to a boiling point they lodged themselves in her throat. Nothing passed her lips but the dying tones of an honest heart.

Darion led them to their room in silence. There, Jacquelyna stepped in, her head hanging and the king's daughter clutching the folds of her skirt. Darion started to shut the door but Jacquelyna grabbed its edge and held it open.

"Do you still love me?" she asked. Darion's rigid gaze wavered. "If you hate me so much then why are you here?"

"Be ready tonight," he said. He closed the door.

## XXIX.
## The Lost Highwayman

Darion locked the door and sighed in a bitter relief. He leaned himself against the wall and slowly slid down and buried his face in his hands. For a while he stared at the crack beneath the door. A sliver of light split by a dark shadow reflected underneath. The shadow remained unmoving. For several agonizing moments Darion fought the urge to rush through and hold Jacquelyna in his arms. He shuddered off that desire. Now was not the time for love or lust, or to fall prey to one's emotions. He needed to keep his soldierly demeanor for all their sakes. Perhaps if they returned to Paris safely, he could indulge himself with the idea, but not now.

The shadow beneath the door vanished; Jacquelyna no longer waited by the door. Darion lingered a while longer, wondering what she wanted to say when he asked about Sergeant Barrière. Her eyes had screamed out to him in a hidden pain, but for some reason she couldn't put them to words. Or wouldn't, perhaps. Darion never knew Jacquelyna to keep secrets or fail to speak her mind. If there was something she wasn't telling him, it had to be for good reasons. Not that it made not knowing any easier.

The highwaymen returned shortly before sunset to the tune of jovial jesting and swearing. They dismounted with looks of relief on their faces, though they'd have just a few hours before mounting up once more for an evening of raiding wealthy coaches along the road. Greed was a highwayman's vice, but at least it gave Darion and Peppin an opening to free Jacquelyna and the king's bastard.

Bauvet shook off the cold as he stepped in. He let his eyes adjust to the light before approaching Darion by the stairs.

"Where are our guests?" he asked.

"Their quarters. I gave Simon a short reprieve so he could get some much needed rest."

Bauvet rubbed the edge of his beard. "Where's he now?"

"Staring blankly at the door, I'd imagine."

Peppin entered, stealing Darion's attention from Bauvet. He adjusted the saddlebags over his shoulder.

"Your friend there has a bit too much love for the taverns," Bauvet grumbled. "Instead of helping out, we found him passing the time in the Hotel de Mâle."

Darion flashed a feeble smile. "I'll speak to him about it."

Darion went to Peppin and led him away from where the rest of the men gathered.

"I hear you were almost caught," Darion said.

"Eh, it was nothing. They just caught me with a mug of wine in hand is all."

"Andre wasn't too impressed."

Pep shrugged. "Good thing we won't be here too long for it to matter."

"You spoke with Monsieur Leclair?"

"Everything's arranged, Gascon. He'll have three horses saddled and waiting for us when we arrive."

Darion patted his old friend on the back. "Good work, Pep."

"You expect anything less?" Darion shot him a flippant look. "Fuck you, Gascon. Oh, and we ran into another one of your other brothers in arms while in town."

Darion's brow crinkled. He didn't remember any of the Falcon Highwaymen missing when he and Peppin arrived. His mind raced through the list of names and faces, while his gaze followed the path from Peppin's stubby finger to the chateau door. A ghostly man stepped in, dressed in black from head to foot with the exception of a scarlet sash around his waist. His face was pale and gaunt, swathed in pockmarks along his cheeks, and a raven black beard trimmed to a perfect point at the chin. His eyes were alarmingly bi-colored, one blue and the other a sickly green. At his hip rested a well-used cup hilt rapier. He carried his saddlebags and another long rapier over his slender shoulders.

Darion's skin crawled.

"What's the matter, Gascon? Looks like you've seen a ghost."

"Worse, I think. That's the fellow who tried killing me in the Bastille."

Peppin's eyes widened. "Jesus Christ. You serious?"

"I don't know his name, but I can tell you that he's trouble and dangerous."

"Why's he here?"

"No idea, Pep."

"Think he'll recognize you?"

The Spaniard turned, spotting Darion. He leveled his gaze at Darion as if trying to penetrate the Gascon's deepest thoughts. He blinked and then did the same with a few others before moving up the stairs.

"Let's hope not."

# XXX.
## Duty & Desire

The Louvre teemed with laughter, music, and the rhythmic patter from thirty couples dancing in unison. By a long table full of food and drink stood a handful of other men and women of the gentry enjoying the refreshments and reveling in their conversation. Their gold and silver trim, lace, beads, and jewels shimmered under the soft glow from the chandeliers. Lecroix's white brows creased over his eyes as he surveyed the room. The queen sat on a velvet covered chair and bounced the prince Nicholas Henri on her knee. She smiled as she watched her favorite, Galigai, dance and twirl with Concini among the throng of others. The Duc d'Epernon stood nearby, a finely crafted chalice in his jeweled hand, chatting with Don Pedro.

All of court seemed gay that evening. All except for Francois Bassompierre who stood by a table full of fruits, meats, and sweets. His arms were crossed, and he tapped a single finger furiously against the side of his goblet. The courtier's eyes were fixated on His Majesty laughing and drinking next to a pretty young girl. Duc de Sully stood not far off from the king, munching on some cheese and fresh bread.

"I'm surprised to see you here," Véronique's velvety voice said. The chevalier closed his eyes for a moment. He had hoped not to run into her again–at least for a little while. He turned.

"Véronique."

Her eyes amplified. She placed a hand over her breast. "That's Comtesse du Jardin when we're in public, Chevalier."

"Of course, Comtesse. My mistake." He bowed before facing the crowd. "And what is all this?"

"A celebration. What else does it look like?"

She hid a smile behind the rim of her chalice.

"You know what I mean, Véron... Comtesse. What's the celebration for?"

"A distraction for the king."

"Who's the young woman he's speaking with?"

Véronique chuckled. "That young girl is Monsieur Bassompierre's fifteen-year-old betrothed, Mademoiselle de Montmorency."

Lecroix's gaze returned to the disenfranchised courtier. He shoved a small pastry in his mouth and washed it down with a large quaff of his drink. All the while his eyes remained fixed on his love and his sovereign. Lecroix probed Véronique for more information, but she merely smiled and raised her glass in a silent toast.

"How goes your own investigation, Chevalier?"

"Not well. I managed to get the messenger to reveal himself, but I blundered it."

"You've grown delicate."

Lecroix's ears burned. "I'm not the same bold soldier I used to be, madam. The pen is my weapon of choice now. Not the sword."

"I can see that. Sadly, Jacquelyna's life depended on you."

Lecroix growled softly between his teeth. Véronique started away. The chevalier followed. "And I've done my best, Comtesse. What have you done to secure her life and liberty?"

"I came to you, which I now see was a grave mistake. I can only hope that your nephew is more competent." Her eyes flickered in eager interest. "What brings you here if not the soirée?"

"I came to report in with the Duc de Sully."

"You cannot tell him about Señor Gonzalo." Lecroix took a deep breath and told her all with a single traitorous glance. "You already have, haven't you?"

"I had no choice, Véronique. It's my duty."

"And if the duke decides to tell Henry, His Majesty will assemble thirty thousand men and lead them to Spain himself. He's already threatened Don Pedro with the prospect of war. Is that what you wish to see? France back at war? A war we cannot win?"

"What would you have me do? Play the mute?"

"I asked you to wait."

"I couldn't withhold that information from my king. You know that. You know me."

"I asked you to trust me. Does the duke know of my involvement?"

"I kept you out of it even when His Grace ensured me a prime quarter in the Bastille. Your name is safe."

Véronique swallowed her rage as best Lecroix knew she could.

"Any blood spilled because of your loose tongue is on your hands, Chevalier. Good evening."

Her skirts rustled as she stormed to the corner of the room where her husband, the Comte du Jardin, conversed with acquaintances. Lecroix fixed the stiff collar of his doublet before traversing around the couples dancing and clapping their hands. Duc de Sully now joined the king and Mademoiselle de Montmorency in their conversation.

"Your Majesty. Your Grace. Mademoiselle," Lecroix said, bowing to the party. "Pardon my intrusion, Your Majesty, but may I steal the duke from you for a moment."

"By all means," Henry said, his joyous demeanor souring. "Everyone else seems comfortable enough to steal that which is most precious from me."

"Your Majesty, I didn't mean–"

Henry waved him off. "It's fine, Chevalier. I know what you meant and please excuse my poor manners. I haven't been myself as of late."

Lecroix bowed and followed the duke to the corner of the room, away from the noise of the party. Both men kept their eyes fixed on the dancers and for any possible unwanted intruders into their conversation.

"What news?" Sully asked.

"We encountered the messenger yesterday night."

"And?"

"He escaped." Sully fully faced the chevalier and leveled a silent reproach. "We did manage to injure him."

"That does us no good, Chevalier. I told you not to return to court until you had something to report."

"And I am, Your Grace. Alas, it's not the report I wish I had. I'm afraid that thread is at its end."

Sully smoothed the ends of his mustache. "This is not good. Not good at all. This misfortune has the king in such a tizzy that he's considering this double marriage with Spain."

"It also means Jacquelyna is good as dead."

Sully sipped his wine.

"The poor girl had no right ever coming to court. I can't allow myself the luxury of lamenting her position, Chevalier. I have my hands full as it is with His Majesty. His mistress has left court because of the abduction. So between that and his daughter being at the hands of treasonous rogues, he's been in a foul mood. I fear he'll lash out at the first target he sees."

"What should I do?"

"Nothing. You've done quite enough, Chevalier. I'll send patrols out to hunt this injured man of yours, but it's moot when we don't know who he is or even what he looks like. I can assume you didn't get a good look at him."

"He was wearing a mask and a hood, Your Grace."

"Of course he was."

Lecroix gestured to the king and the girl speaking. "And the young mademoiselle?"

"His Majesty's only source of merriment at the moment."

Lecroix scouted the room. Véronique feigned a smile at a gentleman speaking with her, but she kept her steady gaze on the chevalier. Lecroix could see the reproach in her amber eyes.

"You know more than you're leading on, don't you, Chevalier?"

Lecroix pulled at the sleeves of his doublet. "Sadly, I do not."

The duke's jaw stiffened. "You've grown quite a credit with the crown, Chevalier, but I must confess you're almost at your limit."

"What will you tell His Majesty?"

"I'll tell him of Spain's connection. I don't want to, but I see little choice in the matter."

"His Majesty will call for war, Your Grace."

"And if I don't and he makes a pact with Spain, France will be thrust into civil war. I've worked too hard, seen too many friends die over religion to see it happen again. Peace and freedom came at a heavy price, Chevalier. You know that as well as anyone. Better France point its swords at Spain's throat than at each other's hearts. I'll do my best to delay any rash action by the king, but this is a very personal matter to him, and a matter of honor for France."

# XXXI.
## The Honor of Thieves

Darion unsheathed his rapier and inspected the blade from tip to tang. A few dark smudges defaced it, early signs of rust from the elements and being handled. The hilt was slightly better off, though it lacked the usual matte luster he preferred. His dagger, too, needed work near the foible. He took a deep breath and ground his teeth. He hated seeing his steel in such a state, but between his holiday in the Bastille and escape from Paris, he had little time to keep up maintenance.

He sat in an old wooden chair and grabbed a whetstone from his pouch. There he took it to the edge of his rapier and slid it down the length of his blade. His sword sang back to him in a thankful, metallic hum. He did thus until his sword had a razor's edge to it once more. He then moved on to his dagger, giving it a sharp blade free of burs. Lastly he gave his wheellock pistol an assessment, cleaning the barrel and examining the intricate gears of the firing mechanism. There was a good chance he'd need to brandish his weapons tonight; he wanted to make sure his tools were up to the task.

When he finished, he stared outside and enjoyed the red, purples, and blues of the evening sky. His room fell dark as the trees swallowed the last few sunrays.

That's when he noticed the orange glow from a lantern illuminating part of the wall. He didn't hear the door open nor anyone enter, but there stood a menacing figure just inside the doorway to his room. The hair on the back of Darion's neck prickled.

"It is beautiful is it not?" the Spaniard said in a dark, raspy voice.

"Like a painting," Darion replied, his own voice marked with distrust.

"We have sunsets like this every evening in Madrid. A gift from

God for being so loyal to Him and His faith. I've noticed your sunsets here aren't usually so colorful. Do you know why?"

Darion remained still as a creature hoping its predator would pass without notice. "I don't suppose I do."

"It's because your land is full of heretics."

"I'm afraid we haven't been acquainted, señor. You are?"

"My name is Gonzalo Yanez de la Cruz de Madrid."

"You're far away from home, señor."

"I go where God leads me."

Darion snickered. "And he brought you to the French countryside to steal alongside highwaymen?"

"He brought me to a land needing cleansing and with men willing to do the work."

Darion's smile vanished. It was the sort of talk that bewitched France into religious civil war.

"You don't seem pleased," the Spaniard said.

"My father was killed in the religious wars."

"Pray tell, which side did he fight?"

"The Huguenots." Darion caught a slight but rapid dilation of Gonzalo's bi-toned eyes. "Is there a reason you're here, señor?"

"Your captain asked me to fetch you. He has some urgent business to discuss with everyone." Darion nodded and reached for his sword and dagger. "No need for that. Capitán Tremear is very eager to address everyone." Darion considered the Spaniard's forced, rigid smile. He reached for his belt once more. "Please, señor, I insist."

The Spaniard threw back the edge of his long cloak, revealing a silver-mounted pistol that hung from his waist. Gonzalo's hand never reached for the pistol, but its disclosure was clear. Darion didn't like the idea of being near this Spaniard unarmed, but if Gonzalo wanted to kill Darion then and there, he would've done it when he silently slipped into Darion's quarters. Honor didn't seem Gonzalo's virtue.

"Since you insist."

The Spaniard stepped sideways allowing free passage to the door. Darion slipping past the swordsman, never taking his eyes off Gonzalo.

Jean-Henri and Charles waited in an adjacent room, armed with sword and dagger, and cloaks worn loosely over their shoulders. All three men surrounded Darion like guards escorting a prisoner to the noose. They led Darion to what used to be the chateau's solar, but now used as a general meeting room for the highwaymen when planning raids and holdups. The far-end wall was mostly tall windows that distorted the view of the moon and starlight. Candles burned in a few lanterns along the near wall, illuminating Captain Tremear and the rest of the highwaymen in a weak, yellow glow. They gazed at Darion as if they had never seen him before. Only three men were missing.

Jean-Henri and Charles stepped in front of the doorway, blocking it.

"Now that everyone is here..." Tremear began.

"Where's Pep, Andre, and Simon?" Darion interjected.

"No worries. They're on the way. There was a little... *mishap* in the wine cellar."

Darion surveyed the room. Every man was armed with sword and dagger, and a few even had their pistols dangling from their rough leather belts. All, that is, except for himself. Darion let his right arm drop to his side, prepared to reach for the small knife hidden beneath the bell of his boot. He considered these men to be his brothers—perhaps even closer than his actual blood brother—but even brothers were known to turn when Fortune or Favor seduced them to do so. And right now Fortune was dangling a giant mound of gold in front of the Falcon Highwaymen.

"Señor Gonzalo has just returned from Paris and on his route back came across a unit of king's men. Part of the Forty-Five Guardsmen to be exact." The men murmured to one another. Darion's brows furrowed. "You seem shocked by this, Gascon."

"Why wouldn't I be? I figure you would've taken measures to prevent being found."

"Indeed. Bring him!"

Jean-Henri and Charles parted from the doorway; Bauvet and Simon entered dragging Peppin between them. Pep's face was battered, but he still bared a crooked, albeit bloody, grin on his face.

"The hell did you do to him?"

"Questioned him. Your friend here was seen conspiring with the innkeeper, no doubt to tell the king's men where we are. Is that not right, Monsieur Cyclops?"

Peppin smiled. "Suck my short, fat–"

Simon struck Peppin across the jaw, shutting Peppin up.

"Dammit, you fucking shits! He's not working for the king! I can vouch for that."

"I have no doubt you would," Tremear said, "but your own word and loyalty is also in question."

The collective gaze of the highwaymen fell upon Darion with like murderous eyes. Darion felt his legs petrify. There was no use keeping up pretenses.

"All I want is Jacquelyna, Tremear. I don't give a fig about the king's bastard."

"Your uncle is an emissary for the king; you're an old companion of the Forty-Five's lieutenant, who is now hunting us like a pack of wolves; you have an intimate relationship with the queen's mistress, and you were miraculously freed from the Bastille. You still expect us to believe all you want to walk away with is the woman?"

Darion glanced at Gonzalo standing motionless in a strip of shadow. Surely he told Tremear all this. His arrival and Tremear's epiphany was too coincidental otherwise. But how the Spaniard knew all this and why he was even here still eluded Darion.

"That's all. On my honor."

The men laughed. Tremear twirled a dagger in his hand.

"The honor of a thief? Trust me, Gascon, I know how much our honor is worth, and it's far less than what we're being paid for this venture. Both the woman and the bastard are worth a pretty coin and to take her away from the men is as good as stealing gold from their purses."

Grumbling from the men grew louder like a rolling storm in the distance.

"But I'm not a prejudiced man," the captain continued. "It is the men's pockets you wished to take from, so it's the men that will decide your fate. So what say you, my fine gentlemen and scoundrels? Do we let the Gascon walk?" Everyone remained silent, the ringing of sword, dagger, and buckles clinking together providing the only noise–an ominous tune at best. "Or do we show him how thieves handle thieves?"

"Kill him! Shoot him! String him up by his balls!" the men yelled. A few daggers were even pulled from their sheaths.

This was why Darion never believed in fairy tales. Why he never wanted to be a hero. In real life heroes die. Heroes get shot down or skewered like a pig. And while heroes waited at Saint Peter's gate with nothing but poor tales to show for their valiant efforts, the villains and cheats of the world live on to rule and flourish. Darion was always sure his demise would come at the tip of a sword or the barrel of a pistol. He just never expected it to be like this.

*All we have is hope and steel.*

Darion wanted to laugh at his father's favorite maxim. He had no steel, and hope was as foolish a sentiment as heroism. Then again Delerue Père died a hero's death. A fool's death. In many ways, hero was just another word for fool, and that's exactly what Darion was, he thought—a fool.

Tremear displayed his hands palm up. "The men have spoken. Take the Gascon and his one-eyed friend here to the river and kill them. It'll be easier to dispose of the bodies."

Someone struck Darion in the back of the head before he could reach for the knife in his boot. A few more punches and kicks flew and Darion fell limp, his eyes hazed over with grey. Darion and Peppin's hands were lashed together and they were marched through the large, open fields that encircled the chateau beyond the old walls. In the distance Darion heard some of the men hoot and holler in excitement.

The honor of thieves indeed.

## XXXII.
## A Change in Plans

A knock came at the door as Jacquelyna reached for the hidden breeches and doublet. It was too early for Darion and Peppin to come get her and Gabrielle, nor did she hear thundering of hooves from the horses as the highwaymen set out for another hunt. She stuffed the clothes back under her cloak just before the jingling of keys signaled the door being unlocked and opened. The highwayman captain stepped inside with a lantern in hand. Gabrielle retreated behind Jacquelyna's skirts.

"Knocking now are we?"

"Just trying to be polite," Tremear rumbled. "I know how you ladies of the court are particular about your manners."

The highwayman smiled, but the scar near his lip made it grotesque and nauseating. He hung the lantern on a peg against the wall. The flame from the candle danced, accentuating the captain's gritty features. He grabbed a chair resting by the small writing desk and dragged it near the bed, its feet shrieking as it scraped against the floor. Jacquelyna fumbled with her hands.

"Enjoying your stay, I pray?"

"What do you want, monsieur?"

"I wanted to speak with you about your plans."

"Plans? What plans?"

"Your ill-timed plans of escape."

Color drained from Jacquelyna's face. "I... I don't know what you're talking about."

Tremear reached for the cloak laying on the bed and threw it back, revealing the folded doublet and pants underneath. "Who brought you these, I wonder."

"No one. I always had them with me."

Tremear bellowed in laughter. "You're an awful fucking liar, mademoiselle. A surprise coming from someone of the court. Perhaps they don't breed your lot as well as they used to." She tried averting her eyes. He leaned forward, forcing his gaze upon her. "Do you think I'd just accept a new face to my band of men without keeping a close eye on him? Especially when he was recommended by that Gascon yokel?"

Jacquelyna fiddled with her hands. "What do you want, monsieur?"

"I want to ease your mind. You no longer have to stress over the idea of escape. As we speak, your daring Gascon champion and his one-eyed companion are being marched to their deaths. Soon they will be bloated and floating down the Seine."

"I don't believe you."

Tremear shrugged and strode to the window. He leaned against the wall and looked out, pointing a gloved finger to something outside. Jacquelyna stepped next to him. Just being near Tremear made her stomach churn, but she nearly purged her dinner as she gazed to the dark horizon. Five figures moved slowly across the field, three on horseback and two walking, all encased in a glow of torchlight held by two of the horsemen. She gasped and covered her mouth with a trembling hand.

"No, no, no. You can't. You can't. You can't. Please, Captain. Please, I'll do anything. Let them go. Please, monsieur."

The captain rubbed his chin. His eyes raked her from top to bottom and back again. An ember of lust sparked in the highwayman's gaze, and a part of Jacquelyna almost regretted her proposal. But if it meant saving Darion... She closed her eyes and recoiled as the captain reached out to touch her.

"We must talk, *Capitán*."

Jacquelyna's eyes flashed open. She recognized the swordsman in the doorway. His somber attire was matched only by the coldness of his bi-colored eyes. It was the Spanish ambassador's lackey. A shiver ran down the length of her spine.

"Can it wait?" Tremear asked.

The Spaniard didn't say a word. He merely stood in the shadow of the doorway with the face of a gravedigger. The captain groaned before his eyes undressed Jacquelyna a second time.

"I need you to prepare yourself and the bastard for travel," he told her.

"Why?" Jacquelyna asked.

"We're leaving."

"I don't understand."

"You don't need to. We leave within the hour. If you're not ready I'll slit your throat and leave you for the crows. Understand?"

Tremear stormed out without waiting for an answer. The Spaniard lingered at the doorway a spell, his eyes emotionless and probing beneath the shadow of his hat. He then backed out and shut the door.

"Are we going to see Mother?" Gabrielle asked.

Jacquelyna pulled the young girl close and stroked her hair. It wasn't until now that Jacquelyna noticed her hand shaking uncontrollably.

"Almost, my darling. We need to make one final stop first."

"I miss Mother and Madame de Mailly."

Jacquelyna cringed. She took Gabrielle's small, blue cloak off the wall and clasped it along the front of the young girl. Gabrielle flashed a grin, the first since their whole ordeal. For a moment Jacquelyna felt a ray of hope.

She reached for her cloak laying on the bed. Tremear had left the doublet and breeches there. Jacquelyna considered putting them on, grabbing Gabrielle and trying their chances alone in the cold, provincial night. But as she reached for the garments, she heard the echo of two pistol shots in the distance.

It shattered what little hope she had in her.

# XXXIII.
## A Change in Plans

The Seine River was a short ride away, but they were forced to march to their deaths while the highwaymen rode their mounts. Darion's head throbbed with each step, but at least the pain would be all over soon enough. From beyond the trees, the sound of the river racing foretold an icy crypt.

"What I wouldn't give to have my fat ass back in the Bastille," Pep quipped.

Darion chuckled making his head throb worse.

"Least this is the death we expected, eh, Pep?"

"Fuck that. I planned on dying ass naked in bed after just having the romp of my life."

"Shut your mouths," Bauvet said. He gave Peppin a quick kick to the flank. Pep staggered, then glared at the highwayman. Soon they came to the tree line. Bauvet, Simon, and Jean-Henri dismounted.

"Which one do you want?" Jean-Henri asked, inspecting his pistol.

"Not Darion, I suppose," Simon answered.

"I'll do both," Bauvet said. Simon and Jean-Henri looked at each other and shrugged. "Watch the horses."

He grabbed Jean-Henri's pistol and pulled his own from his saddle holster. With the barrel of his wheellock, he gestured for Darion and Peppin to continue on.

The Seine glimmered in the moonlight, the crests shimmering like polished steel. Darion shivered as a breeze picked up off the water. How much colder could death actually be?

"On your knees," Bauvet ordered.

"Since when did we go to murdering innocent folks and getting involved in political conspiracies?" Darion asked.

"Since it put coin in our pockets. Now on your knees. Both of you."

"So you sold your soul for a few extra years of freedom?"

Bauvet put the spanner to the wheel shaft and cranked it.

"There are few things I wouldn't do to save my own ass, Darion. I didn't do anything another man wouldn't have. And what about you? What did you have to say or do to buy yourself a measly few days of liberty? Bring back the woman you love? How's that turning out for you, eh?"

Bauvet put the spanner to the second pistol.

"You know," he continued, "I recognized her as soon as I saw her. At least I thought I did. When we attacked the caravan she huddled around the king's bastard, refusing to give her up. Her courage was inspiring for a woman, and when she was forced from the child's side her brooch popped off. I noticed it was in the shape of a wolf with a sapphire eye. The same damn brooch you wouldn't stop talking about when you drank too much. Between that and her fine looks I figured it was your old belle. So I convinced Tremear to spare her. Wasn't until I learned her name later that I was sure of it. I found it odd you didn't help her escape when you had the chance, but I suppose you realized she'd never get far."

"Jesus Christ, is he always this verbose?" Peppin asked.

Bauvet scowled and turned the spanner. The click gave Darion gooseflesh.

"I just wished that you trusted me, Gascon. Maybe we could've worked something out and you wouldn't be in this damn mess. But now you'll have to settle with having just your life intact."

Darion raised his eyes from the ground. "What?"

Bauvet unsheathed his dagger and cut Darion and Peppin's bonds. He then aimed a pistol skyward and fired. The crackle split the air and sent an icy tremble through Darion. The highwayman then fired the second pistol in a similar fashion.

"Don't say I was never a merciful man."

"What is this all about, Andre?"

"I'm sparing your life. What does it look like?"

"Why?"

The highwayman shrugged. "Perhaps I feel like I owe you one. Perhaps I feel like shit about what's happening. Perhaps I'm having a lapse in resolve to send you to whatever shitty afterlife we're all bound for. Who knows?" He stuffed the two pistols into his belt. "I'd get moving and quickly now, before Simon and Jean-Henri decide they want to see two corpses floating down the Seine."

# XXXIV.
## Hotel de Mâle

Pontoise was several leagues away, and with no horses it made for a very long and frigid hike through the French countryside. The moon was high and the stars glimmered against a clear, dark sky. Fortunately the night air was calm. Neither Darion nor Peppin had a cloak—what does a corpse need with a cloak, after all?—and the only thing keeping them from freezing to death was their constant walking. Neither man spoke a word as the hours went by. Speaking meant spending energy, and energy was one thing neither man had much of at the moment. Darion never knew so long a time to go by without Peppin uttering as much as a word or cursing under his breath.

Of course all good things must come to an end.

"What's our plan, Gascon?" Pep asked.

"What plan?"

"I figured you'd been plotting something in that head of yours all this time. You've been as quiet as a nunnery."

"Our plan is to get to Pontoise, sit by a fire, and then go home."

"That's it? What about Jacquelyna? And the king's bastard?"

"We tried and failed. We're lucky enough to get out of there with our blood still flowing in our veins."

"So what do you design to do next, eh?"

Darion pushed a branch out of the way, revealing a wide horizon. The sky was easing to day, and he could feel the air warming against the skin of his face. Just down a slight snow-covered hill was a dirt road. He took a deep breath and soaked in the openness before him.

"I have no idea, Pep. Maybe go to Quebec City."

"Quebec City? What the fuck are you going to do in a wasteland of a colony?"

"Does it matter?"

"Yes, it fucking matters. You're just going to walk away and let Jacquelyna stay at the mercy of those bastards back there? I know you consider them friends, Gascon, but they just tried to have us fucking killed. No doubt they'll slit Jacquelyna's throat if it comes to it."

"I told you, Pep, we tried and failed at almost the cost of our lives. I lost one life to her already, I won't lose another."

"Bullshit. You fucking did that to yourself."

Darion glared at Peppin from over his shoulder. "You know nothing of it, Pep. Don't pretend like you do."

"Oh, I know plenty of it. You got yourself into a stupid duel with that sergeant asshole, and, the night before, you ran away from camp. Not a goodbye to me, to Antoine, to Jacquelyna. You left your friends and left your comrades in arms. Because of that Antoine almost died. Do you understand all that?"

"Perfectly, Peppin. But I couldn't go to the duel and call it off. I couldn't face the man Jacquelyna loved, and grovel and apologize."

Peppin crossed his arms and laid a dubious frown thick on his face. "That what she told you? That she loved the sergeant?"

"She denies it. But what other explanation is there? It's obvious she was trying to protect him."

Peppin shook his head as it hung between his broad shoulders. "For a man so clever you can be quite the fool. She wasn't trying to protect him. She was trying to protect you, you goddamn idiot."

Darion burst out in mocking laughter. "Protect me? From Sergeant Barrière? You're going to have to do better than that, Pep."

"He put two feet of steel through the right side of Antoine's chest."

"Antoine was never a great swordsman, Pep. A fine soldier. A good shot. Could march an army through a sewing needle, but not very apt duelist."

"He's better than you ever give him credit for. Either way, it was still *your duel*."

Darion threw his arms up in exasperation. "What does this have to do with Jacquelyna?"

Peppin opened his mouth to speak but nothing passed through

his chapped lips but the cold plume of his own breath. Darion squared off with his friend.

"Pep, what aren't you telling me?" Peppin doffed his cap and scratched his balding scalp. His single eye looked all over the field, road, and horizon for an answer—or perhaps reconciliation. "Tell me, Pep."

"I promised her I wouldn't tell you, but what good is a secret if it might get her killed, eh?" He took a deep breath. "She was with child when she begged you to call off the duel. Your child."

Darion shook his head. "Fuck you, Pep. Don't jest with me like that."

"It's the truth, Gascon. She feared for your life because of that. She didn't want her child growing up fatherless. Almost did."

"Almost?"

Peppin frowned. "After you left, her condition..."

Peppin's voice trailed off, but Darion could fill in the blanks. Darion wasn't even sure why, but he shoved Peppin. Pep shook off the blow, but Darion shoved him again. This time Peppin pushed back. Darion lunged, grappling his friend by the shoulders. He jerked Pep to the side and the two men rolled down the hill and across the snow, wrestling and swearing, and throwing half-hearted punches. It wasn't long before Darion felt Peppin give up the fight. He stared past Darion. Darion followed Peppin's gaze. Surrounding them were fourteen horses and horsemen, fully armed, and with long, crimson capes around their torsos. A few of the riders parted making way for another Guardsmen with a dark beard and a pale, scowling face.

"Figures I'd find you two here," Castel said.

"Fuck me," Darion mumbled.

"Took you fucking long enough," Peppin said to the lieutenant.

Darion gaped at his friend. "What do you mean?"

Peppin pushed Darion off before getting to his feet. He brushed the snow and dirt off his clothes and greeted Castel warmly.

"Got my message then?" Pep asked.

"I did, though I'd appreciate it if you didn't send your mistress to the palace next time."

Peppin grimaced. "What's wrong with Marguerite?"

"Mortar Marguerite? Where do I need to begin?"

"What's he talking about, Pep?" Darion asked.

Peppin scratched the back of his neck. "I may or may not have told Marguerite to tell Antoine where we were heading."

Darion's blood boiled. "You did what?"

He lunged once more at Peppin, but a handful of the Forty-Five had already dismounted and seized Darion before he grabbed his friend.

"That Gascon temper will get you killed one day," Castel said. "I'll have to be sure to put extra locks on your cell next time now that you're an escape artist." The lieutenant turned his attention to Peppin. "How far is it to where they're holding the king's daughter?"

"A few leagues."

"We leave at once. You'll lead the way, Peppin. As for you, Darion, two of my men will escort you back to Pontoise where you won't leave your room until I return." Peppin started to protest, but Castel quieted him with a single gloved finger. "Not a word of it, Pep. You and Darion played your parts, but I could still use your shot, Pep."

"My harquebus is back at the highwaymen's hideout."

Castel motioned to one of his men, and a finely crafted harquebus was passed over to the lieutenant. He held it out for Peppin.

"It's not made for your eye, but it's the best we can do for now."

Peppin inspected the gun, checking the pan and serpentine, and the ease of the trigger lever. He shook his head and scowled, and then, after considering his options, shrugged.

"It'll do, I suppose."

"How very kind of you to think so."

"I still say we should bring the Gascon."

Castel eyed Darion standing between two Guardsmen. Darion kept his face passive and his mouth shut. There was no use trying to persuade the lieutenant one way or the other. It'd only make things worse.

"He'll be lodged in Pontoise. For now. We can discuss his future another time. We have work to do."

Two Guardsmen were assigned to watch Darion while the rest headed west to the highwaymen's hideout. A pit the size of Paris form in Darion's stomach.

"Come, man," one of the Guardsmen said, giving Darion a shove in the back. "Time to move."

The two Guardsmen bound Darion's hands and led him between their horses. They were closer to Pontoise than Darion realized. Within a quarter of an hour, he saw the town in the distance.

"The lieutenant says you're a deserter," the second Guardsmen said.

"The lieutenant has a good memory."

"He's been far too merciful to you, if you ask me. If it was up to me, I would've had you shot on sight."

Darion said nothing. He couldn't refute that answer. Knowing why Jacquelyna begged him to call off the duel and knowing that his deserting nearly cost Castel his life saddled enough guilt on Darion.

The three men arrived in town a half hour later. Darion's legs felt like pudding and his stomach ached. A woman outside Hotel de Mâle dumped a chamber pot across the ground. She smiled upon seeing the two king's men but knit her brow when she spotted Darion, lashed and shackled, between them.

"We need lodgings for at least a day. And some food. Same for our horses," a Guardsman said. The woman continued to eye Darion. "Don't worry about him, madam. He'll give you no trouble. Promise."

Her expression didn't change, but she nodded and opened the door. "This way, messieurs."

The inside of the Hotel de Mâle was still shrouded in the early morning shadows. A few rays of sun beamed through old windows, scattering the light in the room. One table, however, fell at the heart of the sunlight. The Guardsmen untied Darion's bonds and shoved him into the corner. The Guardsmen sat across from him. They took off their hangers and leaned their swords against a couple of chairs next to them. Darion watched intently.

"I'd be dead before I'd see you holding my sword," the taller of the two men said.

Darion leaned back in his chair. He had little interest in escaping. Considering how he had been living his life, and the things he did to Jacquelyna, his friends, and his comrades in arms, rotting away in the Bastille was a fitting end. If anything, it was a tad merciful for a dishonorable man.

The barmaid wiped her hands on her apron. She continued to look at Darion with an inquisitive gaze.

"My husband has some suckling pork on the spit, but it won't be ready for a few hours," she said. "I do have some leftover fowl and raw vegetables, and some bread, of course."

One of the Guardsmen gestured that the menu was adequate. The woman lingered, staring at Darion. He saw a silent plea in her eyes. Her gaze then flickered to the kitchen. Darion thought he saw two eyes peering behind the door as she passed through.

"Messieurs," Darion said in a low voice. "I think we have a problem."

The Guardsmen smiled. "That so? And what would that be?"

"There's someone staring at us from the kitchen."

"Probably the cook. You're a horrible liar, you know that?"

"You don't understand. The innkeeper's wife looked alarmed."

"No doubt she knows who you are and *what* you are."

"That's not what I mean."

Darion stood. The Guardsmen countered the same and grabbed the pommel of their rapiers.

"Sit down, monsieur. Don't give me a reason to send you to your maker."

The kitchen door opened. The woman returned with a plate full of cold meat, carrots, beans, and half a loaf of bread. Before the door swung closed, Darion spied a silver glint inside, the hilt of a sword or perhaps the muzzle of a pistol.

"Shit," Darion said.

Two men burst through the room, pistols brandished, and masks drawn over their faces. They fired two shots before the Guardsmen even knew what was happening. One struck the king's man square in the head. Blood and brain matter splattered across the table and floor. The second assailant's shot struck the innkeeper's wife in the shoulder. Her face flared in pain and she toppled against a chair. The plate and the food in hand flew in the air all around her. The two attackers dropped their pistols and unsheathed their swords. Darion picked up the dead Guardsman's rapier, ignoring the irony, and drew it. The second Guardsman unsheathed his weapon and faced Darion.

"This is your doing isn't it?"

The Guardsmen thrust at Darion's chest before he could refute the answer. Darion beat the blade away and lunged past the guard to parry a thrust from the masked assailant. He bound the rogue's sword over and shoved him back toward his companion. Despite their masks, Darion knew exactly who they were. Hell, how couldn't he? He fought with them the past few years.

"What the hell are you doing here?" Darion asked Charles and Jean-Henri.

"We could ask you the same thing, Gascon," Jean-Henri said. "You're supposed to be dead!"

The two highwaymen drew long daggers from beneath their cloaks. Darion's hand went to do the same when he remembered he didn't have one. The highwaymen bared bloodthirsty grins, then charged forward.

The massive Jean-Henri, his long rapier held high over his head, hacked at Darion's face. Darion voided and deflected the cut with the edge of his sword. A spark flew as the blades ground together from hilt to tip. Jean-Henri followed up with a horizontal slash. Darion ducked beneath it but lost his balance and crashed backwards into the table and chair. Murderous bliss glinted in the highwayman's eyes. He cocked his arm back to thrust at Darion's chest, but the Gascon swordsman kicked at a nearby chair. It toppled over and slammed into Jean-Henri's knees. The highwayman groaned and leaned forward to keep his balance. Darion grabbed the highwayman's sword with his gloved hand and thrust upward with his own blade. Jean-Henri's cloak provided some resistance, but it wasn't enough to overcome the force behind Darion's attack. The sword slid through the highwayman, and he dropped to his knees. But he wasn't dead, and he wasn't done fighting. Like the seasoned soldier he was, the highwayman flashed his dagger at Darion's face. Darion barely got his forearm in the way to parry the blow. The dagger's edge ripped through the sleeve of his doublet and shirt and into his skin.

Darion groaned and withdrew his sword from the highwayman's chest. In the process, he let go of Jean-Henri's rapier. The highwayman drew it back and thrust it forward like a bolt of lightning. Darion beat at the blade and leaned to the side, letting the tip glide past him and into the wooden floor. He then cut at Jean-Henri, embedding the edge of his blade into the man's fat neck. Darion could see the alarm and fear in Jean-Henri's beady eyes. Darion pushed the blade forward and then hauled it back. The blade tore through the man's fatty flesh. Blood spurted between the highwayman's gloves as he tried to hold close his wound. Darion put a boot to Jean-Henri's ribs, knocking the highwayman to his side. Crimson pooled around him.

Darion grunted as he pushed himself to his feet. The Guardsman and Charles were still fighting, swords and daggers flashing and clashing in the corner between the shadows and the streaks of the tavern. Blood trickled down the guard's arm. He barely parried the highwayman's attacks with large, circular movements of his blade. Darion picked up Jean-Henri's dagger from the floor and snuck behind the highwayman. He wrapped his arm around Charles' face and lifted as he drew the dagger the length of the man's neck. Darion held him there as blood teemed over his glove, warming his hands. The highwayman dropped his weapons and scratched at Darion's arms and face, but he quickly grew weak. Darion let go, letting the highwayman's corpse drop to the floor. The Guardsman gawked at Darion, sweat glistening on his brow. He said nothing.

Darion crouched over the innkeeper's wife sprawled on the floor. She was alive, and though in agony, the injury to her shoulder wasn't fatal. At least not outright.

"Get her a physician," Darion said. He wiped the blood off the rapier and dagger. He unbuckled Charles' sword belt and strapped it around his own waist. He then sheathed his weapons and picked up the discharged pistol on the floor.

"Who are they?" the Guardsman asked, finally breaking from his shock.

"Two of the men you're after." Darion quickly inspected the pistol before stuffing it into his belt.

"What were they doing here?"

Darion opened the kitchen door, praying to find the innkeeper huddled in the corner for fear of his life. Alas, the old man was hunched over a cutting board, a butcher's knife in his back.

"Tying up loose ends."

Darion kicked Jean-Henri's massive corpse over. The man's eyes were still open, but cloudy. Darion hesitated a moment before rummaging through the highwayman's pockets and pouches. In a small purse he found some shot and the gun's spanner. He took it off the highwayman, as well as the small powder horn from Jean-Henri's belt. He closed the highwayman's eyes and remained there a moment in silent memorial.

"You can't go," the Guardsman said. "You're under arrest."

Darion peered over his shoulder, no sign of humor or geniality in his bold blue eyes. He gestured for the Guardsman to look around him. Four bodies lay strewn across the floor surrounded by blood, two of them by Darion's hand. He waited until the king's man swallowed the lump in his throat and agreed with reason.

# XXXV.
## Gold & Steel

"I appreciate you stopping by, Chevalier, but I have no use for you. Not at this moment, at least."

"Nothing, Your Grace? Nothing at all?" Lecroix asked. After his blunder with the highwayman messenger, the chevalier felt like he needed to do something to make restitutions. Since, clearly, wielding a blade wasn't something he was well skilled in anymore, he turned to the one thing he could do well. "No assignment is too trivial."

Duc de Sully closed the large ledger he was working on when Lecroix first disrupted him. The duke's keen, blue eyes reflected over the chevalier in a way that made him uneasy. The duke sighed and stood and placed a friendly hand on Lecroix's shoulder.

"Jean-Girard, you've been an ever loyal member of His Majesty and this court. We all owe you a debt of gratitude and your services will be called upon once more, I'm sure. However, you've been under a lot of strain lately. I'd be remiss to further burden you with another task."

"It's no burden, Your Grace. I assure you."

Again Sully's gaze probed the chevalier. He nodded as if he saw the hidden truth Lecroix wished to hide.

"Very well. Be it war or peace, I'll need someone I can trust to return to the Low Lands. Prepare to return by week's end."

The chevalier bowed. "Any thought on which the king will choose?"

The duke shook his head and moved to the large windows overlooking the courtyards. He crossed his arms behind his back.

"I managed to keep His Majesty from taking any rash actions

after learning about Spain's connection with the kidnapping, but he has a temper as strong as any man I've ever known. He won't stay idle for long. Fortunately, the one vice of his that I've so long loathed has proved useful for once."

Lecroix joined the duke by the windows. King Henry IV crossed the courtyard with a mantled Mademoiselle de Montmorency beside him. The king gestured wildly in story, and the young girl laughed behind a pale hand.

"And how does the girl's intended take all this?" Lecroix asked.

"As well as a courtier can when a king seizes what belongs to him. Monsieur Bassompierre is no fool. There are many women of note to court, but only one king of France."

Lecroix bowed once more before placing his hat on his head and leaving the Louvre. He crossed the Pont Saint-Michel. A biting gust assaulted him off the Seine River, overpowering whatever warmth the sun emanated from above. Lecroix wrapped his cloak tighter around his shoulders. He was pleased to know he hadn't fallen out of favor with the king and duke, that they still valued his services and emissary skills.

He saw a man on bended knee speaking with his daughter. She was crying, and the man leaned forward to catch her gaze. He said something to her, she nodded, and he pulled her in close to his chest. A little excitement drained from the chevalier's blood. He continued on, navigating through the packed streets patched with snow.

As he turned the corner off Rue de Saint-Andre, he spied a young woman with dark hair walking arm in arm with an older gentlemen. The two laughed, and she pecked the old man on the cheek with a light kiss. His eyes lit up. A wide smile materialized beneath his heavy white beard.

Lecroix's stomach churned once more. He leaned up against a post along the street. His pains subsided after a few moments, but anytime he thought of the father and daughter, or the young woman and old man, a painful cavity returned in his gut.

"Monsieur, are you well?" a young boy asked.

Lecroix looked at him as if he saw the answer scrawled upon the child's face.

"Yes. I'm fine. Thank you."

He tossed the boy a coin and marched off, rejoining the crowd of

Parisians in the long and narrow streets. He felt like a ghost, letting his feet take him while his mind floated in the clouds. He didn't stop until he came to the very street where he'd crossed blades with the masked messenger.

Lecroix knocked at the Comte de Gien's modest city dwelling, but no answer came. He knocked a second time, but still the lodgings remained still and silent. The chevalier peered through one of the windows. No candles shone, no fire burned, and no soul stirred within. He sighed and headed home. Perhaps a hot drink and meal would help calm his stomach.

Outside his apartment, he found a tall man with broad shoulders knocking at his own door with a wooden cane. When no one answered, the man limped his way back into the street.

"Jules?" Lecroix said. He jogged after the servant. "Monsieur! Monsieur Venadeau!"

The count's sole servant whipped his head around upon hearing his name. Lecroix nearly was taken aback at how pale and strained the man looked.

"Oh, Chevalier Lecroix! Thank God! I came as fast as I could."

"I just tried paying the count a visit. What is it? What's wrong?"

"The count set up another meeting with the messenger."

"What? How?"

"I don't know, Chevalier, but I left to buy supplies this morning and when I returned he was gone. The house was in shambles, and I found a note on the door telling me to bring the money owed, lest they slit the count's throat. I didn't know what to do."

The servant thrust the crumpled note into Lecroix's hands. He read it. The highwaymen wanted double the amount for the count and his daughter and wanted every *sous* by nightfall. Jules was to meet with the highwaymen, alone, in the heart of the Cour de Jussienne, one of the city's *Cour des Miracles.*

"You did very well, Jules."

"We don't have the money, Chevalier!"

"I know."

"What do we do?"

"We have no choice but to meet with him."

"But how do we pay them?"

Lecroix feigned a comforting smile for the old soldier.

"I'll take care of it. Have no fear. Meet me at the Cour de Jussienne tonight, and bring that harquebus of yours. Just to be safe."

Lecroix gave Jules a friendly pat on the back, but the warm smile on his face vanished as the servant hobbled away. It was more money than he and the count had combined, and the Comte de Mauriac was still away on business. The chevalier rushed into his apartment, grabbed his sword hanging above the hearth and headed back into the cold.

He found Nicholas Joubert at the same table at the same inn he did a few days back. Sunlight poured through the window, illuminating the plate and mug in a bright, white glow, but Nicholas's face remained hidden mostly in gloom. He invited Lecroix to sit with him all the same.

"What can I do for the marvelous Chevalier d'Auch this afternoon?" he asked.

"I need your help."

"With what?"

"An extraction."

Nicholas crossed his arms. "Of whom?"

"Seigneur Marcel Brocquart, the Comte de Gien."

"I'm unfamiliar with that name."

"He's an acquaintance of my nephew. An honest man who had his daughter kidnapped by some brutes, and now he, too, has fallen into their grasps."

Nicholas chuckled. "My apologies for the rudeness, but it seems the Brocquart's have a fondness for being whisked away."

"This is serious, Nicholas."

The old soldier cleared his throat. "You're right. My apologies, my friend. What do these *thieves and brigands* want?"

"Coin. A lot of it."

"So why not pay them and be done with it?"

"That's the problem. They're asking for too much."

Nicholas's eyes flickered. "That so?"

"The count is a poor man, and even my small pension isn't enough to make up the difference."

"I see."

"It's why I've come to you."

Nicholas lowered his brow. "Jean-Girard, I love you as a brother, but I'm as poor as your count friend. I've barely been getting by taking odd jobs here and there. It hasn't been easy."

"I know, I know. That's not the sort of help I'm asking."

"What is then?"

Lecroix flashed a grim smile. Nicholas was one of the finest blades he ever knew, and if he had to draw his own sword to free the innocent, he couldn't think of a better man for the task.

"I need your sword-arm," he said, patting the old soldier on the arm. Nicholas winced and flinched back with a moan. "My apologies, Nicholas. I didn't realize you were hurt."

Nicholas grabbed his arm. "It's nothing. Just a small accident while working at a butcher's shop recently."

"A butcher's shop?"

"Like I said–hard times, odd jobs."

"Then I retract my request. I cannot ask you to do this while injured. In fact, it was a poor request to begin with. I'll go."

Lecroix stood, but Nicholas reached out and grabbed him by the sleeve.

"It's fine. Truly, Jean-Girard. It's just tender. Are you sure there's no way of paying them?"

"Lord knows I've prayed to find the money. I want no bloodshed, but I don't know what these men will do if I don't."

"Who else are you bringing?"

"Just myself, and the count's manservant. He's quite the marksman."

Nicholas leaned back into his chair. His face fell into the shadows. A familiar and grave look glinted in his eyes. "I will join you, but on one condition."

"Name it."

"Bring what money you can anyways. I've dealt with these types of fiends before. Perhaps I can negotiate the release."

Lecroix nodded. "Meet me on the outskirts of the Cour de Jussienne tonight."

The chevalier stepped into the flowing tide of men, women, and children going about their business. He saw a large, stalwart man leaning against the side of the building across the road. No sword protruded beneath his cloak, but his eyes seemed fixated on the inn. Lecroix wondered if he was being watched.

He sped up his walk, moving people aside to get to the small clearing in the middle of a nearby square. He hopped up on a small wall and gazed down the road to see if the mysterious sentinel followed, but the man kept to his post.

Lecroix sighed but not in relief. He was beginning to think he was going mad.

# XXXVI.
## Friends & Foes

Darion peeked over the edge of several fallen logs outside the perimeter of the highwaymen's chateau. For five long years he used to call it home, but it felt like he was looking at it for the first time and in a much more ominous light. The facade looked older and grittier, struggling to survive beneath the enormous vines that rooted themselves in the cracks and crevasses of the stone wall. It did little to weaken the august of it, however. Tall towers trust themselves into the grey sky and the barren field that laid between the forest and the fortress seemed like an eternal deathtrap for anyone hoping to storm the structure. How did he ever call this place home?

Outside the chateau roamed the Forty-Five Guardsmen's horses, most not stabled and just left loose to wander the grounds. Darion's eyes narrowed at the sight. Good soldiers, especially the king's elite, wouldn't have been so careless with their mounts. They were also much further from the chateau than he'd expect, as if something spooked them into putting a little distance between them and the manor.

Darion primed and loaded the pistol. He cranked the span and stuffed it into the saddle holster before remounting the horse he took from the Hotel de Mâle. He wasn't sure if the horse belonged to Charles, Jean-Henri, one of the Guardsmen, or the poor innkeeper himself. He just knew there were far more horses than riders at the inn and that he needed to get to the chateau as quickly as possible.

He put his heel to the horse's flank and galloped to the chateau. As he pulled up he could hear the muffled noise of clashing steel, men yelling, and occasional gun fire.

Darion leapt off his saddle, and drew his sword and pistol. A

Guardsman stumbled out of the chateau. The man's face was clammy and eyes unfocused. He clenched his red stained chest with one hand and reached for the doorframe with the other. Alas, he missed and fell face first into the patch of mud. Darion dragged the soldier out of the way before peering inside. The chateau was too dark and smoky for Darion to see the action. A few muzzle flashes glowed through the gloom, but it did little to aid Darion's vision.

He took a deep breath before plunging into the chaos. Smoke from the gunshots burned his eyes and nostrils. He scouted for Peppin or Antoine amidst the fighting, but with all the smoke, it was hard to tell one silhouette from another. A man charged at Darion from the left, growling and sword stretched outward. Darion leveled the pistol and, without pausing to see if he were friend or foe, fired. The man's head jerked back, and he plummeted to the ground. Darion dropped the pistol beside the body and drew his main gauche.

A second figure materialized in front of him. Darion barely parried the thrust with his sword, and he sliced sideways with his own dagger. He missed, and his assailant let out another barrage of thrusts and cuts with both sword and dagger. Darion retreated and voided each attack but not without feeling a few cut through his cloak or glance off his thick jerkin. Darion had more time to recognize his attacker this time. It was Pierre, one of the younger and newer members of the Falcon Highwaymen. The young man's teeth gnashed and a thin veil of sweat covered his face. He pushed a relentless attack, but in his impatience he overextended on a lunge. Darion parried with his main gauche, bound the man's sword down and under with his rapier and his sword into the young man's chest. Pierre yelped and dropped his sword to grab the blade embedded in him. He then thrust out with his dagger in a desperate attempt to even the carnage, but Darion extended his main gauche. The two hilts clashed. Pierre struggled before dropping to the ground.

"Peppin!" Darion yelled, drawing his sword from Pierre's chest. "Peppin!"

Darion surveyed the scuffle before him. Highwaymen in their dark, grimy clothing crossed blades with Guardsmen and their brilliant, crimson cloaks. Several members from each faction lay dead or wounded on the ground. The quarreling of steel echoed off the walls in a deafening chorus of mayhem and ruin.

"Peppin!"

A Guardsman turned and faced Darion. His eyes went to

Darion's shoulder, bare of a crimson cloak. A murderous frenzy glinted in the soldier's eyes. Darion held up his hands.

"I'm on your side, monsieur."

But the Guardsman was beyond thought and reason. He lunged. Darion parried with a quick beat of the blade. The king's man redoubled and missed, but his momentum threw him forward. He flashed out his dagger. Darion met it with the large guard of his rapier, leaving the two swordsmen locked together.

"I'm on... your... side," Darion growled, using all his strength to keep the Guardsman weapons at bay.

"You're a traitor!" The Guardsman head-butted Darion, knocking the Gascon back in a dizzy haze. The king's man readied for another lunge at Darion when a silver gleam emerged from his chest. The Guardsman looked down at the sword dripping with his own blood. His face shaded in surprise.

Darion shook the cobwebs from his head. Simon grinned from over the Guardsman's shoulder. He yanked his rapier back through the guard's torso. His face grew long and eyes broadened when he saw Darion before him.

"You– You're supposed to be dead. I heard the shots. I was there!"

"Simon–"

Simon dropped his sword and retreated into the cover of the smoke and gloom of an adjacent room.

Darion took off his cloak and threw on the crimson cloak of the dead Guardsman. Bad enough to be attacked by the highwaymen; he didn't need the Forty-Five after him, too.

"Peppin!"

"Over here!"

Darion found the one-eyed soldier crouched behind a pillar, ramming a ball down the barrel of his harquebus. Darion rushed over as another salvo of pistol and harquebus fire came from above and whizzed by his head. Someone cried in a death throe behind him.

"Pep–"

"Fancy meeting you here, Gascon." Peppin glanced up from his loading and smiled. "Nice cloak you got there. Red suits you. Brings out the mayhem in your eyes."

"What the hell happened?"

"The chateau looked deserted. No horses in the stables and no lights in the halls. Didn't see a soul through the windows either. Antoine ordered a quick rest while we try to figure out our next move. We stepped in here and they rained a tempest of lead at us. It's been shit ever since."

Peppin whipped around the pillar and fired at a group of highwaymen perched above. He turned back and sneered.

"Dammit."

"Miss?"

"Hit him in the shoulder. Fucking sights are off. Royal arms at its finest. I need my own gun."

Peppin pulled the match cord from the firearm's serpentine and primed the pan with some powder.

"Where's Antoine now?" Darion asked.

"He took four men down the hall. They were going to try to sneak around the highwaymen up top. Haven't heard from him since and considering that the fucking bastards are still raining hell on us..."

Peppin shrugged, not wanting to continue his thought. Neither did Darion. He untied the pouch of shot and powder horn around his waist and laid them beside Peppin.

"You'll need these more than I will."

Peppin winked as he finished stuffing the ball shot down the barrel. He then reattached his match to the serpentine.

"Ready?"

Darion nodded. Peppin swung around the pillar and fired, giving Darion a few moments reprieve to rush out of the kill pocket. Between the thundering shots and light flashing from the guns it reminded Darion of nights weathering out a lightning storm. Only he didn't fear being struck by lightning as much as he did by a lead ball.

He made it to the adjacent hall and took note of the carnage behind him. Two of the Guardsmen were down and groaning. A third lay lifeless on the floor, a lead-shot hole between the eyes and his cap beside his head. Another two of the Forty-Five were huddled beneath overheads to shield themselves from the harquebus fire from above. The rest of the men clashed steel against steel with the highwaymen in a macabre scene. He needed to clear that second floor firing line.

He spied Castel taking refuge beneath the stairs and wrapping a cloth around his left arm. Darion rushed to him, taking advantage of the lull in gunfire.

"What the hell are you doing here?" Castel asked. "Why in damnation are you wearing that cloak?"

"Saving your ass," Darion quipped. "And the cloak is so your men don't stab me in the back."

"You know much on that subject, I reckon."

"This isn't the time, Antoine." He gestured to the lieutenant's wound. "How bad is it?"

"I'll live if we can get out of here. We're pinned down here and the top of stairwell is barricaded. We can't make a direct attack. We need another approach."

Darion poked his head from under the stairs. Benches and other random furniture were piled at the top of the staircase. With the open lobby and the highwaymen's superior position, Darion and the Guardsmen were no better than sitting ducks.

"Is there another way up?"

Darion nodded. "Through the great hall and in the kitchen is a stairwell leading to the second floor. If we can get there we might be able to sneak up on them. We'll still need to cross that firing squad though."

He pointed to the row of three highwaymen crouched behind overturned tables from the mess hall. They sat patiently, waiting for the Guardsmen to rear their heads and to riddle their bodies with lead and burned powder. The lieutenant surveyed the situation.

"You're mad, Gascon." The lieutenant whistled to get the attention of his men across from him. "Give us some cover!"

The small band and checked their firearms and nodded.

"Ready, Antoine?"

"This better fucking work. Fire!"

The Guardsmen unleashed a volley that sent the highwaymen ducking behind their cover. It wasn't much, but it gave Darion and Castel enough time to make their move. They charged forward, their cloaks billowing behind them. One of the highwaymen popped his head over the table, brandishing an harquebus ready to fire. Castel fired his pistol instantly, striking the highwayman and sending a spray of blood on the two men next to him. Darion and the lieutenant plunged their swords and daggers forward, piercing their adversaries before they even thought of defending themselves.

Darion kicked the table aside. His head felt light as he saw the three men—three companions—dead on the ground.

"Lead the way," Castel said. Darion didn't hear the lieutenant. He just kept staring at the three bodies. Castel smacked him on the shoulder. "Gascon. Let's go!"

Darion broke from his trance. They sprinted through the great hall and kitchen reeking of old wine and spoiled broth. They leaped up the staircase two steps at a time. Around the corner were six men leaning over the railings, unleashing hell on the Guardsmen below. Darion turned to Castel. For a moment he thought he saw a smile on the lieutenant's face.

"Which side do you want?" Darion asked.

"The usual."

This time it was Darion who flashed a smile. Of course it would be the cold thundering of gunfire to thaw the lieutenant's demeanor.

Silently, they rushed from behind the walls, and in an instant Darion had three feet of steel through one of the highwaymen's back. The man gasped before fully realizing his end was upon him. Darion thrust his dagger at the next man in line. Fear flashed in the rogue's eyes just before the point of Darion's dagger buried itself in his neck. Darion pulled his weapons free in time to deflect a cut from the third highwayman. He readied himself for another attack when the man's right eye exploded. Blood and matter sprayed and he fell to the ground.

"Fucking asshole! He moved!" Peppin bellowed from below.

Darion took measure of how the lieutenant faired. One of his foes lay squirming on the ground, pressing his hand against a large puncture wound in his gut, but the other two engaged the lieutenant furiously. Castel did his best to fend off the duo's attacks, parrying with his finely polished swept-hilt and rat-tailing his cloak at the scoundrels' faces to keep distance. But his cloaked arm tired thanks to his wound, and his parries grew wilder.

"Antoine!" Darion yelled as he rushed to his old friend's aid.

The lieutenant unraveled his cloak and threw it over the head of one of the highwaymen. Like a well-practiced dance, Darion and Castel both lunged. Castel ran through the fellow with the cloak over his head and Darion the man's counterpart. Both bandits slumped to the ground in drawn out groans.

A loud crash came by the stairs. Peppin and the remaining Guardsmen, covered in blood and sweat, spilled onto the balcony.

## XXXVII.
## Burdens

Jacquelyna didn't sleep well, but she rarely did in carriages. The bumps and jostling from the poor French country roads made it nearly impossible for her to drift to slumber. Being surrounded by men who'd sooner slit her throat than look at her only added to her restlessness. Gabrielle didn't have that issue, however. She slept like a babe, and Jacquelyna often wondered if the king's daughter knew the full weight of their situation. Jacquelyna hoped she didn't.

Hours went by without stopping for food or drink or even to warm their chilled bones. The quietness slowly clawed away at her sanity. She couldn't stop thinking of Darion and Peppin. She wanted to weep for their passing, but she had no tears left to spare. Mourning would wait. She still needed to escape. Heroes were a thing of the past, if they existed at all, she mused. No longer could women depend on the chivalry of men; she could only depend on herself.

She looked for any opportunity to escape or get word out on the direction they were headed. For miles she saw nothing but open fields and patches of forest. Eventually her restlessness faded. She fell to sleep, curling up in a fur blanket Bauvet gave her.

When she awoke, she pulled back the thick, black curtain of the carriage. The sky was bright and taking into account the sun's path, they were traveling north. The coach stopped at a small village she didn't recognize. Bauvet opened the door.

"Follow me."

She nudged Gabrielle awake. They trailed Bauvet to an inn. Captain Tremear and the Spaniard forced patrons out with the ends of their pistols. Only the innkeeper, his wife, and their daughter remained.

"Sit there," Bauvet said, pointing a gloved finger to a table near the fireplace.

"Will you kill me, too, if I don't?" Jacquelyna asked. "I hear you've gone from killing defenseless women to your own friends."

"You don't know anything about it."

Bauvet gestured to the seat again. This time Jacquelyna obeyed, though not before shooting a curious glance at the highwayman. Gabrielle sidled up beside her and burrowed herself underneath's Jacquelyna's arms. Poor girl was beginning to look ragged, her hair in disarray and gown soiled at the hem. Jacquelyna shuddered at the thought of what she looked like.

The innkeeper's wife appeared from a side door carrying a plate, a few cups, and a jug. She placed them down and looked at Jacquelyna with a face that said she knew the predicament but was in no position to do much about it. Even so, Jacquelyna felt a warmness from the woman and appreciated the first sign that the whole world wasn't against her.

"I'll fetch some meat and bread for you all," the woman said. She bustled through the side door. Meanwhile, Bauvet pulled off his gloves, tossing them on the table. He unbelted his sword and rested it carefully against the edge of the table. He sat on a bench, poured himself a tankard of wine, and threw his head back, downing the whole draught in a single go. In the morning light Jacquelyna noticed how pale the highwayman seemed and how fixated he was on the dark liquid before him. Something burdened him. He poured himself a second glass.

The woman returned a few minutes later and slopped a pile of roasted fowl, and boiled carrots and beans on the plate.

"Let me know if you need anything else." She wiped her hands on her already soiled apron. Jacquelyna poked at her food while shooting fleeting glances at Bauvet chomping down on a leg of meat.

"What is it?" he asked.

"Have you heard from my father, yet?" She raised her mug to her lips in hopes of masking her own anxiety.

"I'd imagine our riders will catch up with us soon enough with an answer."

"And if they come without any coin?"

"They will."

"What if they don't?"

The burden in his eyes lifted, replaced with an irritated gaze. "Why wouldn't they?"

Jacquelyna's heart beat faster. She didn't want to betray the fact that her father was nearly *sous*-less, but the highwaymen would learn that soon enough. She was already bound for death even if she was the only one who knew it. Her only chance of life and liberty was in her gaoler, a scoundrel in his own right but one who showed some compassion. Alas, Bauvet was also the man that murdered Darion and Peppin. And for what? Wealth?

She clammed up and ate a small piece of the pheasant. Bauvet dropped the remainder of his food into his dish.

"'Steeth. He's not paying is he?"

"I didn't say that."

"It's written all over your damn face. Shit, shit, shit." He took a depth breath, and his lips tightened. "How's this possible? Your father is a count, a damned bastard of the aristocracy. How's he not paying, eh?"

Jacquelyna hesitated. "He spent his last *livre* securing me a position among the queen's maids, to better position me to find a well-off suitor. I am not wed and my father is poorer than any of you. So you see there is no ransom to be had."

Bauvet ran a hand through his dark hair. "It looks like I've done nothing but delay the inevitable."

"Not if you let me go."

"I would just be trading my own neck for yours. You're a fool if you think I'd take that deal."

She shuffled across the bench next to him. Close to him. So close that the stench of horse, leather, and sweat almost overwhelmed her. His heavy brows furrowed, but there was a glint of lust that she hoped for. She put a hand on his shoulder. He considered it with a long, teeth-grinding thought. But instead of taking it into his own, he slid it off.

"Let me give you a little bit of advice, mademoiselle. Don't whore yourself out. Not to me. Not to your Gascon love. Not to anyone. It's not worth the few extra breaths in this godforsaken shithole of a country."

Jacquelyna's fists balled. "You might as well take that pistol and shoot me like you did Darion."

Bauvet turned pale as snow. "I didn't shoot him."

"It's appalling enough to be at your mercy, at least have the decency to not lie to my face. I heard the shots."

"And shots have funny ways of not reaching their targets, mademoiselle. I *did not* shoot Darion or his one-eyed friend. I let them go. Told them not to come back."

Jacquelyna's heart fluttered a moment. "You... what?"

"I know you think us heinous dogs and you'd be right on that account, but Darion's a friend of mine. I don't have the habit of killing friends."

"He's... alive?"

The front door flew open, and Tremear stepped in. He gestured with a quick motion of his head for Bauvet to come over. The two spoke a few low words by the door. Jacquelyna used the distraction to grab a knife off of the table and slide it between the folds of her cloak.

Bauvet returned to the table, his face tense. He belted his sword, pulled on his thick black gauntlets and left without a word. Through the window Jacquelyna saw Bauvet peer back in as he passed by.

Tremear plopped himself down on the bench across from Jacquelyna. He ripped off a small piece of meat from Bauvet's plate and tossed it in his mouth.

*Darion alive? Peppin, too?* She suppressed a smile and instead picked at her meal. For a moment hope blossomed in her heart, but as pleased as she was that her friends were unharmed, she hoped they wouldn't return for her. They came too close to making the ultimate sacrifice for her. She couldn't live with herself if they tried again and failed.

Hooves thundered against the frozen ground, shaking her from her thoughts. Five men in black clothing and wide hats dismounted. She didn't recognize them, but they looked no less dangerous than the men who were holding her captive.

"Ah," Tremear said, also gazing out the window. "Your new overseers."

## XXXVIII.
## Confession

"They're not here," one of the Guardsmen said. "Not a sign of them."

Castel fumed. "Where the hell are they?"

"Jacquelyna and the king's daughter were here when we left, Antoine," Peppin said.

"Where could they have gone? Gascon, where would they go?"

Darion had been leaning against a wall, his sword and dagger finally sheathed. A few of the Guardsmen had lit small lanterns to brighten the room. So many cuts and bandages on the men. So much blood on the floors. He pushed off the wall with his foot and crossed his arms.

"I don't know," he said. "This was the only hideout we had."

"Well, there must be another one!"

"I don't know of one, Antoine. I don't know where they went. Don't you think I'd tell you if I did?"

Castel glowered. "Get that cloak off your shoulders. You sully the name of the Forty-Five by wearing it."

Darion had almost forgotten he had the Guardsmen's cloak still on. He fiddled with the satin cord and let it fall into his arms. The lieutenant snatched it from him.

"Are any of the highwaymen still alive?" Castel asked.

"No, Lieutenant," a Guardsmen said. "They've all gone to Saint Peter's Gate."

Darion felt nauseous.

"And how are highwaymen so well armed with harquebuses?"

Darion shrugged. "Most of the lot are former soldiers, but only one or two had an harquebus. A handful of others had pistols."

"There was a hell of a lot more than a couple of harquebuses and pistols. I've seen armies less well equipped. 'Sblood. Search the chateau, top and bottom. Look for anything that might lead us to their next stop. A missive. A note. A map. Horse or coach tracks. Anything. Go. Go!"

The Guardsmen set about their tasks. Darion and Peppin lingered.

"What do you want us to do, Antoine?" Peppin asked.

"Just stay out of my hair." Castel stormed off.

"As you wish, *Monseigneur*," Pep said with a mocking bow. His eye lighted in alarm. He pointed at Darion's jerkin and doublet. "Jesus. That your blood, Gascon?"

Darion looked down. His grey leather jerkin and blue doublet were tainted in a dark cherry-tinged stain. There was a lot on him, and if it were his own, he'd probably be dead.

"Eh, no. It's not. Least I don't think." Darion checked himself for extra holes. Nothing to worry about, anyways. He looked around at the bodies collapsed on the floor. "Nice shooting, by the way."

"Bah! I missed my mark on this whore's son." Peppin kicked one of the corpses in the ribs. "Royal issue guns just don't do it for me. The accuracy is too unpredictable, not to mention it's not built for my eye. I just hope my harquebus is still here. I hid it beneath my bed."

"You want to go check?"

Peppin thought for a moment. "I'll help you with these bodies first."

⚜⚜⚜

Four. That's how many of the Forty-Five were dead in the ambush. Another four were injured. It left just five remaining Guardsmen—including Castel—Peppin, and Darion alive and well enough to continue on. Darion and Peppin dragged the corpses outside. Someone would have to retrieve them later for a proper burial. The ground was still too hard for digging.

After the Guardsmen, the highwaymen were lined up side by

side. Darion looked at the faces of each man. There was Pierre and François, Jules, Theodore, Eugene, Bernard and Gilbert, Roland, Matthieu and Raymond, Alain, Yves and Luc. Each man he ate with and drank with and fought beside, thieved with, and laughed with. And now he killed them. And all for what? For a woman's love? For a chance at redemption and lost honor? And what did the highwaymen fight for exactly? There was no gold to be found with the king's bastard, and gold was the only true motivation for thieves and highwaymen. It all made little sense to him.

Darion lowered his brows as he went through the column of dead. Something was awry. He raked through the faces of the dead highwaymen once more, looking for the pale-faced, fair-haired swordsman. Someone was missing.

Darion rushed into the chateau, ignoring Peppin's inquiry into what was wrong. By the sleeping quarters, Darion spotted a thin trail of blood. A few drops here, a few drops there. It zigged and zagged through the chambers and halls, away from the heat of the fighting, and to Darion's own quarters. The door was ajar and the handle covered in half-crusted blood. Darion unsheathed the sword and dagger. He stood by the door, listening for motion. He took a deep breath before pushing it open slowly with the tip of his blade.

The room was dim. Sunlight fought its way through the lone window, lighting two dusty boots by the wall. Darion approached slowly, sword outstretched to protect from a sudden charge. He found Simon slumped against the wall, his left arm draped across his stomach, trying to keep his innards where God put them. The highwayman's face was pale and slick in sweat. Like a man waiting his turn with the reaper.

"Figured if you survived you'd come back here looking for your toys," Simon said. He coughed and winced. Darion spotted his sword, main gauche, and pistol all resting on the table by the window where he left them. "I thought about shooting you as you entered, but what good is a pistol against a ghost?"

"Indeed."

"So are you? A ghost?"

"Does it matter?"

Simon flashed a sickly grin. "I suppose not. I'm a dead man anyways."

Darion sat down beside the highwayman. For a minute the two

men didn't say a word to each other.

"What was this all about, Simon? What is this all for?"

"Gold, Gascon. Always gold."

"That's horseshit. We've always been able to get gold other ways. Easier ways. Ways that don't involve king's men and the entire band being slaughtered."

Simon tried to shrug. "Maybe we wanted more. Maybe our greed got the better of us. Maybe we... maybe grew tired of living like pigs rotting in shit our whole lives."

"More lies."

"Maybe not." Darion considered his friend a moment. Even if what Simon said wasn't the whole truth about their motivation, he was definitely sincere in his remarks. "And what about you, Gascon? How much did the king pull out of his coffers to get you to turn on your friends, eh?"

"I'm not working for the king."

Simon coughed up a bloody laugh. "You're a fool if that's so. Who are you working for then?"

"No one. Jacquelyna is just an old friend of mine."

"She must've been a fine piece of sheet loving for you to betray us."

That word again. Betrayer. A deserter to his country. A traitor to friends. And now a traitor to his highwaymen brethren.

Simon groaned as he tried to shift his seat. Blood oozed between his hands and onto his woolen breeches. Darion checked the wound with a few fingers. He cringed.

"That bad, eh? I could've told you that." Simon's hazy eyes searched Darion. "Took a knife to the gut as I was backing away from you. Barely held myself together to get here. So, in a way, you're the reason I'm bleeding all over your floor."

Simon flashed a mordant, scarlet smile.

"I'll fetch for a physician." Darion headed for the door.

"Don't bother, Gascon. I'm lost anyways. Best a damn physician can do for me now is make me suffer for a few days."

"You'll suffer for a few days either way."

"Not if you take care of me."

Simon gestured to the table and the well-oiled pistol. Darion's mouth fell ajar.

"I'm no executioner, Simon."

Simon's tongue lapped up the blood around his lips and beard.

"There are about a dozen of your closest friends downstairs who say otherwise. How about as a favor? You do me in good and in return I tell you everything you want to know. Good luck getting that deal from corpses."

Darion rushed out of his quarters. He couldn't believe what Simon was asking him to do. At least with the other men they were armed and fighting back. But Simon? He was still alive and breathing, albeit barely. It was a high cost for what he needed to know. But what other choice did he have?

His answer came in the form of closing the door.

"Ask your questions, Gascon."

"Where is Jacquelyna?"

"Being escorted by the captain, Andre, and that Spanish devil to some location outside of Caudebec."

"Where near Caudebec?"

"No idea. We were told to deal with the Guardsmen and then go to a Fontenelle Abbey at Saint-Wandrille-Rançon."

"Who were you to meet?"

Simon shrugged and coughed up another catarrh of blood. "We were told he'd find us."

Darion accepted the answer with a nod. "One more question."

"Get on with it then."

"Why Spain?"

Darion wasn't sure why he asked that question. He didn't care for politics or intrigue, but part of him wanted to know the reason behind all the blood and death. Maybe it would console him when the death masks of his friends would later haunt his dreams.

Simon shook his head. "It's not Spain."

"What do you mean? Spain's behind this aren't they?"

"Not directly."

"Then who?"

"I don't know."

"How do you know it's not Spain then?"

"Because when Andre was freed from prison, he was approached by three men. Two foreigners and one Frenchman. One of the foreigners was that Spanish devil."

"And the other two?"

Simon's breathing grew more labored. "He says he doesn't know."

"Do you believe him?"

"Does it matter?" It didn't. Not really, anyways. If Simon didn't know then Simon didn't know. "Anything else you wish me to confess?"

Darion shook his head and inched his way to the table. He hesitated before picking up his pistol. His sharp blue eyes looked over the weapon, studying it from butt to muzzle. Every chip, every scratch, every dent had a story. Many times he fired it in self-defense, but never in execution. This story wouldn't leave a mark on the pistol, but it would leave a dark spot on Darion's conscience.

"Get on with it, will you?" Simon said.

"You sure?"

"If you keep dawdling I'll bleed out before you get the chance. Do it already."

Darion saw the resignation in Simon's eyes. Any sense of fear must've spilled out on the floor with the highwayman's lifeblood. Darion cranked the wheel of his pistol. It locked with a click. Darion shuddered.

"Where do you want it?"

Simon tapped his hand over his left chest. "And make sure it doesn't misfire."

Darion leveled the pistol at Simon's chest and gazed sorrowfully at Simon. The man's eyes were harsh now but wavering, like he was damming back a flood of emotions rising within him. Simon did his best to keep his lips from quivering. So did Darion.

"You made a promise, Gascon. Do it."

Darion closed his eyes.

"Forgive me," he whispered.

# XXXIX.
## Cour de Jussienne

Chevalier Lecroix made one final stop by the Comte de Mauriac's Parisian apartments, but a servant there said the count wasn't expected for another couple of days at the earliest. With little gold in his purse he'd have to turn to cold steel, unless Nicholas could somehow manage to negotiate with the highwaymen's messenger.

The moon rose to take watch for the night, the air grew frigid, and the stars twinkled knowingly of the future.

Lecroix sheathed his weapons, threw on a padded leather jerkin over his wool doublet, and draped his long cloak over his shoulders. He toyed with the notion of bringing his pistol, but he still hoped this situation would end peacefully. Dressing for a small war wouldn't help keep men's heads about them. After he finished dressing he grabbed the leather satchel hanging from a chair and slung it over his shoulder.

He found Jules standing in a halo of moonlight. He was dressed in all black, and his harquebus was wrapped up in an oilskin leather.

"Monsieur," Lecroix said.

"Chevalier." Jules doffed his old hat, its brim drooping downward at every side. The servant's eyes poured over his surroundings, searching and scanning for who knows what. All signs of the feeble manservant were gone. In its place glowed the unmistaken bearing of a gallant soldier. Lecroix positioned himself next to Jules. The streets had thinned out. Most of the rabble strolling by now wore steel at their hips or shifted from one shadow to the next, thieves looking for a late and lonesome straggler to prey upon.

"Who else are we waiting on?" Jules asked.

"Just an old friend and a good swordsman."

"And the satchel?"

"What money I could scrounge up. I still hope we can negotiate Jacquelyna and the count's release."

"Little faith in that. There's no honor among these thieves."

A cold gust blew and Lecroix hiked the collar of his cloak. Nearly an hour passed, and Nicholas was still nowhere to be seen.

"We can't delay much longer, Chevalier. This could be our last chance to get the count and Mademoiselle Brocquart."

As much as Lecroix wanted Nicholas there, Jules was right. They needed to go and go now. "Follow me."

Men at home in the moonlight shot wary glances at the chevalier and the manservant. A few stepped out of their way while others held their ground. In a district known for its rags, Lecroix stood out like a sore thumb. It had been a long time since he stepped foot in the *Cour des Miracles*, and the attention he and Jules were inundated with made his skin crawl.

They came to a rundown building at the corner of an unpaved street. No light shone from within, and half the windows were shuttered and boarded up.

"You sure this is it, Chevalier?"

"The note said the old butcher's shop at Cour de Jussienne. This is it. See if you can sneak around the back, but don't enter until you hear my voice. I want this knave well distracted before we make any final moves. We don't know what we'll find in there."

Jules threw off the old leather cover of his harquebus and hobbled his way into the shadow of an alley. Lecroix thought he saw movement at his peripheral, but he couldn't make out anything but the dark silhouette of trees and posts. He took a deep breath and entered through the front. Even in the bitter cold, the large shop still reeked of rotten meat and stale blood. The stench nearly bowled Lecroix over. He began to wonder if more than just pigs and goats were slaughtered there.

Faint gleams from the moon trickled its way through cracks and crevices of the butcher's shop, speckling the floor in a crisscrossing maze of silver light. He stepped around some wooden cartons. There he found the Comte de Gien illuminated in the poor glow of a tallow candle, gagged and roped to a chair. As he drew closer he noticed the count's face was bloody and eyes were shut.

"Mother of Jesus." Lecroix rushed to the count and checked for life. Slow but steady breaths emanated from Gien. Lecroix started to untie the count's bonds when he heard the floor creak behind him. He reached for his dagger and whipped around. He was met with a familiar, smiling face. "Jesus Christ, Nicholas. You scared me."

"Did you bring the money?" Nicholas asked.

"I did, but it's not even half what they're asking for."

"How much?"

Lecroix shrugged. "Barely a hundred *sous.* Help me untie the count."

"Dammit. That's not enough."

"I know, but it appears the messenger has left his roost for the moment. We can get the count out of here without an incident."

The chevalier was so distracted by the need to free the Comte de Brocquart, that he barely registered the cross grimace on his friend's face.

"I'll hold the satchel," Nicholas said. "You get the count."

Lecroix tossed Nicholas the leather bag, but as he turned to free the count, something struck him as off about his old companion. He remembered Nicholas's injured arm, this sudden appearance at the rendezvous, and his obsession with the payment. A cold tingle skulked up the chevalier's spine.

"How did you find us?" Lecroix asked.

"What do you mean?"

"I mean, how did you know to find us here?"

Nicholas chuckled. "Are you growing senile? You showed me the letter."

Lecroix shook his head slowly. "I showed no one that letter."

"Then you must've told me."

"I told you to meet me at the edge of the Cour de Jussienne. I mentioned nothing about this butcher's shop."

Nicholas flashed a wayward grin before throwing back his cloak. Lecroix reached for his dagger, but Nicholas had already leveled a pistol at his head.

"Keep your blade in its sheath, old friend. No need for this to get messy."

Lecroix slowly brought his hand away from his side. He stared at Nicholas. He could scarcely believe his eyes.

"You used to have a sense of honor."

"I told you earlier, Jean-Girard. Times are tough and honor doesn't put food in my stomach. I work odd jobs."

"Like working for Spain?"

The old soldier's face twisted in a coarse scowl. "'Steeth, no. I piss on their damn graves. Every last one of them."

"Then who do you work for?"

"It doesn't matter."

"It matters very much, Nicholas. You know your highwaymen friends have the king's daughter?"

Nicholas shrugged. "The highwaymen are no less a pawn than I am."

"What do you mean? A war could start because of this."

"Good. I've been idle far too long. So have you. A little cannon fire would be good to heat the blood again."

Lecroix gaped. It seemed time had eroded Nicholas's sense of gallantry and duty. All that was left was a shell of a man drunk with greed and a desire for death. But Lecroix's inquiries went deeper than just trying to figure out Nicholas' motives. He was buying time until Jules arrived.

"What happened to the once honorable man I used to know?"

Nicholas roared in laughter. "Don't play that game with me, Jean-Girard. You know very well this is how I truly am. It's you that never had the stomach for the life. To do what needed to be done. It's why I had no qualms about killing the Duc and Cardinal de Guise, while you ran away to an abbey to shade your guilt."

Jules should've arrived by now, or, at the very least, Lecroix should've been able to smell the saltpeter of the servant's match cord. Something was wrong, and he made the mistake of letting his eyes wander, betraying his worry.

"Are you looking for your limped friend? I'm afraid he won't be joining us."

"What did you do to him, Nicholas?"

"Me? Nothing. He's alive. Or he should be if he didn't try to resist."

Nicholas whistled. A man appeared through a door on the second floor. He was armed with a sword and dagger, and a pistol stuffed in his belt. He looked like a hell of a brute, a true son of the *Cour des Miracles,* and it probably took him little effort to overpower Jules.

"The servant?" Nicholas asked.

"Alive. Unconscious." The man stepped down the stairs.

"There. You see? I'm not wholly the monster you think me to be, Jean-Girard. Not all of us have the luxury of a royal pension anymore. Some of us still need to get our hands dirty to survive." Lecroix could nearly taste the venom of Nicholas's words. "Be glad that I left the count in one piece for you."

"We should kill them all," Nicholas's partner said. "I don't like the idea of leaving—"

A laced glove shot out from the darkness, wrapped around the man's neck and lifted his chin, exposing his vulnerable stubbled throat. He gasped and raised his hands to his defense. But a flash of silver kissed his neck, leaving a dark crimson streak in its wake. The brute fell to his knees, his eyes revealing all the regret in his mind. Blood spewed out onto his hands and around him on the moldy floor.

Nicholas gaped before his soldierly training kicked in. He realigned his aim, but the shadowy figure had already pulled out the pistol from the dying brute's belt and fired. Nicholas reeled backwards with a groan and fell against a wooden pole.

The muzzle flash had lit the room in a brief but bright light, revealing a woman in an emerald cloak and hood. Lecroix ogled. Even when the woman stepped into a streak of silvery light, he almost didn't believe his eyes.

*Véronique.*

She shot the chevalier a callous glance through a lacey veil covering her face. She tossed the pistol aside and crouched next to Nicholas. A heavy flow of blood flowed between his fingers pressed against his chest.

"Now," she said, "who hired you?"

"Go to hell, bitch," Nicholas sputtered. "I know who you are."

Véronique flaunted a wicked grin. With a flick of her wrist she sent a long, slender dagger into his groin. Nicholas's eyes flared, and he bit his lip already dripping with blood. He writhed in pain until it became too much. He let out a loud, drawn out groan.

"For all that's holy, Véronique," Lecroix said. "Stop this!"

The chevalier knew her life as a member of the Flying Squadron was split into two. The public life of an honest, polite, and dutiful maid of the queen, and the private life of a spy, working in the shadows to reach the queen mother's ends. She led many men to their demise, but never in a thousand years did Lecroix imagine her playing the part of an assassin.

"Who hired you?" she asked again in a calm, motherly voice.

Nicholas clenched his teeth. Véronique twisted the blade. He cried out until his eyes started to haze over. Lecroix stepped forward, but Véronique held out a single finger, stopping him in his tracks. She relented the blade and life seeped back into Nicholas. His face alternated between rage and anguish.

She reached for a parchment that stuck out from his doublet. With his free hand, Nicholas tried swatting her away, but Véronique flicked her wrist, slicing him across the hand. He recoiled, and she pulled the paper free. She moved to a broad stream of moonlight and quickly read the letter's contents. She shot a fleeting glance at Nicholas before folding up the parchment and hiding it in her cloak.

Lecroix rushed to his old friend's side. "Nicholas..."

"Well, then..." the latter replied. His eyes became hazy and a final breath softly passed through his blood caked lips.

Lecroix rested there, his eyes fixated on the corpse of his once friend and fighting companion. He almost didn't notice Véronique slipping away.

"Wait," he said. She stopped, but the edge of her cloak and hood were visible from the shadows. "Show me the letter."

She turned for the door. Lecroix seized the pistol resting next to Nicholas's lifeless body and cocked the spanner. Véronique spun, her eyes fiery like a mother in disbelief when her child steps out of line.

"Are you threatening me, Chevalier?" she asked.

"Whatever is in that letter satisfied your curiosity, therefore it's piqued my own. It's a matter of state."

"And will you shoot me if I don't? Would you, the great Chevalier d'Auch and emissary for His Most Christian Majesty, shoot a defenseless woman in the dark?"

"If I must."

Véronique chuckled. "I think not, but here. Have it. I know all that I need to know."

Lecroix went for the parchment like a man reaching over a viper. He grabbed it and retreated to the light to read it. Its contents weren't too revealing, merely giving orders and explaining the nature of Nicholas's contract. Unsigned, of course. He turned it over to look at the seal. His body nearly froze on sight. On it was a large cross patonce with a sword to its left and an opened hand to the right–the seal of the Catholic League.

Lecroix raised his eyes in alarm. Véronique had seemed so calm and unsurprised by the revelation, and he wanted to know why. But she was gone, vanished into the shadows whence she came. He stood there a moment, stupefied, until he heard the muffled moans of the Comte de Brocquart trying to break free from his bonds.

# XL.
## Fontenelle Abbey

If Darion didn't know better, he would've expected Lieutenant Castel to have him executed then and there. His crime? A long list of them if one were to listen long enough to the lieutenant. This time Castel was irate that Darion dispatched Simon before he could question the highwayman himself. At least the lieutenant's rage tempered when Darion gave the location of a meeting point between the highwaymen and their employers.

"Your dead friend there had better been telling you the truth," Castel said as they rode out. Only two of the Forty-Five ventured on with the lieutenant, Darion, and Peppin. Three healthy men were left behind. Two tended to the wounded; the other raced back to Paris for reinforcements and transportation for the injured men.

They arrived at Saint-Wandrille-Rançon, a small commune on the banks of the Seine River, after the sun set. Fontenelle Abbey sat in the heart of the community, but it wasn't what any of them expected. The abbey lay in ruin. Large blocks of stone collapsed from the face and surrounding pillars, while old timber were left splintered and blackened by fire. No doubt this place, like so many, fell victim to the religious wars. Darion wondered how many abbots died in the process.

Darion tethered his horse to a post. He turned back as the other men did the same, but amongst the grey and black of the torched abbey, the Guardsmen stood out like blazing beacons.

"Take the cloaks off," he said.

One of the men scoffed. "I don't take orders from you."

Darion turned to the lieutenant. "Antoine, whoever the Falcon Highwaymen were meant to meet is expecting grubby highwaymen, not the crimson cloaks of the king's Forty-Five. He may run if he suspects anything."

"Do as he says," Castel ordered.

"But, Lieutenant, we'll freeze."

Castel whipped his head around. Whatever look he gave the men frightened them straight. They shed their cloaks, wrapping them into tight bundles and hiding them beneath the back of their saddles. A breeze picked up. The Guardsmen wrapped their arms around themselves and shivered. Darion unlaced his wool cloak and held it out to one of the men.

"Put this on and stay with the horses."

The soldier gaped at Darion. He thanked Darion almost sheepishly, and wrapped himself in the thick wool.

Darion led the way through the crumbled façade of the abbey. Wind whistled through the openings of the cloisters, and the steel at his side clinked together. Peppin walked next to him, his harquebus back in his hands and a smoldering match cord around his wrist. His face had grown grim in recent hours.

"You haven't said very much since the chateau," Darion said.

Peppin shrugged. "Haven't had much to say. Just looking forward to getting this shit over with, so I can go back to Marguerite."

"I'm sure she'll be pleased to see your mug again."

"She'll probably kick my ass for leaving in the first place."

Darion slapped him on the shoulder. "Don't worry, Pep. I'll tell her how you saved my ass." Peppin grinned.

The internal courtyard was a garden of death. Charcoaled lumber was scattered around uprooted thorn bushes. Stone benches were shattered into pieces. A statue of the Virgin Mary beheaded and smashed lay next to a neglected fountain now covered in dirt, moss, and vines.

Peppin gathered some kindling and started a fire. The men huddled around it, chewing on dried chicken and vegetables they scrounged up at the chateau. A cold hour went by.

"You sure this is the place, Gascon?" Castel asked.

"This is what Simon said."

"How do you know he wasn't playing you for a fool? He might've just told you a tall tale to get you to end his suffering sooner."

"I know you don't think highly of these men, Antoine, but they're not all bad people. Some are just trying to get by."

"By turning traitor to their country?"

"By doing whatever they need to survive. I don't approve of their actions. I merely understand their reason."

Castel scoffed. The fire crackled and popped and warmed the men as they ate. Darion leaned himself up against a stone pillar. The night sky was bare of clouds, and he took the quiet moment to soak in the stars glimmering between the veil of dark stains above.

"Seems we got company," Peppin said. He pointed to a soft light in an upper floor window of the abbey. The lieutenant got to his feet.

"No, I'll go," Darion said.

"Like hell you are, Gascon," Castel replied.

"You don't know anything about the Falcon Highwaymen. I do. If they question you they'll know they've been misled. We could lose our only lead."

"You screw this up, Gascon, and I swear..."

Darion crossed the courtyard. The abbey was dark as sin, but at the far end of the room shone a candle next to a broken down door. Carefully, Darion walked across the priory floor, stepping over upturned stones, and around half-crumbled pillars. Several small candles illuminated the stairwell in a dim, yellow glow. Darion's footsteps echoed as he climbed to a small chamber.

A man in a long brown cassock stood at the far end. As Darion entered he saw the glint of steel on either side of himself. Two men stood on guard, resting their hands on their swords.

"We expected more than just five of you," the frocked man said.

"We took causalities."

The man turned and studied Darion a moment. "You are not Simon. Where is he?"

The image of Simon's corpse burned in Darion's mind. He shifted uncomfortably. "He didn't make it."

"Quite unfortunate." The man pulled out a folded parchment, sealed in red wax. "You will find your captain at the Chateau de la Rose. Present this to the guards and they'll let you in."

Darion took the note, but before he could ask any questions, the abbot and his two sentinels were moving through a hidden side entrance. It opened and closed with a stony grunt, leaving Darion alone in the candlelight.

He returned to his party still huddled around the fire. Castel stood with arms crossed and his boot tapping the cold ground.

"Well?" he asked.

Darion held out the parchment. The lieutenant snatched it with an annoyed hand. His eyes grew to the size of saucers.

"By all the saints," he mumbled.

"What? What is it?"

"Do you not recognize the seal?"

"No."

"It's the device of the Catholic League, Darion. We long thought they were disbanded, but apparently we were mistaken."

Darion shuddered. The Catholic League was a major opponent during the civil wars. They pressured King Henry III into constant aggressions against his Huguenot subjects and constantly threatened to undermine the power of the crown. Henry III had hoped to vaporize that threat with the assassination of the League's two senior leaders—the Duc and Cardinal de Guise—but all it did was stir the hornet's nest, and cost the king his own life.

It was only after Henri of Navarre rose to the French throne, converted to Catholicism, and defeated the remaining League outposts did the venomous sermons, religious grievances, and cries for continued war dwindle. It had been a little more than a decade since the last League resistance. Now it appeared the League weren't wiped out but merely went into an extended hibernation.

"Are the men you met still here?" Castel asked.

"They disappeared through a hidden entrance along a wall. It's how they got past us without us hearing as much as spurs jingling in the distance."

"Think it leads to where Jacquelyna is?" Peppin asked.

"If it did, they would've just taken us there. They said the captain is at the Chateau de la Rose. Jacquelyna and the king's daughter must be there. Tremear wouldn't abandon them."

"The king must know about this," Castel added, his gaze still fixated on the paper in his hand. He headed for the horses as if the matter was settled.

"We don't have anyone to spare, Antoine," Darion said.

"And if we fail in our mission His Majesty may never know who's truly behind this."

Antoine stuffed the paper into his saddle bag and let loose the rein tied around a tree. Darion grabbed him by the arm.

"Are you listening to me, Antoine? This might be our last shot at freeing Jacquelyna and the king's daughter before another civil war breaks out."

Castel wrenched his arm free. He was clearly exasperated, but he nodded.

"Remy will take a note back to the highwaymen's chateau," the lieutenant ordered. "No doubt, our men are still there. Hopefully some reinforcements will have arrived by then, too."

Castel scribbled a short note and tied a ribbon around it. He handed it to the young Guardsman who leapt into his saddle, and spurred his horse south from the abbey.

"I hope you have a good fucking plan in that head of yours, Gascon," Peppin said in a murmur. "There's just four of us now."

"True, but you're about as wide as two," Darion quipped. Peppin smirked but Darion could see the worry in his friend's eyes.

"You know where this Chateau de la Rose is?" Castel asked.

"It's not far. A little south from here."

"Any idea how many men we might run into?"

"No. There's just Andre and the captain left from the highwaymen. And that Spanish viper. With any luck that's all we'll run into."

"Three against four ain't so bad," Pep said with some relief. "Especially with the element of surprise."

"The monk I met was guarded by two well-armed men I've never seen before. We have to assume there are more like that where we're going."

"So how are we getting in?"

"With that note."

Castel chuckled. "You plan on having us just walk through the front door?"

In truth, Darion wasn't sure what his plan was. He shrugged. "We shouldn't delay further," he said.

# XLI.
## Comte de Mauriac

"We may have bigger problems than the Spanish, Your Grace."

Jean-Girard Lecroix said as much as he stood before the Duc de Sully once again. The duke had been enjoying his breakfast with Francois Bassompierre—an appetizing meal of honeyed bread and smoked fish—but any pleasure the duke took in his morning repast dissipated with the chevalier's arrival.

"What do you mean?" Sully asked.

Lecroix reached into his doublet and pulled out the parchment. Sully wiped his hands on his breeches and snatched the paper from Lecroix's glove. He shot the chevalier a wary look as he spotted the drops of blood that speckled the paper. He turned the note over, to the side with the seal, and the rage and fear rose in the duke.

"Mother of God," he mumbled.

"What is it?" Bassompierre asked, dabbing a napkin to his lips.

"Our worst dreams realized."

He flipped the parchment open and read its contents. Bassompierre's steady gaze tried probing Lecroix for some sort of information. The chevalier merely shook his head.

"What is it?" Bassompierre asked again.

Duc de Sully rubbed his temples before burying his face into his hands. He then looked up at Lecroix like a man who had just been read his death sentence. He handed Bassompierre the letter. The courtier's face paled instantly.

"Mother of God, indeed," the courtier said. "The Catholic League has returned?"

"Alert the king and tell him I'll meet with him presently."

Bassompierre dashed through the side doors without as much as a bow.

"Paper. I need paper. And ink." Sully rushed to the main doors, his long silk and fur robe billowing behind him. He threw them open and thrust his head into the antechamber. "Ink! And paper! Quickly now!"

He sat back at the table and shoved the plate of bread, the bowl of honey, and the dish of smoked fish into a corner of the tabletop. A servant hurried in, carrying the necessary items for the duke. Sully dipped the quill into the well and scrawled a dispatch across the paper, finishing it with some powder to dry the ink. He raised his hands and looked around.

"Wax. Wax. I need wax. Quickly!"

The servant returned a moment later with a stick of red wax. Sully folded the letter into thirds and then melted the stick over a candle. He let some of the wax drip on the paper, licked his ring, then pressed it into the red blob.

"Take this to the Hôtel de Loudun," the duke told the servant, "and hand it directly to the Comte de Mauriac. No one else, understand?"

Lecroix perked. "The Comte de Mauriac has returned?"

"Late last night, and he was in great haste to get back into the saddle to find Mademoiselle Brocquart and the king's daughter. Alas, we had no real lead beyond that lone Spanish swordsman, but this goes well beyond Spain now. Well beyond. This changes everything, Chevalier. If the Catholic League is truly reforming and are behind this, well..."

The duke got lost in his own sea of thoughts. After wading through them, he shook his head.

"Does anyone else know of this letter's existence?"

Lecroix swallowed as he thought of Véronique standing among the butcher's shop's shadows, a bloody dagger in one hand and a smoking pistol in the other. What was her role in all this? Whose side was she for?

"Just the Comte de Gien. I was able to extract him last night, but he has no knowledge of the contents."

The duke nodded. "I need to dress before the count arrives." He vanished into a side room and returned several minutes later. By then,

Bassompierre had also returned, and the active sergeant of the Forty-Five had been summoned. The large oak dinner table was cleared of food and drink, and servants brought in rolls of maps and pewter figures. Soon the duke's eating area transformed into a small war room.

The large decorative doors opened. A herald stepped through.

"The Comte de Mauriac!" he announced.

All eyes turned to the door as the count strode through, dressed in a brocade silk doublet and tall leather boots. He wore a blackened cuirass over his doublet and a long, rich wool cloak hung from a single shoulder. An elegant sword hung at his side and glimmered in the morning light. Under his arm he carried his polished helm.

"You have news of Jacquelyna?" he asked in full stride.

"Somewhat," Sully said. "Last night the Chevalier d'Auch intercepted a letter of an agent involved in the kidnapping."

"Is it the Spanish? If so, lend me an army and I will march into the heart of Madrid to get her back if I must."

"Calm down, Martin. It's not the Spanish. At least, not entirely."

Sully tossed the paper down on the table. The count and the Guardsman sergeant inspected the seal.

"This can't be right," Mauriac said. "The League dissolved fifteen years ago. This has to be some Spanish trickery."

"Let us hope you're right, monsieur, but this feels authentic to me. If the League is allowed to grow they could throw us right back into civil war."

"We must stop them then. Does the note say where they're camped? Or who their leader is?"

"I'm afraid not. We're still in the dark in regards to where. At least we know who we're up against. It's not much, but it's better than where we were yesterday."

The count punched the table. "So where is she?"

Young. Hot blooded. Lecroix had seen that disposition on the faces of many young generals and princes of France. The same type of men who led France into blood and fire for decades.

"We don't know. I wanted to alert you because of your strong familiar ties with the Comte de Gien and his family. And also because you are familiar with the nobles of court."

"You think there are traitors in our midst?" Lecroix asked.

"Court is the best place for them. To hide. To observe. To learn. At the very least we should keep a watchful eye on those with previous connections to the Catholic League."

"Agreed," Bassompierre chimed in.

"Shall I dispatch the men to follow your suspects?" the sergeant asked.

"No," Sully said. "We don't want to spook the roost."

"Then what are we to do, eh?" the Mauriac asked. "Sit on our thumbs?"

"While Henry was fighting for his coronation, we received rumors of several League bases in the French countryside." The duke's long, slender fingers brushed the edge of the map and stopped at three distinct areas. "One outside of Tours. Another somewhere in Brittany. And a third along the coast of Provence. We should start our searches there."

"That could take months. None of those locations are specific enough for a proper search, and it's been fifteen years. They could've moved elsewhere. Somewhere more secret. More secure."

"It's all we have to work with at the moment."

The count hung his head and grunted. "What's your plan then, Your Grace?"

"We dispatch three companies. One led by you to Brittany. One by Monsieur Bassompierre to Tours. And the Chevalier to—"

The duke was interrupted by the doors opening. A Guardsman staggered through, held up by the duke's servant. His riding boots were caked in dirt and mud, his doublet and cloak tattered and disheveled. His face was covered in grime and dried blood, and his eyes carried the burden of a poor night's sleep. The sergeant met the Guardsman partway. They spoke briefly. The Guardsman pulled out a rolled up note from his glove and handed it to the sergeant.

"Get yourself a drink, monsieur," the sergeant said. He then presented the note to Sully.

"What news?" Mauriac asked.

Sully read the letter. "The Forty-Five under Lieutenant Castel's lead has befallen a great misfortune. They were ambushed by the highwaymen and took heavy casualties. In the end, they prevailed. Not all was lost, however. In the process, they learned of a possible second location of the abductors. They're heading there now but could use reinforcements."

"I will go," Mauriac said.

"As will I," Lecroix added.

"Sergeant," Sully said, "prepare a full retinue of your men. You are to ride out with the Comte de Mauriac and the Chevalier d'Auch. Hand pick your best men. Take all of them if need be."

"We'll be ready within three hours," the sergeant said.

"Make it two," the count interjected.

The sergeant bowed and left.

"I will prepare my things," Mauriac announced to the rest. He then faced Lecroix. "I shall meet you at the Guardsmen Gate in less than two hours."

The chevalier nodded. The count marched out, his long cloak trailing behind. Lecroix remained behind.

"I understand the need to keep a keen eye out for traitors at court, but I also fear it'll turn the court against one another," Lecroix said.

"I understand the concern, Chevalier, but we will keep this knowledge secret for now," Sully said. "It should minimalize the chance of potential damage."

Lecroix inclined his head. "Your Grace, is there any mention of my nephew in that letter?"

"I'm afraid not."

"I see."

"Is there anything you'd have me do, Your Grace?" Bassompierre asked.

The king burst through the side doors, half dressed and a look of rage on his face. He stormed toward the three men.

"There is, in fact. Help me keep a level head about the king." He turned to Lecroix. "You best get going before you get caught in the king's tempest. You have your orders, Chevalier. Don't fail me."

# XLII.
## The Hero in the Mirror

The windows rattled. The wind howled. It was as if the outside world was trying to shake free Jacquelyna's and Gabrielle's bonds. But if the world wanted them free it'd need to do more than just rattle the windows. It'd need to blow the roof off the chateau and whisk her away back to Paris. She smiled sadly—another childhood fantasy destroyed.

The moon shone bright and full. Branches of the willow trees swayed and rustled, adding to nature's symphony blustering in the night. She closed her eyes and listened, praying for some news to be carried on the wind, but she heard nothing. That, surprisingly, comforted her. Bauvet said the riders sent to her father should've been back by now. Yet no one had come to the chateau.

That wasn't entirely true. A small group of men came and went from the chateau during the course of the evening. They didn't look like the highwaymen. These new men were different. They were better dressed, their swords were nicer in design and polished to a sharp sheen. Guards posted outside bore fringed halberds, and they all carried themselves with a different air than the highwaymen. A bit more arrogance—or perhaps righteousness. These new men weren't common thieves and bandits, she mused. Whatever danger she was in before didn't compare to her new predicament.

The door latch unlocked. Bauvet and Captain Tremear stepped in and moored themselves on either side of the doorway. A third man, tall and wearing a long cloak with gold and silver trim along the edges, stepped between them. Beneath his cloak Jacquelyna spied a doublet of blue and green silk with slashed sleeves and fine hose. He rested a jeweled hand upon his rapier. Its golden hilt glimmered brighter than the lantern illuminating him. He peered at her with startling blue eyes beneath a tall crown hat. Around his nose and mouth he wore a large cloth, shielding his identity from her. But from the way he gazed at her, Jacquelyna was sure they'd met before.

Tremear displayed Gabrielle Angélique and Jacquelyna like they were exotic beasts at a zoo. Bauvet looked on with reservation, but this new man, this masked gentleman gazed at them both with a severe and calculated indifference.

The masked man never said a word. He merely nodded occasionally as Tremear briefed him on what had taken place and the precautions put in place to keep the king's men at bay. And all through it the masked gentleman remained stoic. The only time any sense of emotion stirred in him was when Tremear mentioned having to execute Darion and Peppin for being king's agents. A cold fire burned in this gentleman's eyes, but he seemed satisfied enough with the traitors' ends. Then he left the room, followed by the captain. Bauvet lingered a moment, his eyes full of remorse, but he did not speak. He then left and closed the door behind him.

Whistling permeated through the door, followed by a wooden chair being dragged across the floor. Her custodian for the evening, no doubt.

Jacquelyna gazed into the mirror to find a face tired and fatalistic. Her hair, usually in tight curls beneath her bonnet, fell loosely about her shoulders. Her face was dusted with dirt and grime, and heavy, dark bags hung below her eyes. The flickering from several candles on the table only seemed to accentuate her flaws. It amazed her that this was the same face that so many men tried to woo. She almost didn't recognize herself. Yet it was the face of the only person she could trust, the face of the only person who could free her from her shackles now. And if she failed, at least she would do so knowing she didn't sit idly by while others controlled her fate.

Her plan was simple: sneak past her guard and slip out the side door with Gabrielle. The stables weren't far from the chateau and a horse could probably fit through the gap in the stone wall that blocked them from the countryside. If she could get to the nearest town, she could hire a ride back to Paris. To home. To safety.

The key would be sneaking passed her guard. Part of her hoped it wasn't Bauvet. In this den of vipers, he was the closest thing to a friend she had. But he had done nothing to ease her and Gabrielle's condition, so she wouldn't shed too much of a tear if it was. What she feared more, however, was that the Spanish swordsman was her caretaker. His distant and unsympathetic gaze chilled her to the core, and she heard the whispers among the highwaymen about his prowess with a blade. If there ever was a devil in human form, she was sure he was it, and she didn't find comfort in the idea of having to get by him. Anyone else, even Captain Tremear and his vicious grin, would be preferable to the Spaniard.

She paced back and forth for what felt like an eternity, her fingers fidgeting and hands trembling. A few times she gazed upon Gabrielle sleeping soundly on top of the bed. For a moment she considered waking the young girl up, just in case they needed to make a hasty retreat, but she decided against it. What she was about to do was not meant for such young, innocent eyes.

She lifted the cloak from a wide, velvet covered chair, revealing the kitchen knife she smuggled from the tavern. She looked at it longingly. The steel gleamed in the candlelight, and the serrated edge of the blade seemed to yearn to do its work. As a young girl Jacquelyna lived for her mother's stories of gallant knights and mythical swords. She often imagined herself being whisked away by such a brave gentleman, to live happily ever. It wasn't until now, as she stood in the dim room with nothing but her reflection and the kitchen knife for true company, did she understand why so many men raced to pick up the sword.

She breathed deep and went to the door. She knocked.

"What?" a gruff voice said from the other side. A Frenchman. She was relieved.

"I... I need to take care of some business," she replied.

"What? What business?"

"The type that a gentleman shouldn't ask of a woman."

There was a moment of silence. "Use the blasted chamber pot."

"There isn't one."

"Like hell there isn't."

"I'm not lying. On my honor. Come and look if you don't believe me."

The chair feet scraped against the floor. Metal jingled as the guard futzed with the lock and latch. Jacquelyna stepped back as the door swung open. The guard wasn't overly tall nor as gruff as he sounded. His beard was neatly trimmed, and he wore what looked to be a new leather jerkin over a clean black doublet and breeches.

"Did you check under the bed?"

"I tried, but it's not easy to bend over in this dress."

The guard rolled his eyes and made for the bed. Jacquelyna's heart began to race. Every fiber in her being screamed for her to forget her plan and to play it safe and submissive. But she beat that fear back into the darkest corner of her soul and watched as the guard dropped to a knee he looked under the bed.

"Hand me a candle." Jacquelyna hesitated. "A light, dammit."

She grabbed a candle and handed it to him. He lowered it under the bed.

"It's right here where it should—"

Jacquelyna plunged forward with the knife, sliding it into the guard's neck. The next sound to pass his lips was him squalling in pain. He reeled back and reached for the hilt of the knife. Blood spewed out from the wound. Jacquelyna turned white and backed away. The guard groaned and yowled like a mewling pup, and she feared one of the other men would hear him. She grabbed a pillow from the bed and placed it over his mouth. His eyes flared in surprise as she forced him to the floor. With one hand she held the pillow and with another she ripped the knife from his throat and shoved it between his ribs. She pulled it out and drove it in once more. And again. And again. She didn't stop piercing the guard until he grew limp and silent.

Jacquelyna began to sob. She stared at the corpse and the dark fluid pooling beneath him. His eyes were still wide but empty, and lips permanently frozen in fear. It chilled her to her very core. She sat there, numb and mindless. Gabrielle awoke with an irritated groan.

With blood-slicked hands, Jacquelyna pushed a few strands of hair from her face. She threw on her cloak, wiping her hands as best she could, and then grabbed Gabrielle's cloak.

"It's time to go see your father," she said in an unsteady voice.

The little girl rubbed her eyes, then looked at Jacquelyna curiously. "Father is here?"

"Not here, but we're going to go see him now. Here, put this on." She wrapped the girl's cloak around Gabrielle's shoulders and fastened it at the front with the brooch. Jacquelyna futzed over her own cloak when she noticed Gabrielle staring at the guard's corpse.

"He's just sleeping," Jacquelyna said, forcing a smile. "We need to be very quiet not to wake him or anyone else. Understand?"

Gabrielle nodded. Jacquelyna led the girl by the hand across a small chamber down the hall. They did their best to stick to the shadows, rushing from dark spot to dark spot like chapel mice. They made their way down a set of steps. Jacquelyna poked out her head from the doorway. The room was empty. The only signs of life came from long shadows escaping the great hall down the corridor.

She squeezed Gabrielle's hand. "This way, darling."

There was a back entrance that led to the side courtyard. Jacquelyna had paid close attention to the layout of the chateau and its manor when they arrived. Once outside Jacquelyna and Gabrielle could easily sneak to the stable and ride off into the night.

Jacquelyna pushed open a large oak door. It groaned on its hinges. Jacquelyna guided Gabrielle down a flight of stone steps. The wind blew harshly, slicing right through her cloak and the fabric of her dress. She shivered, but at least she was outside, away from Bauvet. Away from Captain Tremear. Away from the new swordsmen and the Spanish viper. It was a small step but a start. Torches illuminated iron gates at the bottom of the steps and behind it, one of the willow trees swayed, begging her to follow.

A callous hand grabbed her from behind. She tried to scream—why, she didn't know—but a dark hand muffled her voice. The man gripped her tightly against himself. She could smell the garlic on his breath.

"Ssshh," he said in a low voice. "I'm not going to hurt you. Shhh." She continued to struggled. Gabrielle backed away slowly into a shadowy corner. "You need to stop fighting me. Stop it, dammit."

Jacquelyna wouldn't stop struggling. She reached in her cloak and felt the wooden grip of the knife. She pulled it out and blindly drove it behind her head. The man released her and grabbed her wrist before the blade hit its mark. He wrenched her arm, and the knife clanged against the ground. She moaned softly in pain and backed toward where Gabrielle was. She had to protect the child. She *had* to protect the girl.

"For the love of God, woman," the man said, stepping into the pale light. "It's Andre."

"What are you doing out here?"

"I could ask you the same thing but that would be silly, wouldn't it?" Jacquelyna eyed the gate. She could still try to run for it. She wouldn't make it, of course, but at least she'd die trying, she thought. "Don't even think about it. There are a few other men just around the corner keeping watch."

Bauvet's brow furrowed. He pulled back the edge of Jacquelyna's cloak, revealing the dark, bloody stain on her dress.

"'Steeth," he mumbled. Jacquelyna grabbed Gabrielle and turned for the gate. Bauvet slid to his left, blocking their path. "No."

Anger and desperation swelled within her. If she didn't escape now, there was no escape at all.

"I won't go back in there," she said in a determined and resolved tone. "I won't, so you either take that dagger and plunge into my heart right now or let me through."

Bauvet narrowed his eyes in contemplation. He stood there, still in the cold breeze, but the wind nor the highwayman's piercing gaze bothered Jacquelyna. For once she felt in control in her life. Too bad she wouldn't live long enough to enjoy it, she thought.

"No, I won't let you through. But I won't murder you either."

"Then what?"

He bit his lower lip.

"Shit," he said, his voice resigned. "Follow me."

He took off without waiting, walking briskly up the stairs with his cloak billowing behind him. For a moment Jacquelyna had half a mind of grabbing Gabrielle and running through those iron gates, but something compelled her to follow Bauvet. He could've called for the guards if he wanted. She picked up the kitchen knife, took Gabrielle by the hand, and followed. Through the back entrance they went and down the corridor guarded by the long shadows. Bauvet was taking them past the great hall where she could hear the men's merriment taking place. He stopped before they reached the hall. Urgency tinged his face.

"When we get to the hall I'll step into the doorway to block people's vision. You and the girl hurry by as fast as you can, understand?"

Jacquelyna nodded and took a deep breath. She placed a hand over her heart trying to escape her chest. Bauvet filled the threshold with his body and his enormous wool cloak. Jacquelyna and Gabrielle hurried across. As she passed, she glanced into the room filled with the men drinking and gambling.

Bauvet spun from the doorway. "Let's go. And quickly now."

Jacquelyna and Gabrielle kept to the shadows of the hall while Bauvet led the way. He pushed open a small oak door and back into the cold night.

Hooves rumbled in the distance and Jacquelyna froze. What if that was one of the highwaymen messengers returning with news that her father wouldn't pay the ransom? They'd surely go to her room right away and find her gone. It didn't give her much of a head start. They'd probably cut her down this time—just like Madam de Mailly.

"This way, mademoiselle," Bauvet said.

She followed at a pace as brisk as the wind in her face. Just ahead was the stable cast in a silvery glow from the full moon. There was nothing but open space between them and the stables, and she prayed to God and all the saints that none of her captors were star gazing through the windows.

Like rabbits they scurried across the open field, Bauvet leading with one hand on the hilt of his sword while Jacquelyna dragged a weary Gabrielle along.

"Wait here," Bauvet said at the mouth of the stable. "I'll saddle a horse for you."

Jacquelyna wrapped the cloak tighter around her shoulders. Her eyes fixated on the chateau, looking for any sign of movement or being spied upon. But it seemed the festivities were kept mostly on the opposite side of the chateau. Only a single room was lit up in a yellowish glow, but thin curtains were drawn over the window, and no one yet had peered between them.

A band of clouds passed over the moon. The stable and field fell into darkness. Jacquelyna's fingers throbbed and her ears pricked. How she and the child would survive the night's ride in the elements, she didn't know. What she did know was they had to try.

Bauvet returned a few minutes later with a brown mare prepped and saddled to leave. But something was wrong or perhaps just different with the highwayman. She saw a glimmer of sadness in the highwayman's battered face. Yet he tried to hide that melancholy behind a veil of calmness.

"Head south. There's a town there where you can get provisions. Here's a few coins for it." He handed Jacquelyna a small purse. "It's not much but it's something. You can tell the Gascon he can pay me back someday."

"Thank you."

The highwayman helped her to the saddle and then lifted Gabrielle and placed her in front of Jacquelyna.

"Take care of Darion will you? He's a good man. Probably better than the rest of us lot."

Jacquelyna frowned. "I'll see what I can do. And if you ever leave here, well..."

Her words trailed off and not because she couldn't muster the courage to finish them. Just beyond the highwayman a silhouette shifted. At first the man was barely visible, just a black imprint on a blacker background. But as he continued forward and into a patch of moonlight his features fell into focus—a sharp, aquiline nose, sunken and scarred cheeks that betrayed the bearer's harsh life, and perfectly trimmed beard in the shape of a spade. But what truly frightened her was the brooding and somber gleam that appeared in the man's bi-colored eyes. Jacquelyna gasped and the sudden appearance of the Spaniard even forced Bauvet to retreat a step.

"What are you doing here?" Bauvet asked. He held out his arm as if to protect Jacquelyna and Gabrielle from harm, even though they remained safely mounted on a horse.

"I could ask you the same thing, señor," the swordsman replied. "A bit late for a ride, señorita, no? Especially in this cold and covered in all that blood."

Jacquelyna remained silent. She didn't want to gratify the Spaniard with any sort of response. Or perhaps she was too scared to say a word.

"Turn around, Gonzalo," Bauvet said. "Turn around before it's too late."

A subtle smile slipped onto the Spaniard's lips. He threw back the edge of his black cloak, revealing two long rapiers.

"There is still time to save your body and soul, señor. Hand over the girls and all will be forgiven and forgotten. Otherwise, prepare to spend eternity in Hell for helping these two heretics."

Bauvet peered over his shoulder at Jacquelyna and Gabrielle. He looked exasperated, and Jacquelyna wondered if he would follow through with his promise—turn them over to save his own skin.

"Ride. And ride hard," he said. He gave the horse a hard slap on its rear, sending the beast and its two riders galloping across the field, nearly trampling the Spaniard in the process. They made it to the edge of the chateau when two guards with halberds appeared in their way. They took defensive postures, bracing their weapons by their feet and aiming them straight for the horse. She pulled on the reins, and the horse neighed wildly. Gabrielle cried.

Jacquelyna reached for the knife at her side. Maybe she could surprise them like she did the last guard. But four more armed men came rushing from behind the two sentinels. One man she could surprise attack, two would be pushing the limit, but six men was an impossibility.

The four new swordsmen drew their swords. The soft, leather noise each blade made sent Jacquelyna's heart deeper into despair.

"Secure these two," one of the guards said.

"As you wish," a familiar voice answered.

Two blades materialized through the guards' chests. They dropped their halberds, and their mustachioed faces twisted in surprise before collapsing to the ground. The swordsmen stepped into the moonlight. One lifted the brim of his wide hat.

"Time to go," Darion said.

## XLIII.
## A Song of Swords

The metallic song of swords rang out not far from where Darion stood. He peered into the darkness but only caught a few glimpses of silver flashes here and there.

"What's going on back there?" Peppin asked.

"Not sure," Castel said, "but I don't care to stick around long enough to find out."

"It's Andre," Jacquelyna said, her eyes full of worry. "He's fighting that Spaniard. You need to go help him."

"What?" Darion asked.

"He helped me get as far as I did. You need to help him, Darion."

"We don't have fucking time for this," Castel said. "We have what we came for. We need to move before more men arrive."

The lieutenant's face was grim and grew darker with each moment they delayed. Darion shot a glance at Peppin who raised his eye in a way that suggested he was of the same mind as Castel. But the most somber of the group was Jacquelyna. There was a pleading tenderness in her sapphire eyes that softened Darion to the core. He knew it. She knew it. He hadn't seen that look since the night she beseeched him to give up his duel with Sergeant Barrière.

"Shit," Darion mumbled. "I'm a damn fool." He turned to Castel. "Get them out of here and back to safety. I won't be far behind."

He took off running.

"Darion, wait!" Castel said.

Darion didn't answer and didn't look back. He just hoped that

Castel still hated him enough to abandon him to whatever ill-fate lay ahead.

The ringing of steel on steel became louder. The flashing of silver swipes grew more regular. He heard men grunting and swearing. Clouds left the room, revealing a dismal scene. Bauvet wielded his rapier in one hand while he pressed the other tightly against his chest. He flashed his maimed arm out when he needed to reinforce a parry, but he'd press the arm right back to his chest thereafter. Bearing down on him was the Spaniard, wielding two long, cup-hilt rapiers that dripped red like venom from a viper's fang. He flicked one blade out that Bauvet parried and then thrust with the other. Bauvet threw out his maimed arm and took another blow across it. He cried out and stumbled back a step.

Darion used the shadows to his advantage. As he fell into range, he lunged at the Spaniard, hoping to catch him off guard. Alas, moonlight hit the edge of Darion's blade, betraying his presence. The Spaniard spun and parried, but not before the tip of Darion's sword embedded itself into the swordsman's forearm. The rogue bellowed an oath in his native tongue and struck out with a quick downward thrust from his other blade. Darion, unprepared for such a quick riposte, used his free arm to fend off the attack. The rapier's cold edge grazed Darion's arm, making his flesh prickle and burn.

"What the fuck are you doing here, Gascon?" Bauvet said. "I thought I told you to never come back."

"You know how well I take orders, Andre." He threw two sweeping cuts to keep the Spaniard at bay.

"Go now! Jacquelyna and the bastard are already gone."

"She's the reason I'm here helping your sorry ass."

Darion wanted to display a comforting grin to his friend, but his eyes were preoccupied with the Spaniard who renewed his attack. Darion had hoped his thrust would've at least disabled Gonzalo's sword arm, but the Spaniard lifted both blades without a care. Darion reached behind his cloak and drew the main gauche resting by his kidney. He knew he'd need every inch of steel he could get.

The Spaniard's blades flared in and out, alternating between cuts and thrusts in a whirlwind fashion. Darion had faced many fine blades in his short time, but this Spaniard was leagues beyond any of them. Every time Darion moved to exploit an opening the Spaniard countered, closing him off and locking the line.

The Spaniard's teeth set in a white, amused sneer. His blade work was so fine and crisp that Darion couldn't even risk rushing forward to shank him in the gut. Darion would more likely skewer himself on the Spaniard's sword.

Like a bolt from Zeus, came a bright flash and a thunderous boom of an harquebus. The Spaniard reeled back, one of his swords flying out of his hands. Darion whirled around to find Peppin standing there with a wide, crooked grin about his face.

"If you're done playing, Gascon, we got to move."

"Guards! Men of Truth Faith and Sword!" the Spaniard yelled, retreating and checking his wound. "To me!"

The chateau doors burst open and out poured a handful of half-dressed men armed with swords and daggers.

"Shit," Bauvet said. "We're not going to be able to outrun them."

"Pep, we could use a little distraction," Darion said.

"Already on it." Peppin pulled from his pouch two small grenades. He put his match cord to one fuse and blew. It sparked and sizzled in a bright light. He handed it to Darion and prepared a second grenade. "Don't fail me now, my loves," he said, giving the second grenade a kiss. "Peppin wants a big boom."

They lofted the grenades into the middle of the Leaguers. The men's faces whitened. They stumbled and scrambled to get away from the iron balls. Even the unshakable Spaniard felt the need to put distance between himself and the explosive.

Darion, Peppin, and Bauvet were halfway to the ruined wall when the grenades exploded. The trees ahead of them reflected the sharp light. Darion's chest rumbled from the shockwave. It spurred them to move faster.

When they reached the wall Darion glanced at the mayhem behind them. Most of the swordsmen had managed to escape the blast area, but a few were still close enough to be knocked down by the force. There was chaos among their ranks, but Darion knew that wouldn't last long. Captain Tremear was out among them now, along with a cloaked and masked figure. Darion and Bauvet mounted one horse and Peppin the other. They put boot to flank, and the horses darted through the small wooded area toward the main road.

Peppin's "loves" bought them some time. Darion just prayed it was enough.

# XLIV.
## Choices

Jacquelyna paced back and forth by a large window, peering into the distance. She hoped to hear horses charging from the horizon, but the night remained still and the horizon vacant of both friend and foe.

"You shouldn't stand so close to the window, mademoiselle," Castel said. He pulled a heavy red curtain over it. She looked at him crossly. "Wouldn't want anyone to see you. Besides, the fire's warmer."

She turned toward the fireplace. The innkeeper's wife poked at the fire, sending the flames into a slight frenzy. In front of the fire lay Gabrielle. Her eyes were fighting against the sleep that was trying to envelope her. The stress and excitement of their situation had eluded the young girl. Fortunate for her, Jacquelyna thought.

They had arrived at the inn at Caudebec in quick time. Horses were needed, and they took refuge in an inn while new mounts were procured. Jacquelyna pulled the curtain back a little to peer out over the moonlit road.

"We can't delay," Castel said. "Once carriage and horses are set we need to leave."

"Carriage? Won't that slow us down?"

"It's the safest way to transport you and the princess. I dare not ride that long and hard with the girl on a saddle unless I absolutely must."

"What if those men overtake us?"

"The more reason to leave as soon as we can."

"What about Darion? And Peppin?"

Castel hesitated. "They're good fighters, Jacquelyna. With any luck they'll get out of there intact."

"We shouldn't have left them there."

"They bought us some precious time. Besides, they know the way back to Paris. I will admit I suspect Darion will head anywhere but there."

A creased formed in Jacquelyna's brow. "Why's that?"

The lieutenant looked at her oddly. "Because he's a deserter, and a highwayman that attacked an emissary of the king. He's a wanted man, and if he's lucky, he'll get a quick death. He'd be a fool to return to Paris."

"You can't let them do that, Antoine. He's your friend!"

"He hasn't been my friend for many years. You know that."

"Do his efforts to rescue me and Gabrielle mean naught?"

The lieutenant took off his hat and looked at her with a serious eye. "Perhaps if he did all this for the king it would. But it wasn't anyone in the king's employ that freed him."

She shook her head wildly. "I don't understand. What does it matter what his motives are?"

Squeaking of the floor boards in the next room interrupted their conversation. Castel pulled the pistol from his belt and readied it–just in case–but it was a Guardsman. He was young and handsome, but with a look of a man who could handle himself in a fight. Jacquelyna recognized him from guarding the king at court, but she hadn't a clue what his name was.

"The coach is just about ready, sir," he said.

Castel turned to Jacquelyna. "I'm sorry, but we need to go. For her sake." The lieutenant gestured to Gabrielle sleeping soundly by the fire. So peaceful. So innocent. She had suffered greatly and unnecessarily as it was. Jacquelyna knew she couldn't let her own wants and desires rise above Gabrielle's safety.

Jacquelyna moved to where the young girl slept and shook her awake. "Come, darling," she said. "It's time to go see your father."

The young girl smiled and reached out with her hands. Castel dropped to a knee and picked her up, holding her tightly against his chest and shoulder.

Four grey horses led a small black coach. The horses stamped on the ground, as ready to leave this wretched place as Jacquelyna was.

The young Guardsman stood next to the door of the coach while holding the reins of a beautiful white horse. He opened the coach upon seeing them.

"Thank you," Castel said. He stepped partially into the carriage and laid Gabrielle down on the seat. He grabbed an extra wool blanket offered by the innkeeper's wife and laid it over the young girl. He turned to Jacquelyna. "I'll be riding by your side the entire way. Gregoire will be leading your team."

Jacquelyna nodded and swallowed her despair. She was about to step into the coach when she caught the sound of clamoring hooves in the distance. She moved around the coach to get a view.

"Jacquelyna," Castel said, "we must be going immediately."

She peered at the horizon. Following on a cold breeze emerged the silhouettes of two dark figures on horseback racing toward them.

"Riders are coming!" Gregoire said. "Two of them! No. Make that three. Three men. Two horses. A scouting party?"

"If so, they won't be returning with any information to report," Castel said. He pulled his pistol from his belt and grabbed a second one from his saddle holster. Meanwhile, Gregoire readied his harquebus and took refuge at the edge of the coach. "Get ready to fire on my mark. Jacquelyna, get in the carriage. Should any more than these two appear I'm sending your coach off without us, understand?"

Jacquelyna nodded but didn't move. Something told her they wouldn't be traveling alone. One rider was short and portly while the other was lean and carried a second, broader man with him.

"Hold your fire, you assholes!" Peppin's voice boomed.

Jacquelyna yelled. Gregoire tried to hold her back, but she slipped past him and to the approaching horsemen.

"Darion! Peppin!" she said. "I thought we'd lost you."

Darion bared a meek but pleasant grin. His blue gaze then reached the lieutenant. "We have about a dozen or so Leaguers on our tail, and they're not exactly in a sociable mood."

"Leaguers? The Catholic League?" Jacquelyna asked.

"It's a long, complicated story, love," Peppin answered.

"We can't stay here," Darion continued. "Is the coach ready?"

"Yes," Castel said.

"Then we need to move. And quickly!"

Castel spun on his heel. "You heard him! Go! Move! To Paris!"

Gregoire leapt to the coach seat. Jacquelyna lingered, hoping to catch Darion's gaze before they left. She noticed a distant glint in his eyes, like he was lost in the sea of his own thoughts.

"Get in the coach, mademoiselle," he said, finally. "We can't linger longer."

She frowned but got into the coach. She had spent so much time in a carriage that she had grown sick of them. She would've preferred to have walked back to Paris if wasn't for the fact they were being hunted down. At least this coach was taking her toward liberty and not captivity.

Bauvet labored his way into the coach. He sat across from her and the king's daughter. He closed the door and almost immediately a whip cracked. The coach rumbled forward; Bauvet lurched and groaned.

"You're injured," Jacquelyna mused. He pressed a bloody arm against his chest and his breeches were also stained red.

"What gave it away?"

"Don't be a child. How bad is it?"

"I can't move my fingers."

"Anything I can do?"

The highwayman shrugged. "Not unless you're a physician. Or a barber-surgeon. Or perhaps a miracle worker." Bauvet adjusted his seating with some agony. "Darion said you sent him to get me."

"You risked your life for me."

"So you risked sacrificing the Gascon?" He chuckled softly.

"You could've handed me back over, but didn't. I couldn't leave while you got cut down."

Bauvet leaned his head against the wall and closed his eyes.

Darion was riding not far from her side, his eyes fixated coolly toward home. The steel of his sword and dagger clanged together as his horse clattered through patches of moonlight. She noticed a certain stoicism about him that she had not seen before. She had seen him laugh, seen him fumble through in his nervousness, seen him smolder in the embers of his own anger, but rarely had she seen the hardness in his eyes, the rigidness of his jaw and the calmness of body. She only heard about that side of Darion from his friends on the nights when they drank too much wine and shared too much of their tales. She couldn't help but smile thinking of those stories. Peppin told them the best, of course—drunk or sober. She wanted to call out Darion's name and thank him for what he had done, but fleeing from a band of cutthroats wasn't exactly the most opportune time for it. And there was another matter—perhaps even more important—that she needed to discuss with him.

The coach and three horses raced through the countryside. The sound of thundering hooves, horses breathing heavy, and the wooden wheels of the carriage creaking were her symphony toward freedom. Once in a while Jacquelyna would pull back the coach's curtain and look out. The sky once so dark and foreboding began to lighten in the distance. Morning was just around the corner, and with that Paris and safety from the highwaymen and the Leaguers.

They pulled into a small village. The coach came to a stop but no one opened the side door. She heard the Guardsman, Gregoire, step down from his seat and shuffle off, as well as the scuffling of boots on frozen ground from the others.

"Wait here," Bauvet said. He looked sickly, but he exited the coach nonetheless, albeit with a groan, and closed the door behind him.

Jacquelyna huddled herself in the corner to keep warm, figuring someone would alert her as to what was happening. But no one did. She heard a knock and then muffled voices. She pulled back the curtain of the coach. Darion had a hand on a stable boy's shoulder. He spoke to the boy in a calm but serious tone, though Jacquelyna couldn't make out exactly what he was saying. He then gave the boy an encouraging push, and the stable boy jetted off like a rabbit.

He turned to the rest of the company, his shoulders sagging with fatigue—or was it dejection? Jacquelyna couldn't tell. She wasn't used to seeing Darion in either state. He spoke with the rest of the group—Peppin, Antoine, Bauvet, and Gregoire. Their voices were soft and hushed at first but quickly grew louder and more agitated. They were trying to figure out what to do next, and it didn't seem like any of them had a clear plan. Jacquelyna glanced at Gabrielle. They needed to get the king's daughter back to Paris. That's all that mattered to Jacquelyna now. That's all that ever truly mattered.

Jacquelyna opened the coach door. A cold breeze greeted her, and she tightened the cloak around her body. The men's bickering stopped as she approached. They glanced at her and each other as if their conversation was a grand secret and had nothing to do with her. She scowled at the thought.

"What's the matter?" she asked.

They all remained quiet a moment.

"Nothing," Castel said. "Get back into the coach, if you please. It's warmer there."

"It's cold everywhere, Andre. Besides, I want to know what's happening? Did we lose the highwaymen? Or Leaguers. Whoever they are?"

"No," Darion said, crossing his arms. "They could be upon us any moment."

She looked at them all in disbelief. "Then why are we just standing here?"

"We need fresh horses, but they don't have enough for us all."

"So?"

"With the coach it means they'll overtake us regardless. We can't run."

"Nor can we make a stand," Peppin sighed. "We're far outnumbered."

"What if we barricade ourselves in the inn?" she asked.

"We're almost out of ammunition," the lieutenant said. "We wouldn't last ten minutes before they busted through the door."

Silence again overtook the group. The men's eyes darted between them as if what they said was enough, and Jacquelyna should return to her coach and wait for them to come upon a plan. She knew that, but she didn't budge. She had been through too much, fought too hard to get herself free to put her fate back into the hands of someone else—even if they were honorable loved ones.

Her eyes scanned the horizon. To the east there were a few rolling hills. It would provide some cover but not much and not for very long. To the south were flat open fields. To the west were more large hills. She knew from her days riding the countryside as a child that the highwaymen would surely see them from the hill, regardless of which direction they traveled. Her brow then crinkled. Perhaps they could use that disadvantage to their benefit.

"I have an idea," she said.

Castel cracked a smile. "That's all well and good but—"

"Let her speak," Darion said. Castel glowered.

"We need to distract the highwaymen," she continued, ignoring their childish bickering. "We need to make them think we're somewhere that we're not, right?"

Peppin chuckled. "Did you learn some sorcery while you were gone because that's what it would take, deary."

"What if we sent the coach running east. The highwaymen would see it and make chase, would they not?"

"They won't fall for that," Castel said. "There's too many of us."

"They don't know how many of us there are, right? For all they know there's just me, Pep, Darion, Andre, and Gabrielle."

The lieutenant gazed at her eagerly. "And what do we do while we send a coach charging aimlessly into the dawn?"

She shrugged. "Wait for them to take the bait?"

"You know how much I care about your opinion," Peppin began, "and it's a fine plan and all. A fine plan except that—"

"It'll work," Darion said. Everyone looked at him with wide eyes. Even Jacquelyna was surprised by the vote of confidence. "It'll work. The Leaguers will make chase and it'll give us time to head back to Paris. By the time they know what is happening it'll be too late."

"Perhaps, but—"

"It'll work. We need to get everyone in the inn now though."

Castel relented with a nod. He headed for the innkeeper who was still rubbing the sleepiness from his eyes. Jacquelyna entered, followed by Gregoire who carried a sleeping Gabrielle, and Bauvet limped in tow. Gregoire laid the young girl on some blankets near the hearth and posted himself by the backdoor, harquebus in hand. Bauvet dragged a chair across the floor and slumped into it near one of the windows. His wounds seemed to have stopped bleeding, but he looked like hell.

Jacquelyna looked outside. Darion and Peppin spoke by the coach. Darion had his arms crossed and his face, dirty and bearded, held a grim expression about it. Peppin's eyes were animated; he scratched the back of his neck and shook his head in a pessimistic manner. At the end of their conversation, Darion gave Peppin a hard slap on the shoulder, but Peppin drew him in for a friendly embrace. Peppin then shrugged and headed for the inn, his head hung between his broad shoulders. He looked up toward the window only briefly, but it was long enough for Jacquelyna to see the look of despair on his face. Something was wrong. Very, very wrong.

She rushed out of the inn, nearly bowling into Peppin as she did.

"Jacquelyna," he said. But it was no use. All of this was because of her and she needed to fix it—whatever *it* was.

"You sure you want to do this, Gascon?" Castel asked Darion, holding the reins as Darion lifted himself up into the driver's bench.

"It's the only way, Antoine."

Darion caught a glimpse of Jacquelyna advancing and gestured to the lieutenant. Castel stepped to intercept her, but she pushed through him.

"What are you doing?" she asked Darion. In truth she knew what he was doing, but she couldn't believe it. She didn't want to.

"Doing what I must to keep you all safe," he said. Darion didn't look at her; his eyes were fixated on his boots. "It's my fault you're all in this mess."

"It's not. It's not, Darion. You're not the one that set this up."

Darion shrugged and glanced up. She saw softness in his eyes. They seemed to have much they wanted to share but didn't. She wondered if her own eyes betrayed her thus, betrayed her true feelings, and the secret she kept from him. She almost spoke out in sheer desperation, but he blinked, and his eyes turned cold once more. He turned to the lieutenant.

"See that she's safe, eh?" he said.

Antoine placed a closed fist over his heart. "My honor, Darion."

"No!" Jacquelyna grabbed the edge of the coach and tried to pull herself up. Darion held out a hand to stop her. "No!"

"Come now," Castel said grabbing her by the shoulders and pulling her back. "Don't be foolish."

"No!" She felt her heart swell in pain. "No! No! No!"

Darion cracked a whip, and the horses started trotting away. Jacquelyna tried to fight the emotions rising within her, but she failed. She was too tired, too emotionally drained to find any more strength. She fell to her knees, tears streaming down her face as the horses sped up into a gallop.

# XLV.
## A Fine Plan

It was a fine plan, Darion thought. A damn fine plan. Setting up a ruse to trick the Leaguers into chasing an empty carriage while Pep, Jacquelyna, and the rest slipped away under what little darkness was left of the night. It was clever, devious, and—albeit a bit—the best option available. Darion just saw one fatal flaw in Jacquelyna's plan—the horses. He didn't trust the horses to run hard enough, long enough, or in a straight enough path on their own to convince the Leaguers that the coach they were chasing held Jacquelyna and the king's bastard. It needed a little human guidance to work.

Not that Darion wanted to be the man driving the coach to its inevitable doom. He knew there was no safe haven in the direction he was traveling, not with four tired horses and a band of angry and radical swordsmen nipping at his heels. It would be only a matter of time before they leapt upon him like a pack of wolves. He volunteered himself because it made the most sense. He was a condemned man anyways. At least this way meant he could die with a sword in hand and not a noose around his neck. Perhaps he'd even earn a shred of honor back.

He cracked the whip, sending the horses in a speeding frenzy. He wasn't sure how much longer the beasts could gallop at this pace, nor did he have any idea how far they could take him before stopping from exhaustion. He just hoped the answer was far enough.

The frigid air nipped at Darion's face, chapping his lips and skin. In a way he looked forward to a little swordplay. It would get the blood flowing; he might just feel warmth one last time before the icy hands of death embraced him.

He glanced over his shoulder. Along the ridge of a tall hill he could see the silhouettes of more than a dozen riders barely lit against the dark western sky. They scanned the area. Darion hoped they would see him and the coach rushing south toward Ivry. If not, things could get ugly for everyone he left behind–Peppin, Jacquelyna, the king's daughter. Even Antoine would find a cold, metallic end if the plan didn't succeed.

"Shit."

The band of horsemen split into two parties–half heading toward him and half heading toward the village. Apparently the Leaguers were fine with hedging their bets. It was far from ideal, but at least it meant Peppin and company would only have to take on half the riders. It gave them a fighting chance.

There was nothing more Darion could do for his friends. He had his own hide to look out for now. He urged the horses on. With a jolt the coach raced faster south. The sky to his left began to lighten.

He looked back over his shoulder. Six riders bore down on him, gaining ground while rolling hills and open fields lay on either side of the coach. Not exactly prime hiding territory. Up ahead he spied a line of trees, not thick enough to take refuge in, but the road narrowed at its mouth. It would funnel the riders, forcing them to ride close together and hopefully retard their progress. It could give him a little more distance. And distance was time–something he was desperately short on.

*Ffffffzzzzzzzzzzzzz!*

A lead ball whizzed by Darion's head–an unmistakable warning–and the thundering of half a dozen horses galloping just behind him filled his ears. He could almost smell the sweat and steel of each rider. A familiar scent, it now reeked like death itself.

A grey and white muzzle of a horse thrust into Darion's peripheral. He turned to see the rider garbed in black staring back at him. The man lifted his head, revealing a wide and unkempt mustache, stubble cheeks, and pale blue eyes framed by heavy bags beneath them. He leveled a pistol and Darion braced for the worst, but instead of pulling the trigger, the fellow jerked back on the reins, nearly sending himself and his mount toppling onto the frozen ground. Darion looked forward in time to make a slight course adjustment. The coach fled into the forest. Darion looked back and saw the horses and their riders struggle to funnel their way into the trail. Darion sighed. He bought himself a little time.

Alas, the forest wasn't very deep nor overly thick. Most of the woods lay further east of the trail and after a few minutes of traversing the narrow, dark road, Darion and his team of horses lurched back into the open air. Up ahead, however, he saw a small barn reaching skyward from a deserted farm. It wasn't a grand fortress, but Darion wasn't expecting to run into one either. He just wanted a place to make a final stand and to take a few miserable souls with him. He reckoned they were all bound for the same table in Hell anyways.

"Whoa!" He pulled on the reins and leapt off the coach before it came to a complete stop. The Leaguers were close. He could see every scowl and grimace, see every scar, scratch and wrinkle, and feel every glint of hate in their eyes. It nearly froze Darion solid. He wondered if he ever wore such a look on his face as he thieved on rich men. Did he ever look so cold and callous?

Two pistol shots were fired. Darion leapt over a broken-down fence, and bolted into the old barn. He closed the large wooden gate as another lead ball struck the boards.

"Goddamit," he muttered. He looked around. The barn was eclipsed nearly in darkness. Only a few strands of early morning light shone through cracks in the wall and ceiling. One of these gleams illuminated an old, moldy ladder against the side wall. Darion rushed to it and with careful hands and feet climbed up to a second-level loft. He heard horses stop outside of the barn. He peered through a small gap in the wooden panels. The Leaguers surrounded the coach with bare steel in hand. They threw open the doors and glanced at each other with looks of confusion.

Tremear rode in and pulled on the reins. The Spaniard, Gonzalo, was with him. The captain looked at the men with his usual stark gaze.

"What is it?" he grumbled.

"The coach is empty," one of the men said, "and we only saw one man flee into the barn. No one else."

Tremear's eyes narrowed. He looked over his shoulder and back at the barn. A cold chill ran the length of Darion's spine. He knew Tremear couldn't see him, but it sure as hell felt like he could.

The Spaniard turned his horse around.

"Where do you think you're going?" Tremear asked.

"I'm going after the heretic girls and whoever is harboring them. This Gascon of yours means nothing to me."

Tremear balled his fists. "Take one of the men. Make sure you get the king's daughter or don't bother coming back."

The Spaniard didn't say a word but put spurs to his horse and galloped away. One of the riders soon joined him in the distance, leaving just Tremear and three Leaguers to deal with.

# XLVI.
# Hope

"Put out that fire."

"It's fucking freezing, Antoine," Peppin said.

"We can't be having the Leaguers know anyone is awake."

The lieutenant went outside while Peppin headed for the hearth. He broke the logs up and tossed some dirt on top to slow the burning down. Jacquelyna sat there, her legs huddled against her chest. She thought of Darion and how her foolish plan had sent him to his death. Peppin laid a friendly hand on her shoulder.

"How's he doing?" Peppin asked. He gestured toward Bauvet.

"Not well," Jacquelyna said, searching for her voice. "He says he can't feel his fingers. He looks like death."

Peppin frowned. "Is he still bleeding?"

Jacquelyna shook her head, but in reality she didn't know.

"It'll be a little while before the riders show up, if they show up. Go check up on him, eh? Get him some water."

Jacquelyna stared at Peppin for a moment, before realizing what he was doing. She needed something to keep her mind off doom and off Darion. She grabbed a pitcher from a table, and poured some water into a mug. She brought it over to Bauvet, but it took some effort for him to sit at an angle appropriate for drinking. He nearly spat the liquid out.

"Jesus," he croaked. "Water?"

"You look awful, monsieur. You need it."

"What I need is that bottle of wine over there."

Jacquelyna grabbed the open bottle and handed it to him. He

pulled the cork out with his teeth and spat it on the floor. He brought the bottle to his mouth. Streams of violet-red poured out of the corners of his lips, trickling down his beard and onto his doublet and cloak.

"Where's Darion?" he asked.

"Gone."

He looked at her from beneath heavy, creased brows. Then a light went off in his eyes.

"He took the coach?"

Jacquelyna nodded. He chuckled.

"What's so funny? He's gone to his death most likely."

"It's such a Gascon thing for him to do." The inn door swung open. The lieutenant returned with the stable boy and the innkeeper.

"Get back to your rooms," the lieutenant told them. "Don't make a peep and don't answer the door. If you have any guests, I'd recommend making sure they do the same. Understand?"

He tossed the innkeeper a small pouch of coin which seemed to ease the man's consent. Castel shuffled them up the stairs before taking his position by the door.

"How much shot do you have left, Pep?" he asked.

Peppin, sitting by a window, glanced into a leather pouch hanging from his belt.

"Four. You?"

"Five."

"What about your man in the back?"

"Three."

Peppin blew gently at the end of his match chord to keep it burning. He rested his harquebus against the wall and walked over to Jacquelyna.

"Here," he said, holding out the pistol. "It's one of Darion's. I'm sure he'd be happier if you had it for some protection. I won't bother asking if you know how to use it. It's already loaded."

Jacquelyna took the wheellock and nestled next to Gabrielle. The fire was almost out now. The room fell into a frigid shade of blue.

"Here's the plan," Castel said. "We wait for the riders to hit the top of the hill and pray to God that they see Darion and the coach riding hard away from here. If they make chase, we wait fifteen minutes before saddling back up and rushing to Paris."

"And if they don't take the bait?" Peppin asked.

The lieutenant hesitated; it was a scenario none of them hoped for. "Gregoire takes Jacquelyna and the king's daughter to Paris while you and I give them some cover."

A crooked grin appeared on Peppin's face. He picked up his harquebus and peered to the hilltop. It felt like forever before something aroused his interest.

"Here we go," he said.

Jacquelyna tightened her grip on the pistol.

"How many?" Castel asked, moving toward the window.

"Twelve by my count."

Castel pulled a corner of the curtain back and looked out. "Dammit. They're not moving."

Jacquelyna's heart raced. She crawled across the floor to the window.

"Stay back, Jacquelyna," the lieutenant ordered.

"It was my idea that either has doomed us or Darion. I need to see which."

Castel relented. Jacquelyna moved the edge of the curtain away. The sky had turned a blue-grey and snow on the grass began evaporating, creating a thin layer of fog in the village and hillside. On top of the hill were twelve or so small black dots. They sat there, unmoving for a minute. Jacquelyna imagined they were debating over whether or not that the coach held what they were looking for. The group split into two parties. Half went in the direction of the coach; the other half headed toward the village.

"'Sblood," Castel swore.

"Six is better than twelve," Peppin said.

"Six more than I'd like." He shifted his attention to Jacquelyna. "Take the girl into the kitchen. There's a side door there. Once the fighting starts I want you to run like the wind to the stable. Get on that horse and you don't stop until you reach Paris. I'm going to send Gregoire with you. He's a good man. Good soldier. He'll look after you."

"I understand, Antoine." Jacquelyna stuffed the pistol under her arm before leading Gabrielle into the kitchen. She pushed open the door a smidge to watch. Peppin continued at the windows, updating them on the riders' location. The lieutenant went back to his post, standing flush against the wall by the door. It took about another ten minutes or so before they heard the riders pull into town. She prayed they'd keep on going by.

Alas, Providence didn't see fit to bestow them such fortune. The horses stopped and spurs jingled as the riders drew near. Eventually the pale light beneath the front door was blotted out by a shadow. Someone knocked.

Peppin and Castel didn't move a muscle. Another knock rapped at the door, but still the two men remained still and silent. A third knock was pounded, and after more silence, a deep voice cursed. A flash of pale light appeared beneath the door before the shadow returned and the door kicked open. The wooden frame splintered and cracked under the blow. A man in a long cloak stepped through, his eyes instantly noticing Bauvet slouched in the corner. But before he could say a word or react, Castel drove his dagger into the man's neck. The rider gasped and stumbled onto the floor. Castel reached around the corner of the door with his pistol and fired. Jacquelyna wasn't sure if the lieutenant hit his mark, but he rushed away from the door and ducked behind an overturned table to reload. Peppin broke the glass of the window near him, thrust his harquebus out and fired. He smiled. A sure sign that he hit his intended target.

"Go, Jacquelyna!" Castel yelled. "Move! And take Gregoire!"

Jacquelyna swallowed the lump in her throat. She grabbed Gabrielle by the hand and pulled her up. The young girl cried out in pain, but Jacquelyna didn't stop to apologize. They rushed out of the kitchen to the back area where Gregoire remained on guard.

"This way, mademoiselles," he said. He opened the door, harquebus at the ready, and led them toward the stables. Fog was growing thicker. The sound of pistol and harquebus fire amplified the austere morning.

Four horses, saddled and ready, were tied at the edge of the stable. Gregoire unwound the reins of one of the horses. A shot was fired, splintering the wood next to the Guardsman's head. He flinched. The horses reared and neighed. Gregoire spun and leveled his harquebus at the knave who shot at him, and pulled the trigger. The Leaguer's face twisted, and he fell to his knees. Almost instantly a second shot was fired. Gregoire jerked back while a stream of blood left his chest. He slumped against a post, breathing heavily. Gabrielle screamed.

Jacquelyna spied around the corner. A man in black approached, but to her relief it wasn't the Spaniard. He dropped his harquebus and drew his rapier.

"Hide in the back," Jacquelyna told Gabrielle. The young girl whimpered. "I'm not leaving you. I promise."

The young girl nodded and sprinted into a dark corner. The swordsman continued to toward them, though he did so with some hesitation. She looked at the pistol in her hands. Darion's pistol. She waited until the swordsman got closer before she jumped out from the shadows. The rogue flinched at seeing her before him, arms outstretched with the pistol pointed at his chest. Jacquelyna gritted her teeth closed and screamed as she pulled the trigger.

The recoil from the pistol was stronger than she expected. Her arm jolted back, and she nearly dropped the pistol in the process. When she opened her eyes she saw the swordsman still standing. A wide grin spread on his face. Her shot missed, and she was sure she wouldn't be taken as a prisoner this time. The Leaguer approached with more confidence in his purpose. His rapier gleamed sickly between wafts of fog.

She stumbled into a post. Behind the swordsman she saw light grey splotches fade in through the fog. The splotches grew darker and darker, and the sound of thunder rolled through the town. Then came the terrifying roar of men. More than fifteen horses and riders in crimson cloaks emerged from the fog. Their swords were drawn and glinted in the early light. One of the horsemen swung his broadsword downward and struck Jacquelyna's assailant just as he turned to see the commotion. The blow split the man's skull in two, scattering his brain matter across the lawn.

The pistol and harquebus fire ceased and in its stead was the singing of swords clashing and the Leaguers trying to escape. But each rebel was cut down as quickly and as maliciously as the first. Soon the ground was littered with heaps of blood, wool, and flesh.

"Jacquelyna! Jacquelyna! Jacquelyna, where are you?"

Jacquelyna's heart fluttered. "Martin! I'm here, Martin!"

The Comte de Mauriac pull on the reins of his horse. He leapt from the saddle and sprinted toward her. She ran just as fast to him and into his strong and warm embrace. He squeezed her so tight that it almost hurt against his armor. But she didn't care. She felt safe.

"My dear Jacquelyna. I thought I lost you."

"I'm so glad you came."

"I left as soon as I got word. I would've come sooner, but–"

"I know. I know. I just want you to hold me right now."

He did. She smiled while tears streamed down her dirty face. She couldn't remember the last time she had a reason to smile.

"Where's the princess?" Jacquelyna and the count broke their embrace. The Chevalier d'Auch, approached with bare blade in hand. "Where's the king's daughter?"

"In the back of the stable," Jacquelyna said.

The chevalier gestured to two Guardsmen to fetch the girl.

"Where's Darion?" he asked, his eyes now eager and full of worry. "Where's my nephew? Where's my son?"

# XLVII.
## Steel

Darion rushed toward the opposite end of the barn and crouched behind a few haystacks. He doffed his hat and checked his pistol to make sure everything was in working order. Part of him wished he brought both pistols, but he knew Peppin and Jacquelyna would need it, even more so now since their plan hadn't worked as they had hoped. But if Tremear wanted Darion so badly, he'd have to come in and get him. So Darion waited and waited. It took a few minutes before the men outside were able to break open the door with a strong kick from one of the horses. Tremear strode into the barn followed by the three Leaguers. None had weapons drawn, but one of the horsemen held a torch that lit up the end of the barn in a bold, orange glow.

"Gascon!" Tremear said. "Gascon, I know you're in here. Come on out of hiding so we can have a little chat."

"Go to hell!" Darion yelled.

Tremear's head cocked to the side as if he was trying to pinpoint exactly where Darion took refuge. He flaunted a sarcastic frown.

"Oh, I'm sure I'll be there soon enough, but I'm willing to wager you'll already be down there long before I'm cold and in the ground."

"I have other plans, Tremear."

Again the captain cocked his head. His peered into the shadows of the barn. Light from the flames burning at the end of the torch glinted in Tremear's dark eyes. He looked even more foreboding than usual.

"A clever ruse you concocted. Leading us away from the real coach, so the king's daughter and your friends could escape. Clever and madcap. But all the same just as honorable. In fact, I'm moved to present to you one final offer."

Darion kept his eyes fixated on the highwaymen. He hoped they'd step deeper into the barn and within his pistol range, but they remained steadfast at the edge.

"And what offer may that be?"

"I offer you a quick death if you come out of your quaint little hiding spot right now. If not, it'll be long and painful."

"Doesn't seem like much of an offer to me."

Tremear crossed his arms. "You betrayed us, and traitors don't deserve anything better than being sent away from this world with lead or steel. Simple as that."

"Fuck you, Tremear."

"Oh come now, Gascon. There's only one of you and four of us. Even if you have a pistol with you you'll get one shot off before you're cut to ribbons. I also promise to do the same to that pretty girl you so stupidly tried to save tonight, too, unless you come out now."

Darion's knuckles turned white as he squeezed his fists. The captain and the three Leaguers weren't deep in the barn, not close enough for Darion to have an accurate shot with his pistol. Worse yet, he had only one shot. He needed to make sure it counted.

"Why don't you come in further where I can see you better. Maybe we can work out some sort of an arrangement."

Tremear chuckled. Darion didn't expect that line to work, nor did he even bellow it in a serious tone; he was just trying to buy himself some more time to think of a way out.

"I'm quite comfortable right here, Gascon. I'll tell you what. You take all the time you want in deciding if you're going to come out with or without a fight. We'll be waiting for you outside." Tremear shivered exaggeratedly. "But damn is it cold as a whore's tit in here, eh? You must be freezing."

"You'd be surprised how warm the hay can be."

Tremear flashed a malevolent, sardonic smile, and Darion couldn't but help shudder at the sight.

"Ah yes, the hay." Tremear turned to the man holding the torch and nodded. The man stepped further into the barn; the bright glow from the flames lit up their area in a deep, orange tint. At three separate haystacks he put his torch to the straw. The hay lit up with a great roar and crackle, and Darion shielded his eyes from the bright blaze of the fire. When he looked down he saw Tremear glaring up at him with the face of a devil. Shadows from the inferno danced all around him. For the first time ever, Darion saw how truly comfortable Tremear was when in control, when on the verge of a decisive victory and eradicating an enemy. "So take all the time you need, old friend. It is truly up to you if you wish to be buried in one piece or have your ashes scattered in the breeze."

Tremear mockingly tipped his hat before leaving the barn inferno. The three Leaguers followed, walking backwards with one hand on the hilt of their swords. They closed the barn door behind them.

Darion leapt to his tired, aching feet. Half the barn was ablaze. He could hear the straw sear, and the wood planks crack and pop under the intense heat. It was a chorus of hell and a thickening cloud of black and grey smoke filled the loft.

He needed a plan, but first he needed some air. He rushed to the rickety ladder and started to descend. Spiraling trails of smoked rose into his face, burning his eyes and his lungs, while the acidic smell of searing wood and hay singed his nostrils. He coughed as his feet hit the ground. He dropped into a crouch to get as far below the smoke as he could.

By now more than half of the barn was a raging inferno. His eyes darted around him for another way out—a window, a side door, anything he could shoulder his way through and not have to face the men on the other side. Alas, the windows were small and boarded up, and he found no side doors. There was only the one way out, and it was straight through the devil.

A stream of sweat flowed from Darion's brow. Heat from the flames roasted him inside his heavy doublet, leather jerkin, and wool cloak. He refused to die by the fire, cooked like some plump pheasant. He was sure he would spend the rest of eternity in Hell's flames. The fire could wait. Besides, he was a former soldier for France and a highwayman. There was only one proper way of dying—with sword in hand.

He untied his cloak and drew his rapier. He was going to need all the tricks of his trade if he was going to take a few souls to Perdition with him.

*All we have is hope and steel.*

He buried his shoulder into the wooden door and forced it open.

As he came into the cool, fresh morning air, he leveled his pistol in front of him and fired. The Leaguer's head jerked back as he raised his hands to his jaw. Darion wasn't sure if it was a killing shot, but it definitely was enough to incapacitate the lout. He tossed his smoking, discharged pistol at a second swordsman, stopping the fellow's advance and giving Darion a few, but precious, extra seconds of space. He then whipped around holding his cloak out, so it spread out wide, catching air like a sail, and threw it at the third advancing highwaymen. The wretch put up his arms to deflect the cloak, but the heavy wool was too much to glance away. The cloak enveloped him. He stumbled back. Darion set to throw a killing blow when he saw Tremear charge forth with naked steel in hand.

Darion aborted his attack and unsheathed the main gauche that hung at his back. Its guard was covered in nicks and scratches from previous fights, and Darion had no doubt it—and he—would earn a few more scars before all was said and done.

Tremear laid his attack on heavy, throwing a barrage of thrusts at Darion's face and arms. Darion parried them but was unable to answer with any successful attacks of his own. Outnumbered now three to one, Darion needed to be on the offensive, but Tremear's attacks were too well placed to present any definite openings. Soon two of the other swordsmen came to reinforce the captain. Darion had to parry and move as fast as he could muster.

Through the chaos of clashing steel, Darion assessed his foes. The two Leaguers had proper sword training. Their moves were quick, fluid, and deliberate as if they just stumbled out of a fencing salon. It made them deadly, but, fortunately, it also made them predictable. Then there was Tremear. Cold, calculating, and unyielding in his attack. What the captain lacked in training he made up for with a maliciousness found only in seasoned soldiers. The three men continued their assault. Darion parried most of the blows with his sword and dagger, but a few cuts and thrusts glanced off the thick hide of his jerkin. One the Leaguers lunged. Darion threw out his dagger, but the cold burning sensation of steel forced its way into his skin and muscles. He grunted, but he couldn't stop moving. Stopping meant death.

Tremear and the Leaguers fought like boars. The swordsman to his far left, the man he threw the pistol at, overreached on another a lunge. With a quick circular motion of his wrist Darion parried the attack. He then stepped to his left pushing his adversary's sword into

Tremear's blade. With two swords tangled, Darion reached out with his dagger and sliced open the Leaguer's forearm from elbow to wrist in a diagonal cut. The bastard cried out in agony, and his sword clanked against a small stone on the ground. At quick glance, the cut looked deep. Darion was sure he must've hit a tendon or two. It meant one less blade he had to deal with.

Alas, it came at a cost. As he stepped to slice the man's arm he exposed his flank to Tremear and the third swordsman. Tremear's blade was tied up, but the remaining Leaguer's sword was free to strike. The rogue lunged, aiming the cold tip of his rapier at Darion's ribs. Darion twisted his body to void and threw out a wild, uncontrolled sweeping parry to counter the attack. He got a piece of the blade with his own, but not enough. Searing pain raced through him. He bellowed and staggered back.

He pressed the fingers of his dagger hand over the wound. It felt mostly superficial, no internal organs pierced, but it bled like a sieve. He readied himself once more as Tremear and the swordsman advanced. Their swords glistened silver and Darion saw crimson drip from the tips.

"It didn't have to be this way, Gascon," Tremear said with two large sweeps of his sword; Darion retreated to keep distance. "You were one of us once."

"Times change, I suppose," Darion replied. "I never saw profit in harassing young girls." He slid back, blocking two short thrusts from the Leaguer swordsman. Clanging blades and the burning barn provided for austere music as the sun began to rise in the distance. Darion riposted, but it was easily pushed aside. Tremear took the moment to counter with a quick shot of his own.

Pain. Blistering pain sped through Darion's leg and up his spine. He felt his head grow light. For a moment he thought he'd lose consciousness. But he kept his wits about him, and made to step back and regain his distance. But as he shifted weight to his left leg he fell straight to the ground, his leg numb.

"Goddammit!" he yelled. He shuffled back along the cold ground. Tremear and the swordsman advanced slowly with wolfish grins.

"Oh, God's got nothing to do with it I'm afraid," Tremear said. "Just justice being dealt with the only way this world knows–with loaded guns and tempered steel."

Darion slid back a few more feet and looked around him for something, anything that could help him out of this mess. But all he found was loose hay and a burning barn. Not the things one conjures a miracle out of. At least he took a soul with him and ruined another's fighting career. He had hoped to have taken Tremear with him, but, as they say, *c'est la vie*.

The swordsman with the maimed hand now joined the group, holding his rapier in his left hand instead.

"Are you done fighting, Gascon? Or shall we add a few more holes in your miserable body?"

Feeling crawled back to Darion's leg. With much effort, he rose to his feet. It was a futile move, more to show an air of bravado than anything else. His leg was practically useless at the moment. He looked at the three men. Flames from the inferno glinted and danced in their eyes. He knew he was lost, but he wouldn't stand there and be slaughtered like a chicken. They'd have to earn this kill. He did his best to take an on guard stance. Tremear threw up his arms, flabbergasted.

"Dammit, Gascon. You always were a—"

Something broke the captain from his words. He stopped and let his eyes scan the horizon. His two men did the same. And then Darion heard it, a faint whinny that made its way through the sound of scorching fire roaring just a few feet away. The two Leaguers turned around just in time to see Death reach its hands out toward them.

"*Darion*!" A stout horseman materialized through the thinning fog, an harquebus already cocked in hand. The fellow discharged it on sight. It struck between one of the swordsmen's beady, dark eyes. Blood and brain splattered everywhere, some landing on Darion's boots. The horseman leapt from the saddle and wrestled the second swordsman to the ground. It was Peppin, and while the Leaguer fought fruitlessly to throw his assailant off him, Pep pulled out a silver-hilted dagger from beneath his cloak and buried it into the man's chest.

Tremear seemed to be as much in awe of the spectacle as Darion. With the highwayman captain's head turned Darion threw a thrust aimed to send Tremear to meet his maker. But he stumbled over his wounded leg, and instead of entombing his sword hilt-deep into the captain's chest, he buried a heavy shoulder into Tremear.

They stumbled and tripped over their swords and sheaths,

tumbling into the burning barn. Darion groaned as he lifted himself onto his hands and knees. He shook his head hoping to shake some sense back into himself. His head felt light; he lost more blood than he first realized.

He felt a hot, prickly sensation and a drop of sweat run down his ribs beneath and into his open wound. Everything was engulfed in flames, and the smoke was so thick he couldn't see five feet in front of him. A loud snap came from above. Wooden beams and some roof tiles fell, blocking most of the barn door entrance. A ball of fire erupted as the wood hit the ground. Darion recoiled back from the intense heat nipping at his face.

He remained crouched to keep his head below the rancid smoke. His irritated eyes darted around the barn, hoping to find another exit created by the fire, but his gaze couldn't pierce the thick, black smoke that spiraled from every direction. He also didn't see Tremear anywhere. He wondered for a moment if his old captain had darted out of the barn before the beam and ceiling collapsed. Darion found his sword resting near a pile of smoldering hay. He crawled to it and reached out. As his fingers began to enclose around the grip, a black blur appeared from the smoke, smashing into Darion's face. He reeled back and grunted as he fell.

Tremear materialized before him from the smoke, his eyes rigid and mustache singed at the end. He held his arm high and sword coiled back, aimed at Darion like a scorpion ready to strike. Darion kicked at Tremear's leg. The highwayman captain swore and fell to his hands and knees. Darion sprang forward and tackled Tremear. His wounds and tired, aching body didn't faze him now. He threw a few punches before wrenching the sword from the captain's hands. Tremear struck Darion across the jaw. The sword flew out of Darion's grasp and bounced away into the billowing smoke. The two men grappled and rolled, surrounded by smoldering hay and splintering wood. They exchanged blows with their fists, their elbows, their heads. Darion had to fight for his life many times but never had it been so dirty or so brutal.

Darion landed a few swift blows to Tremear's face, dazing the captain. In a flash he grabbed hold around Tremear's neck, squeezing it tighter and tighter. Complete, unadulterated rage pumped through Darion's veins. Moments went by before he realized what he was doing. He loosened his grip just a smidge as he contemplated if he should finish murdering Tremear, his old comrade and captain.

Tremear's face turned to a deep livid. His eyes bulged from their sockets. Beneath the flakes of skin and blood, Darion's own fingers were white as snow. The captain clutched and slapped at Darion's arms and wrists, struggling to break through Darion's vice-like hold, but he couldn't. Darion had locked down. He could feel Tremear's pulse start to slow and throb, the captain's heart and veins working overtime to pump blood to the brain.

Then Tremear changed tactics. He threw several quick blows to Darion's ribs, right where there was a red stain from a sword thrust. Darion grunted with each jolt, clamping his jaws shut to keep from screeching in the agony that surged through him. He redoubled his efforts in trying to strangle Tremear, his fingers nearly going numb from squeezing so tightly, but the captain kept punching Darion's ribs. The punches grew more furious as the captain inched to the tipping point. If Darion could only hold on a little longer...

Tremear launched a final punch into the growing stain. He twisted and dug his knuckle into the wound. It was too much for Darion to bear. He fell back and covered the wound with one of his arms. Before he could recover, Tremear was upon him, unleashing a flurry of blows that made Darion recoil in defense. There was nothing he could do to stop the captain's relentless attack but hope to weather the storm. But each punch sapped energy from his being. He wondered how long he could hold out. His head grew light and his body convulsed from the punches. He wanted nothing more than to curl up, close his eyes and sleep... and sleep... and sleep...

He teetered on the verge of unconsciousness when a loud crash lured him from the darkness. He opened his eyes, his vision hazy. A dark figure stood at the threshold of the barn, the beams and debris pushed aside. In the haze of pain, the columns of smoke swirling around him Peppin looked no more than a shadow watching over him. He raised what Darion assumed was an extended arm. A shot fired. Tremear whirled backward, deeper into the barn and disappeared into the smoke and fire with a bloodcurdling scream.

Darion started to crawl for Peppin's silhouette. He only made it a few miserable feet before collapsing. His eyes fluttered as he struggled to stay conscious. He reached out as the figure raced toward him, but his vision blurred, his strength waivered, and he was quickly enveloped in darkness.

# XLVIII.
## Don Pedro's Reward

Don Pedro Alvarez of Toledo, the Marquis de Villafranca, woke up early. He wanted to see the sun rise on the day of his victory. The day he outwitted Duc de Sully. The day he humbled the Bourbon king and brought victory to Spain and God.

He sat down and reread the letters he got from the Duque de Lerma—King Phillip's favorite statesman—demanding results or to return to Spain ashamed. A shrill smile grew across the marquis' bearded face. Don Pedro had gotten word that the highwaymen had arrived safely at their new hideout with the Leaguers. And with no word from the king's men, victory was imminent. If King Henry wanted to see his precious daughter again, he'd have to give in to the demands. There were few greater family men in the world than Señor Henry Bourbon. It seemed that the Duque de Lerma would get his wish, and Don Pedro his rewards.

A knock came at the door.

"Enter."

A short, young usher strode through. "Excuse me, Excellencia, but the Duc de Sully is here to speak with you."

Don Pedro nodded. He expected this.

"See him in, and ready my coach."

The usher bowed and rushed out. The Duc de Sully entered. He wore a short-rimmed black felt hat with a few feathers protruding from its band. His eyes were weighed down by heavy bags. The corner of his lips drooped toward the floor. He looked terrible, like a man who hadn't slept in days, anchored down by the heavy burdens of a king's minister. From the fresh, black stains on the duke's fingers the marquis had conjured images of Sully huddled over his desk by candlelight, working fervently on the basis of a new treaty with Spain. It would be needed to keep Huguenot renegades in check once their precious Edict of Nantes was eradicated and they became outlaws once more. It'd also give Spain the time and space it needed to suppress the rebels in the Low Lands, and unite the Spanish Netherlands.

Finalizing such a treaty would, of course, take some time, but it'd be worth it in the end and sealed in a grand double marriage. Don Pedro would give all the silver and gold to see the smug grins wiped from the French heretics' faces.

"Your Grace," he said with a friendly bow. "A pleasant surprise to see you at my quarters so early. Will you come in for a morning drink?"

Sully looked him over. Though he seemed teetering on the verge of exhaustion, his eyes didn't lose much in terms of their scorn.

"No. Thank you." He looked past Pedro and into the room. His eyes seemed to glisten in alarm for a moment, or perhaps it was just the rays of sun through the window. "I've come not to visit, but as a messenger."

Don Pedro stroked his full beard to keep from betraying his excitement. "Messenger? What sort of business deserves such a high and noble messenger such as yourself?"

"A royal one, and one of war and peace, I'm afraid." He closed his eyes and rubbed his temples. "His Majesty wishes to speak with you about an urgent matter concerning our two nations."

"I see." Don Pedro stepped into his apartment, expecting the duke to follow. But when he turned Sully remained at the door's threshold, nearly in silhouette from the bright light pouring in behind him. "Is it regarding his daughter's kidnapping?"

"His Majesty is finishing up with another appointment, but will expect you there promptly thereafter. As you would expect, the king is in a foul mood."

"I will go presently then."

Duc de Sully considered the marquis for a moment before leaving. Don Pedro shut the door. His thick beard expanded as he smiled, revealing a row of bright ivory teeth. He sat down at his desk and wrote a letter to his wife, telling her of his triumph, and apologizing for his delay in returning home. He chuckled to himself, quiet at first until it rolled into a full bellow. He picked up his robe, black with bronze and orange trim, and threw it over his shoulder.

He strolled with an extra spring in his step, like a young man on the verge of his first conquest of love.

*Finally, I will have brought that heretic king to his knees.*

Don Pedro came to a large waiting area outside of the throne room. The usual courtiers, guards, nobles, maids, and foreign emissaries were in attendance, gossiping among each other as they were wont to do. They all parted for him as he strode in. He nodded to a few of the faces he saw, but he didn't stop to talk to any of them. He had a battle to win. He was prepared to give France—as they say—*le coup de grâce.*

A young man dressed in a black and white doublet and hose entered from a side door. He carried a gold hilted sword upon a blue pillow with a field of golden fleur-de-lis. It was the king's sword. Like a hawk, Don Pedro swooped toward the carrier, throwing back the folds of his robe to reveal the bronze silk lining beneath. He doffed his cap, fell to a bended knee and pressed his lips to the hilt.

"Now," he said in a loud voice that carried throughout the chamber. "I am a happy man, having kissed the sword of the bravest king in the world."

The chamber doors opened, and the Swiss guards parted their halberds from the entrance. Francois Bassompierre strode out in fine attire of blue velvet with gold trim and a stiff ruffled collar. He made his way across the chamber, twirling his mustache with each step. He rested a ringed finger on the pommel of his sword.

"Excellency, His Majesty the King will now see you," he said.

Don Pedro followed the courtier into a smaller antechamber to the throne room. In a pool of warm sunlight, movement caught his eye. He turned as he trailed Bassompierre. In the yellow halo stood two figures. The first he didn't recognize at all. The fellow was short and corpulent, with a grubby beard and a stained cloth wrapped around his head to cover an eye. His clothes were caked in blood and dirt, and a military broadsword hung at his hip. He stood with a crooked, knowing grin behind a young woman who looked barely better. One was a young woman with long black wavy hair that fell below her shoulders and a black cloak wrapped tightly around her body. Her face was pretty, though darkened with dirt and grime, and her lips were chapped from cold winter winds.

Then he realized who the young woman was—Jacquelyna Brocquart, one of Marie de Medici's ladies. He feared the plan had failed until he remembered that the highwaymen were ransoming her off to her father. Perhaps the count finally found the coin to free his daughter.

He was about to move on when he spied a third figure with them, a young girl with golden, disheveled locks and a warm, animated smile children save for their loving parents. His blood ran cold. Clearly his eyes played tricks on him.

"The king's daughter," he uttered.

"Hmm? Ah yes, she arrived early this morning," Bassompierre said. Don Pedro nearly jumped out of his skin. He hadn't realized he spoke aloud. "The Guardsmen rescued her and Mademoiselle Brocquart. Bloody exploit from the looks of things. It's amazing anyone survived."

Before Don Pedro could say another word, Duc de Sully ushered the girls and the one-eyed man through a side entrance.

"Are you coming?" Bassompierre asked.

Don Pedro whipped his head around. The courtier stood before closed doors. Pedro nodded and gave the antechamber one final look, half expecting to see the king's daughter standing there but in a ghoulish form.

He entered the large throne room. Its floors were a finely polished marble, its walls decorated with paintings of French kings long past, and a high ceiling with golden inlay. Banners with the royal arms hung from the rafters, and several candle chandeliers lit the room warmly. Per decorum, the Forty-Five Guardsmen were there, standing in several rows along each wall of the room. Beside the throne stood several other Guardsmen, their clothes ragged and dusty, and some with bandages or slings supporting injured limbs. They looked like they had been through hell, and their gazes only intensified the marquis' apprehension.

"Ah, my dear Don Pedro, step forward," King Henry said with a smile.

The ambassador did so, his gaze jumping from one Guardsman to the next. They had murder in their eyes.

"Your Majesty, I am told you wanted to speak about an urgent matter between Spain and France. I, for one, hope it is the beginning of peaceful relations between our two great nations."

The king leapt to his feet and met Don Pedro at the bottom of the velvet steps. He held out his hand. Don Pedro pressed his lips to the royal ring.

"Of course! I, too, would love nothing more than for France to enjoy the prosperity of peace. You may have noticed that my daughter is back, safe and sound."

"I did, sire. A blessed miracle from God."

"I know not if God had his hand in this matter, but I do know these men behind me did. They bled and some even died to see that my daughter was returned safe to me."

Don Pedro's gaze met those of the dirty and battered Guardsmen. He felt the rage of their gaze and heat rise beneath his collar.

"Your Majesty is fortunate to have such loyal men at your disposal."

Henry's face grew harsh. "I prefer to not dispose of them at all, monsieur. When they returned they had some interesting and startling news to report. Apparently one of your retainers was among the kidnappers."

Don Pedro's mouth fell ajar. "Good Lord in Heaven! I had no idea. I admit, in secrecy, I sent him off to find your daughter. I had hoped if we found her it would improve relations between our countries. I had no notion that he would betray my orders."

"Of course not. Why would you suspect him of being a traitor when his reputation has always been that of a loyal and militant servant of Spain?"

The king smiled. Don Pedro struggled to think of what to say next. "I shall send a party to find him at once. He will be dealt with severely."

Henry waved his hand, brushing the idea aside. "Don't concern yourself with it, ambassador. My men will find him. Have faith in that. You, my friend, have more important matters to occupy your time."

"Sire?"

"You'll need to figure out how to convince your king why peace with the Low Lands is paramount for all parties involved."

Don Pedro stared at the king and, for the first time in his long life, was at a loss for words. Henry gazed back with sturdy eyes before gesturing to the door.

Pedro bowed and turned slowly. Had he really just lost the battle and the war? What happened in the short day between the highwaymen claiming victory and King Henry announcing, in different terms, Spain's defeat?

As he made his way through the waiting room full of courtiers, soldiers, servants, and emissaries, he felt their collective eyes fall on him. The room was quiet as a convent, but soon waves of whispers blew across the room like a gentle breeze. His embarrassment turned into anger. He stormed to his apartments.

"Pack my things!" he ordered one of his servants. "We leave tomorrow!"

"For where, Excelencia?"

He ground his teeth. "For Spain."

He slammed the doors to his quarters and threw himself into a chair by the window. Most of his room remained covered in darkness except for a long band of sunlight teeming through the window. He leaned over the arm of the chair and rubbed his temples. He then reached to pour himself a drink when a shape shifted in the shadows. *Assassins! The king!* He jumped up and reached for his sword.

"Don't bother, Marquis de Villafranca," the shadow said.

Don Pedro recognized the voice as one of the masked officials of the Catholic League. He sighed in relief and fell back into his seat.

"Where's your associate?"

"Busy. Busy cleaning up messes."

"Your men. Your idea. Your mess."

The masked man's eyes hardened at the accusation.

"You came seeking an impossible task. We told you as such when we began to move pieces for you. You let your ego get in the way of the reality of the world we live in. Your one flaw, señor, is that you tricked yourself into thinking Henry would ever bow to the idea of a Franco-Spanish alliance. Alliances are cheap. They're easily bent, forgotten, betrayed, and ignored. How naive of you, señor. For as long as King Henry of Navarre draws breath he will do nothing but look for ways to humiliate Spain. Today, he did just that, though I suppose history will never learn of this little indiscretion."

"Why aid me then?"

The man gave it a thought, then shrugged. "We needed to test our resources and that of the king's. He's well looked after. As well as we could've predicted. There is more at stake here than a simple alliance between France and Spain. An alliance wouldn't turn France Catholic. There is only one way to turn France Catholic."

# Epilogue

Voices crept in the darkness. At first they were incomprehensible, just sounds jumbled together. Like the incoming tide, the voices grew closer and closer, louder and louder. Their words became clearer in his mind. At first it was just a few words among a storm of noises, then a few phrases—an "over here!" and "fetch physician"—and at last full thoughts. Slowly, he crawled out of the darkness, the words and voices like a hook at the end of the line.

Darion opened his eyes. Light flooded him, blinding him at first so instead of darkness he saw only white. Then a gentle shadow passed over him, relieving him of the bright light. As his vision fell back into focus, he saw brilliant sapphire eyes staring back at him. A few long, raven locks tickled his nose. The woman smiled.

"You're safe, Darion."

And then he fell back to sleep.

The next time he woke up, he was greeted by a different pair of eyes but just as sweet and just as welcoming. He tried getting out of bed, but Catherine de Lesset placed her hands on his shoulders.

"Easy, monsieur. You still need rest."

"How did I get here?" Darion croaked. His throat burned.

"We pulled your lucky ass out of the fire," a growly voice interjected. Darion turned and smiled. Getting up from a wooden chair was Peppin. Next to him was Uncle Jean-Girard.

"You were having trouble breathing," his uncle said. "We feared you wouldn't make it."

"You looked like shit. You still do."

Darion chuckled before grimacing and grabbing his ribs in pain.

"I feel like shit," he joked.

"I'll get you something to drink," Catherine said. She trotted out the room.

"Did you make it back fine?" Darion asked.

"Touch and go there at the end," Peppin said. "But the chevalier here and the rest of the Forty-Five showed up. They cut the bastards down just fine."

"How did you find me?"

"After reinforcements arrived, me, your uncle, and Antoine all set out to find your hairy ass. We saw the plume of smoke in the distance and where there's smoke there's Gascon fire."

"What about Tremear? Last time I saw him he fell deeper into the barn."

Jean-Girard and Peppin exchanged glances.

"That barn was nothing but a pile of ashes after we got you out of there. Unless God Himself pulled him out of the jaws of Hell, I'd imagine the captain's bones are mixed with the dust and cinders."

Darion sighed, a mixture of relief and sorrow.

Jean-Girard put a warm, familiar hand on Darion's shoulder.

"I'll check in on you tonight," he said.

"Leaving already?" Darion asked.

"I promised Jacquelyna I'd fetch her when you awoke. She's been visiting you as often as she can, but her duties to the queen take up much of her time. I also must pack."

"Where to?"

His uncle flashed another smile. "The king wants me return to the Low Lands to finalize the treaty. Plus, I think Spain and the Low Countries will need an intermediary to resolve their issues."

"No war then?"

"Not today."

Jean-Girard grabbed his hat and cloak off the chair and left.

"No war. No coin," Peppin said, crossing his arms. "Not good for men like you and me."

Darion chuckled, but it quickly turned into a cough. His lungs burned and ached, and his throat felt parched as Hell. Catherine returned, however, like an angel bearing a flagon of wine and two mugs.

"Thank you, darling," Pep said with a wink.

Catherine curtsied and left, lingering at the doorway before smiling and passing through the door. Pep poured two drinks and gave one to Darion.

"To your marksmanship," Darion said.

"To your damn Gascon luck."

Darion sipped the wine. The cool liquid rushed down his throat, quenching his thirst and rejuvenating his body. He felt life rush back into him. His gratification was short lived, however, as his mind drifted to Jacquelyna.

"She came to find you, too," Peppin said, seemingly reading Darion's mind, "despite that noble shit, the Comte de Mauriac's, best protests. She's always been a willful woman, Darion, but something changed in her during her abduction. There was a fire in her belly that not even a tempest could dowse. You should talk to her."

Darion took another sip of his wine.

"What happened to Andre?"

Peppin cringed. "To be true, not sure. Last time we saw him, he was practically as white as a sheet, slumped in the corner of the inn. When we got back from finding you he was gone. Quick search of the area found nothing. No body. No tracks. No idea where your friend disappeared to, but he didn't look well." Peppin threw his head back, downing his drink. "Probably for the best. He was bound for the noose anyways."

Darion frowned. Pep was right, but in that moment he remembered his own situation. Pep grabbed his belongings and headed for the door.

"Leaving, too, Pep?"

"I promised Marguerite I'd come visit her for dinner. I don't dare be late. She's still right pissed at me."

He shot Darion a mischievous wink and left.

⚜⚜⚜

The sun started to set when Jacquelyna arrived. Darion, in his Gascon stubbornness, was trying to get out of bed. He hated being locked indoors, let alone bedridden. His ribs and arms ached as he shifted into a sitting position at the side of his bed. He finished putting on his boots when a knock came at the door.

"Enter."

Catherine opened the door and backed away, letting Jacquelyna in. Darion took the moment to take in her beauty. She was dressed in a fine blue silk dress that brought out the bold color of her eyes. Her hair was washed and combed, and her face scrubbed free of the blood and grime collected from her unfortunate adventure. Only her chapped lips from the cold winds hinted of her ordeal.

"You're supposed to stay in bed, monsieur," Catherine said.

"Had plenty of that." He groaned as he stood. "Need to stretch my legs."

"I can come back later," Jacquelyna said.

"No. I was going to take a short walk if you wanted to join me."

She nodded. The two stepped out. Darion was almost thankful to feel the cold against him. At least the air was fresh. Darion was slow to move. Each step felt laborious and painful. Even his ribs ached as he stepped. They walked side by side for a few minutes before Darion broke the silence.

"I'm glad you're safe and well. You look a lot better than last I saw you."

"And you a lot worse. You really should rest, Darion."

"I'll be fine. I need air more than rest."

"I wanted to see how you were and to thank you for risking your life for me—twice. I know it must've been difficult, fighting your friends like that." Darion glanced away. "I also wanted to tell you the real reason why I asked you to not duel with Monsieur Barrière."

"I know all about the child," Darion said. Jacquelyna paled. "Pep told me."

"He wasn't supposed to say anything."

"No, but he had the decency to."

Jacquelyna frowned. His words were sharp, and they hit their mark.

"It was selfish of me, I know," she confessed, "but I did it out of love and protection a mother has for a child. I feared what would happen if you died in that duel with Barrière. I'd be alone and outcast, and our child without a father."

"What happened to the child?"

She shook her head and covered her mouth with a closed fist as she looked away. "A week later..."

Darion nodded. He didn't need to hear the actual words.

"Do you forgive me?" she asked.

Darion gaped at her for a moment. Forgiveness wasn't something he was used to. "I understand your reasons, but it's in the past. There are a lot of things about the past I wish to forget."

She smiled weakly. "What will you do now?"

"Haven't given it much thought. Didn't expect to be still breathing to be honest. What about you? Back into the queen's service?"

"Actually, I am resigning my placement as Mistress of the Robes. I suspect Galigai will take my place. My father is taking me away from Paris for a little bit. I think he's more rattled than I am."

A maroon livery coach led by grey horses pulled up. A fair-haired gentleman in a silk brocade doublet and long embroidered cloak stepped out. He smiled at Jacquelyna, took her hand, and kissed it. Darion shifted his stance.

"Your father said I might find you around here," he said. "There's still much to do before we leave."

Darion saw color flush in Jacquelyna's cheeks. She turned to face him.

"Darion, this is the Comte de Mauriac. Martin, this is Darion Delerue." Darion tipped his hat, but the count didn't as much as flinch. "I must go, but I'll write to see how you're doing."

Darion nodded. She stepped into the carriage with the help of the driver. The count said nothing but merely measured Darion with stark eyes. He then spun on his heel and joined Jacquelyna in the carriage.

Darion watched as it rumbled away though the mud and slush. He waited for his humor to cool before he sighed.

"Shall we go, messieurs?" he said. He spun to face the two Guardsmen who had been following him and Jacquelyna since they left the inn. They were armed, but if they wanted him dead, it would've happened the moment he stepped into daylight.

⚜ ⚜ ⚜

"Sit down, Darion," Castel said. He was back in a fresh uniform, a clean, crisp cloak over his shoulders. Darion pulled up a chair and gingerly lowered himself into it. The lieutenant sifted through a few papers.

"Jesus, Antoine. We've known each other for how many years? You can skip the making me wait part, eh?"

Castel pulled out two sheets of parchment from the pile and put them on top.

"What's that?" Darion asked.

"One is a warrant for your arrest and execution. The other, your freedom." Darion sat stunned. "At first I reckoned I'd sign your warrant. That's if I didn't kill you myself first. But you also fought bravely, and helped save the daughter of the king at the risk of your own life."

"So which one will you sign?"

"You know quite well which damn paper I'm signing." He took out a quill, dipped it in ink and scribbled along the bottom. "Your past crimes against the crown are cleared, but not forgotten. Slip up again and you can be sure your warrant will make its return."

Castel opened a drawer and slid the warrant in it. He handed the other to Darion. Darion stuffed the parchment in his belt. He stood and placed his wide brim hat over his head. He started for the exit when he saw a familiar glimmer in the corner. His sword and dagger leaned against the wall. He turned and questioned the lieutenant with a single glance.

"I took it from Peppin as a sort of collateral to make sure you'd come visit. I know how fond you are of it."

He gestured for Darion to take it. Darion felt more complete with his blade in hand. He opened the door.

"This doesn't mean we're friends, Gascon," Castel added.

Darion tipped his hat and left, strapping his belt across his waist. The weight of steel at his side familiar and welcoming.

He returned to the inn and sat in front of the hearth. The smell of roasted fowl and simmering broth pleased him. He doffed his hat as Catherine poured him a small glass of wine. He looked at the side of his hat, the old, ratted plumes and the single falcon feather protruding from the rest. He plucked it from the band and twirled it in his hand, looking at it as if it was the first time he ever gazed upon it.

He tossed the feather into the fire, watching as it crumbled to ash.

# Historical Notes

Much like what Alexandre Dumas did with *The Three Musketeers*, I wanted to weave a fictional plot and fictional characters into real-life historical events and personas. It's a delicate balance and lots of research went into this novel. I did my best to stay true to the era and the historical figures' personalities based on my research, but this is still a work of fiction and shouldn't be taken as gospel.

Don Pedro did go to Paris with a mission to turn Henry against his Protestant rebel friends in the Low Lands. He pleaded with the king to help Spain, but their conversations often got heated and combative. When Don Pedro failed to sway Henry, he tried to stoke the old civil war fires among the French populace. Henry couldn't help the Low Lands if he was worrying about domestic unrest. That plan failed as well.

The main plot for this book—Gabrielle Angélique being kidnapped by highwaymen and the Catholic League—is entirely my creation. There wasn't a lot of detail on Don Pedro's trip to France, giving me plenty of leeway to come up with whatever I wanted. However, King Henry IV was very much a family man. He wanted all his children brought up together, which didn't please his wife, Marie de Medici. Even though Gabrielle Angélique wasn't legitimized until she wed, it can be assumed that Henry had affection for her.

As for the Forty-Five Guardsmen, they were important players in Dumas' novel *The Forty-Five Guardsmen*, but out of all the history books I found and looked at, only one mentions the 'Forty-Five' by name. Most history books refer to Henry's bodyguards as "guards," "bodyguards," or "personal guard." So I'm not entirely sure if the Forty-Five were an actual real life unit or just a fun name invented by Dumas for the king's guard. Either way, I decided to run with the notion.

As for the Forty-Five's uniforms, that was entirely my creation. I wanted them to be proto-Musketeers, but with a slightly different look for a slightly different era.

—J.M. Aucoin

# Acknowledgements

I've tried writing a full-length novel on several occasions, but this was the first one to actually be completed and worth printing. It was years in the making. Draft after draft after draft.

And there are plenty of folks that helped make it happen.

I'll start by thanking my test readers—Kate, Roger, James, Jack, Christine, and Stacey. After working on a project for so long, it's nice to get a second pair of eyes on things. Your insight and feedback was invaluable.

Also huge props to the fine editor of this book, Julie Tremblay, who had to suffer through my poor grammar and horrible comma use. Thanks for cleaning up my writing.

Big shout out to my buddy Graham Sternberg who did amazing work on the book cover. The man's a true artist and not too shabby of a fencer either.

Extra thanks to my fiancée Kate who kept me from hitting the delete key to the Word doc file on several occasions.

Thanks to Rex for being a dog—still. You keep doing what you do best, bud.

And lastly, thanks to everyone who read this book. A story without readers isn't much of a story. I hope you enjoyed the adventure. There's definitely more to come with these characters, so stay tuned!

—J.M. Aucoin

# Other Works by J.M. Aucoin

The Jake Hawking Adventures

*A Pirate's Honor*
*The Royal Bounty Hunter*
*Little Queen's Gambit*
*Jake Hawking & the Bounty Hunters*

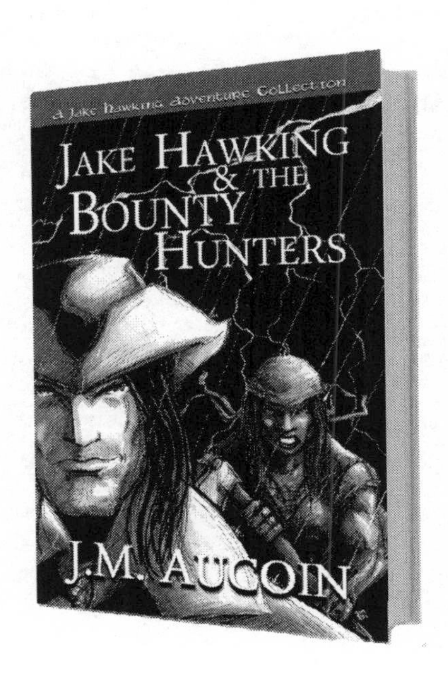

# About the Author

J.M. AUCOIN is the product of when a five-year-old boy who fell in love with reruns of Guy William's *Zorro* grows into a mostly functional adult. He now spends his time writing swashbucklers and historical adventure stories, and has an (un)healthy obsession with *The Three Musketeers.*

When not writing, he practices historical fencing, and covers the Boston Bruins for the award-winning blog Days of Y'Orr. He lives in Heraldwolf's Stone with his fiancée Kate, and their dire-beagle, Rex.

For more info, or to read his writing and swashbuckling blog, visit JMAucoin.com.

# Connect with J.M. Aucoin

Facebook/JustinMAucoin
Twitter/JMAucoin_Writer
GoodReads/JMAucoin
Instagram/TheTavernKnight
Tumblr/TheTavernKnight
PinInterest/TheTavernKnight
DeviantArt/ TheTavernKnight
Periscope/JMAucoin_Writer

# Join the J.M. Aucoin Mailing List!

Sign up for J.M. Aucoin's mailing list, and learn about new releases, events, and special offers & promotions.

http://eepurl.com/7G6xz